MASQUERADE
of the
HEART

ALSO BY KATY ROSE POOL

Garden of the Cursed

The Age of Darkness series

There Will Come a Darkness
As the Shadow Rises
Into the Dying Light

MASQUERADE

of the

HEART

KATY ROSE POOL

HENRY HOLT AND COMPANY

NEW YORK

Henry Holt and Company, *Publishers since 1866*
Henry Holt® is a registered trademark of Macmillan Publishing Group, LLC
120 Broadway, New York, NY 10271 • fiercereads.com

Our books may be purchased in bulk for promotional, educational, or business use. Please contact
your local bookseller or the Macmillan Corporate and Premium Sales Department at
(800) 221-7945 ext. 5442 or by email at MacmillanSpecialMarkets@macmillan.com.

Library of Congress Cataloging-in-Publication Data is available.

First edition, 2024
Cover illustration by Michael Rogers
Book design by Samira Iravani
Printed in United States of America

ISBN 978-1-250-84668-6 (hardcover)
1   3   5   7   9   10   8   6   4   2

ISBN 978-1-250-36320-6 (special edition)
1   3   5   7   9   10   8   6   4   2

To Mom & Dad
For being far better parents than anyone in this book

———————————

ONE

Warm rain poured over Marlow as she stood outside the towering front gate of Falcrest Hall.

The gate was shut, its iron finials piercing the dark-gray sky like fangs. Invisible wards snaked through the bars to keep unwanted visitors out.

And Marlow knew she was just about as unwanted as they came.

Clutching a bouquet of deep-violet blooms to her chest, she raised her other hand to press the button of the enchanted intercom. A crackle of static burst from the speaker, and then a prim, flat voice answered, "Falcrest Hall is closed to visitors at this time."

Marlow cleared her throat. "I have a delivery."

There was a pause on the other side of the intercom. Marlow tugged her hood closer to her face—she knew her image was being projected to the head steward, or whoever it was she was speaking with.

"One moment," the steward said curtly, and then the intercom clicked off.

Several long, silent minutes passed, the rain steadily pounding down on Marlow in sheets. She was far beyond drenched, and despite the sticky heat, she started to shiver.

Just as she was beginning to suspect that the steward planned to leave her dripping and shaking until she eventually gave up, she spotted a figure coming down from the main steps of Falcrest Hall.

Through the heavy downpour, Marlow could only discern the figure as a dark smear against the gray sky, until they were just a few dozen paces away.

Marlow's heart dropped into her stomach.

Amara stepped up to the gate. She was dressed entirely in black, from the sculptural cape she wore over a columnar gown to the enchanted umbrella that floated just above her, shielding her from the downpour. Every line of her clothing, her severe makeup, even her shining raven hair, was aggressively polished.

Marlow could not help seeing her own bedraggled appearance through Amara's eyes—her tangled, damp blond hair, the plain, ill-fitting clothes she'd taken from her old wardrobe in Vale Tower, her pale face lined with shadows from too little sleep.

Amara's wine-red lips lifted into a snarl. "What? Have you come here hoping to finish my father off?"

Marlow swallowed thickly, letting the flowers drop to her side, and with them, any pretense as to her purpose here. "I came to speak to Adrius."

An incredulous laugh barked from Amara's mouth. Her dark eyes blazed. "You are *never* going to see or speak to anyone in my family ever again."

Marlow didn't let herself flinch from the deep hatred in Amara's gaze. She knew there was little point in arguing—Amara had no reason to hear her out. As far as she knew, Marlow had just tried to murder her father in cold blood.

She should have known coming to Falcrest Hall would be pointless, but she *had* to try. Adrius's life might depend on it.

"Please." She gripped the bars of the gate. "I just need five minutes. Please."

"And give you a chance to dig your claws into him again?" Amara scoffed. "Never."

2

"I wouldn't have come here unless it was important." Marlow's knuckles were turning white with the force of her grip, as if letting go of the gate would mean giving up on this foolish mission.

"Oh, is it?" Amara said mockingly. "Well, if it's so important, then why don't you tell me?"

Amara didn't know about the Compulsion curse Adrius was under. She may have suspected something—at least Silvan had thought so—but she didn't know the full truth. And Marlow wasn't going to spill the secret to her. Adrius may have been Amara's brother, but like her father, Amara saw him as something that needed to be controlled.

There was no way in hell Marlow was going to hand that control over to her.

But as Marlow looked at her face, she began to see the cracks in Amara's armor. The faint shadows under her eyes. The reddish tint to her cheeks and nose that made it apparent she'd been crying.

Amara couldn't know about Adrius's curse, that much Marlow was firm on. But Amara wasn't as emotionless as she tried to appear. Her father was dying somewhere inside Falcrest Hall, and as horrible a man as he was, Marlow could see that Amara's grief for him was real.

She deserved to know the truth about who had tried to take him from her.

"It's about your father," Marlow began.

Amara's face twisted with undeniable fury. "*Don't* talk about my father."

"I know you hate me," Marlow said, desperation seeping into her words. "And you have every reason to. But you don't know the whole truth about what happened. If you'd just listen—"

"Marlow?" a voice called over the drum of the rain.

It had come from behind Marlow. She and Amara both turned to see who was there.

Marlow's heart slammed against her ribs as her gaze landed on Vale.

He stood beneath the shelter of his own enchanted umbrella, cobalt-blue suit blending almost seamlessly into the gray clouds behind him. His warm, boyish features were creased with concern, his gray eyes trained on Marlow. She had last seen him only a few hours ago, in the living room of her apartment in Vale Tower, where he'd embraced her as Marlow finally put the pieces together about what he'd done.

He stepped toward her. "Marlow, what are you doing here?"

A chill skittered down her spine. "Did you follow me here?"

Vale's brow wrinkled with confusion. "Of course not. Amara is hosting a dinner for the heads of the Five Families and the Falcrest vassal houses."

Marlow turned back to Amara in surprise. It hadn't even been two days since her father was attacked, and Amara was already hosting a *dinner*?

Then again, maybe it made perfect sense. She noted the tension in Amara's jaw. This dinner wasn't just a social occasion. Amara's grief was real, but so was the political reality of the Five Families. And if Marlow knew one thing about Amara, it was that she always put strategy above sentiment. With her father lying half-dead, Amara would be under pressure to shore up the Falcrest family's power before someone took advantage of their weakened position.

"So?" Amara asked, ignoring Vale completely, her gaze searing into Marlow. "What is it you wanted to tell me?"

Marlow could feel Vale's eyes on her, too. A hysterical, desperate urge welled up in her. She wanted to grab Amara through the bars of the gate and say, *It's him, he's the one responsible for your father's attack, don't let him in, don't let him near Adrius, please, Amara.*

She choked down the words. Vale had no idea that Marlow knew anything about what he'd done—anything about the Compulsion curse he'd placed on Adrius, the order he'd given him to stab his own father in the heart. And it had to stay that way, until Marlow could figure out what he was really up to.

She lowered her gaze, uncurling her cold, wet fingers from the bars of the gate. "Tell Adrius I'm sorry," she said, and then turned away and retreated into the downpour.

"Keep her the hell away from my family!" Amara snarled at Vale.

Vale didn't even acknowledge the demand. His gaze was pinned on Marlow, gray eyes dark like storm clouds. He stepped toward her and laid a hand on her shoulder before she could pass.

Marlow braced herself against a shudder.

"We'll talk about this tomorrow," he said in a grim tone.

Talk about *what*? Marlow showing up at Falcrest Hall in the most foolish of fool's errands? Her back teeth clenched against the anger building in her gut, but she forced herself to meet Vale's gaze with a nod.

Vale returned her nod with satisfaction and then patted her once on the shoulder and released her.

It took all her willpower to turn away and allow Vale to walk through the gates of Falcrest Hall, knowing that Adrius was somewhere inside. Knowing he was still under the Compulsion curse. Knowing Vale was the one who had cast it.

And not knowing just what Vale would do with that power.

TWO

The first course had already come and gone by the time Adrius made his entrance to the dining room. He could still see the remnants of some fussy appetizer involving candied figs and thinly sliced cured meat.

"Adrius," Amara greeted him from the head of the table. The crease beside the corner of her mouth announced her displeasure. "I didn't realize you were joining us."

Adrius sauntered past the seated guests, swiping a random glass of wine off the table as he went to flop down in an empty chair to Amara's left. "Are you kidding? I wouldn't miss it."

Truthfully, he *had* decided to skip this little gathering, intending to spend his evening getting so exquisitely drunk he couldn't see straight. But at some point, staring down at the bottom of an empty bottle of wine, he'd abruptly decided that actually, a dinner with the heads of all the most important families in Caraza *did* sound like fun—if only because he knew his mere presence would wreck whatever plan Amara was furiously trying to execute.

Ever since the day of the wedding, Amara had done her level best to ignore Adrius's entire existence, and he was finally sick of it.

He smiled blithely at her over the rim of his wineglass and turned his attention to the guests. Representatives of all the Falcrest vassal houses were seated around the table, as well as the heads of the other Five Families—Zeno Morandi, Dahlia Starling, and Cormorant Vale.

Missing, of course, was the Delvigne family. While still nominally one of the original Five Families, Adrius's mother's family had long been subsumed by the Falcrests.

"So!" Adrius said brightly, wine sloshing out of his glass and splashing onto the fine tablecloth. "What are we all talking about?"

"Actually," Amara said crisply. "We were discussing you. And I really should thank you for proving my point so succinctly." She turned to address her guests. "As you can plainly see with your own eyes, Adrius is hardly fit to take over Falcrest family as heir."

Adrius gave an exaggerated wince. "Not going to sugarcoat it, are you?"

A balding man with a thin nose and spectacles cleared his throat. Adrius recognized him as Jean Renault, the head of one of the most powerful of the Falcrest vassal houses. Adrius had always found him to be criminally uptight and stuffy, but he did hold a lot of sway with the other vassals. "While we appreciate your candor and your opinion on this matter, we do have to wonder—what is it exactly that makes *you* fit to take over? Your brother was the one Aurelius named as heir. Clearly, *he* felt Adrius was up to the task."

Adrius could sense the tension in Amara as her jaw tightened. But her voice was even when she replied, "My father made that decision before Adrius decided to disown the family."

Renault looked at Adrius. "Is that true?"

Adrius shrugged. The truth of it didn't matter—what mattered was whether Amara could successfully convince these men that it was in their best interest to put her in charge. She'd failed to convince their father of that—and Adrius supposed he was at least a little curious to see if she'd fare any better with these men.

"It is," Amara said. "The night before my wedding, Adrius walked out of Falcrest Hall and declared he was never going to return. I believe both my husband and Lord Vale can attest to this." She glanced to her other side, where Darian sat, ever the dutiful husband.

"He did spend that night at Vale Tower," Darian confirmed.

"When Adrius walked out of Falcrest Hall, he renounced any claim as heir," Amara went on in a cool, authoritative voice. "Therefore, the *only* person with any legitimate claim to the Falcrest family is me."

The heads of the vassal houses seemed to take a moment to absorb this, glancing around at one another. Finally, Renault spoke again. "We appreciate your position on this, but surely you can understand our . . . hesitation in putting a teenage girl in charge of the Falcrest family."

"With all due respect," Amara said coolly, "it is not your decision to put me in charge or not."

Renault narrowed his eyes. "Yet I think you'll find that if the vassal houses are not confident in your leadership, you may lose our support altogether. We need to think of our own families' fortunes, which are intimately tied up in the Falcrest family operations." He shot a quick glance over to Zeno Morandi. "We might need to consider whether our interests might be safer in someone else's hands."

Adrius stifled a snort. The threat was clear. If Amara didn't capitulate to the vassal houses' demands, they would pull their investments from the Falcrest family altogether and find somewhere else to put their money. If even a few of the biggest vassals pulled out, others were sure to follow.

"I assure you," Amara said in an icy tone, "I am more than capable of running the Falcrest family. I've been preparing for this duty my entire life."

She sounded brutally calm, but it wasn't enough to fool Adrius. He'd known her for eighteen years, and he knew how to tell if she was angry. And right now, she was *furious*. She hated that she needed approval from these people, who she no doubt considered beneath her.

"If it would make the vassal houses more comfortable," Vale cut in from down the table, "perhaps a solution can be reached. Perhaps a . . . level of oversight might put some of your concerns to rest?"

Adrius raised his eyebrows. He wasn't sure what Vale's angle was here—knowing him, he might genuinely be trying to help Amara, oblivious to how deeply resentful she would be of the offer.

Renault, on the other hand, looked intrigued. "Oversight?"

Vale bowed his head. "Amara and my son are married now. As her father-in-law, I would be more than willing to step in until she gets her bearings."

"*Step in?*" Zeno Morandi spat. His lip curled as he turned to Renault. "Surely you can't be considering this. To put the head of another one of the Five Families in charge of the Falcrest family is utterly ludicrous. A clear conflict of interest."

"Calm down, Zeno, no one said anything about being put in charge," Vale cut in placatingly. "This would purely be an advisory role. Temporary, of course. Amara would still retain full control."

"Oh, please," Morandi scoffed. "This is a clear grab at power, and the other Families won't stand for it."

"Ah, well, that's something you'd know about, isn't it, Zeno?" Vale asked.

Adrius couldn't help but smirk. He'd never much liked Morandi, had always thought him to be just as cruel and ruthless as Adrius's father, only twice as cowardly.

Morandi's beady eyes narrowed. "What are you implying?"

"Rumor has it the Morandi family is looking to acquire the Falcrests' most talented spellwrights and part of the Falcrest Library collection," Vale replied. "Don't you think it's a little crass to be sniffing around Falcrest Library while the Falcrest patriarch lies dying?"

"You want to talk about what's *crass?*" Morandi spat. "How about harboring the very person who attacked Falcrest in the first place, and then turning around not two days later to try to wedge yourself into a position of power?"

Adrius flinched. Even if Morandi hadn't said her name, the mention of Marlow made the room feel suddenly airless.

"The courts," Vale said slowly, "will determine who is at fault for the attack."

His gaze flickered to Adrius for the briefest of moments. A sick unease rocked through Adrius. Did Vale know the truth—that it wasn't Marlow who had stabbed Aurelius, but Adrius? Had Marlow told him?

Adrius grabbed clumsily for his wine and took another long sip. Even *thinking* of Marlow made his chest tight.

"Gentlemen," Renault cut in. "We are here only to resolve the matter of who is in charge of the Falcrest family operations. That is all. Now, from my perspective, Lord Vale's oversight would, I believe, put to rest some of our misgivings. Otherwise, perhaps control of the Falcrest family could be put into some sort of trust with the vassal families, at least until Lord Falcrest, uh . . . recovers."

A heavy silence followed his words. Adrius dropped his gaze to the tablecloth in front of him. The wine he'd spilled was dark red against the white linen. It almost looked like blood. Nausea rose in his gut, and he shut his eyes.

No one sitting at the table thought recovery was where Adrius's father was headed. Least of all Adrius.

"No," Amara said stiffly. "No, that won't be necessary. I would be glad to welcome my father-in-law's input, if it would put the vassal families at ease."

Her voice sounded syrupy sweet, but Adrius could hear the venom in it.

"Before we decide," Renault said, "I'd like to hear from Adrius. After all, he is the *actual* heir. Do you have anything you'd like to add?"

Adrius pulled his mouth into an ugly, vicious smile and pushed to his feet. "I say you can burn down Falcrest Library for all I care."

𝒯*he light was* on at the end of the hall. Adrius hadn't expected that. It was late, dinner long since over, their guests already gone, the household staff retired for the night. Adrius should have been in bed, too. But these days he hardly bothered, knowing he wouldn't fall asleep until the early hours of dawn, if at all.

Instead he was here, in his father's wing. And it seemed he wasn't the only one who'd been drawn here tonight.

Through the half-open doorway, he could see Amara's back as she sat bent over their father's sickbed. She was speaking in a low, gentle voice, but Adrius couldn't make out the words.

Adrius stepped toward her, his shoes clicking against the polished tile floors.

Amara straightened, whipping around to face him. Her eyes were rimmed red. She'd been crying. Adrius knew she hadn't been getting much sleep, either.

Aurelius had not woken since the day of Amara's wedding. There were countless spells and enchantments keeping his body alive, but none that could completely heal the wound that festered in his chest. The wound that Adrius had carved into him.

Adrius had avoided walking down this hallway for the past two days, but something had drawn him here this evening. It wasn't until he looked at his sister's face that he realized what it was. He'd come in search of the grief he could see so clearly reflected in Amara's eyes.

"What are you doing here?" she demanded.

Adrius lingered just outside the doorway, holding back from stepping inside. "I came to see how he's doing."

"What do you care?"

Adrius didn't answer. He didn't *have* an answer. Amara was right—he didn't care. He didn't feel anything.

"You've spent more time worrying over that *murderer* than you have worrying about your own dying father," Amara hissed. "It's *sick*."

Marlow isn't a murderer, Adrius wanted to say. *I am.*

He had plunged a knife into his own father's chest. And when he looked down at that pale, still face, Adrius felt—nothing.

This is why he chose me. The thought surprised Adrius. Ever since his father told them that he'd named Adrius heir, Adrius had wondered why. But now he saw the answer, stark and terrible in the cold light of his father's sickbed.

Because as much as Amara wanted to be like their father—ruthless and unflinching—it was Adrius who was most like him. It was Adrius whose heart was as cold and hard as the ice in his father's chest.

And for all her armor and her viciousness, Amara wasn't a killer like them.

"You need to choose a side, Adrius," Amara said, rising to her feet.

"What are you talking about?"

"I'm talking about *Vale!*" Amara snarled. "He is making a play for Falcrest Library."

"You're paranoid," Adrius replied. "All he did was agree to advise."

"You are so godsdamned naive," Amara replied. "He got your little girlfriend released from jail, did you know that? For all we know, they cooked up the plan to murder Father together."

"That's—Amara, come on, that's—"

"I'm not going to sit around while Vale tries to wrestle control of the Falcrest empire from me. I'm going to make my own moves." Amara's lips curled into a grim smile. "And you're going to help me. No more sitting out, Brother."

THREE

Sometimes, when Marlow was particularly stuck on a curse-breaking case, she would sit down and make a list of everything she knew. It was a way of calming the chaos of her mind and focusing her attention not on the questions swirling through her head but on what she needed to do next.

So, the day after her unsuccessful visit to Falcrest Hall, Marlow sat at her mother's writing desk and made a list in her mind of everything she knew. The first item was *Adrius doesn't know Vale is the one who cursed him.*

She'd failed in her attempt to talk to Adrius yesterday, but she hadn't given up hope of getting a message to him. Amara couldn't possibly keep him locked up in Falcrest Hall forever. Marlow would just have to wait for an opportunity.

The next item on the list was *Swift hasn't gotten in contact.*

It had been two days since she'd instructed him to go to the Black Orchid to seek refuge from the Copperheads. Marlow assumed he would have heard about her arrest, and likely that she was now at Vale Tower. He was probably worried about her, and she hated to worry him. It also made her uneasy that he hadn't found a way to contact her here—what if she'd been wrong, and the Black Orchid couldn't be trusted? What if he'd never even made it to them?

The third item on her list was *Adrius is still cursed.*

By now, she had less than two weeks to figure out where Vale was hiding the curse card and burn it before the Compulsion curse on Adrius became irreversible. And she didn't know where to start.

A knock at the door startled her from her thoughts. Vale's voice floated in through the door. "Marlow, it's me. May I come in?"

Marlow went to the door and pulled it open. Vale stood smiling on the other side. A fresh wave of disorienting unease rocked her every time she looked at him—part of her finding comfort in his familiar, affectionate demeanor, and the other part of her disturbed by the ease with which he put on that facade.

"I wanted to talk to you about last night," he began, hesitant but firm. "I don't think it's a good idea for you to leave Vale Tower."

Vale's tone may have been gentle, but his words told her she was basically a prisoner here. Her grip tightened on the doorknob.

"At least, not on your own," Vale went on with a tight smile.

Marlow forced her body to relax. "I'm not really used to answering to anyone."

"I know that," Vale said softly. "I'm not enough of a fool to think that just because I'm your father I can walk in here and tell you what you can and can't do. But I do want to keep you safe. And right now, with everything that's going on, the safest place for you is here. At home."

Home. This tower might have been home once. It wasn't anymore.

"What were you even doing at Falcrest Hall?" Vale asked. Marlow studied his face, trying to decide whether he suspected her true motive for going there. He had no reason to believe that she knew about Adrius's curse, much less that he was the one who had cast it, but still her heart pounded at the thought of being found out. Before she could come up with a satisfactory answer, though, Vale lowered his voice and asked, "Were you there to see Adrius?"

Marlow tugged her lower lip between her teeth. Her mother used to say that the easiest way to con someone was to show them exactly what they expected to see.

Vale seemed to think Marlow was a lovesick teenage girl. So she would be a lovesick teenage girl.

She nodded, blinking rapidly as if holding back tears.

"My dear," Vale said consolingly. "I didn't want to be right about him. But it's better that you found out now. No matter what he might feel for you, he will never put you first. It's not his fault—not really. He's just not capable of it. He's too much like his father."

Marlow swallowed the lump building in her throat. She may have thought she was faking her tears for Vale's sake, but the pit in her stomach said otherwise. Part of her—a part she wasn't proud of—wondered if Vale might be right about Adrius.

"Why don't you join the family and me for dinner this evening?" Vale offered.

Marlow wiped her eyes with the back of her hand. "Don't you think it's a bit soon for that?"

"Not at all," he answered. "Truthfully, it's long overdue."

"I only got here two days ago."

He gave her a fond look. "I mean, we should have done this years ago. If I'd only known who you were back then . . . if your mother hadn't been so intent on keeping her secrets . . ." He shook his head. "I suppose it's no use thinking of what could have been. The important thing is, we know the truth now. It's never too late to do things right."

It was chilling to hear Vale talk of "doing things right" when he had Adrius under a curse to follow his every command.

"You have no reason to be nervous," Vale went on. "I've already explained everything to Elena. Whatever resentments may exist, they are mine alone to shoulder."

Vale may have seen it that way, but Marlow somehow doubted his wife agreed. Still, as much as Marlow had no interest whatsoever in sitting down to a family dinner, this was clearly something Vale wanted her to do, and she *did* have an interest in staying on his good side.

"Let me just freshen up," Marlow said.

Vale smiled, pleased by her acquiescence. "Of course. We'll be waiting for you down in the family apartments. You know where to find them?"

"Sure," Marlow agreed. She'd never once set foot inside the Vale family's private apartments when she'd previously lived in Vale Tower, but she knew where they were. "I'll be right down."

Vale offered her one last, twinkling smile and then left the room.

Marlow went to her old wardrobe and found several dresses she'd left here over a year ago, only one of which still fit. It had a long-sleeved silver bodice and a tiered, midnight-blue skirt beaded with pearls. As far as Evergarden dresses went, it was fairly subdued, but Marlow still felt completely overdressed for dinner.

Even if it was dinner with three people who probably would've preferred that Marlow never existed, and the man who Marlow had just recently learned was both her father and an unrepentant monster.

But if Marlow was to stay in Vale Tower long enough to break Adrius's curse, she was going to have to play along.

She should be used to playing a role by now. Before, it had been the role of Adrius's besotted girlfriend. She'd simply traded that role for this one—Vale's long-lost daughter, desperate to forge a connection with a family she had no rightful claim to.

Once she'd dressed, she left the apartment, locking it behind her, and took the elevator up to the Vales' private apartments.

The elevator let out into a grand but tasteful foyer, with a pair of cushioned chairs that looked as though they'd never been sat in, and a few vases with carefully manicured greenery. On the far wall hung a gold-framed portrait of the four Vales—Silvan and Darian in front, Vale and Elena behind them. They all wore varying shades of blue, and all four of them were smiling.

Through the arched doorway, Marlow could see the dining room, with a well-appointed table laid out beneath a sparkling crystal chandelier. A lone figure sat at the table, his ice-blond hair bright beneath the lights, the familiar blue coil of his pet snake curled around one arm.

Silvan's gaze shot up as Marlow entered the room.

Marlow felt like she was seeing his face for the first time. He was her *brother*. Half brother.

He mostly took after his mother, his elegant, sharp features a contrast to his father's softer, boyish looks. But his eyes, while pale blue in color, were precisely the same shape as Vale's. As Marlow's.

As soon as those eyes landed on her, Silvan leapt to his feet. "What the hell are you doing here? Aren't you supposed to be locked up somewhere?"

Marlow paused on the threshold of the room, momentarily stunned. "He didn't tell you?"

Silvan's eyes narrowed. "Who didn't tell me what?"

"Your father got me released," Marlow said.

"He *what*? Why would he do that?"

So it seemed Vale had spoken to his wife but had neglected to have the same talk with his sons. Part of Marlow was horrified. Another part of her could not wait to see Silvan's reaction to finding out they were related.

And then a third part—the part that was constantly devising plans in the back of her mind—had Marlow rushing over to him.

He leaned away from her instinctively, eyeing the silverware as if he thought she might take hold of a butter knife and try to stab him.

"Have you seen Adrius since the wedding?" Marlow asked. "Is he all right?"

Silvan stared at her with suspicion bordering on outright hostility.

"*Is he all right?* That's your question? You tried to kill his father and you want to know if he's all right?"

"Look, it's—complicated," Marlow said. Silvan knew about the curse. Marlow could try to explain that Adrius had been commanded to attack his own father, and that she'd only taken the blame to protect him. As much as Silvan had always grated on Marlow's nerves, she trusted that his friendship with Adrius was genuine. There was no part of her that suspected Silvan had the slightest inkling as to who his father really was and what he'd done. But she also knew he had no reason to believe Marlow's side of the story, and this was hardly the time or place to try to convince him.

Instead she said, "Can you just tell him to come see me the next time you talk to him?"

"I'm not your messenger boy," he sneered.

Marlow had thought that perhaps rescuing Silvan from a dozen Copperheads might have softened him toward her a little. Clearly, that had been wishful thinking. "Silvan—"

"Oh, good, you're here." Vale's jovial voice rang into the room.

Marlow looked up at the open archway that led to the Vales' private quarters and found Vale with his wife at his side. Elena Vale was a thin, pale woman with the same fine, fair hair as her youngest son. She was even shorter than Marlow, and everything about her seemed small and delicate. Next to her husband, whose broad frame and boisterous manner made him seem larger than he actually was, she looked particularly diminutive. Her green eyes swept coolly over Marlow and Silvan, giving nothing away.

Silvan whirled on his parents. "What's going on here?"

"Your father has some news to share," Elena replied mildly.

"Where's your brother?" Vale asked, glancing around the room like his eldest son might be hiding in a corner somewhere.

"Forget Darian," Silvan hissed. "What is a killer doing standing in our dining room?"

"Silvan!" Vale exclaimed, aghast. "Marlow, I am so—"

"It's fine," Marlow cut in quickly. "I'd be suspicious of me, too."

"Sorry I'm late, Father, Mother." Darian's voice carried into the room seconds before he emerged from the hallway, looking a little harried. "Amara brought in some new healers to work on her father and I didn't want to leave her while—"

He stopped speaking abruptly as his gaze landed on Marlow.

"Darian, have you met Father's new guest?" Silvan asked. "You might recognize her from your wedding. She was the one holding the bloody knife and standing over your dying father-in-law."

Marlow considered the wisdom of fleeing Vale Tower and taking her chances in the Marshes. She was pretty sure no torture the Copperheads devised could be more excruciating than this.

"Marlow is not a murderer," Vale said with authority. "If everyone would please have a seat, I'll explain."

Darian obeyed, shuffling into a seat across the table from Silvan, shooting Marlow wary glances. Elena swept past her and sat beside her youngest son, her hand briefly pausing to comb through his long hair— an unexpectedly tender gesture.

Vale went to Marlow's side, clasping his hands on her shoulders and facing the rest of his family. Marlow shivered. "First, to address the crocodile in the room—Marlow is completely innocent. She was merely at the wrong place at the wrong time."

"She told everyone she did it!" Silvan exclaimed. "We were all there."

"She lied to protect the real culprit," Vale replied smoothly. His words had the air of a rehearsal—and that's exactly what it was, Marlow realized. Vale was trying out the lie he would feed to the rest of the noblesse nouveau in order to clear Marlow's name. And the first test was to see if Vale's own family would believe it.

Darian looked at Marlow seriously. "Marlow? What really happened?"

She felt Vale's eyes on her. This was a test for her as well, then—to see if she would go along with his lie.

Marlow believed in the truth above everything. That was what she wanted to tell them all—these people who thought they knew Vale so well, and yet had no idea what the man was really capable of. She imagined speaking the words into the room. *The real culprit is Vale. He cursed Adrius and compelled him to stab his own father.*

But as long as Adrius remained under the Compulsion curse, she couldn't reveal the truth. It would put him in too much danger. And unless she had proof that Vale had cast the curse, who would believe her?

If she doubled down on her own lie—that she was the one who had stabbed Aurelius—Vale would surely begin to wonder why she was going to such lengths to protect Adrius.

She met Darian's earnest gaze. He had the same boyishly handsome looks as his father, but his eyes were all his mother's: bright, clear green like chrysanthemum leaves. She had the sense that unlike Silvan, he hadn't made up his mind about her yet. But she knew whatever she said in this room would find its way back to Amara, who no doubt was already plotting how to get Marlow locked up for life. Marlow didn't want to give her any more ammunition, if she could help it.

She had to choose her words—her lies—carefully. "It—it all happened so fast," she said. "Lord Falcrest was angry with Adrius for disowning the family. But he blamed me for it. He'd tried to poison me the night of your candle-lighting ceremony. And when he saw me at the wedding, he threatened me again. I—I was scared. I grabbed the knife to defend myself and—I don't know exactly what happened in the scuffle, but—" She broke off, burying her face in her hands as if she couldn't bear to go on.

Vale patted her comfortingly. "It's unfortunate and tragic that Aurelius's rage forced Marlow to fend off his violence—but we have all seen just how intractable Aurelius's temper can be."

"That doesn't explain why she's *here*," Silvan said with a snarl.

"Well," Vale said. "This will likely come as a shock. It came as a shock to me, too, when I first learned it. But the truth is . . . Marlow is my daughter."

Darian's eyes went wide. Silvan looked vaguely nauseated.

"Your . . . ," Silvan began. "No. No way. This is . . . you *can't* be serious. This is a joke, isn't it?"

Trust me, Marlow thought, *I'm just as thrilled as you are.*

"I . . . ," Darian began, his forehead creased in confusion. Then he blurted, "But Marlow is younger than me. You . . . that means that you . . ."

He trailed off, apparently unable to even voice the conclusion that his father had been an unfaithful husband. He looked *crushed*.

"Marlow's mother and I have a complicated history," Vale said. "I have never claimed to be perfect. And while I regret many of my actions, particularly those that have caused pain to you and your mother, I hope that you can see beyond my own transgressions and welcome Marlow into our family. She deserves to get a chance to know us and she doesn't deserve to be punished for my own misguided actions."

Elena cleared her throat primly. "Boys. I know this is difficult to take in. I was just as shocked and upset as you are when I learned. But your father is right—Marlow is not to blame."

Something about her tone rang false to Marlow. When she looked at Elena, she felt she could see the true anger seething beneath her calm mask. Marlow didn't know her well, but she knew Evergarden, and she knew the kinds of calculations the noblesse nouveau made. Elena would have understood that trying to make Vale reject Marlow and cast her aside would only create more discord between herself and her husband. She'd chosen instead to make him believe she would accept his illegitimate child—born of an adulterous affair—in order to avoid alienating herself from her main source of power and status. Either Vale didn't see his wife's true fury, or he chose to ignore it.

Marlow saw it, though. She saw it very clearly. And she knew that just because Elena was putting on this act for her husband and her sons didn't mean she would take this affront lying down.

"It's not her fault her mother was an immoral, wicked woman," Elena continued.

Marlow had to grind her teeth together to keep from snapping at Elena that she should take a look at her own husband if she wanted to see what an *immoral* and *wicked* person really looked like.

"Well, you know what they say," Silvan spat, pushing away from the table. "Like mother, like daughter."

He stalked out of the room, oozing disdain with every step.

Darian shook his head and stood from the table, too. "I'm sorry. I—this is too much. I'm sorry."

He walked off, and Elena rose to follow him.

When they were gone from the room, Vale turned to Marlow with a doleful look.

Marlow summoned a smile. "Well. I think that went great."

FOUR

When Marlow woke the next morning, there was a breakfast tray sitting on her dining table, with a note next to it from Vale requesting that Marlow join him for tea that afternoon. The request made her already dark mood darker.

She hated being all but trapped in Vale Tower. She hated being forced to make nice with people who would probably rather that she disappear off the face of the earth. She hated having to pretend that looking at Vale didn't make her skin crawl.

She wanted to see Adrius. She wanted to talk to Swift.

Instead she was stuck here, picking at a tray of fruit and sweet bread, stewing in her own uselessness. She'd made two unsuccessful attempts to contact Adrius, and it had now been three days since she'd seen Swift. With every passing moment, she was more anxious to make sure he was safe.

A green light beside the front door caught her attention. It took her a moment to remember the light flashed to indicate when she had visitors down in the lobby of Vale Tower. She scrambled to the door, tripping over the rug in her haste to get there.

It had to be either Swift or Adrius. Who else would come to see her?

"Hello?" she asked into the brass speaker.

"Marlow, it's Gemma."

Marlow froze, one hand hovering over the intercom button. ". . . Gemma?"

She couldn't think of any reason Gemma Starling might come to see her, except—maybe Adrius had put her up to it? Maybe he *did* want to get in contact with her but couldn't come himself, so he'd sent Gemma in his place.

"Can you let me up?" Gemma asked impatiently.

Heart starting to race, Marlow pressed the button that would allow Gemma entry up to Marlow's floor.

Before Gemma had even knocked twice, Marlow wrenched open the door.

"Did Adrius send you?"

Gemma always looked glamorous no matter where she went, but there was something different about her appearance today. Her hair was a dark burgundy, almost black, and her lips were painted a deep blood red. Her expression was more serious than Marlow had ever seen her.

"Why would Adrius send me?" Gemma asked.

Marlow's heart sank. "I—I just thought he might, is all. How'd you know I was here, then?"

"Silvan told me. We went dancing last night and he spent almost the entire night ranting about you." She paused. "Is Vale really your father?"

Marlow nodded. "I only found out two days ago."

An awkward silence descended, heavy with everything Marlow wasn't saying.

"Um, do you want to come in?" she asked. "I can make tea."

Gemma's gaze swept through the apartment. It was certainly very lavish by Marlow's standards, but she imagined to Gemma it must seem quaint compared to the luxury she probably enjoyed at Starling Manor.

"I'll come in," she said at last, stepping across the threshold. "But I'm not here to stay. I just . . . I came because I had to know the truth."

Marlow closed the door behind her. "You mean about what happened at Amara's wedding."

Gemma nodded. "I couldn't let myself believe that you'd do something so . . . so heinous. And when I saw you standing there holding that knife I just—it felt like I never really knew you."

Marlow folded her arms across her chest. She'd never been completely honest with Gemma—she couldn't risk it. But she'd been surprised by how much she actually did like her once she'd gotten to know her.

"What do you want me to say, Gemma?"

Gemma drew herself up straight, looking Marlow in the eye. "Did you go to that wedding planning to kill Adrius's father?"

Marlow knew why this was Gemma's first question. The only reason Marlow had gotten into the wedding in the first place was because she'd convinced Gemma to take her as her guest. Gemma had even been grateful—she'd needed someone to console her while she watched the girl she loved marry someone else. And now Gemma wanted to know whether Marlow's sympathy had been genuine, or just a ploy to enact her own murderous scheme.

Marlow couldn't tell her the entire truth, but she didn't have to lie. "No. I went because I wanted to see Adrius. That's all."

"But that was your knife, wasn't it?" Gemma asked. "You *brought* it there. Why would you do that, if you weren't planning on—"

Marlow bit back a laugh. "Gemma, I always have that knife on me. Or I used to. You can ask Adrius, if you don't believe me."

Gemma looked bewildered. "Why?"

"I'm from the Marshes," Marlow replied simply. "It's basic safety over there."

"Oh," Gemma replied, as if she hadn't considered that Marlow might be accustomed to facing dangers Gemma had never conceived of. "Then what really happened, Marlow? Why did you do it?"

"To protect Adrius."

That much, at least, was true. She hadn't stabbed Aurelius, but she *had* taken the fall for it in order to protect him.

Gemma looked down. "The papers are saying something different."

Marlow's pulse jumped. Of course the papers were speculating about this—it was the most scandalous thing to happen in Caraza in decades. But somehow Marlow hadn't thought about what they might be saying about *her*.

It was with some trepidation that she asked, "What are they saying?"

Gemma swallowed. "That Vale manipulated you into it."

That, Marlow hadn't been expecting. "What? The papers think Vale is responsible?"

"It's just rumors and speculation," Gemma replied. "No one knows anything for sure, but when you look at all the pieces . . . they do seem to add up to something. I mean, he *did* bail you out of jail immediately. That much is public record." She looked up at Marlow again. "Although I guess if he really *is* your father, I can see why he might not want you sitting in jail."

Marlow hesitated. "The truth is . . . complicated, Gemma." It was the same non-answer she'd given Silvan. "Even I don't have all the pieces yet. But what I did—*why* I did it. It was to protect Adrius. That much, you have to believe."

"I do," Gemma replied softly. "But I don't think *you* understand. Whatever this is about—whatever really happened—it's not going to matter."

"How can it not matter?" Marlow asked. The truth was the truth— even if Marlow couldn't reveal it to Gemma, it still *mattered*.

"This is Evergarden," Gemma replied. "The truth is malleable here. If enough people *think* something is the truth—or even just pretend they think it is—then that's enough to *make* it true. If people think Vale used you as a pawn, if they think I was in on the plan—since I'm the one who brought you to the wedding—then they're going to think that Vale is making a power grab, and that the Starlings are backing him. And if they think that, then it becomes justification for retaliation. Relations between the Five Families have been peaceable for a while now. But it seems like that's about to change. This isn't just about you and Adrius. It's about the Five Families. It's about the fate of Caraza."

Gemma was right—this was bigger than Marlow knew. And the only ones who knew the real truth were her and Adrius.

"What did Adrius say happened?" Marlow asked.

Gemma shook her head. "He won't talk about it at all. At least, not to me."

In the last seconds before her arrest, Marlow had ordered him not to tell anyone what had really happened. She couldn't have him undermining her story and potentially revealing the Compulsion curse, exposing himself to even more danger.

"Is he all right, though?" she asked. "I mean—you've seen him, haven't you? Does he seem okay?"

Gemma hesitated. "I've seen him."

"Does he know I'm here?"

Gemma's gaze shifted away from her. "He knows."

And he hadn't done anything to try to contact her. Marlow ignored the sudden knot in her stomach.

"Can you pass on a message to him? From me?" Marlow asked. "It's important."

Gemma looked distinctly uncomfortable. "I . . . can try, but he says he doesn't want to see you. He said he . . . wants to put you out of his head. Entirely."

Marlow's heart stuttered in her chest. She had put her own life on the line for him, and this was how he saw fit to repay her—by cutting her out of his life. *Again.*

She couldn't help but think of what Vale had said, just after the wedding and Marlow's arrest. *When reality sets in, he will leave you to hang and do what he must to protect himself and his reputation. That is what the Falcrests know. That is who they are.*

It was too much like the first time he'd abruptly stopped talking to her. But—no, she couldn't let herself enter a spiral of doubting herself, doubting him. He had real reasons to still be angry with her. After all, she'd used the Compulsion curse against him not once but twice now. If he was still angry at Marlow for ordering him to tell her the truth, she couldn't quite find it in herself to blame him.

She shoved aside her hurt. Adrius might want to forget her, to stamp out his feelings for her, but Marlow's mission was more important than whatever desire and resentment existed between them. She *had* to warn him about Vale.

Gemma bit her lip, her gaze flicking up to meet Marlow's. "I'm sorry, Marlow. Truly. I mean, I know better than anyone what it feels like to be abruptly dropped and watch the person you love get engaged to someone else."

"Engaged?" Marlow asked, stumbling over the word.

Gemma's eyes widened. "Oh. You don't—I thought you knew. It's all over the gossip columns. This morning, Adrius announced his intention to find a wife. He says he'll make his choice before the year is out."

Marlow's heart plunged into her stomach. A *wife*? Here Marlow was sticking her neck out for him and he was looking for some other girl to marry.

But what had she expected? That she would break the Compulsion curse and he'd just fall into her arms, declare his undying love, and they'd run off together happily ever after?

She was such a fool. She was the Moon Thief, and he was the Sun King, and at the end of the ballet he returned to his shining court and she was left an outcast in the dark, ruined by her own heart. That's how the story ended. That's how it *always* ended.

"Oh," she said faintly.

"I'm sorry, Marlow," Gemma said again.

"No, I . . . ," Marlow said. "I didn't expect him to . . ."

Gemma snorted. "Remember who you're talking to. It's okay. You can be upset."

Marlow glanced at her. Gemma was intimately familiar with what it felt like to be cast aside by a Falcrest while they pursued a more *suitable* match.

But unlike Amara and Gemma, Adrius and Marlow were never *actually* together. Adrius may have felt something for her, he may have truly cared for her, but that didn't mean he'd give up his family, his future, to be with her.

Gemma cleared her throat. "The, um, the rumor is that he's going to use the Falcrest Midnight Masquerade to start looking for potential suitors. Every girl in Evergarden is conspiring to catch his eye."

"They're still throwing that?" Marlow asked. It was supposed to be held in four days' time, on the third day of the Masquerade Moon.

Which was less than a week before Adrius's curse became permanent.

"I think Amara wants to show Evergarden that they're not going to retreat from society after the . . . tragedy." She shot an almost apologetic look at Marlow. "Or maybe Amara is just trying to get Adrius married off as quickly as possible to strengthen their weakened position."

Either way, the masquerade presented an opportunity for Marlow— one she'd be a fool not to take.

"Gemma," Marlow said, "how do you feel about helping me crash another Falcrest party?"

———————

After Gemma left, it was already time for Marlow to meet Vale in his office parlor for tea. She wasn't exactly looking forward to another awkward meal pretending to play doting daughter, but at least she might be able to weasel out some information about what he might be plotting.

To Marlow's knowledge, this was meant to be an informal teatime between father and daughter, but when she arrived in the parlor it was laden with towers of little cakes and sandwiches, enough food to feed at least two dozen people. A decorative teapot sat in the center of the table, with flower petals swirling in the golden tea.

"Marlow! I'm so glad you could make it," Vale said with a smile as she entered the room. "Please, have a seat. Help yourself to whatever you like."

Marlow paused in front of the table. "You're not expecting anyone else, are you?"

Vale blinked, and then, glancing at the overladen table, let out a loud chuckle. "I may have gotten somewhat carried away. I wasn't sure what kind of tea cakes and sandwiches you prefer."

Marlow's favorite thing to eat with tea was a particular type of chocolate biscuit she purchased from a boat near the Bowery Spellshop. Swift would sometimes bring her one on his way into work. A sudden pang of longing hit her when she thought of Swift, and the Bowery, and even grumpy Hyrum.

"This looks great," Marlow said, sitting down at the table across from him.

Vale selected a sugar-dusted cookie with a center of ruby-red jam from the tower on the table. "Have you had these before? They're my absolute favorite."

Marlow shook her head and plucked one off the tower, nibbling an edge. "It's good."

Vale smiled. He tapped his spoon against the teapot, which lifted off the table and poured golden liquid into her cup.

"Sugar cube?" Vale asked, motioning toward a dish of sugar spun into intricate little flower shapes.

Marlow accepted one and dropped it into her cup.

"I wanted to apologize for last night," Vale said. "I truly didn't think that my sons would react the way that they did."

Marlow shrugged. Clearly, he'd wanted their dinner to result in a tableau like the one Marlow had seen in the Vale foyer—one big, happy family, united and eager to accept Marlow into the fold. The fantasy of that happy family meant that Vale would never have to confront the messy consequences of his affair with Marlow's mother.

"Silvan's never really liked me," she said. "I'm not surprised he wasn't exactly thrilled to find out we're secretly half siblings."

Vale seemed even more troubled by this. "He'll warm up to you," he said firmly. As if he could will it to happen simply by saying it.

Marlow did not actually think Silvan would "warm up" to her under any circumstances—she wasn't sure he had ever "warmed up" to anyone in his life. He was ice all the way through.

"There's something else I need to discuss with you," Vale said, setting his teaspoon down. "Emery Grantaire, the City Solicitor, stopped by this morning to speak with me regarding the Falcrest case. He informed me that his office intends to move forward with the charges against you. They will be setting a date for a preliminary hearing in a few weeks."

Vale's tone was frustrated, and Marlow wondered if he'd tried to persuade Grantaire to drop the charges altogether. But given that she'd confessed to the attack, it didn't seem plausible that they could let her go free—especially not with Amara on the warpath.

She didn't regret taking the blame, but at the time, some part of her had thought she'd find a way to escape the consequences. Now, with a hearing on the horizon and Amara's fury fresh in her mind, she wasn't so sure.

She swallowed. "What does that mean exactly?"

"The city will present the charges against you to the heads of the Five Families, who will then vote to determine whether the case will go to trial."

"Why would the Five Families be the ones to vote on that?" Marlow asked.

Vale raised his eyebrows, surprised by the question. "A provision in the city's charter states that any criminal trial involving a member of the Five Families will be handled by their own."

Gods below. Marlow had never been under any illusions that there was justice in Caraza, but this provision all but guaranteed that the Five Families were untouchable in the court of law. It made Marlow think of what Gemma had said about how the truth didn't matter—what mattered was what the Five Families wanted, and what they chose to believe in order to get it. If it was in their interest to send Marlow to prison for the rest of her life, they wouldn't hesitate to do it. Whether she was actually guilty or not didn't matter.

She sipped her tea, eyeing Vale. Wondering if it came down to it, whether he would step aside and let her be locked up if it meant he'd get away with cursing Adrius.

But maybe this was a good opportunity to test him. Just a little—not enough that he would suspect she knew anything.

"Gemma came to see me today." She was pretty sure Vale already knew that—she doubted anyone came into Vale Tower without his knowledge. But volunteering the information would begin to build trust between them.

"Are the two of you . . . friends?" Vale asked.

Marlow nodded. "She told me there have been rumors in the papers. About me. And . . . you, I suppose."

"There are always rumors in the papers," Vale said dismissively.

"This one said that you're the one behind the attack," Marlow said bluntly. "I didn't read the article. It all seemed so ridiculous."

She kept her gaze locked intently on Vale's face, searching for any sign of guilt or fear.

Vale set his tea down and closed his eyes. "Perhaps not so ridiculous."

Marlow nearly capsized her cup.

"I'm afraid I know exactly where this is coming from."

Marlow didn't dare move, her heart pounding. Was Vale really about to admit everything he'd done? Just like that?

Vale exhaled a slow breath. "Amara must be behind these rumors."

Marlow's heartbeat returned to its normal pace. Not a confession, after all. Of course it wasn't. Why would Vale ever risk telling Marlow the truth? "Amara?"

"She made a bid for control of the Falcrest family," Vale said. "The vassal families were . . . uncomfortable with her proposition. They requested I be instated as a temporary adviser. I believe Amara was very unhappy with the provision. This rumor is her way of lashing out."

"I thought Adrius was supposed to be heir," Marlow said. She had overheard Amara and Aurelius arguing about it the night before the wedding. Vale had also mentioned it to Grantaire, as proof of Adrius's guilt.

"That was Aurelius's intention," Vale agreed. "But Amara claims that Adrius abdicated his role as heir when he left Falcrest Hall and disowned his father. The vassals probably did not want Adrius as heir in the first place. They can sense some of the other Families beginning to circle, now that Aurelius is . . . incapacitated."

"Other Families?" Marlow echoed.

"The Morandis, chiefly," Vale said. "Before the Falcrests took over the Delvigne family, the Morandis were the most powerful of the Five Families. With Aurelius out of the picture, Zeno Morandi believes he can reclaim their status. They're no doubt looking to persuade some of the Falcrest vassals to invest in them instead. If they can siphon off enough of their support, they may even succeed in acquiring the Falcrest's most talented spellwrights, or even parts of the collection at Falcrest Library."

Marlow studied Vale carefully. He very well might be telling the truth—the Morandis likely *were* trying to wrestle some power from the Falcrests now that they were without their patriarch.

But maybe that was what Vale wanted, too. Was that the reason he'd cursed Adrius in the first place? To try to take over the Falcrest family? And if so, to what end?

"Truthfully, I find all of this petty power play and infighting between the Families tiresome," Vale said with a sigh. "I often wonder whether the city would be better off without it."

Marlow pressed her lips together to keep from blurting out her immediate response to that, which was a wholehearted agreement.

"Gemma said there's mostly been relative peace between the Five Families," Marlow said. "But that that could change if they believe there's more to the attack on Aurelius."

"She's right about that." Vale looked grave. "That's why I think it's time you reconsider taking the blame for what happened. Especially now that there are false rumors swirling."

Marlow sat back in her chair. *And what did really happen?* she wanted to ask. But she couldn't let Vale think that she knew anything about his own culpability. Let him think she believed in his innocence. She might be lying about stabbing Aurelius, but so was he—and the harder he pushed to get her to admit the truth, the more suspicious it looked.

"I told you what happened," Marlow said stubbornly. "Aurelius threatened me, and I defended myself. I don't know why you think I'm lying."

Vale did not look fazed. "Right this very moment, what do you suppose Adrius is doing? He's out in Evergarden, looking for a *wife*. He does not care about you the way you care about him, Marlow."

Marlow couldn't deny the twinge of resentment she felt at the reminder of Adrius's search for a *suitable match*.

"Adrius can do whatever he likes," she replied. "It doesn't change the truth."

"He wouldn't do the same thing for you," Vale pressed. "You know he wouldn't."

Marlow swallowed down the bile in her throat. Because the news about Adrius's search for a wife more or less proved Vale's point. "It doesn't matter what he'd do."

Vale kept his gray eyes trained on her a moment longer, giving Marlow the sense that he was trying to figure her out. Then he rested his hands on the table in front of him, and in an entirely different tone, said, "I don't want to continue to argue with you, Marlow. Let's discuss more happy topics, shall we? How are you settling in here?"

"Just fine," Marlow said. "It almost feels like I never left."

A lie, but a small one that hopefully Vale wouldn't clock.

"Good," Vale said warmly. "I'm glad. I want you to feel at home here."

"It's only . . ." Marlow trailed off, biting her lip.

"Yes?"

"Never mind," Marlow said quickly. "It's nothing."

"Marlow, whatever I can do to make you feel more welcome here, just name it."

Marlow nodded. "Vale Tower is lovely, of course. It's just that I've been here for a few days now and I'm feeling rather . . ."

"Cooped up?" Vale suggested. "I understand completely. I was much the same at your age. I used to sneak away from Vale Tower at every opportunity."

"I just need an afternoon out, I think," Marlow said. "Gemma invited me to go shopping with her on Pearl Street tomorrow."

Vale looked uneasy. "Usually I wouldn't hesitate, but I do worry about you being out in Evergarden alone given . . . everything. Why don't I accompany you? I should be able to free up an afternoon tomorrow, or perhaps the next day."

"That's very generous," Marlow said. An idea began to form in her mind, and before she'd thought it through she barreled on, "But maybe you're right about Silvan warming up to me. Maybe if we spent more time together . . . ?"

"Well," Vale said, clearly pleased by Marlow's desire to bond with his son. "There's an idea! I'll make sure he makes time to escort you to Pearl Street tomorrow."

Marlow did not imagine Silvan would be the least bit enthusiastic about this outing, but that would only make it easier for Marlow to get rid of him.

FIVE

When Marlow had agreed to go shopping with Gemma, she hadn't realized that it would be such an *event*. Shopping, to Marlow, meant walking up the Serpent causeway to wander around the Swamp Market, or popping her head into the pawnshop next door to the Bowery.

Shopping to *Gemma* meant an elaborate pre-shopping brunch at Ambrose Teahouse, followed by post-brunch, pre-shopping drinks on Ruby Bridge, followed by manicures and facials at Sunrise Salon (where they plied them with more sweet, fizzy drinks), and finally a private appointment at not one but *five* different ateliers, where they were served even more fizzy glasses of sparkling wine, tiny porcelain cups of tea, and little bite-sized cakes sprinkled with rose petals and gold flakes. Gemma told her that all the maisons on Pearl Street were usually booked months in advance of the Falcrest Masquerade, but that they'd made time for Gemma, the fashion darling of Evergarden.

Marlow had no doubt that was true. She wouldn't be surprised if the maisons paid *Gemma* to wear their creations. Once Gemma wore a dress by a particular maison to an event, that maison could be sure to be flooded with requests for the next year. They'd probably fall all over themselves to do anything she asked.

Silvan met them at the first of the ateliers. He barely said a word to Marlow, merely glared in her direction and occasionally made snide comments to Gemma about how ridiculous Marlow looked, pretending like she'd ever fit in with the noblesse nouveau. Marlow was a little surprised he'd even gone along with this—she'd assumed he'd make some excuse to his father, or if not, he'd at least part from their company at the soonest possible opportunity.

But to her irritation, he stuck to them like glue. Thankfully, he waited outside in the display room while Marlow got fitted for a dress at the final atelier.

"We have a selection of masks if you'd like to take a look, Miss Starling," the attendant offered. "Perhaps that will help narrow down the style for the dress."

"No, thank you," Gemma replied. "We'll be commissioning her mask from Madame Delphine."

"Ah, very good," the attendant said approvingly. "They do fine work there."

"Gemma, I don't need—" Marlow began, but Gemma waved her off.

"Trust me, Marlow, a custom mask is worth the expense," Gemma interrupted. "You don't want to show up to the masquerade wearing the same thing as Opal."

"Isn't Opal a friend of yours?" Marlow asked.

Gemma didn't answer. "We'll go onyx for the mask, I think." She stood behind Marlow, arranging her hair around her face. "And not that your natural color isn't great, but I really think a darker color will suit you *so* well. Maybe a dark toffee or, *ooh*, a deep aubergine?"

Gemma flitted about, comparing different fabric swatches and holding them up to Marlow's face. Marlow felt a little like a doll that Gemma got to play dress-up with.

"Whatever will make me the least recognizable," Marlow said, lowering her voice so the attendant wouldn't overhear. "No one's going to know we were here getting a dress for the masquerade, are they?"

"Relax, I made the appointment under my name and the maisons are very good about keeping their clients' business private," Gemma assured her. At Marlow's confused look, she added, "It's a bit of a game for the gossip magazines to try to suss out who's wearing who at high-profile events like this. The maisons know to keep tight-lipped until the reveal at the party. Everyone wants to make a big splash, so the maisons know if they leak the designs, or even *who* they're designing for, they risk getting blackballed. Especially if it's for the Falcrest Masquerade." She waved one of the sample masks over her face. "Half the fun is the mystery of it."

"This is a whole lot more . . . intense than I ever thought," Marlow said. So much scrutiny at this party meant it would be harder to slip in unnoticed. But it wasn't like she had another plan to talk to Adrius. She glanced at the clock hanging on the wall above Gemma's head. "How much longer are we going to be here?"

Gemma blinked at her. "Why? You have somewhere you need to be?"

"Sort of."

"You can't rush beauty, Marlow," Gemma declared, fluffing Marlow's hair with her fingers. "But . . . I *suppose* I can finish finalizing the designs without you. Assuming you trust my taste."

"Better than I trust my own," Marlow assured her. "Tell Silvan I felt faint or something and went back to Vale Tower."

"I'm guessing you're *not* heading back to Vale Tower?" Gemma said.

Marlow just smiled. "Thanks, Gemma."

She started to get re-dressed, but not in the gauzy day dress she'd come in. Instead, she put on an old pair of her mother's black pants, a fitted gray top, and a dark-blue jacket. She laced up a pair of brown boots and then ducked under the curtain of the fitting room to sneak out the back.

And ran directly into Silvan.

"I thought you were in the display room," she blurted.

He raised an eyebrow. "And I thought you were shopping all day with Gemma."

"I didn't feel well," Marlow said. "Overdid it on the sparkling wine, probably. Too rich for my poor, peasant stomach."

Silvan narrowed his eyes. "Then why don't I escort you back home?"

"Oh, no, I'm sure you have way better things to do," Marlow said, trying to slide past him to the door. "I'll be fine."

Silvan turned and leaned his hand on the door before she could pull it open. "Where are you really going?"

Marlow looked skyward, stifling an irritated sigh. She missed the days when Silvan wanted absolutely nothing to do with her.

"Look, we both know you'd rather be literally anywhere else right now," Marlow said. "So why don't you make both of our lives easier and just let me go. Your dad will be none the wiser."

"Not a chance," he sneered. "I know you're up to something, and I'm going to find out what it is."

Marlow cursed herself for choosing the wrong brother as her decoy. Darian would've bought her flimsy lie in a heartbeat.

"Fine, you got me," she said, raising her hands in surrender. "I *am* up to something, but I swear to you it has nothing to do with you, or Adrius."

"Then what is it?" Silvan demanded.

"I just said it has nothing to do with you," Marlow retorted. "So that makes it none of your business. I'll meet you at Ruby Bridge at sunset so we can go back to Vale Tower together."

She turned to go, but before she could get far she felt something wrap around her wrist, pulling her back toward Silvan.

"What—?" She looked down and saw his pet snake, Bo, trying to slither his way up her arm, still curled around Silvan. Effectively handcuffing them together. "Please tell your snake to get off me."

"No," Silvan replied stubbornly. "Not until you tell me what it is you're plotting."

"I'm not—*gods below*, fine." She rolled her eyes. What did it matter to her if Silvan knew what she was doing? As long as it got him off her back. "I'm trying to track down Swift."

Instead of the bored, uninterested reaction she'd expected, he leaned in toward her, his blue eyes bright and intense. "What do you mean track him down? Where is he?"

Marlow blinked, bewildered by the urgency in his voice. "I don't know—that's why I have to track him down. I haven't seen him since before Darian and Amara's wedding. Leonidas—you remember Leonidas, the one who tried to feed your fingers to his pet crocodile?"

Silvan's jaw twitched, almost a flinch, like he was trying not to relive that night at the Blind Tiger. "I remember."

"Well, he declared open season on us in the Marshes," Marlow explained. "I was supposed to meet Swift somewhere safe. Obviously, that didn't happen. And he hasn't contacted me, so I'm just—I need to make sure he's okay."

"You think the Copperheads got to him?" Silvan asked. There was absolutely no trace of his usual sneering derision in his voice.

"No," Marlow said quickly. Although the truth was, she didn't know. It was certainly a possibility—just not one Marlow wanted to think about for long. There was also the possibility that the Black Orchid had done something to him, since Swift wasn't even supposed to know about them.

Silvan seemed to hear the doubt in her voice, because he asked, almost anxiously, "You're not planning on going back to that place, are you?"

"You mean the Blind Tiger?" Marlow asked. "Not if I can help it."

"All right," Silvan replied, pulling the door open. "Then where are we going?"

Marlow could only gape at him for a moment, before she recovered herself. "*We* are not going anywhere."

"I'm already here, aren't I?" Silvan replied waspishly. "I'll come with you."

Marlow was thoroughly baffled by his insistence. She'd already told him this had nothing to do with him—why was he trying to involve himself? Unless he didn't believe her and thought there was a chance she really was plotting something nefarious.

Marlow knew she wasn't going to get another opportunity as good as this one to sneak off to see the Black Orchid. And there were only a few hours of sunlight left—she didn't want to waste any of this precious time arguing with Silvan. She wanted to find Swift.

"Fine," she agreed at last. "But stay close, keep your mouth shut, and *do not* get in my way."

The Mudskipper Teahouse was located inside an old garment warehouse in the Industrial Quarter. The interior was a cavernous space, with high brick walls and a glass ceiling supported by exposed steel beams. A wall of windows looked out over the canals. From the looks of the clientele seated at the spindly iron tables scattered throughout the open floor, the Mudskipper catered mainly to factory workers and shipbuilders.

Marlow could blend in easily enough, but Silvan in his blue silk jacket was more than a little conspicuous. She pulled him over to a table in the corner and flagged down a waiter to order a pot of tea. Silvan ordered a smattering of tea snacks, which surprised Marlow until they arrived and Silvan began feeding them to Bo.

"So," Marlow said, blowing the steam on her cup of tea and casting about for some topic of conversation so she and Silvan weren't simply steeping in hostile silence. "What do you know about this business with Adrius looking for a wife?"

Silvan shrugged. "I don't understand half the decisions Adrius makes. Dating you, for instance."

That dredged a laugh from Marlow.

"This, though." Silvan shook his head. "This really doesn't seem like him."

But didn't it? Adrius had turned his back on Marlow once before, and his reason had not been cruelty but cowardice. She couldn't be surprised that faced with the same choice, only with much higher stakes, he'd made the same decision. Looking for a wife would signal to the other noblesse nouveau that he'd cut ties with Marlow.

"It was the smart move," Marlow said.

Silvan eyed her. "Yeah," he agreed. "Like I said. It really doesn't seem like him."

There was something Silvan wasn't saying, and it wasn't hard to figure out what it was. It was just a little irritating that Silvan had thought of it before her.

Adrius was still under the Compulsion curse. Meaning that everything he'd done—refusing to see Marlow, announcing his intention to find a wife—might not be by choice.

Amara could have gotten to him and issued the orders—whether or not she knew he'd be compelled to obey them.

Before Marlow could say anything in reply, a man pulled a chair up to their table and sat down, helping himself to Silvan's food.

Marlow recognized him instantly. It was the same man who'd once tailed her all the way through the Swamp Market. When she'd confronted him, he'd warned her away from asking questions about the Black Orchid.

"Can we help you?" Silvan demanded, sounding somewhat scandalized.

"I'm Gray," the man replied.

"I'm—" Marlow began to say, but he cut her off.

"Marlow Briggs," he said, like they were old friends. "What brings you to the Mudskipper?"

"Viatriz said I could find her here," Marlow replied carefully.

Gray eyed Silvan.

"Oh, don't worry, that's just my brother," Marlow said cheerfully.

Silvan shot her a powerful glare. "*Half* brother."

Marlow smiled sweetly. "I'm looking for my friend Swift," she continued. "He came in here a few days ago. Or he was supposed to, anyway. Dark hair, one arm, very handsome, hexed you outside the Swamp Market?"

Silvan glanced at her sharply.

"I know who you're talking about," Gray agreed through a bite of biscuit.

"So he *is* here," Marlow said in relief.

Gray wiped his mouth. "No. I remember him from the Swamp Market, but that's it. He hasn't come through here."

Marlow's heart dropped. "Are you *sure*?"

Gray looked annoyed.

"I want to talk to Viatriz," Marlow insisted. She may not have trusted the woman, but she trusted this guy even less. "I have information that may be of interest to the Black Orchid. But I'll only talk to her."

Gray sighed, looking like he was weighing the headache of continuing to deal with Marlow against the possible consequences of bothering Viatriz with this. "Wait here."

He slipped off to the long, narrow bar that lined one side of the teahouse and leaned over to whisper something to the man behind it. Marlow watched as the other man's eyebrows rose steadily, and then he cast a quick glance over to Marlow and Silvan. A moment later, Gray returned with a teacup, which he placed in front of Marlow.

"Drink this," he said, and did not elaborate further.

Marlow gave the teacup a wary glance. The liquid shimmered slightly. The tea was probably enchanted somehow. Or cursed.

"You want to see Viatriz, drink the tea," Gray said impatiently.

Silvan scoffed. "Yeah, you're going to have to give more of an explanation than that if you expect—"

He broke off as Marlow raised the teacup to her lips and gulped down the liquid. In any other circumstance, she probably would have done more to make sure she hadn't just knocked back a cup of poison, but right now she didn't know where Swift was, and she could feel panic setting in.

The tea was warm going down, but Marlow didn't feel any different after drinking it. She raised her gaze back to Gray, who gave her a quick nod. "Come on, then."

Marlow stood to follow him, as did Silvan.

"You're not invited," Gray said to him.

Silvan sneered. "Why, because I didn't drink your mystery tea?"

"Yes," Gray replied simply, and then led Marlow across the tearoom toward the back wall of windows.

Marlow saw something that hadn't been there before—between two of the windows, a brick archway in the middle of the wall, with a staircase leading down into seemingly nowhere. The staircase must have been concealed by an illusion enchantment—and the tea Gray had given her allowed her to see through the illusion.

The stairs led them down into some kind of basement, dimly lit and wafting with smoke. Musty bookshelves formed partitions, creating small, private alcoves throughout the room. In one of them, two Pento players frowned over their tiles. A phonograph piped out brassy music in the corner.

Gray led her all the way back to where a velvet sofa sat flanked by two wooden stools.

Sitting on the sofa, a cigarette smoldering in one hand, was Viatriz.

Gray leaned into her, murmuring a few words that Marlow didn't catch.

"Thank you, Gray," she said to him as Marlow perched on one of the stools. Viatriz raised an eyebrow in Marlow's direction. "I guess the rumors are true, then. We'd heard you managed to slip out of custody. Not sure I really believed it until now. Gray says you have information for me."

Marlow nodded. "But first I want to know where Swift is."

"As I'm certain Gray already told you, we have no idea where your friend is," Viatriz said. There was a thread of sympathy in her voice that made Marlow feel like her words were the truth. "I'm sorry."

Marlow ground her teeth together to keep back the scream that wanted to erupt from her throat. Swift had to be safe. He *had* to. If the Copperheads had gotten ahold of him . . .

Well, Marlow was already wanted for one murder.

"I know you have eyes and ears all over the city," Marlow said. "If you hear *anything*—anything at all—"

Viatriz nodded. "We'll let you know." She cleared her throat. "So. This information—was that just a ploy?"

"Not a ploy. It's about my mother."

Viatriz leaned forward. "You found her?"

Marlow shook her head, her next words sticking uncomfortably in her throat.

"No," Viatriz said abruptly. "No, there's no way."

Marlow clenched her hands in her lap, tears burning in her eyes, unable to reply.

"Cassandra's too smart to get herself killed."

That was what Marlow had thought, too. The last thing Cassandra had wanted was to become a victim of this city. But Marlow was beginning to think there was no way to escape that fate. Not for people like them.

"Who was it?" Viatriz asked, an unexpected fire in her voice. "The Copperheads?"

Marlow swallowed. "Falcrest."

Viatriz swore. "He found out she stole the grimoire."

Marlow nodded.

"He must have it, then," Viatriz said. "All that, and he still—"

"He doesn't have it," Marlow said. "Mom said she destroyed it."

"How do you—?"

"I saw her," Marlow said. "Not—not since that night. But I saw Caito's memory of that night. I saw what happened. I saw her—" Tears sprang into her eyes again and Marlow battled them back. She couldn't bear to remember what she'd seen in Caito's head. Her mother's fall into the canal. The long minutes Caito had spent waiting to see if she would surface.

The devastation that had torn through Marlow when she hadn't.

"I'm sorry you had to see that." Viatriz's gaze clouded over with genuine sympathy. "But your mother must have lied to Caito."

"What do you mean?"

"There's no way to destroy the grimoire, not with just one person, not in just one night," Viatriz said. "There are powerful enchantments on that spellbook. Knowing Cassandra, she probably found a place to stash it until the heat died down."

Whatever Cassandra had done with the grimoire, it had ended up in Vale's hands. But Marlow wasn't willing to share that with Viatriz just yet.

"Well, I just wanted to let you know," Marlow said, standing from the stool. "Mom didn't betray you to the Copperheads like you thought. Falcrest got to her."

"You blame us," Viatriz surmised.

"I blame Falcrest."

"Then I guess he got what was coming to him," Viatriz said. "Is that why you tried to kill him?"

Marlow flashed a wan smile. "Don't believe everything you read in the gossip magazines, Viatriz."

"Oh, really?" Viatriz asked. "Then I shouldn't believe what they're saying about you being the daughter of Cormorant Vale?"

Marlow froze.

"So it *is* true. You know, I always thought there was more to Cassandra's relationship with him than she let on," Viatriz went on. "I should've known."

"I only just found out," Marlow said.

"Well, that's awfully lucky for me," Viatriz replied.

Marlow eyed her. "What does that mean?"

"It means that now that you're a Vale, you have access to Vale Library," Viatriz replied. "That makes you useful to me."

"And why would I do any favors for you?"

Viatriz stood abruptly and went to a cabinet that stood against the wall. She opened it, revealing shelves and shelves of spellcards, organized and labeled meticulously. Viatriz pulled a few off the shelves.

"I'm guessing you don't have a good way to get the kind of spells you need in Vale Tower," Viatriz said, holding out the spellcards. "But the Black Orchid—we've got plenty of spells. And we're happy to share. In return for your help, of course."

Marlow hesitated to take the cards. "My help with what exactly?"

"Nothing dangerous," Viatriz said. "Nothing even *difficult*. We just need a way to smuggle something into the library without detection."

Marlow was still on the fence about whether the Black Orchid could be trusted. And she was all too aware that this was likely how Cassandra's association with them had started—a simple favor here and there, until suddenly she was stealing a forbidden grimoire from Falcrest Library.

Marlow knew how that had turned out.

She reached for the spellcards and looked through them. A Lockpick spell. An Eavesdrop enchantment. An Immobilizing hex.

"You don't have to make a decision now. Here." Viatriz held out two more spellcards—Disguise spells. "Consider this a gesture of goodwill. You want more, you come back here."

Marlow added them to the stack and slipped all five spellcards into her pocket. "I'll think about it."

SIX

"*So where is* he?" Silvan asked, keeping pace as Marlow marched back through the Mudskipper and onto the muddy road.

"I don't know."

"If these people don't have him, does that mean the Copperheads do?"

"*I don't know.*" Frustration and fear sharpened her tone. She whirled toward him. "Why do you even care?"

Silvan huffed, looking off toward the canal. "What do we do now?"

"Now you go back to Evergarden," Marlow told him, stomping down the stairs that led to Cannery Dock. "Field trip's over."

"Where are *you* going?" Silvan countered.

Marlow didn't need to think particularly hard about that. She was going to turn over every rock in the Marshes to find Swift. "To get answers."

"Well, I'm coming," Silvan declared. "If you wind up getting killed and your body gets dumped in the canals while you were supposed to be out shopping on Pearl Street with me, my father will eviscerate me."

"I doubt that," Marlow said. "But I'm not going to waste time arguing with you."

She jabbed the light at the end of the dock, which flickered green to grab the attention of passing water-taxis. It didn't take long for one of them to pull up to the dock.

Marlow slid onto the bench seat.

"Take us to the Swamp Market," Marlow directed the driver. She reached into her pocket for the two Disguise spellcards Viatriz had given her.

"Here," she said, handing one to Silvan.

"What am I supposed to do with a Disguise spell?" Silvan asked.

"What do you think?"

"Is that really necessary?"

"The minute we show our faces in the Marshes, the Copperheads are going to be all over us," Marlow said briskly. "So yeah, it's really necessary."

Silvan glared, but he cast his spellcard as Marlow cast her own. She watched his hair darken, his features changing minutely, until he no longer looked like Silvan at all. She knew her own features were doing the same subtle shifting. She'd used Disguise spells before on cases, although rarely, because they were expensive. The fact that Viatriz had freely handed her *two* was definitely her way of showing off the Black Orchid's resources.

"The spell only lasts two hours," Marlow told him. She nodded to the snake coiled around his arm. "You should hide Bo."

Silvan dutifully coaxed Bo into his sleeve, where he curled around his bicep, an unassuming lump.

They wound through the familiar, muck-filled waterways of the Marshes until the crooked causeway of the Serpent came into view.

The Marshes was like a living creature, its waterways like veins and arteries, the rickety ladders and rope bridges its sinew. And the Serpent was its long, crooked backbone, connecting the disparate enclaves together.

The waterways surrounding the Swamp Market were snarled with traffic, so Marlow had the boat driver let them off at a dock that splintered off from the main branch of the Serpent.

It felt—well, not *good* exactly, but at least familiar to be back here after being sequestered at Vale Tower. Ironically, the rickety, swaying dock felt like the most solid ground Marlow had been on in days.

"What are we doing here exactly?" Silvan asked.

"Paying a visit to an old friend," Marlow replied. "Don't wander off."

Silvan's glare effortlessly communicated that roaming into the morass of unwashed Marshes-dwellers was the very last thing he wanted to do. His gait was stilted as they joined the crowds flooding into the Swamp Market proper, climbing down ladders and crossing unstable dockways that wove between the boats.

Every first day of the month, the center of the lagoon the Swamp Market occupied was cleared out to make way for the Swamp Brawling arena. It was the biggest monthly event in the Marshes, drawing crowds of thousands who flocked to the piers and plankways and even on top of boat cabins and ladders to watch the spectacle.

Marlow bought herself and Silvan tickets to spectate on one of the floating platforms surrounding the main arena. She also stopped to buy a paper cone of fried shrimp tails, which she munched while shepherding Silvan to their platform. She kept an eye on the crowd around them, searching for anyone wearing the telltale bronze snake tattoo that marked them as a Copperhead. Even though she and Silvan were disguised, she still wanted to stay clear of them.

The Swamp Brawling tournament drew big crowds, and it was the one place in the Marshes where members of the various gangs regularly mingled in uneasy peace. As no single gang had ever managed to gain control of the entire Swamp Market, it was a neutral territory in their unending turf wars.

"What the hell is this?" Silvan asked, eyeing the elaborately costumed dancers in the center of the arena, who were already chanting, stomping, and gyrating, hyping up the crowd in advance of the match.

"*This* is the finest entertainment the Marshes has to offer." Marlow shook her cone at him. "Shrimp tail?"

Silvan made a face like he would rather jump off the platform, but Bo poked his head out of his sleeve, black tongue flicking in interest.

"If we're here just so you can get me to leave, it's not going to work," Silvan informed her.

"Darn, there goes my plan." She dumped the last of the shrimp tails and flattened the paper cone between her hands.

Suddenly, the crowd around them erupted into impassioned cheers and chants. Down in the ring, the first competitor was making their entrance.

They stood around six and a half feet tall, with long, dark hair and tattoos covering nearly every inch of their muscular body. Their face was painted with red and black paint, and they wore an elaborate costume, with swamp reeds hanging down their back and a skirt woven from moss.

The fearsome Brash Buccaneer.

The Brash Buccaneer pounded their chest and roared at the crowd. The crowd roared back. Around the ring, the dancers ululated and shook their hips.

Four shirtless men entered the ring, a long, narrow cage held aloft on their shoulders. Slowly, they lowered it to the muddy ground and backed away.

The Brash Buccaneer pounded their chest again.

The cage opened. A seven-foot-long crocodile crawled out.

Marlow glanced at Silvan and saw that he had gone even paler than usual.

"Are they really going to fight that thing?" he asked in alarm.

His question was answered when the crocodile made a shockingly fast lunge for the Brash Buccaneer. They backflipped out of range. The crowd hollered its approval.

The crocodile and the fighter circled each other slowly, the creature's tail whipping back and forth behind it. Suddenly, it struck again. This time, the fighter threw themself to the side and then rolled onto the crocodile's back, grasping its long snout firmly between their broad hands. Crocodile jaws, it was said, were incredibly powerful when they snapped closed on their prey. But when they used those same muscles to try to *open* their jaws, they were very weak.

Keeping their grip on its snout, the Brash Buccaneer forced the croc's head up, using their powerful arms to hold it in place.

Silvan looked even more alarmed than before. "Are they hurting it?"

Marlow blinked in surprise. "You're worried about the *crocodile*?"

Silvan shot her a glare. Marlow supposed that it actually made sense—Silvan didn't really like most people, after all, but he'd always had an affinity for deadly, cold-blooded creatures.

"Don't worry," Marlow assured him. "It's a show. The crocodile is trained for this."

In the ring, the Brash Buccaneer forced the crocodile's jaws open, and then lowered their head between its sharp teeth. The crowd stomped and cheered and chanted in delight.

The Brash Buccaneer pulled their head away and then swung around to pin the beast on its back. The crocodile thrashed wildly beneath the fighter as the crowd gleefully counted down from five, their voices rising to a deafening crescendo as they reached *one*.

As soon as the announcer called the match, Marlow and Silvan shouldered through the crowd toward an elaborately decorated fanboat moored to one of the surrounding piers. The rest of the crowd was homing in on the ring, where the Brash Buccaneer was making their victory lap before exiting as the dancers stepped back in. Marlow watched the Brash Buccaneer swagger up the gangway to their boat, which was festooned with bright red feathers, dyed swamp reeds, and violet bioluminescent lights strung up in fishing nets. The deck of the boat had been arranged into a lounge-like area, with a plush couch and a hammock where the Brash Buccaneer reclined with a few scantily clad companions, smoking a fat, cherry-tipped cigar and eating fresh oysters off the shell.

"Nice friends you've got," Silvan hissed under his breath.

Marlow pulled him to the end of the gangway, where they were stopped by a burly bouncer with a glinting gold tooth.

"What do you think you're doing?"

"We just want an autograph," Marlow said excitedly, thrusting out the flattened shrimp tail cone. "Please, my brother and I have been waiting for this match for *weeks*! The Brash Buccaneer is our *favorite* Swamp Brawler."

She elbowed Silvan.

He coughed. "Big, big fan."

The bouncer eyed the shrimp tail cone. Marlow had written a note on it during the match, but it was folded over so the bouncer couldn't see.

"Fine," he said at last, snatching it from her hand. "Wait here."

He walked up the gangway, boarded the fanboat, and handed the note to the Brash Buccaneer.

Marlow watched as they read it, expression transforming from lazy indulgence to full-on confusion. They glanced up, gaze finding Marlow.

Marlow waggled her fingers.

The Brash Buccaneer motioned Marlow and Silvan to approach, and then waved off their companions.

Marlow took a seat on the couch across from them. Silvan sat gingerly beside her, pulling his limbs very close to his body as though afraid to let them touch anything.

"Marlow Briggs," the Brash Buccaneer said slowly. "Didn't think you'd show your face here."

Silvan nervously eyed Marlow.

"Well, technically, I'm not," Marlow said, gesturing at her disguised features.

The Brash Buccaneer's face cracked into a brilliant smile. "You got me there! How *are* you? I heard a rumor you were in jail!"

"Aw, well, you should know even jail time can't keep me from cheering on my favorite Swamp Brawler," Marlow said, grinning back at them.

"And who's this cutie?" the Brash Buccaneer asked, throwing a wink in Silvan's direction.

Marlow stifled a laugh at Silvan's rattled expression. "That's my brother."

"Stop saying that," Silvan hissed.

"Oh, don't mind him," Marlow said breezily. "He seems prickly, but deep down he's—well, actually, he's pretty much just terrible all the way through."

Silvan glowered poisonously.

"What'd you think of the match?" the Brash Buccaneer asked. "Pretty great, right? Did you see my new finishing move? The crowd *loved* it."

"One of your very best performances," Marlow agreed.

They went back and forth for a few minutes, reliving the most exciting moments of the match, Marlow making sure to shower the Brash Buccaneer with praise. Silvan glanced between the two of them, looking increasingly bewildered by the conversation.

"So, listen," Marlow said after a few minutes. "I need your help with something."

"Of course! Anything for you!" the Brash Buccaneer said, beaming. "After all, if it weren't for the curse you broke, there wouldn't *be* a Brash Buccaneer."

"I just did what I could," Marlow said airily.

"So, what is it you need? Front row tickets to the next match?"

Marlow smiled faintly. "I need to know if you've heard anything about the Copperheads picking up Swift."

The Brash Buccaneer's exuberant smile flickered out. "That . . . isn't something I can help you with."

"Because you don't know anything, or because you don't want to tell me?" Marlow pressed. The Swamp Brawling matches were awash in dark money from the street gangs. As one of the top competitors, the Brash Buccaneer had regular enough contact with the gangs to know of any rumors circulating.

That was one reason Marlow had chosen them to talk to today. The other reason was that they were the person she'd figured would be most amenable to helping her and the least likely to betray her.

But it seemed they weren't quite amenable enough.

The Brash Buccaneer leaned in, lowering their voice. "Marlow, if anyone finds out I talked to you about the Copperheads . . . especially when they've offered a reward to anyone who brings you to them . . ."

"There's a *reward* now?" Marlow grumbled. "You've got to be kidding."

"They really have it out for you," the Brash Buccaneer said uneasily.

"And for Swift," Marlow said. "So if you *do* know something . . ."

The Brash Buccaneer looked at her for a long moment and then heaved out a breath. "Godsdamnit. You know I can't say no to you. Fine. I haven't heard anything about the Copperheads and Swift."

"Are you sure?"

"Nothing about the *Copperheads*," the Brash Buccaneer said again, giving it more emphasis.

Marlow's eyes widened. Someone else, then. "The Reapers?"

"I may have a friend who deals curses for them who heard from one of their household staff that they've got a new guest over on Reaper Island."

"What the hell do the Reapers want with Swift?" Marlow asked.

The Brash Buccaneer shrugged. "It's just what I heard."

Suddenly, the sound of raised voices crested over the din of the crowd. Marlow, Silvan, and the Brash Buccaneer turned toward the source of the commotion.

"You spineless, cheating swamp rat, I'll—"

"*Cheating?* You accuse *me* of cheating?"

"Well, I'd expect nothing less from a Copperhead."

Marlow's gaze locked onto two men squaring off in the middle of a gangway. One of them, she noted, had a bronze snake tattooed around his neck. A crowd had formed around them, watching the two like they were another Swamp Brawling match.

"Rich words," the Copperhead snarled, "coming from the mouth of a Reaper."

The Reaper shot off a hex toward the Copperhead, dark-purple glyphs zinging through the air. The Copperhead fired one back.

"Should we leave?" Silvan asked, tense at Marlow's side.

"Reapers and Copperheads are always getting into scuffs," Marlow replied dismissively. Both gangs knew it was too much of a risk to get into any real conflict here. "The Swamp Market is technically neutral ground. So once they've gotten a few licks in they'll go their separate—"

The Reaper fired another spell, this one a ghastly green that ricocheted off a nearby boat and into the brackish water. A wave of mud rose around the Copperhead, engulfing him before splashing back down over the gangway.

There was a stunned pause from the spectators. And then, a moment later, hexes fired from all directions toward the Reaper still standing there.

Chaos exploded over the crowd. Before Marlow could even move, hexes were hurtling through the air, uncaring of who was caught in the crossfire.

She grabbed Silvan's arm. "Okay. *Now* we should run."

SEVEN

Marlow pulled Silvan through the chaos, ducking under flying hexes and scrambling over the boats and rafts and plankways that comprised the Swamp Market. She had no real plan for where she was going other than *away* from the fighting—only she had no idea what direction *away* was.

The market quickly became a snarl of panicked boats unmooring themselves, trying in vain to flee from the chaos as the crowd swarmed the few vessels capable of rowing away. Marlow watched as dozens more people went splashing into the churning morass of the market.

"What do we do?" Silvan demanded.

Marlow's mind raced. The waterways were way too choked with traffic. The Pavilion cable car station would be swamped with people trying to flee.

She spotted an abandoned river barge half sunk into the mud at the edge of the Swamp Market. A rusted old chassis that probably hadn't moved in years. "In here."

She grabbed hold of the rope ladder and started to climb up the side, Silvan at her heels. She swung herself over and onto the main deck, which was tilted at such a dramatic angle that she had to sit with her knees bent and her feet in front of her hips to slide down to the lower side.

From this vantage point, she could see more clearly the chaos of the market around them. Over on the Swamp Brawling platforms, a group of

Reapers and a group of Copperheads were still locked in combat, flinging hexes and curses at one another with abandon. Meanwhile, the crowd was trying its best to vacate the arena, knotting around various choke points of the market's crisscrossing walkways. Many of the boats in the center of the market had already been abandoned, the water too grid-locked to allow much movement.

Marlow scanned desperately for an exit route.

There.

A small dinghy floated off the northern edge of the market, moored to a crooked, rotting dock. Getting to it would mean going against the crowd and back toward the fighting, but that was a risk they were going to have to take. Quickly, she charted their route through the labyrinthine market.

"See that boat over there?" Marlow said, pointing it out to Silvan. "That's our way out. Stay close and move fast."

Before he could reply, Marlow climbed over the barge's gunwale and onto the elevated dock below it. From there, they were able to cross a rope bridge to the crow's nest of another boat, down the ladder, and onto a lower dock. The crowd had started to thin here, but they still had to fight their way through.

And just as Marlow spotted the dinghy ahead of them, a loud *crack* and a scream filled the air. The dock buckled beneath the stress of the stampede. Behind Silvan and Marlow, the wooden dock gave way, plunging dozens of people down into the muddy waters below.

Marlow seized Silvan's arm and pulled him forward. She could feel the dock continuing to crack beneath them, but they were *almost* there, almost at the boat. She could see it ahead.

And she could see someone else heading straight for it, too. A brawny man with a scruffy beard and dark hair that fell in tangles to his shoulders. He darted toward the boat's mooring, untying it from the dock. On his bare shoulder, Marlow saw a silver tattoo of a scythe.

A Reaper.

She didn't think. She just reached for the Immobilizing hex Viatriz had given her and aimed.

"*Congelia!*"

The Reaper went stiff and then collapsed to the ground.

The dock gave way beneath Marlow's feet. She let out a scream, clawing at the rotted wood planks, fingernails digging in to keep her from falling into the water below. "*Silvan!*"

He was two steps ahead of her, and at the sound of his name he turned, bewildered, and then spotted her. Skidding to a halt, he reached out and grasped her hand, pulling her to safety.

Without missing a beat, Marlow sprinted to the dinghy and launched herself into it, Silvan at her heels.

The Reaper still lay immobilized on the dock. Marlow hesitated—and then cut the mooring, sending them adrift.

"Thanks for saving me," she said to Silvan. She lifted a paddle and handed the other to Silvan. "I guess we're even now."

Silvan made a dismissive noise. Then, after a moment, he said, "That was pretty ruthless back there."

"Yeah, well, that's the Marshes for you," Marlow replied.

He squinted his eyes. "No, I meant you. Hexing that man."

Marlow stared at him. He sounded almost . . . disapproving. Like she'd done something wrong. And coming from Silvan, that was—well, it was almost laughable. "That man was a Reaper. He would've killed us, or worse."

Silvan shrugged. "Still."

They rowed in silence, the chaos of the Swamp Market fading into the distance.

Things were worse than Marlow had imagined. The conflict between the Reapers and the Copperheads had existed for as long as Marlow had been alive, but it had never been *this* destructive. People would get hurt—people had *already* gotten hurt. Marlow couldn't help but feel a wave of guilt. She wasn't the sole cause for the war between the gangs, but would things have gotten this bad this quickly if not for her?

If she hadn't pissed off the Copperheads so egregiously, they wouldn't have declared open season on her and violated their territory agreement with the Reapers.

And now the Reapers had Swift. She didn't know what that meant, what they were planning to do with him, but it could be nothing good.

"If we don't get back to Evergarden by sundown," Silvan warned, "my father is going to send a search party for us."

Silvan was right. And soon enough, their Disguise spells would wear off.

As much as Marlow wanted to storm Reaper Island and find Swift, she knew she'd never make it past the dock unless she figured out a plan to get in.

Hold on, Swift. I'm coming for you, she promised. And then she turned the boat toward Evergarden.

O*ver the next* three days, Marlow plotted Swift's rescue, sneaking away from Vale Tower every chance she could and cashing in just about every favor owed to her to gather as much information as she could about the Reapers. She tried not to think about what Swift might be enduring as their prisoner.

And, while she waited for her opening to sneak onto Reaper Island, she had a masquerade to attend.

She returned to Vale Tower to find Gemma already standing inside her apartment, a large box leaning up against the wall.

"And just where have you been?" Gemma demanded as Marlow opened the door.

"I was running an errand," Marlow replied, bewildered. "Did we have plans?"

Gemma gaped at her. "Please don't tell me you *forgot* about the Midnight Masquerade."

Marlow blinked. "I didn't forget about it. But isn't it . . . you know. Later tonight? As in, hours from now?"

"Exactly," Gemma snapped. "We're already behind schedule." She herded Marlow toward the washroom. "Your dress and mask were delivered to Starling Manor this morning. Now, I already drew you a bath— go get in, and do not forget to wash your hair. I'll meet you out here when you're done."

Marlow undressed and carefully stepped into the tub. The bathwater was gently perfumed with something floral and sweet, frothy with thick pink and lavender bubbles that glistened in the light. It was, of course, the perfect temperature, enchanted to remain that way no matter how long Marlow stayed in. Marlow wanted to ask why there was glitter in the bathwater, but she wasn't entirely sure she wanted to know the answer.

Despite Gemma's insistence that they were running behind—how *that* was possible, Marlow couldn't fathom—she took her time. There was a variety of different creams and soaps and serums that definitely hadn't been there earlier that day, but absolutely no instructions as to what they were meant for. Marlow tried a bit of each, rubbing them onto her skin and combing them into her hair. She had never felt so confused by the mechanics of taking a bath. Back in the Marshes, she'd cleaned herself using a spigot and basin attached to the outside of her flat—she was lucky if she had a Warming spellcard to heat the water.

When she was reasonably sure she was clean, she slipped on a silk robe that hung next to the door and went back into the living room, where Gemma was standing by Marlow's mother's writing desk, the chair pulled out.

"Sit."

Marlow obeyed.

"Now, normally," Gemma said, combing through Marlow's wet hair with her fingers, "I would have brought over my personal beauty consultants to help with this transformation. But I realize the fewer people who know you're going to the masquerade, the better, so you'll just have to make do with me."

She grinned at Marlow in the mirror.

"Since your face is mostly going to be covered by the mask, we won't go *too* excessive with Illusion spells," Gemma said. "But we definitely need to pick a new eye color—yours is too distinct. So gray they're almost purple. But what do you think—green? Brown? Amber?"

"Whatever you think is best," Marlow replied.

Gemma selected a spellcard with a gilded illustration of an eye. "*Cambiare.*"

Cornflower-blue glyphs floated out from the spellcard and surrounded Marlow's head in a pale halo. When they dissipated, though, nothing had changed. Marlow's eyes were the same stormy gray.

"Huh," Gemma said thoughtfully, looking at Marlow's reflection. "That's weird. Must have been a dud card." She shuffled through her other cards. "Maybe brown, then?"

Marlow caught her wrist. "Wait." She turned around to face Gemma. "Look again."

Gemma's eyebrows shot up in surprise. "They're blue. Bright blue."

"It's the mirror," Marlow explained. "It was my mother's. It's called a Mirror of Truth—it sees past illusions. Shows things as they truly are."

"Well, that's not going to be particularly helpful to us today," Gemma remarked.

"I have another mirror in my bedroom," Marlow said. "I'll switch them."

She gripped either side of the mirror and unhooked it carefully from the wall. She then hurried into her bedroom, switching out the Mirror of Truth for the unenchanted one that hung above her dresser.

When she returned to the living room with the other mirror, Gemma was staring at the wall with an odd expression on her face.

"What's wrong?" Marlow asked.

Gemma just pointed. The part of the wall where the Mirror of Truth had hung had a small square carved out of it, forming a kind of compartment. A hiding place.

Marlow's heart drummed in her chest. There was only one thing inside the compartment. A small, leather-bound notebook.

Marlow reached for it without even thinking about it. Her hands shook.

"It must have been my mother's," Marlow said faintly.

"Is it a journal?" Gemma asked.

If this really was a journal, then maybe Marlow could finally understand the choices her mother had made that had led her to her death. Maybe she could finally understand who her mother was beneath all the deceit and confidence tricks.

But when she opened the notebook, she saw that it was filled with pages and pages of some kind of chart. The first column listed dates, stretching back for several years. The second column listed names. The third column was filled with numbers in neat, round sums in the ten thousands. The last column also contained sums, although they were uniformly smaller than the first sums. Marlow paged through the whole thing, but that was all that was in there.

She felt foolish for imagining she'd just found some kind of secret diary Cassandra had left that could explain everything. All her secrets, laid out in ink for Marlow to ponder.

But that kind of closure was as much a fantasy as the thought of somehow finding her mother alive. And that fantasy had been dashed to pieces the moment Marlow had peered inside Caito's memories and seen her mother's tragic fall into the canals.

But if this wasn't a diary, what was it? Marlow paged through it again, but slower. She recognized some of the names. Lyam Zarconi. Ginevra Thorn. Aldrik Hargrave. They were Vale spellwrights. The two columns of numbers looked like they could be amounts of money—some kind of payment?

"It's just records," Marlow said to Gemma.

"Records of *what*?"

In a flash, Marlow remembered what Bane had told her about Cassandra taking a cut from Vale spellwrights who were selling curses on the black market in exchange for not turning them in. Her stomach knotted. Had she just discovered evidence of her mother's extortion scheme?

She looked at the chart again, her heart sinking. The two columns of sums glared up at her. Thousands of pearls that Cassandra had bled from rogue spellwrights. Profit that she'd made from the curse trade. And the second column was—what? Another cut of the profits, perhaps? Someone else Cassandra had been paying off to keep the scheme going?

This was pointless. What did it *matter* that Cassandra was blackmailing Vale spellwrights? What would Marlow gain by solving another mystery that, in the end, wouldn't change the fact that her mother was dead?

Nothing. It would do her no good.

She clapped the ledger shut and shoved it back into the compartment.

"Whatever it is, it doesn't matter," Marlow said harshly. "It's not like it can bring her back." She hung the mirror over the compartment and sat back down in the chair. "Let's just finish getting ready."

Gemma looked a little startled by the flatness of Marlow's tone, but she nodded, picking up a hair comb.

Over the course of the next few hours, Gemma played handmaiden to Marlow, buffing, polishing, brushing, and primping her within an inch of her life.

When she was done, Marlow hardly recognized herself—which was, of course, the whole point.

Her dress was a shimmery, iridescent material that Gemma told her was made out of mother-of-pearl. Her mask was a delicate black filigree, interlaid with pearl and clear crystals over the eyes and in the center of the forehead. Gemma had colored her hair midnight blue, so dark it almost appeared black unless it caught the light, with highlights of silver. Her lips were painted dark, with just a smear of iridescent shimmer to them. When Marlow donned the mask and looked at herself in the mirror, she felt entirely transformed—no longer Marlow Briggs, but instead some enigmatic, elegant girl who could sweep anyone off their feet with ease.

"What do you think?" Gemma asked, looking smug.

"I barely recognize myself," Marlow said—though she wasn't sure how she felt about that.

"Ah, almost forgot," Gemma said, and then laid a string of pearls around Marlow's bare neck. "Finishing touch."

Marlow stared at the girl in the mirror. She looked like noblesse nouveau. She looked like the daughter of one of the Five Families.

Which, Marlow had to remind herself, she was.

"Ready?" Gemma asked, offering her arm.

Marlow rose and took it. "Ready."

The hallway leading inside the Grand Ballroom of Falcrest Hall was already overflowing with revelers when Marlow approached, her heart in her throat. Hundreds of noblesse nouveau made their way down the hallway, dressed in extravagant clothes and sparkling masks.

Marlow knew that Adrius would be the center of attention tonight, so step one was to get close enough to talk to him. Step two was to get him alone without revealing who she was—if Adrius really *had* been ordered to stay away from her, then the moment he realized it was her it would all be over.

How exactly Marlow was going to accomplish that, she hadn't quite figured out.

Slowly, following the ebb and flow of the crowd, Marlow made her way into the ballroom. Two staircases swept down from either corner of the room, joining together onto a landing framed by a magnificent gilded arch and backed by a huge window that looked out on the glittering Caraza cityscape.

It was on that landing that Marlow spotted Adrius, a glass of chilled wine in his hand, holding court amidst a large coterie of admirers. Even wearing a mask of gold, it was impossible to mistake him.

It had been over a week since Marlow had stood in the same room with him. Even here, over a hundred paces away, her breath caught at the sight of him. He wore a shot silk jacket that seemed to change color as it reflected the ballroom lights—pale gold at some angles, turquoise and bright carmine in others. A lock of burnished brown hair fell over the edge of his mask.

Girls spilled down the staircase, waiting in line to get a chance to speak with him. With no other recourse, Marlow joined the line, attempting to blend in. She couldn't quite stop herself from wondering which of them would succeed in catching his eye—or if someone already had.

To Adrius's right stood Silvan, looking as bored as ever in a shimmering emerald suit. He hadn't even worn a proper mask, but instead had one painted on in silver. It did nothing to obscure his features, of course, but Marlow figured that was probably the point. Silvan wasn't one for facades.

For perhaps the first time ever, the sight of Silvan made Marlow feel more relieved than resigned. At least it meant that there was someone close to Adrius who could step in and intercede if any of these girls unwittingly issued a command that Adrius otherwise would be forced to follow.

But the figure standing on Adrius's other side filled Marlow only with dread. It was Amara, dressed in deep red and black, her face half-obscured by a ruby mask. She appeared to be acting as a gatekeeper for the girls, allowing only those who passed muster through to speak to Adrius. The ones she found lacking—by some criteria known only to her—were quickly sent right back down the stairs.

Which meant Marlow was going to have to get past her, without Amara realizing who she really was.

And if Amara saw through her disguise, well—Marlow didn't want to think what she might do to her.

EIGHT

Adrius pressed his fingers against his throbbing temple, his vision going fuzzy at the edges as he looked out at the opulent ballroom, the swirl of elegant dresses on the dance floor, the glasses of sparkling wine catching the light of the floating chandeliers.

"What was that?" he asked the girl he'd been conversing with. She seemed young—too young to be married off—but he didn't want to seem rude.

"Would you, um, would you care to dance the next song?" she asked in a nervous stutter.

"Adrius and I are very busy greeting our guests just now," Amara cut in smoothly before Adrius could reply. "Perhaps later in the evening."

The girl dipped into a lopsided curtsy and then fled down the stairs on unsteady legs.

"How many more guests must we greet?" Adrius asked his sister, his head pulsing slightly as the lights in the ballroom flickered from gold to red and back again.

"You would think I was asking you to catalog the Falcrest financial records," Amara muttered at his side. "Isn't this your ideal way to spend an evening? Indulging in your vices and charming every girl in sight?"

He couldn't deny it. There was once a time when he would have reveled in the extravagance of the masquerade, dancing with as many girls as he could, downing glasses of enchanted wine, letting the attention of the crowd pour over him.

Now he felt as though he would rather be anywhere but here. Everything just felt so . . . tedious.

He fought to keep his attention focused on the girls trying to flirt and make conversation with him. He replied like he was reciting lines. Their comments fell broadly into three categories: compliments, which Adrius returned with a charming smile; condolences about his father, which he dully thanked them for; and invitations to dance, which Adrius invariably accepted, unless Amara refused for him.

But when he led his partners out onto the ballroom floor, he couldn't quite stop himself from letting his gaze linger over the masked guests. He could almost convince himself it was idle curiosity at who was in attendance, or admiration of the exquisite outfits and masks they wore.

But then his gaze would snag on a flutter of dark blond hair, or the edge of a sarcastic smile, and in that split second he couldn't lie to himself.

He was looking for *her*.

Of course, she wasn't here. She had no reason to come, and every reason to stay away. Adrius knew that.

But it did not stop him from looking for her. From wondering if any of the jewel-encrusted masks glittering throughout the room could be hiding her face. It did not stop him from hoping.

"Thank you for the dance," Adrius's current partner said in a smooth, lilting tone. Iris, she'd said her name was. "Perhaps you can come find me later for another."

She let her fingers trail over Adrius's sleeve. Even with the jeweled mask hiding her face, Adrius could tell she was very pretty. Soft brown curls framed a heart-shaped face. Her skin was a warm, sun-kissed brown, and her eyes a startling shade of emerald that matched her dress.

He could take her hand now, lead her through the ballroom doors and into the garden. Press her against the trellis and kiss her.

But he knew he'd only be doing it to drown out the memory of *her*— of another night, another party, a darkened parlor. The heat of her body against his. The scent of summer rain on her skin. The taste of smoke and honey on her lips. The way her hands had pulled him into her.

He had to move on. For real, this time. Because he'd already been here before. A year ago, after Marlow had unceremoniously disappeared from Evergarden and Adrius's guilt and shame had kept him from tearing apart every corner of the city to find her.

He'd told himself then that he would move on and accept the fact that he was too big a coward to ever be worthy of her. He'd distracted himself with whoever he could find, and almost had himself convinced that it was what he wanted.

It had all unraveled the moment he saw her again at the Monarch Theater, looking everything and nothing like the girl he'd spent a year trying to get out of his head.

He tried not to think about what she would think of all this. She would have heard about his public search for a wife by now, and she must hate him again. He wasn't sure he didn't deserve it.

"Perhaps I will," he told his dance partner with a slow, inviting smile. He took her hand in his and pressed his lips to her knuckles. "Or perhaps we can find some other way to occupy ourselves."

She cocked her head at him. "You don't need to do that, you know."

Adrius blinked at her in surprise. Her hand slipped out of his. "Excuse me?"

She waved vaguely. "This act you're putting on. The charming smiles and the flirtatious lines."

"You think it's an act?"

She shrugged. "You don't really seem like you want to be here."

Adrius did not know how to reply to that. The fact that she'd so easily seen through the charade, this girl who didn't even *know* him. It upset him in a way he didn't fully understand.

"Well, you're right," he replied curtly. "I *don't* want to be here, having my motives questioned by some girl I don't even know."

"I wasn't trying to offend you—" she began.

"If you'll excuse me," he said icily. "I must attend to my other guests."

He turned, striding swiftly back to his post on the grand staircase, and did not look back.

NINE

O*ver the last* half hour, Marlow had waited patiently in line, rising steadily along the staircase, inching closer and closer to her destination. Once or twice, Adrius allowed himself to be led onto the dance floor and Marlow was forced to watch him twirl some other dazzling girl around below the floating crystal chandeliers.

And then, at last, she reached the landing of the staircase, and was face-to-face with the last obstacle to getting to Adrius.

"Who are you?" Amara demanded.

Marlow dropped into a delicate curtsy. "Marlena Orsino," she replied, pitching her voice low and adopting a heavy Vescovi accent. She'd perfected it over years of imitating accents with her mother to amuse themselves—and sometimes to run cons. "My father is the marquis of the Bolcini *provenza* of Vescovi. We're visiting your lovely city on holiday."

Amara's gaze tracked over Marlow's mask, and what little of her face was visible beneath it. Marlow's heart thudded—she didn't think Amara would recognize her, but the real risk was that she wouldn't deem her worthy enough to talk to Adrius.

She could see him, just over Amara's shoulder, turned away from the dance floor, speaking to some other girl in a lavender dress and an amethyst mask.

"Is that so?" Amara asked, smiling tightly. "What sort of sights have you been hoping to see, Lady Orsino? All the eligible bachelors Caraza has to offer, perhaps?"

"Well," Marlow said, tucking a strand of dark hair behind her ear demurely. "I was hoping for one dance, perhaps. Just so I can tell my sisters I danced with the Falcrest scion."

Amara laughed. "And while that's very sweet indeed, I'm afraid my brother's time is rather precious," she drawled. "If he danced with every country bumpkin who wandered into our Great Hall, why, he'd be here until dawn."

"Oh!" Marlow replied, going cold. She had to think of some way of getting past Amara. "Well, perhaps—"

"Off you go," Amara said with a dismissive wave. "Enjoy the festivities, Lady Orsino."

"Well, perhaps if Adrius doesn't have time for a dance, I could at least make his acquaintance," Marlow blurted. "My sisters would never forgive me if I came all this way and met only one Falcrest scion."

Amara paused, cocking her head, and for a faltering moment Marlow thought she'd won. If Amara let her speak to Adrius, she would find *some* way to tip him off without raising suspicion.

"That mask," Amara said at last. "It's Carazan made, is it not?"

"I believe so," Marlow replied.

"Curious that a daughter of a Vescovi marquis should have such a mask," Amara said, eyes narrowing behind her own mask.

"I shouldn't think so," Marlow replied. "I bought it on Pearl Street just a few days ago."

Amara smiled. "You bought it? From a shop? See, I happen to know all the ateliers on Pearl Street, and I *know* for a fact that mask is a custom design from Madame Delphine. And they're usually booked out for *months* before the masquerade."

Sweat beaded on Marlow's brow. Damn Gemma and her insistence on a custom mask. And damn Amara—although Marlow couldn't help but be a little impressed by her perceptiveness. If she wasn't so busy making Marlow's life miserable, she might have made a good cursebreaker.

"Y-yes, that's correct," Marlow replied, thinking fast. "I believe the maison who sold it to me said it had been sold secondhand to him. I suppose whoever commissioned it originally decided on a different style."

"Hmm," Amara hummed. "Well, it's beautiful craftsmanship. Perhaps you could remove it, so I might have a closer look?"

Shit. Marlow's disguise wasn't enough without the mask. Amara would recognize her in an instant. Did she suspect that it was her? Or simply that Marlena Orsino wasn't who she said she was?

"Oh," Marlow said, touching her mask and trying to stall. "Well, I—this is a masquerade, isn't it? What would be the fun in taking off my mask so quickly?"

The music in the ballroom swelled around them. Lights cascaded onto the dance floor. Amara's gaze flicked over Marlow's shoulder and held on something there.

Marlow turned and saw Gemma.

She was utterly radiant, spinning through the air, her glittering dress spilling out from her waist like molten silver, her hair fanned out like a flame. The very air around her seemed to shimmer.

Marlow turned back to Amara and saw the way her jaw tightened, shoulders going stiff at the sight of the girl she'd once at least claimed to love. The girl she'd given up to please a father who'd denied her what she most wanted.

Marlow couldn't summon much sympathy for Amara—but she did know how to use Amara's distraction to her advantage.

Her gaze found Adrius over Amara's shoulder. To her surprise, he was already looking back at her, the girl in the lavender dress long gone. Their eyes locked behind their masks. Everything went still. Even the melody of the orchestra seemed to fade beneath the pounding of Marlow's heart.

The last time she'd locked eyes with Adrius, she had been holding a bloody knife in her hand. Despite the mask, despite the disguise, she felt exposed to his gaze.

He swept across the landing toward her.

"This dance is a favorite of mine." He held out a hand. "Indulge me, won't you?"

Marlow nodded, throat suddenly thick, and took his hand. Her heart kicked the moment his warm fingers closed around hers.

"Adrius." Amara's attention was back on them. There was a warning in her voice.

"Surely I can be spared for one dance," Adrius replied flippantly. "Perhaps you should do the same. I'm sure your dear husband could do with some attention this evening."

He brushed past Amara, leading Marlow down the stairs to the dance floor.

They joined the other couples, and Marlow placed her hands gently on his shoulders. Adrius pulled her closer, a hand at her waist.

Marlow shivered.

"I overheard you talking to my sister," he said as they fell into the familiar steps of the dance. "How are you enjoying your visit to Caraza?"

She tried to imagine what a Vescovi noblewoman might think of this city that had been both a home and a snare to Marlow her whole life. "It's overwhelming," Marlow said. "The buildings, the people, the parties—it feels impossible to take it all in."

"Are there no buildings or people or parties in Vescovi, then?" Adrius asked, a flirtatious lilt to the words and a smile tucked into the corner of his mouth—familiar to Marlow in a way that made her ache.

"Not like this," she said. She wondered if he flirted with every girl he'd spoken to tonight. The thought made her feel ill. But it didn't matter—she hadn't come all this way to flirt with Adrius. She had come to warn him about Vale.

But maybe flirting would get her the chance she needed. "Although, I believe the tradition of the masquerade was actually begun in Vescovi."

Adrius's mouth twitched, like he was fighting a smile. "Is that right?"

"Traditionally, couples would pair up and share a dance," Marlow explained. "At the stroke of midnight, the couples would kiss and then unmask each other."

"Well, then," Adrius said, whirling her into a spin as the music swelled around them. "If I'm to be a good host, I should observe your traditions."

He pulled her close, fingers trailing over the open back of her dress, down her spine. Marlow's breath caught.

"It's not midnight yet," she said breathlessly.

"Then we'll have to meet later. When the clock strikes twelve, find me in the gardens, by the crepe myrtles," he murmured. "Perhaps you can show me some other Vescovi traditions."

Marlow took in a shaky breath. Could it be that simple to get Adrius alone? She should have felt relieved by the ease of it, but instead, perversely, her stomach clenched with what could only be jealousy. She'd watched him dance with countless other girls tonight, but she'd told herself it was for show, or because Amara had ordered him to do it.

But no one had ordered him to proposition Marlena Orsino.

Marlow had gone through all this trouble, disguising herself and sneaking into the masquerade under Amara's nose, and Adrius wasn't thinking about her at all.

She crushed her disappointment, her seething jealousy, beneath a bright smile. "I look forward to it."

He spun her again and then the song ended. Marlow dipped into another curtsy and Adrius bowed again.

"At midnight, then," he said, and swept away before Marlow could reply.

Marlow touched her mask. Was this some kind of game? Had he made similar promises to other girls tonight? Was she just one in a long string of clandestine trysts?

It didn't matter, she told herself firmly. Whether Adrius wanted *Marlena Orsino* or not was irrelevant. Once she was alone with him, she could tell him what she'd come here to say and be done with it.

"May I have this dance?" a voice asked.

Marlow turned to find a man in a white mask holding his hand out to her.

There was still over an hour until midnight and she didn't have much else to do. She accepted and let the man whirl her around the dance floor, as Adrius had. He wasn't a bad dancer, nor a bad conversationalist. When the dance was over, another man took his place. Clearly, having received even a small amount of attention from Adrius made Marlow—or rather, *Marlena*—a sought-after dance partner.

As she twirled in the arms of her fifth partner of the night, Marlow glanced across the dance floor and caught sight of Adrius's distinctive gold mask. Her gaze held there for a moment, and it almost seemed as if Adrius was looking back at her.

Then Marlow's partner twirled her and Marlow lost track of him.

At ten minutes until midnight, Marlow made her way off the dance floor and slipped out to the gardens. A fair amount of guests were outside, sipping drinks and getting air. Some were indulging themselves in *other* pleasures, emboldened by the anonymity their masks provided.

Marlow followed the garden path to the quiet copse of crepe myrtle trees, sheltered from view by hedges of roses. From here, she could see the tall windows of the Falcrest ballroom, lit from within like a glowing lantern.

Marlow paced, thoughts running wild through her mind. What would Adrius do when she revealed who she really was? Would he storm off and refuse to speak to her? She had no idea how they had left things. Before the wedding, Adrius had been furious, and she didn't blame him. Maybe he really was done with her. Maybe he hadn't been ordered to find a wife, like Silvan thought. He certainly hadn't seemed to mind flirting with Marlena Orsino, or dancing with any girl who asked.

Maybe this was what he really wanted—to marry some Evergarden girl or daughter of a nobleman. The kind of girl who didn't bring trouble with her everywhere she went.

Ten minutes passed, then ten more. Marlow's thoughts churned.

Maybe Adrius wasn't coming. Maybe he'd gotten a better offer. Maybe—

An arm snaked around Marlow's waist, startling the breath from her chest.

"My apologies for keeping you waiting, my lady," a voice said low in her ear.

Adrius.

Marlow whirled to face him. He'd taken off his mask, his face bared to the moonlight pouring in from between the branches of the crepe myrtle.

After over a week without seeing his face, Marlow was unprepared for the heat that rushed through her at the sight.

"I saw you," Adrius went on, "dancing with all those other people. One might think you were trying to make me jealous."

"I wasn't," Marlow replied, caught off guard by the implication, and his playful tone.

"Good," he said, eyes alight. His hand was on her hip, pressing her gently back against the trunk of the crepe myrtle. Vivid pink blossoms rained down on them.

Adrius was so close under the veil of flowers, his nearness more intoxicating than any glass of wine. His fingers trailed from her hip down her thigh. She could feel their heat through the fabric of her dress. His breath skated over her lips. Marlow let out a shuddering breath, aching to close the last half inch of space between them.

But this—this wasn't right. He wasn't out here with Marlow, he was out here with *Marlena*, and Marlow had made the mistake of kissing him under false pretenses before. She wouldn't do it again.

She pushed him away with one hard shove. *Too* hard, as it turned out, because he stumbled and fell back into a thorny rosebush.

"Ow, Minnow, what the hell!"

Marlow froze, blood rushing into her cheeks. Her heart thudded. "You know it's me?"

He carefully disentangled himself from the bush. "Of course I know it's you! You didn't really think I was fooled by a little enchantment and a silly accent, did you?"

"I . . ." Marlow tried to make her mind start working again.

His expression shifted from the humorous, playful look to something darker. Wounded, almost. "You thought I'd take just anyone out here?" He turned away from her, raking a hand through his curls, disheveling them. With a bitter laugh, he said, "Of course you did."

She'd hardly been speaking to him for a minute, and already she'd hurt him. In a wavering voice, she said, "I didn't know what to think."

He shook his head, jaw tight, fist clenched at his side. "Why are you here?"

Marlow's heart plummeted into her stomach at the frustration in his tone. It felt like an answer. Proof that he was finished with her. That whatever feelings he'd had for her, he had already buried. "I needed to see you."

He turned back to her, eyes wild and burning in the darkness. He held himself with such restraint, it was almost as if he was fighting against something. A breath shuddered through him, and then his hands were on her face, his thumb tracing the curve of her cheek below her mask.

"Gods." The word punched out of him. "I needed to see you, too."

It sounded like a confession. Marlow felt the pull of his heated gaze deep in her belly. She had felt this same pull every time his hands were on her, back when each touch was nothing more than a gambit in their ruse.

His hands went to the sides of her mask. "May I?"

Marlow nodded, unable to look away from him as he gently pushed her mask up and off her face, baring it to the moonlight and his intent gaze.

"I thought I was dreaming when I saw you standing on those stairs," Adrius confessed, cupping her face up toward him.

Her fingers were clutched against his waistcoat—she wasn't sure when that had happened. She closed her eyes, summoning every scrap of will-power she had and pressing her hands against his chest, stopping him inches from kissing her. "I mean, I need to *talk* to you."

Beneath her hands, she felt his chest rise and fall on a breath. "Oh."

She surely wasn't imagining the disappointment that colored his voice. It was almost enough to make her toss her entire plan out the window in favor of letting him press her up against the tree again and kiss her until she forgot her own name. But she knew they only had a brief window of time before his absence from the ballroom was noticed and someone came looking for him.

She stepped out from between him and the tree. "I know who cursed you."

Adrius froze. "What?"

"I figured it out right after the wedding. Remember the cursemarks from *Ilario's Grimoire*? Vale . . . my *father* . . . he has them. I saw them." She paused. "Oh, uh, also, Vale is my father."

"Silvan told me," Adrius replied faintly. "Why would Vale curse me?"

Marlow shook her head. "I don't know what his plan is. But I suspect it has something to do with trying to take over the Falcrest family. With your father dead . . . or at least close enough to it, that puts you and Amara in charge. And if he has you under a Compulsion curse—and Amara now married to his son—that puts him in a good position for a takeover."

Adrius's brow creased. "Vale isn't like my father. He's not power hungry."

"Or perhaps he's just better at hiding it," Marlow suggested. "But whatever his plan is, if he can't get to you, he can't give you orders. So you need to stay away from him from now on—or at least until I find the curse card and break the curse."

"Break the curse?" Adrius echoed, sounding bewildered. "You mean . . . you don't know—?"

"And then you won't have to go through with this," Marlow barreled on.

"Go through with . . . what?"

The confusion in his voice made Marlow's stomach knot. "With *what*? With . . . with finding a wife. Or whatever it was you were ordered to do."

Something flashed over Adrius's face, quick as lightning. Gone before Marlow could decipher it. "Minnow . . . no one ordered me to do this."

The blood drained from Marlow's face. Mortification simmered in her gut, followed swiftly by the heat of anger. He was searching for a wife, of his own volition, his own free will, and yet still tried to kiss Marlow in the shelter of a moonlit garden.

How embarrassing that she'd almost let herself be swept up in the game.

"I thought, after everything, that you were done toying with me,"

Marlow said, crossing her arms over her chest. "Clearly, you still haven't gotten your fill."

"*Toying*—Minnow, you know I was never toying with you," Adrius bit out. "I shouldn't kiss you when I'm supposed to be finding a wife, but I—I saw you on those stairs and I could no longer think of anything else. You're *here* and I thought—I thought I could let myself have this, even if it was only for a night."

"And what about tomorrow?" Marlow asked, her voice trembling. "You go back to the adoring girls lining up to wed you, and I get to read all about it in the morning's paper?"

Adrius shut his eyes. "Tomorrow, I break my own heart."

And what about my heart? Marlow wanted to yell.

"You say such pretty things, Adrius," she said instead. "You did when we were pretending, too. But do you mean any of them?"

"You know I do," Adrius replied, his voice thick like the words had been dragged out of him. There was an edge of anger there, too. Because Marlow *did* know that Adrius had meant everything he'd said to her throughout their fake courtship. He'd confessed as much, when Marlow had ordered him to tell her the truth.

An order she'd issued because she hadn't trusted him. And it seemed, even now, that she still didn't.

Or maybe she couldn't.

"Then why are you doing this?" Marlow asked. To her horror, it came out as a plea. "If you meant it then. If you mean it now."

She wanted Adrius to admit it. Admit that no matter how he felt about her, it wasn't enough to overcome the need to follow the path that had been set for him. As much as he tried to style himself a rebel against the expectations of his father and everyone else in Evergarden, he wasn't really. He wouldn't fight for her.

He'd never fought for anything.

"I *knew* it!"

Amara's voice pierced the fragile silence. Marlow turned to find her marching toward them. Marlow's pulse jumped.

"I knew you were not some Vescovi noblewoman," Amara seethed. She spun on her brother. "Adrius, what the hell do you think you're doing with her?"

"This isn't what it looks like," Adrius said, his voice taut.

"I'm sure," Amara replied, hand on her cocked hip. "Adrius, get back inside, *now*."

"No," Adrius snapped, stepping between his sister and Marlow.

Marlow's heart steadied—and then her thoughts caught up with her. Adrius had just *refused an order*. That shouldn't have been possible. Her breath caught. It *wasn't* possible, unless—

Unless somehow the curse was already broken.

Adrius shot her a glance over his shoulder. His expression was focused, like he was trying to tell her something with just his eyes. He didn't seem surprised by his own ability to defy Amara's order.

"We had an *agreement*," Amara hissed.

"An agreement?" Marlow echoed.

Amara folded her arms in front of her chest. "Yes. Adrius is to find a wife and wed before the year is out."

Adrius turned away from Marlow and did not deny this.

"You agreed to this," Marlow said dully.

"Yes," Adrius said, his voice hollow. "And in exchange, Amara will petition the court to request a full pardon for you."

Marlow was stunned. A full pardon? She had trouble believing Amara would do such a thing. But she didn't deny it, either.

"Tell her the other part of the agreement," Amara said, her voice crisp and cold.

Marlow's chest clenched. Of course there was more to it. Of course Amara wouldn't offer a pardon for so little.

Adrius's face was drawn and pained in the moonlight.

"Tell me," Marlow pleaded softly.

"I can't see you anymore." He swallowed. "Ever."

TEN

It was half past midnight when Marlow left the masquerade, but her night was just beginning. She fled Falcrest Hall on foot, heading straight for the Vale boathouse. No one was around this time of night, and Marlow slipped unnoticed into one of Vale's enchanted canal boats. Tapping the prow of the boat, she instructed it to take her to the Catwalk brothel in the Honey Docks district.

She was glad to leave the glowing lights and cloyingly sweet air of Evergarden behind. What she couldn't seem to manage to leave behind was Adrius's voice, still ringing in her head.

I can't see you anymore. Ever.

When it came to Adrius Falcrest, rage and heartbreak had become so entangled that Marlow didn't know how to separate them anymore. She didn't care that Adrius was only cutting her off to try to protect her. Somehow, that only made her more furious. She was angry with Amara for forcing him into a marriage he didn't want. Angry with Adrius for agreeing to the deal. And most of all, she was angry with herself for being in a position to be used like a pawn against him.

The curse might have been broken, but Adrius still wasn't free. And until Marlow unraveled the mess she'd gotten herself into when she'd taken the blame for Aurelius's attack, he never would be.

As the canal boat speared through the dark water, Marlow wrestled off her mother-of-pearl dress, exchanging it for a pair of simple black pants, a plain blouse, and a duster coat she'd stashed aboard the boat earlier that day. She felt a little bit more in control with each piece of clothing she put on—a little bit more like herself.

She was Marlow Briggs. It might not be a curse she had to break, but she'd find a way to free Adrius—just not tonight. Tonight, she had another mission.

The Honey Docks were bustling with activity this time of night, with patrons stumbling in and out of the many bordellos lined up along the dock. Liliana, one of the Catwalk's most popular girls, was standing at the end of the dock, smoking a cigarette, when Marlow arrived.

"You're late," Liliana said, tossing her cigarette butt into the canal. She sounded more amused than annoyed.

"Sorry. Got held up," Marlow replied, tying up her boat. "Is he here already?"

Liliana nodded, gathering her silk shawl around her shoulders. "Watching the burlesque show while he waits for me. One of the dancers managed to get these off him."

She dangled a set of keys between her fingers. Keys that Marlow knew went to a fanboat moored over on the next dock.

"Thanks," Marlow said, taking the keys. She tucked them into the pocket of her coat and pulled out a hex card from the same pocket. "Here you go."

Liliana took the card and peered down at it. "A Hangover hex? That's it?"

"He won't suspect anything," Marlow said. "He'll just think he drank too much."

A visit to the Black Orchid the day before had furnished Marlow with all the hexes she needed—for a price, of course. If she managed to get through tonight in one piece, she was on the hook to return the favor by helping them access Vale Library.

But she'd worry about that later.

"Seriously, Liliana, thanks for doing this," Marlow said. "I really appreciate it."

"You know I'm always happy to help out my favorite cursebreaker," Liliana said with a wink. "Even if you won't tell me exactly what it is I'm helping you do."

"Trust me, the fewer details you know, the better for everyone," Marlow said. That much was true, but Marlow also knew that if she told Liliana she was about to sneak onto Reaper Island to rescue Swift all by herself, she'd think Marlow had a death wish.

Marlow had never been to Reaper Island, but like everyone who lived in the Marshes, she knew exactly where it was.

It wasn't an actual island, but man-made: a series of platforms connected by narrow wooden walkways, built around the remains of an old ruin of a sunken mansion that had once belonged to the Morandi family, long before the Five Families had built Evergarden. When they abandoned it, the Reapers took it over.

It was fitting, Marlow supposed. In the Marshes, the Reapers were sometimes called the Sixth Family. They were the oldest gang in the Marshes, and the only ones who had anything close to the kind of influence the noblesse nouveau had.

The mansion lay about two miles southwest of Swamp Market, surrounded by crocodile-infested swamp water. The only way to access it was via boat or airship. The entire structure was carefully warded against intruders, and heavily patrolled by Reapers.

It was practically a fortress, almost as secure as Evergarden. Marlow had only one hope of getting in.

Once a week, Lady Bianca, the wife of Nino Ironwood, the Reapers' leader, bathed in goat's milk and honey, which was supposed to help preserve her youthful complexion. She required that the goat's milk be as fresh as possible. So at dawn, one of the Reapers went to fetch it from an upriver farm.

"Where's Bosko?" the confused farmer asked when Marlow arrived in her stolen fanboat.

Bosko was probably facedown in his own sick on the Honey Docks, thanks to Liliana's help.

"Got a promotion," Marlow replied, tying the fanboat up to the dock post. "Looks like I'll be on delivery duty from now on."

The farmer seemed to accept this easily enough—Marlow was, after all, sailing Bosko's fanboat, and he had no reason to suspect she wasn't just another Reaper lackey working her way up the ladder doing grunt work. He loaded the boat with four heavy drums of milk and two jugs of honey and sent her on her way.

It was almost dawn, and here on the quiet, broad stretch of Pearl River, it was almost peaceful. A fine mist blanketed the water as Marlow's fanboat chugged its way to Reaper Island. By the time Reaper Island appeared, a thin sliver of gray light had sliced through the horizon.

Marlow spotted two flatboats patrolling the perimeter of the mansion. They paid her no mind as she maneuvered her boat toward a dock splintering off from one of the main platforms. Through the mist, they could hardly tell that it wasn't Bosko aboard the fanboat.

The Reaper waiting on the dock for the delivery, however, would see Marlow and know in an instant something was up.

So as Marlow maneuvered the boat up to the dock, she grabbed an Immobilizing hex from her pocket. "*Congelia.*"

Red glyphs shot from the spellcard and struck the Reaper. He seized up instantly and crumpled to the dock. Marlow tied up the fanboat and stepped onto the dock, nudging the Reaper onto his back with her foot. He let out a groan.

"Tell me where the Reapers keep their prisoners," Marlow said, her foot pressed against his windpipe.

"Who the fuck are you?" he rasped. "And where's Bosko?"

"Bosko's dead," Marlow lied. "Answer my question, or you'll join him. I'll push you off this dock. This water's not very deep, but that won't matter. You'll sink beneath it, and you'll be close enough to see the surface, but you won't be able to get there. And then it's just a question of whether you'll drown before the crocodiles and the snapping turtles find you."

It was a bluff, but this Reaper had no reason to think Marlow wouldn't make good on her threat.

"I'm just a grunt, I'm not privy to that kind of information," he wheezed.

"That's too bad." Marlow wedged her foot under his ribs and tipped him toward the edge of the dock.

"The old kitchens!" he exclaimed. Marlow paused. "First floor. I don't know anything for sure, but I'd check there first."

Marlow stooped down and searched the Reaper's pockets until she found a ring of keys. "I'll just take these, then, and be on my way."

She stood and turned toward the mansion.

"Wait, you can't just leave me here like this!" he yelled after her.

"You'd better hope your intel is good, because the sooner I find what I'm here for, the sooner I'll lift the hex."

Also a bluff. The hex would wear off in ten minutes no matter what Marlow did.

Which didn't give her a lot of time before the alarm was raised. She hurried across the dock, stepping carefully onto one of the floating platforms that led her to what had once been a second-floor balcony, but was now just above the water level. Marlow climbed over the railing and unlocked the door to slip inside.

The balcony led her into a lavish drawing room, decorated how Marlow imagined a Vescovi palace might look. A huge crystal chandelier loomed above the gleaming harlequin-tiled floor. A grand piano dominated one side of the room, with gilded candelabras and expensive fabrics in overwrought patterns filling the other. It was an ode to old-fashioned luxury, so different from the sleek, modern designs of Evergarden.

She paused at the door, listening for the sounds of footsteps or voices outside the drawing room, before peeking her head out. She stared down a long corridor with a row of windows on one side and a row of doors on the other. This early in the morning, there weren't many people roaming the halls of the mansion, but Marlow knew the second she was spotted, there would be dozens of Reapers bearing down on her.

She crept down the corridor toward a landing that overlooked the mansion's atrium. A sweeping staircase led down, disappearing into muddy water on the ground level. There was no telling what might be lurking below the surface of the water, but if she was going to find Swift she was going to have to brave it.

As she slunk toward the staircase, she heard voices filtering in from some other hallway that branched off the atrium. Marlow's heart kicked in her chest. She could not tell exactly where the voices were coming from, and if she tried to make a break for the stairs, she ran the risk of being spotted. Instead, she seized the knob of the nearest door and wrenched it open, praying she hadn't just made an even worse miscalculation.

The door opened to reveal what looked like a storage room, and Marlow let out a breath of relief, slipping inside and shutting the door silently behind her. Dozens of boxes were stacked from floor to ceiling. Many of them were marked with the Falcrest Library sigil. Curiosity seized her, and Marlow knelt to open the nearest box. She knew what she expected to find—spell ingredients, likely stolen from Falcrest Library.

But instead, the box was filled with spellcards, all of them bearing the Falcrest sigil. No, she realized with a start. They weren't spells. They were *curses.*

What was Falcrest Library doing, making illegal curses?

But Marlow didn't have time to puzzle over it. She filed it into the back of her mind and pressed her ear against the closet door, listening for voices. When she heard none, she eased open the door and darted into the atrium.

"Do you hear something?" A voice sounded from just down the adjoining hallway.

Marlow froze. She was steps away from the stairs, but she was completely exposed.

Without pausing to think it through, she heaved herself over the railing of the landing and dropped down to the water below with a splash.

The water was just deep enough to submerge her. She kicked beneath it, aiming for what she hoped would put her beneath the landing, and swam until she felt a wall at her fingertips. She surfaced carefully, glancing up, relieved when she saw the edge of the landing ahead of her. No one would be able to see her from above.

"There! That splashing sound!" a voice exclaimed from the upper floor.

"Probably just another crocodile," a second voice replied, bored. "They're always slipping past the wards."

Marlow didn't dare move until she heard their footsteps fade away. She didn't have long to search for the kitchens—the Immobilizing hex would wear off in a few minutes, and the Reaper she'd hexed would raise the alarm. She waded as quietly as she could over to a corridor that branched out from the atrium, hoping it led toward the kitchens. The water was shallower here, and by the time Marlow was halfway down the hall, it was only at her waist. She opened every door along the hallway, panic fluttering in her stomach as the minutes ticked by with no sign of Swift.

She forced the panic down. She would find him. There was no other choice.

At last the hallway led her into a formal dining room, with a dilapidated table and a rusted candelabra. She pushed over to a door that led out the adjoining wall of the dining room, and nearly collapsed in relief when she stepped through into a sizable kitchen. Tangled mangrove roots reached through the windows like skeletal fingers. Muddy water lapped at her waist.

"Swift?" Marlow whispered into the room. "Are you in here?"

There was no reply.

Another rotted wood door stood at the other end of the kitchen. Marlow waded over to it and found it locked. She pulled out the stolen key ring and tried one, two, five, a dozen of the keys. None of them worked.

Marlow jiggled the doorknob and raised her voice as loud as she dared. "Swift? Are you in there?"

She pressed her ear to the door and heard a muffled reply on the other side.

Good enough for her. She reached into her pocket and pulled out a Lockpick spell—another gift from the Black Orchid.

"*Aprire*," Marlow whispered. Emerald-green glyphs surrounded the doorknob. Marlow tried it again and it creaked open to reveal a plain room with a simple table and a dozen chairs—maybe an old servants' mess. But

Marlow didn't pay much attention to the details of the room, because hunched in the center of the table was Swift.

He looked up as Marlow entered, his brown eyes wide. "Marlow? Are you really here?"

Relief made Marlow's knees go weak.

"*Gods*, I'm so glad to see you, Swift," Marlow said, pushing through the muddy water toward him. "Are you all right?"

"Oh, fine," Swift replied airily. "Just, you know. Got kidnapped."

Marlow reached the edge of the table and hauled herself onto it, scrambling to pull Swift into a hug. "I'm really sorry about that."

"It's not your fault," Swift replied, hugging her fiercely back. "The Reapers jumped me on the way to the Mudskipper."

"I should've come sooner," Marlow replied, pulling back and shaking her head. "I thought you were with the Black Orchid. I thought you were *safe*."

"How'd you figure out they had me?" he asked.

"Long story, I'll tell you later," Marlow replied. "Did they hurt you?"

She let her gaze scan over him, searching for clues as to what he'd gone through the past few days. His skin looked pale and clammy, his eyes shadowed like he hadn't slept. His dark hair, usually thick and lustrous, looked limp and matted.

But he was alive.

"I'm all right enough to get out of here," Swift replied impatiently. "I assume you didn't sneak into the Reaper headquarters without some kind of plan?"

Marlow pulled out two more spellcards from her pocket. "Endless Breath spells. We're swimming out."

Swift stared at her. "Marlow, there are crocodiles literally *everywhere*."

"I'd rather take my chances with a crocodile than a Reaper," Marlow replied. "But let's hurry, because they're going to be searching the mansion for me soon, if they aren't already."

More than ten minutes had elapsed since she'd entered the mansion—the Reaper she'd immobilized would've raised the alarm by now.

She slid back into the water, Swift right behind her.

"There's a window out in the dining room we can probably get through," Marlow said, shouldering through the door and into the kitchen. With his taller frame, Swift was more easily able to wade through the water and make it to the dining room.

"I don't think we want to go out this way," he said uneasily, staring out the nearest window.

Marlow followed his gaze to the swarm of snapping turtles bobbing just outside the window, each at least as big as a dinner platter with beaks as sharp as knives. "Shit. Okay. This way."

She grabbed Swift's arm and led him out to the corridor that led back to the atrium. She knew instantly it was a mistake.

"There she is!"

Ten paces from them, blocking their exit, was the Reaper she'd immobilized, flanked by three other Reapers.

Marlow pulled Swift back around to the dining room, but two more Reapers stepped out from another doorway.

They were cornered. Marlow had a few hexes in her pocket, but the minute she went for them, she knew she and Swift would be hexed sideways.

"Hands where we can see them!" one of the Reapers demanded.

Marlow raised hers, palms out. Beside her, Swift did the same.

The two Reapers behind them closed in and forced their arms behind their backs.

"Back in the mess?" one asked, indicating toward the kitchens.

Marlow clamped down on a bright flare of terror. If she and Swift were locked up again, there was no one who'd know to come looking for them here.

"No," another Reaper said, a slow smile spreading over his face. "Take them to Lady Bianca."

ELEVEN

The Reapers took Marlow and Swift back up the stairs and through an arched doorway to a parlor. The sun had fully risen by now, and the room was suffused with morning light, gilding the woman who sat on an ornate settee at the back of the room.

Marlow had never met this woman before, but she knew exactly who she was. Lady Bianca, the wife of Nino Ironwood. The rumor was that Nino, in his advanced age, was reduced to a mere figurehead of the gang, while his much younger wife ran things in his stead.

Lady Bianca wore a gown in deep emerald, a string of pearls encircling her slender neck. Her long, silky hair fell in dark waves over one shoulder. Squirming in her arms was a baby, no older than ten months, wrapped in a delicate, lacy blanket.

The baby stared at Marlow with unblinking dark eyes as she and Swift were brought before them.

"I really don't enjoy having my morning interrupted," Lady Bianca said. She waved an attendant over and handed the baby to her. "So let's make this quick, shall we?"

"I agree," Marlow said evenly. "Why don't you let me and my friend Swift go, and we'll be out of your hair for good."

Lady Bianca smiled thinly. "I was told you have quite the sense of humor, Miss Briggs."

Marlow returned the smile blithely. "I promise you, we're way more trouble than we're worth."

"Surely a girl as smart as yourself must understand that having both you and your friend in our grasp gives the Reapers quite the advantage in any negotiations with the Copperheads," Lady Bianca said.

"Negotiations?" Marlow snorted. "Come on, you know Leonidas isn't interested in *negotiating* with the Reapers."

"Perhaps you're underestimating just how much he hates you for humiliating his gang," Lady Bianca suggested. "Twice. Were we to hand you over, it would make this little headache go away for the Reapers."

"You're not afraid it'll make you look weak?" Marlow asked. "Handing us over like you're Leonidas's loyal little lapdog?"

"No, Miss Briggs, I don't think it will make us look *weak*," Lady Bianca replied scathingly. "I do think it would make us look incredibly foolish to start a street war over a girl who's been nothing but a thorn in our sides."

Marlow swallowed a laugh. "The Copperheads aren't going to start a street war with you. You think they have that kind of manpower? They're bluffing."

Lady Bianca tapped her lacquered red nails along the carved wooden armrest. "The fact remains, Miss Briggs, that the Copperheads want you dead and the Reapers have very little reason to want you alive. No reason at all, actually. So perhaps we'll just cut out the middle man and kill you ourselves. That would solve our little problem nicely, don't you think?"

She gestured to the Reapers behind them and then pointed at Swift. "Kill that one first."

The Reaper pulled out a knife as big as Marlow's forearm. Panic seized her as one of the Reapers grabbed Swift by the hair, dragging his head back to expose his throat to the blade.

"Wait!" Marlow cried. "You don't want to do that."

Lady Bianca raised an eyebrow. "And why not, Miss Briggs?"

Marlow sucked in a breath. Cold sweat beaded at her brow. "Because I found something in my mother's things. A list of spellwrights making curses for you. And if I go missing, a copy of that list is going to make its way to the desk of the City Solicitor, along with every reporter in the city. How do you think that's going to affect your bottom line?"

"Now who's bluffing?" Lady Bianca asked. She flicked a hand at the Reaper with the knife. He raised the blade to Swift's throat.

"Lyam Zarconi!" Marlow blurted. "Ginevra Thorn. Aldrik Hargrave."

Lady Bianca froze, growing paler with every name Marlow recited. She raised a hand, halting her henchman.

Marlow waited.

"Perhaps I underestimated you," Lady Bianca said softly.

"You wouldn't be the first," Marlow replied. To the Reaper still gripping Swift's hair, she said, "Can you let him go, please?"

Lady Bianca nodded, and the Reaper released his grip.

Swift doubled over, coughing violently and wheezing in a breath. Marlow went to him on instinct and held on to his shoulder to help him stay upright. Over his head she met Lady Bianca's gaze. "Are we free to go?"

"I'm beginning to understand why Leonidas is so fixated on having you killed," Lady Bianca said dryly. She beckoned over the attendant holding her child and took the baby into her arms. "You can see yourselves out. Little Elio needs his rest now."

⸻

Marlow and Swift didn't waste any time piling back onto the stolen fanboat and leaving Reaper Island behind. As Marlow steered them through the mist, Swift caught her up on his capture by the Reapers and subsequent imprisonment.

"What did they want?" Marlow asked.

"You," Swift said simply. "They sent someone to my room to interrogate me. They used this hex on me . . . didn't leave a mark, but it was some of the worst agony I've ever felt in my life. Like someone was carving out my insides. It's lucky that I really had no idea where you were, because I don't know what I would've told them."

"I should've come sooner," Marlow said again, guilt clenching her chest tight.

"Hey, come on, Marlow," Swift replied. "You had no way of knowing."

"Yeah," Marlow said, "but instead of making sure you were safe, I was just wasting time in Vale Tower, trying to find a way to break a curse that, it turns out, is already broken."

"Vale Tower?" Swift echoed.

"Like I said, long story," Marlow replied with a wave. "And before we get into it, we should figure out where you can lie low."

"You think the Copperheads are still watching Orsella's place?"
Marlow nodded.

"I hope she's all right," Swift said with a grimace.

"You know she can take care of herself." Marlow cleared her throat. She really only saw one solution to Swift's predicament, but it was one she was loath to suggest. All it would do was pull Swift from one dangerous, complicated situation to another.

But she didn't have any other ideas, and after the worry that had almost consumed her over the past few days, she couldn't help but want to keep Swift close.

"You could come back to Vale Tower with me," she said hesitantly.

"Really?" Swift asked. "Would I be . . . allowed?"

Marlow shrugged. "It's my apartment. Sort of."

Swift grinned. "Well, I'd be a fool to turn that down. When else am I going to get the chance to live in Evergarden?"

"Trust me," Marlow replied, "it's not all it's cracked up to be. And before you make a decision, there's something you should know about Vale."

———

Marlow should have known that telling Swift that Vale was behind Adrius's curse would only ensure that Swift insisted he stay in Vale Tower with her. Truthfully, she was grateful. She couldn't deny that having him with her made her instantly feel safer and less alone.

It was still fairly early in the morning when they arrived back at Vale Tower. She doubted anyone was up and about yet—which was why she froze for a solid ten seconds when she stepped out of the elevator and saw Silvan standing in front of her door, knocking furiously.

"Silvan?" Marlow asked.

Silvan whirled around, taking two strides toward Marlow and then stopping abruptly when his gaze fell on Swift behind her. "What are *you* doing here?"

"Nice to see you again, Your Highness," Swift replied, unbothered by Silvan's hostility.

Silvan turned an accusatory glare on Marlow. "I thought that swamp pirate person said the Reapers had him."

Swift turned a curious eye on Marlow.

"They did have him," Marlow agreed briskly. "Now they don't. And if you're done interrogating me, maybe you want to explain why you're pounding on my door first thing in the morning?"

Silvan narrowed his eyes. "Tell me what you did to Adrius last night."

"What I *did* to him?" Marlow echoed in disbelief. "I didn't do anything. We talked for maybe five minutes and then Amara found us together and basically threw me out."

Silvan scowled. "Well, he spent the rest of the night trying to drown himself in a bottle of wine. When Gemma and I tried to drag him back to his room, he refused, and passed out in a rosebush."

Swift stifled a snort.

"And that's somehow my fault?" Marlow asked.

"Yes," Silvan replied stubbornly. "He was *fine* before you came back here, to Evergarden. You—you *broke* him."

"Yeah, well," Marlow muttered. "What do you want me to do about it, Silvan?"

"*Fix. It.*"

Marlow stared at him, stunned by the ferocity in his voice and the lethal glint in his eyes. Not for the first time, she wondered at the fact that Silvan Vale, the boy who seemed to despise just about everyone he met, Marlow most certainly included, had chosen Adrius Falcrest as the one person who deserved his loyalty.

"I can't," Marlow said, her voice breaking a little. It was too honest an answer by far. "Amara's forbidden him from seeing me."

"And you're telling me," Silvan said scathingly, "that you've stood up to two of the most powerful gangs in Caraza, but you're still afraid of Amara Falcrest?"

Swift caught Marlow's gaze, his eyebrows raised.

Well. When Silvan put it like that.

$\mathcal{S}$*weat beaded at* Marlow's brow as she sat in the stands, surrounded by hundreds of other fans watching the courte paume match. The shade provided by the awnings offered little respite from the sticky afternoon heat, and Marlow couldn't help but feel bad for the four players dashing across the court below.

She lifted her gaze to the private tent that had been erected along the sidelines of the court. There she could see Amara, Darian at her side, with dozens of other guests from Evergarden arranged in small groups on cushioned couches, with tables laden with tea, iced wine, and delicate honey-glazed cakes.

Sitting on one of those couches, surrounded by admirers, was Adrius. His posture was relaxed and open, one arm slung over the back of the couch as he smiled and exchanged what could only be described as flirtatious looks with the girls seated around him.

To his left sat another familiar figure, her hair a bright copper beacon even in the shade of the tent. Gemma.

Marlow focused on her, resisting the overwhelming urge to stare at Adrius and scrutinize exactly how sincere his flirtation with the brunette sitting on his other side was.

And then, just as Marlow felt her resolve begin to crack, she saw it—the flash of sunlight reflected off a small compact mirror in Gemma's hand.

Their signal.

Marlow rose from her seat in the stands and wove through the crowd toward the stairs.

After leaving Vale Tower earlier that morning, Marlow had gone to Gemma and told her everything that had happened at the masquerade. Well—not quite *everything*, because Gemma didn't need to know about the curse or Vale. But she'd explained the deal Adrius had struck with Amara and asked for Gemma's help in getting Adrius alone again without his sister's knowledge.

Gemma had been surprisingly enthusiastic about the prospect of subterfuge.

"Amara may have broken my heart, but I'm not going to let her do the same to you and Adrius," she'd said. Then she'd told Marlow about the courte paume match, and how Amara had invited a few dozen of the girls from the masquerade—the ones Amara had evidently deemed worthy of courting her brother.

Marlow reached the bottom of the stands and circled around the court, climbing under the scaffolding of the opposing stands until she was right outside the Falcrests' private tent, hidden from view. She inched her way over to the back of the tent, heart tripping in her chest. She could hear laughter and chatter from within but couldn't make out anything distinct.

Until she heard Gemma's voice float toward her.

"I hate to drag you away, but it'll really just take a minute, we won't miss much," Gemma was saying.

The tent flap fluttered open, revealing Gemma's mischievous smile. She yanked Adrius's arm, shoving him through the opening and toward Marlow.

"Wha—*Minnow*—?"

Marlow clapped a hand over Adrius's mouth before he could make another sound and hauled him around the side of the tent.

"You can thank me later," Gemma whispered with a self-satisfied smile before disappearing back inside.

Leaving Marlow alone with Adrius.

Adrius, who had gotten over his surprise at the ambush, was now glaring at Marlow over the curve of her palm.

Marlow lowered her hand. "Hi."

"What part of *I can't see you anymore* did you not comprehend?" Adrius demanded through his teeth.

The vehemence in his voice chafed, but Marlow pushed down her hurt. "You weren't exactly trying to get away from me at the masquerade."

"You were in disguise," Adrius replied. "And I was—selfish. I shouldn't have done that. If anyone sees you here—"

"Gemma's on lookout," Marlow assured him.

"Why are you even here?"

"Oh, I'm sorry, am I keeping you from your adoring fans?" Marlow said, unable to keep the acid from her voice.

Adrius's already tense jaw clenched down harder. "It isn't like that, and you know it."

She did know, but she still wanted to hear him say it. Wanted him to tell her that none of the girls inside the tent meant anything to him. That he only wanted her.

But none of that mattered as long as he was trapped by Amara.

"Why did you come here, Marlow?" Adrius asked again, but his voice was softer this time, a glimpse of vulnerability beneath his shield of anger.

Why *had* she come? To convince him to give up his deal with Amara, his search for a wife, and choose her instead?

"The curse," she blurted instead. "I need to know how you broke it."

He gave her a look of pure confusion. "I didn't."

Marlow's blood went cold. "*What?* But—at the masquerade, Amara ordered you back inside and you refused. I saw it. Are you saying you're still cursed?"

If he was still cursed, they only had a few days left to break it before it became permanent. Marlow's heart thudded with dread. Had she made a mistake?

"No, I'm not—the curse *is* broken," Adrius said hastily. "You were right about that. But *I* didn't break it."

"Then who did?"

He stared at her. "You."

Her breath hitched. She searched his face, but there was no hint of humor there. He was serious. "That isn't possible. I never even found the curse card. How could *I* have broken it?"

Adrius's gaze dropped. "It was when you kissed me."

Marlow's heart fluttered against her rib cage. "Adrius, that's not . . . curses don't break like that."

It only happened like that in fairy tales. Not in real life.

"Well, this one did." He looked up at her, his eyes dark and heated like molten gold. Warmth bloomed over her skin. "You grabbed the knife. You told me I could never hurt you. And then you kissed me."

His gaze dropped to her mouth. Marlow pulled in a shaking breath, her own eyes drawn to the slight glimpse of his tongue as his lips parted.

Then he pulled away, taking a breath and a step back.

"We can't," he said. "I-I'm supposed to be finding a *wife.*"

The word hit Marlow like a shock of cold water. Anger flashed through her.

"Call off the deal," she said.

"What?"

"Call. Off. The deal. Tell Amara you changed your mind."

Adrius's gaze flicked away from her. "I'm not going to do that."

"Yes, you are," Marlow said. "Because I'm going to prove that Vale cursed you."

"*How?*"

"I'm . . . still working on that," Marlow admitted. "But there has to be someone else who knew about the curse. I don't think he could've made it by himself. A spellwright must have helped him. If I can find them—"

Adrius cut her off with a frustrated sigh. "I don't doubt that you can find proof. If anyone can, it's you. But I don't think it's going to matter."

"You don't think Amara would want to punish the person who's *really* responsible for what happened to your father?" Marlow asked. "I know you both have a complicated relationship with him, but—"

Adrius shook his head again. "She would. But Amara knows there's a good chance if she goes up against Vale, she'll lose. And I think she'd rather see someone get punished than no one, even if it's the wrong person. Besides—you're Vale's daughter. If she thinks she can hurt him by hurting you, then so much the better."

Marlow swallowed. Of course politics trumped truth in Evergarden. That wasn't a surprise, but she wasn't about to give up because of it.

"I'll find a way," she vowed.

"And if you can't?" Adrius asked. "I'm not risking that. I'm not risking *you*."

There was a conviction in his voice that Marlow had only heard a few times from him. It caught her off guard, even now, knowing that his feelings for her were real. But it also stung. "So you'd rather just never see me again?"

Adrius set his jaw. "If it keeps you safe, then yes."

"I didn't ask you to keep me safe."

"And I didn't ask you to take the blame for me!" Adrius hissed. "But here we are."

Here they were, inches apart, with a dozen girls waiting for Adrius just on the other side of the flimsy tent. Marlow could leave it there, let Adrius draw this line between them, let him go back to those girls and the deal he'd made. But she'd never learned how to leave well enough alone.

"Yeah. Here we are," she said. She stepped into him, grabbing on to the lapel of his suit jacket. "After all that pretending we had to do, are you really going to pretend you don't want me?"

"Marlow." His voice was a warning. She could feel his breath on her cheek. But he didn't pull away.

It was foolish, and risky, and Marlow knew only heartbreak lay at the end of this road, but that didn't stop her from needing to go down it. She was drawn to Adrius the way she felt drawn to a mystery—overwhelmed by the need to unravel something even if it unraveled her, too.

"This will only make it harder," he said. "And if Amara finds out—"

"What was it you said to me once?" Marlow asked. "That if you can't control your life, at least you'll have a damn good time living it?"

He swallowed, eyes locked on hers, dark with desire.

"Tell me you don't want this," Marlow said, whispering the words into the shrinking space between their lips. "And I'll walk away."

"I . . ."

She could hear him breathing in the silence between them. She waited for one breath. Two. When he still didn't speak, she let her hand drop from his jacket. Disappointment curdled in her gut, tinged with embarrassment. What had she expected? She'd never had any kind of power over him, not the way he had over her.

She started to turn away.

Adrius seized her arm and spun her back toward him. His lips were on hers before she could so much as breathe. His hand fell to her waist, pulling her close, the other tangling in her hair. Marlow gasped against his lips, her heart slamming in her chest.

He kissed her like he was desperate for it. For *her*. Like she might disappear if he let go.

Heat scorched a path through her veins. She had never been kissed like this before. She was dizzy with it, clinging to him, helpless to the storm she'd just unleashed in both of them.

Adrius broke away with a wounded sound. Marlow let out her own involuntary gasp.

He was still holding her, breathing heavily. "This is a bad idea." But his voice was low and warm and he made no move to let her go. Almost absently, he brushed a lock of hair from where it clung to her neck, slightly sticky from the heat.

Marlow reached up and guided him down to kiss her again.

A bright burst of laughter sounded from inside the tent. She watched the sound break over Adrius, as if he'd forgotten, until now, that they were right up against a tent full of potential suitors.

"Let's go somewhere," he said urgently. "Right now."

"Everyone will notice if you suddenly disappear halfway through the match," Marlow said.

"I don't care." His grip tightened on her waist. "Gemma will cover for me."

The heat in his voice sent a thrill through her. Her hands shook with how much she wanted to say yes, to drag him out of the stadium and back to Vale Tower—or just the nearest storage closet. She wanted him to kiss her again, but maybe even more than that, she wanted to revel in this newfound power—the power to make him want her enough to be reckless.

Instead, she slid her hands to his chest and pressed him gently away. "Tempting. But I've got an errand to run."

"Tonight, then," Adrius said, undeterred. "The Isabella Morandi Museum Gala. I'll be there."

Marlow could guess what he was leaving out. He'd be there with the same dozen girls who wanted to wed him.

"You think you can sneak in?" he asked challengingly.

Marlow smiled. "Come on, Adrius. Don't you know me at all?"

TWELVE

The task the Black Orchid had set for Marlow was simple—get into Vale Library, go to the spellbook archives, and place a book on the shelf.

They hadn't bothered to tell her what the book was for, only that it wouldn't cause harm to anyone, and that any other information about it was on a need-to-know basis.

Marlow had examined the book carefully. It was completely blank inside, and most likely enchanted in some way, but Marlow hadn't seen any signs of a curse, or anything that might hurt someone should the wrong person come across it, so it had seemed to her that the Black Orchid was telling the truth about that.

Her best guess was that it contained a message of some kind that the Black Orchid wanted to get to one of the spellwrights in Vale Library— or perhaps not a specific message at all, but a means to pass messages back and forth without drawing suspicion. In any case, she'd decided it was worth the risk the minute she'd accepted their help and spellcards to rescue Swift, so it wasn't like she could back out now.

Getting in wasn't hard. Her visit to Falcrest Library with Adrius a few weeks ago had taught her that the libraries allowed automatic access to anyone within the bloodline of the family who owned them.

Unlike Falcrest Library, however, Vale Library did not have the same dizzying, enchanted architecture. Marlow supposed it didn't need it— Falcrest Library's collection was many times larger than the physical space the library took up, but the Vale Library collection was not as vast. As a result, Vale Library was far more inviting, with tall, marble buildings arranged around a central lawn that functioned almost like a town square, complete with a tall clock that chimed out the hour.

Marlow had been here a few times before, when Cassandra had first begun working for Vale. Vale had even given her a personalized tour once Marlow had confessed to him her aspirations of becoming a spellwright.

So it was easy enough for her to find the spellbook archives, and easy enough to slip the Black Orchid's book onto the shelf where they'd specified. There were all sorts of wards and enchanted protections to keep anyone from taking a book *off* the shelf without proper authorization, but absolutely nothing stopping Marlow from putting something *on* it.

She was grateful the Black Orchid hadn't asked her to do something more dangerous, given that she would've been in no position to refuse. Her debt was paid now, and all it had really cost her was part of an afternoon. She still had plenty of time to figure out how she was going to sneak into the museum gala that night to see Adrius. Anticipation fluttered in her chest at the thought.

But as she left the archives to cross back through the central courtyard, Marlow decided to put the museum plans on hold for a little longer. Because across the courtyard, marching briskly down one of the walkways, was Vale.

It wasn't completely out of the ordinary for him to be at Vale Library, but the urgency of his gait made Marlow's instincts prickle. Before she'd entirely decided on it, she was crossing over to slip a few dozen paces behind him on the walkway.

At this hour, there were plenty of people milling around the footpaths and covered walkways that connected the buildings together. Marlow briefly lost track of Vale weaving through the throngs of people, but caught sight of him again just as he disappeared into one of the academy buildings. She darted after him into the spacious, sunlit atrium.

Students streamed past them into a large auditorium, but Vale bypassed the auditorium for a set of stairs that led up to a mezzanine hallway.

Marlow slowed her pace as she followed him up the stairs. There was no crowd up here to hide in—just a scattered handful of people making their way across the mezzanine. None of them paid Marlow any mind, too busy staring after Vale.

Marlow's curiosity heightened again. Along the mezzanine was a row of doors that Marlow assumed led to offices of academy lecturers. But she could think of no reason why someone as important as Vale would come all the way here just to meet with an individual spellwright.

He stopped at one of the offices and knocked. Marlow stayed where she was at the top of the stairs, partially hidden behind the corner, and waited. The door opened, but Marlow could not make out who was there. There was a moment's pause as Vale and the office's occupant exchanged greetings, and then they stepped aside, letting Vale in, and closed the door behind him.

Marlow's heart thudded. That prickle of instinct told her this was important—certainly unusual enough to warrant further investigation. But it wasn't like she could stand outside the door, listening in. If anyone saw her there, they'd certainly want to know what she was doing. At the very least, though, she could find out who Vale was meeting and look into them.

Each of the office doors had nameplates stamped outside them. With a deep breath, she hurried down the corridor, as if she had somewhere important to be, glancing quickly and subtly at the office door Vale had entered.

As she read the nameplate, she realized she wouldn't have to spend much time investigating this spellwright at all. She already knew him.

Dominic Fisher, a boy from the Marshes who had astounded everyone when he'd earned himself a full scholarship to attend Vale Academy to become a spellwright. Marlow hadn't known him well—he was a few years older than her and Swift—but everyone in the neighborhood knew the story.

And she'd seen his name even more recently than that. It was written in Cassandra's ledger.

Marlow startled away from the door when she heard Vale's voice rise behind it.

"—you just don't understand what's at stake here!"

The spellwright—Fisher—said something in reply that Marlow couldn't make out.

"Have you forgotten who it was who made all this possible?" Vale's voice rang. "I gave you every opportunity, and this is how you wish to repay that kindness?"

Again, Fisher's reply was too low for Marlow to hear. But she heard Vale's footsteps clear enough as he stomped toward the door. Heart leaping to her throat, Marlow ducked into the neighboring office just as Fisher's door slammed open and Vale came charging out.

She remained there, pressed against the wall, until a moment later she heard a second set of footsteps pass through the doorway. She heard the office door shut and then the sound of footsteps fading down the hall.

She poked her head out of the empty office to see which direction Fisher had gone and nearly bowled into a reedy, slightly haggard-looking woman carrying a cup of tea.

"Can I help you?" the woman asked, blinking at Marlow from behind her owlish glasses. "My office hours don't start for another half hour."

Marlow glanced at the woman, and then at the office she'd stepped into. "Sorry, I think I'm in the wrong place."

"Well, where are you supposed to be?" the woman asked impatiently.

Marlow opened her mouth, an idea forming. "Do you happen to know where Professor Fisher's next lecture is?"

"So as you can see, the effectiveness of a given spell is not just a product of the quality of its ingredients and the skill of the spellwright in assembling them. Two different spellwrights can follow the exact same recipe with the exact same components and produce two spells that are vastly different in strength, potency, and duration."

Marlow sat back in her chair as the students around her in the lecture hall of Vale Academy hurried to scribble this down in their notebooks. At the lectern at the front of the classroom, Professor Fisher's gaze tracked over the students, snagging on Marlow as it had done six times already in the last hour.

"Professor?" A prim-looking girl sitting in the front row held up her hand. Fisher nodded at her to continue. "What is it exactly that accounts for the difference? I mean, couldn't you account for it by the fact that the more skilled spellwright is likely more accurate with their measurements, and therefore the spell works better?"

"You bring up a good point, Miss Bell. They've actually done experiments to test that exact hypothesis. Two spellwrights working on the same spell using precisely the same ingredients. Each spellwright's components were then double-checked by a third spellwright to ensure accuracy. The spells were still different in quality. Can anyone guess why?"

No one raised their hand. Marlow glanced around just to be sure and then lifted her own.

"Yes," Fisher said, nodding at her with a perfectly neutral expression.

"Because no matter how much a spellwright might try to remove themselves from the process, they will inevitably imbue the spell with their own beliefs and intentions and emotions," Marlow said.

The other students shifted in their seats to look at her, some with suspicion.

Professor Fisher smiled. The expression lit up his youthful features. "Exactly. Spellcraft takes more than just *skill*. And no matter how much we may study it, no matter how carefully we may document our processes, magic is magic, and even when we try to control for every possible factor to create perfectly reproducible spellcards, the intention of the spellwright still matters."

His gaze held on Marlow's for a full second before he glanced away.

"That is where I'll leave it for this afternoon," he said. "Please turn in your problem sets by the end of the week. I'm available in my office tomorrow at lunch hour should you have any questions. Your spell presentations start in two weeks, so get working on them now and don't leave them until the last minute."

The students all began moving at once, shoving notebooks into bags and dragging chairs away from desks. Marlow remained where she was, watching Professor Fisher gather his own belongings. By the time he was done, the other students were gone.

"Miss Briggs," Professor Fisher said briskly, approaching the desk where Marlow sat. "What can I do for you?"

"You remember me?"

"Of course," he replied.

"But we only met, like, twice," Marlow said. "And I was nine."

"Yes, well, you're awfully well-known by just about everyone in the city now, aren't you?" Fisher replied pointedly. "Besides—I never forget anyone from the neighborhood."

"You know somewhere we can talk?" Marlow asked, getting to her feet.

"This classroom is empty for the next period," he said.

"Somewhere we won't be . . . overheard?" she asked pointedly. She wouldn't be surprised if the academy classrooms were all outfitted with Eavesdrop spells.

Fisher regarded her with a keen look—one that made Marlow think he was doing to her what she did to her suspects. Trying to read her. After a moment he nodded toward the door. "I could use a bit of fresh air, I suppose."

She followed him out of the lecture hall and into the golden wash of the late afternoon.

"I didn't know you were enrolled in the academy," Fisher said.

"I'm not," Marlow replied. She cleared her throat. "So. You still making curses for the Reapers?"

He turned to her, his dark eyes narrowing sharply. "Am I to understand you're here to pick up where your mother left off, then?"

"Not exactly." Marlow let her gaze drift over Fisher. He really wasn't that much older than her—only six or so years. He was handsome, too: lean and graceful, with warm, dark-brown skin, peat-dark eyes, and a smile that felt like being invited inside for a soothing cup of tea.

He wasn't smiling now. He looked tense, his eyes guarded, his shoulders tight.

"You know, I used to really look up to you," Marlow said. "You were the one they all talked about in the neighborhood. The one who got out. Moved up. Left the Marshes."

A muscle in his jaw twitched. He must be used to hearing this after eight years. No one in the Marshes went to the spell academies—not until Fisher, anyway. He was said to be so brilliant that Vale himself had sponsored him through all four years at the academy—had even paid a stipend to his family during that time just so Fisher could afford to leave them to attend the academy and become a spellwright.

When Marlow had seen his name in her mother's ledger, a part of her, a part she'd thought had long since died, had been crushed. Because Dominic Fisher, the smartest kid the Marshes had ever produced, the boy who'd defied the odds and made something of himself through sheer talent and hard work, had worked his way up to become a spellwright for *what*? To make curses for crime lords to profit off of?

"I guess the Marshes never really leave you, though, do they?" Marlow went on.

He spun on his heel, facing her head-on beneath the shade of a flowering dogwood tree. His arms were crossed defensively over his chest. "What do you want?" There was no trace of the friendly, smiling man, the encouraging mentor, in his voice.

"Information," Marlow replied. "That's all, I swear. I just want to know what you might've heard around here about spellwrights dabbling in magic they shouldn't."

"You're going to have to be a bit more specific," he replied dryly.

"*Ilario's Grimoire*," Marlow said bluntly.

Fisher stiffened. Then his expression slipped into a caustic smile. "Ha, very funny. The grimoire was destroyed centuries ago. Did you really come here to ask me about fairy tales?"

Marlow was *almost* fooled. But he would no longer meet her gaze, and his voice wavered just the slightest bit.

"I have to prepare for my next class," he said briskly, moving to brush past her. "So if that's all—"

"It's *you*, isn't it?" Marlow asked.

Fisher fell silent, watching her with careful eyes.

"You're the spellwright who helped Vale make a—a Compulsion spell." She had to choke the words out. It made a sick kind of sense, didn't it? Who else in this academy was as indebted to Vale as Fisher? Who else owed him their entire *life*, and the lives of everyone he loved?

Fisher pressed his lips into a thin line. Maybe he sensed there was no use denying it.

"How do you know about that?" he asked in a low voice.

"I'm a cursebreaker," Marlow replied, figuring he could put two and two together as easily as she did. "Fisher . . . why did you do it? Why did you help him?"

Fisher set his jaw and looked away. "You really want to know?"

Marlow nodded.

"My father's been a deep-sea fisher his whole life—his father, too. He goes out just before dawn, catches glow-fish for lantern makers. I started going out on fishing trips with him when I was three. Learned to skin a fish before I could tie my shoes. I always thought that would be my life—living in the Marshes, working with my father until eventually I took over."

"But then you got into Vale Academy," Marlow said.

"The whole thing felt like such a fluke," Fisher said, shaking his head. "The schoolteacher who came around to our neighborhood—you remember her, Ms. Crane—she noticed I had a real knack for letters. Started giving me all sorts of things to read. She had a cousin who worked as a custodian at one of the spell academies. He brought me some of the old entrance exams. Every morning I'd go out on the boat with Dad and study those tests while we waited for the morning's catch. When I turned seventeen, Ms. Crane started raising money around the neighborhood for me to take the academy entrance exam. By the time the test opened for that year, she'd raised less than half of what we needed. But then somehow— and I still don't quite know how it happened—Vale found out about what she was trying to do. About me."

"He gave you the money for the exam," Marlow said. It had been the talk of the neighborhood for *months*. Marlow still remembered the careful excitement that had taken over—lucky breaks like that didn't just *happen* for kids like them.

Fisher nodded. "And when I passed, he gave me a scholarship to attend Vale Academy. Took a special interest in me and my education. He was very good to me, for many years. Even invited me to tea once or twice just to see how my studies were going. I was grateful to him."

"So how'd you start making curses for the Reapers?" Marlow asked, folding her arms over her chest.

Fisher wiped the back of his hand over his mouth. "My dad . . . he's an honest, hardworking man. Not a lot of people in this city are. He got taken advantage of by a loan shark—took out some money to pay for repairs on the boat and, well . . . you know how that story goes."

Marlow could guess.

"When he couldn't pay back the debt quickly enough, they wanted to take his sight," Fisher said. "He didn't tell me, of course—didn't even tell my mother. I had to find out from one of the boat crew who overheard him. I begged my father to let me quit the academy to come back and help pay off the debt. He told me he'd never speak to me again if I did. So I did the only thing I could. I went to the Reapers. They knew I was at Vale Library—everyone did. They said they'd see to it that the debt was forgiven, no questions asked, if I came to work for them. What else could I do?"

"You know it was probably a setup," Marlow said quietly. "If the Reapers knew you were a spellwright, they were probably just biding their time for an opportunity to make you one of theirs."

Fisher shrugged. He looked exhausted—even more so than the woman Marlow had encountered upstairs. Fisher's was the type of bone-deep weariness that Marlow recognized well from people who came from the Marshes. The kind of weariness that came when all hope had been wrung out of you. "Yeah, I thought of that. Don't see what difference it makes. Once you're in, they make it impossible to ever get out."

Marlow felt for him. He'd become a spellwright, thinking that it was a handhold to lift himself out of the muck for good. And instead, it became just another way for them to pull him under.

"I did what I had to do to protect my father," Fisher said. "And then . . . well, then your mom came to work for Vale. And she knew enough about the Marshes underworld to know what I'd been doing. And I guess you know how that went."

Marlow's throat felt tight. She knew her mother could be ruthless, but had she really been that cold and heartless? To extort someone like Fisher, who'd just been trying to play the best hand he could with the shitty cards he'd been dealt?

"She didn't ask for money from me," Fisher said. "Guess she knew enough about my situation. Instead she made me an informant. I ratted out dozens of other spellwrights who were making curses on the side to her. When she disappeared . . . I was relieved. Sorry. But it's true. And not long after that, Vale came to me. Told me he wanted help on a special project. I trusted him, and it seemed like a good opportunity. I said yes."

"You're loyal to him," Marlow said.

"I *was*," Fisher replied. "At first, he just needed my help getting his hands on a few ingredients. Then he was having difficulty with the spell itself. It was a complicated recipe with a lot of variables, and everything had to be precisely right. He asked for more and more of my help and . . . eventually I found out what he was trying to do. What spell it was I was helping him make."

Marlow shivered.

"When I learned the truth, I wanted to tell him I was done. That I wouldn't help with something so—monstrous. But I knew I couldn't afford to lose my position at the library. If I stopped being able to make curses for the Reapers, they'd collect on the debt my father owed."

"So you went along with Vale."

Fisher nodded. "I'm not proud of it. I'm ashamed that I had any part in it. But I can't sit here and tell you I'd make a different decision now."

Marlow didn't say anything. It wasn't that she didn't believe Fisher, or think his remorse was genuine. He'd made the same calculation that so many others in this city made—the same calculation that, once upon a time, Marlow's mother had probably made, too. It was like Cassandra had always said—in Caraza, you were either a victim or a survivor. And in Fisher's case, it wasn't his own survival he'd chosen. It was his father's.

But when it came down to it, Adrius had still been cursed and Fisher was at least partially responsible. No matter his motive, no matter how sorry he was, it didn't change what he'd done.

"You know what he did with the curse, don't you?" Fisher asked, raising his gaze to Marlow's. His dark eyes looked haunted. "Do you know who he used it on?"

Marlow nodded. The curse was broken now, according to Adrius. She didn't think she'd endanger him by telling Fisher that much.

He lurched forward suddenly, grabbing Marlow's wrist. "Then whoever it was, you have to tell them. You're a cursebreaker now, aren't you? You have to tell them there's a way to break the curse."

"It's already broken," Marlow said.

Fisher dropped her wrist. "Thank the gods."

"What do you mean, there's a way to break the curse?" she asked slowly. "You mean, without burning the curse card?"

"Yes," Fisher replied. "It was the only thing I could do, the only way I could think to try to . . . mitigate the damage Vale could do. I secretly altered the spell just slightly. Just enough so that, under the right circumstances, it could be broken. A kind of fail-safe."

Marlow's heart lurched. Adrius had claimed the curse broke when Marlow had kissed him. Could there be truth to that? "What kind of fail-safe?"

"It's going to sound strange," Fisher said. "But in all the fairy tales, there's always one thing that wakes the princess from her sleep or restores the monstrous prince to himself, right?"

"What?" Marlow asked.

"True love's kiss," Fisher replied. "It sounds silly, but those fairy tales *are* based in truth. And it turns out it's one of the most common flaws in curse-making. Forgetting to account for strong emotions—like love."

Her face went hot. She cleared her throat. "Well, that's—how do you know if a kiss is *true love's kiss*, anyway? It could be just, you know, a regular kiss."

Fisher shook his head. "The curse knows."

Marlow toyed with the ties on her jacket. She didn't *love* Adrius, that was—ridiculous. She cared about him, of course. And he—

Well, he felt something for her. But *love*?

"Good for you, I guess," she said. "You still helped Vale make a fucked-up curse, which he used to do a lot of fucked-up things. You really feel bad about it? Then help me *fix* it. Help me prove what Vale did."

Fisher's jaw tightened, his shoulders curling toward his ears. "I can't."

"Yes, you can," Marlow said. "Just because Vale helped you out doesn't mean you owe him your loyalty for life. It doesn't mean you owe him your *conscience*."

"That's not—it's not about my conscience," Fisher replied. "It's about my father."

"I can make sure he's protected," Marlow said. "I can make sure the Reapers don't—"

"It's not just the Reapers. Even if we *could* prove what Vale did, even if anyone believed us . . . it won't matter."

"Trust me, I know as well as anyone that there's no real justice in this city, but we have to at least *try*," Marlow insisted.

"That's not what I mean." He bit his lips, looking away. "Look, just— it's better if you just forget about this, all right? The curse is broken, so there's nothing left to do."

Marlow narrowed her eyes. She'd been a cursebreaker long enough to know when someone was being evasive. "What did you argue about?"

The question startled Fisher into meeting her gaze again. "What?"

"You and Vale," Marlow said slowly. "I heard you arguing in your office just before your class. It sounded like he wanted something from you, and you said no."

Fisher's gaze dropped. "You're right. I let him bully me into making the Compulsion curse for him, and now . . . now he wants my help with something else."

"Another spell?" Marlow asked, heart thudding in her chest.

Fisher nodded.

"What?" Marlow demanded. "Something else from *Ilario's Grimoire*?"

Fisher nodded again. "Ilario was interested in how magic itself worked. How, when it came down to it, each spell was a way of rewriting reality itself. Exerting your—or the spellcaster's—will on the world. All his life he tried to figure out the key to it and *why* magic works. He thought if he could figure out that one guiding principle, he could use it as a way to bypass all the rituals and components and ingredients of spellcraft altogether."

A cold dread gripped Marlow's chest. "What does that mean?"

"It means Vale is trying to pick up where Ilario left off," Fisher said. "He wants to create a single spell—*the* spell—that will give him ultimate power over reality itself."

THIRTEEN

The Isabella Morandi Museum Gala was always a lavish affair, the jewel in Caraza's social crown. Guests paid exorbitant fees to attend, and showed up in the most elaborate clothing designed specifically for the event. Dinner was served in the main exhibit hall at precisely twenty-one bells, and then guests were allowed to wander the gallery and mingle.

Adrius was in attendance, as he was every year, as were Amara, Darian, Gemma, and Silvan. But there were plenty of new faces at the event, too—families who might have balked at the price in past years had made sure to secure invitations for their eligible daughters because they knew Adrius would be there, and they weren't about to miss out on a chance to charm him.

As a result, Adrius had spent the majority of the sumptuous dinner fending off advances that ranged from coquettish to brazen, counting down the minutes until dinner was over and he could sneak off to find Marlow.

If she was really coming.

She was, he told himself. Marlow didn't break her promises.

Dinner dragged on for almost two hours, and then they were served cocktails and invited to explore the exhibit. Adrius entered one of the side rooms, sipping his drink and admiring the sculptures. The theme of the exhibit was *In Shadow*. Each intricate sculpture was cleverly lit so that its shadow on the wall portrayed a different image. A flock of birds became a city skyline, a mangrove tree became a woman's face, a bouquet of flowers an outstretched hand.

From across the room Adrius spotted Amara, who sent him a fleeting glare that wasn't difficult to decipher. With a sigh, Adrius turned to the girl closest to him and said, "The sculptures are just lovely, aren't they? Nearly as lovely as that dress."

The girl blinked bright-emerald eyes at him. With a start, he realized he recognized those eyes. This was the same girl he'd danced with at the masquerade, who'd somehow immediately seen through the show he was putting on and known he was simply going through the motions. Iris Renault—the daughter of Jean Renault.

"How long did it take you to come up with that line?" she asked. In her voice, he heard the echo of another. *Does that really work on Evergarden girls?*

"Iris," he said. "It's good to see you again."

"Is it?" she asked, a tinge of sharp humor in her tone.

"I apologize for the way I acted the other night," he said. "It was rude of me."

Her expression softened. "There's no need to apologize," she said. She put a hand on his arm. "I can't imagine what you're going through right now. How difficult it must be, with your father . . . Well, I don't hold it against you, is what I mean."

The gentle sincerity in her eyes made Adrius want to disappear beneath the floor. Iris's empathy only made him feel more hollow. She could summon this human sadness and grief, but Adrius felt nothing. Just an ever-widening blank chasm where any emotion should be.

"Thank you," he said. "I appreciate that."

"Oh, Adrius!" another voice called from several paces away. "Come look at this one!"

Grateful for the excuse to get out of Iris's keen gaze, Adrius followed the sound of the voice, where three girls stood in a cluster around one of the sculptures. One of the girls—Opal, a friend of Amara's—seized Adrius's arm and spent the next half hour parading him around the gallery.

Adrius let the sound of her idle chatter wash over him, occasionally making noises of interest or agreement. They made their way into another room of the exhibit. Adrius studied a sculpture of a hand lit so that its shadow showed the image of a man standing in profile. It was impressive how well the illusion worked—the artist seamlessly able to produce an object that portrayed two seemingly disparate ideas at the same time. An object that was one thing in the light, and another in the dark.

As he started to turn away from the sculpture, something caught his eye. A small, glowing orb of light, like a tiny star, orbiting around the sculpture. Adrius stopped and the light stopped, too, hovering right in front of him.

Adrius glanced at his companions. None of them seemed to notice the light.

Then the light zoomed around Adrius and zipped toward the doorway to the next room before pausing there on the threshold, like it was waiting.

Waiting for Adrius.

"Excuse me a moment," Adrius said to his companions, and then followed the light before they could reply.

The light led him through another room of the exhibit, and then into a side hall that had been cordoned off. With a quick glance around to make sure no one was watching, Adrius stepped over the velvet rope and hurried down the darkened hall.

The light zoomed around another corner and then winked out.

Adrius dashed after it and then skidded to a stop. He found himself in a grand room furnished like a Cortesian noble's parlor room, with a grand piano, a plush divan, and an ornately carved coffee table. Lamps scattered around the space filled the room with a pinkish glow.

Standing there beside the grand piano, lit by the moonlight streaming in through the paned windows, was Marlow. She was luminous, wearing a dress of pale gold, the skirt full but made of some material so delicate it was almost sheer, allowing glimpses of the shape of her body beneath it.

"You're late," Adrius said, advancing on her.

"I was busy," Marlow replied. "Looks like you are, too. There are a lot of girls here."

Her tone gave away very little, but Adrius knew her better than that. "Jealous?"

She pushed herself up onto the piano, legs dangling beneath her skirt. She regarded him with a steady gaze. "I have no reason to be."

"Really."

"Why would I be jealous of all the girls who came here hoping to get your attention," Marlow asked, tucking a finger into his waistcoat and tugging him toward her, "when I'm the one who already has it?"

There was no use denying it. No use pretending that any one of the perfectly nice, perfectly attractive girls in the other room held even a spark of interest for him compared to the wildfire that blazed in his blood when he saw Marlow.

He caught her chin and lifted her face to his. She shivered—the only indication that she was affected by his nearness the way he was by hers. He wanted to make her shiver again, to feel her tremble against him.

He couldn't help but think about the agony of their fake courtship. Every time he'd touched her under the guise of pretending had left him burning. He'd tried so hard not to let her see the power she had over him. That had been the true farce.

"Adrius," she whispered.

"Yes?" he replied, only a little embarrassed at how breathless he sounded.

She turned into him, her lips by his ear. "Sing 'The Bastard King of Corteo.'"

Adrius jerked back, bewildered by the request. He didn't know *what* he'd expected her to say, but it wasn't that. "What? Why?"

Even in his confusion, he couldn't help but admire the curve of her mouth, tilted into a playful smile. "I want proof you're really not cursed anymore. Sing it for me."

He opened his mouth and started to belt out, "*Now the minstrels—*"

She slapped a hand over his mouth. "What are you *doing*?"

"You just told me to," he replied, voice muffled by her hand.

"I thought you said the curse was broken."

"It is."

She looked at him with that watchful, assessing gaze. Adrius craved having that knife-sharp attention, that focus, directed at him.

Slowly, she dropped her hand from his mouth. "Step back."

He did. It was a thrill every time he got to defy an order—but this was a thrill, too. Watching careful fascination bloom over her face.

She dropped down from her seat on the piano. Their bodies were close, close enough that he could feel the whisper of her skirt brushing against the back of his hand. He waited.

She tilted her face up to his. "Kiss me."

He pressed his lips to the soft ridge of her cheekbone. It was barely a kiss.

He heard her gentle intake of breath and then he kissed her again, this time just at her hairline, where a few blond curls tumbled free.

He drew back and looked down at her, watching fascination turn into understanding.

He would do whatever she asked, but that was the trick of it—she had to ask. She had to speak the words and make plain what she wanted.

Because he had wanted this—wanted *her*—for so long, and he had to know for sure that she wanted him, too.

"Adrius."

He kissed her throat, her pulse hot and alive against his lips. He shut his eyes against a flash of memory. Warm red blood. The cold, hard handle of a knife in his grip. The sharp blade pressed against the tender skin of Marlow's throat—the same place where Adrius pressed his lips now.

The sound of her voice, ringing through his ears.

You could never hurt me, Adrius. Say it again.

Her lips, warm and soft against his. The way the kiss had broken him open, narrowing his world to the single point where they touched.

He had *felt* the curse break, although it wasn't until later that he realized it.

"Adrius," she said again. Her hand cupped the back of his head, fingers tangling in his hair. "Kiss me like you mean it."

He let go, covering her mouth with his, pulling her into him and kissing her with all the longing that had been pent up inside him since the day she'd left Evergarden and disappeared from his life.

The feeling of her body against his filled the chasm in his chest with reckless heat and want. He was numb, hollow, *empty*, but not with her. With her, desire coursed through his veins, lighting him up, and all he wanted was *more*.

There was only one way this could end.

He might not have been under a curse any longer, but she'd cast her own spell on him, and he was powerless against it.

Marlow was here, in this moonlit room, here, in his arms, and she wanted him. He kissed her, knowing it would ruin him. Knowing that this would end in a fiery blaze. But he'd rather have the memory of her lips when everything turned to ash.

FOURTEEN

The dock Marlow had asked Fisher to meet at was in the Industrial Quarter of Caraza, close enough to Copperhead territory that Marlow re-enchanted her hair dark just to be safe. She dressed in her old, familiar clothes—high-waisted trousers cut off above the knee and a hooded, sleeveless jacket that would protect her from any sudden rainstorms, though the evening sky looked clear.

She'd told Vale that she was taking Swift over to Starling Manor to have tea with Gemma. He could hardly argue that Starling Manor wasn't safe.

Taking Swift with her to meet Fisher was just strategy. Swift had known Fisher's family in the Marshes, had sometimes helped his father with odd jobs after Fisher left for Vale Academy. Marlow thought maybe the spellwright would be a little more forthcoming with another familiar face there.

Fisher was already waiting for them on the dock when Marlow and Swift's water-taxi pulled up. He held up a hand in greeting as Marlow and Swift disembarked.

"You remember Swift, right?" Marlow asked.

Fisher nodded. His eyes looked a little shadowed. "I heard about what happened to you. With the Copperheads. I'm sorry you had to go through that."

Swift nodded stiffly. "It's in the past now. Thanks to Marlow."

"I heard about that, too," Fisher said. He looked more weary than ever, like maybe he'd never had a proper night's sleep in his entire life. With everything Marlow now knew about him, maybe that was true.

"That's actually sort of why we're here," Marlow began. "I know what Vale did with the Compulsion curse you helped him create. He forced an innocent eighteen-year-old boy to kill for him."

Fisher's eyes went wide, and Marlow saw the moment that realization broke over him. He'd probably read enough in the papers about Aurelius's attack to put the pieces together.

"He's just as bad as the Copperheads," Marlow went on. "Worse, maybe, because no one knows what he's really capable of."

"If you came here wanting more information about Vale, I've already told you pretty much everything I know," Fisher said stiffly.

Marlow shook her head. "I'm here because I'd like your help."

"With what?" he asked warily.

"Stopping Vale."

His eyes narrowed in disbelief. "What?"

"Last time we talked, you told me he was working on a new spell," Marlow answered. "That he was picking up where Ilario left off—trying to master reality itself. We can't let that happen."

Given the power of a Compulsion spell, Vale had forced Adrius to attack his own father. She didn't want to know what he might do with the power to control reality itself.

"What exactly do you think you, or any of us, can do?" Fisher asked. "He's one of the most powerful men in the city. He has an entire library and hundreds of spellwrights at his disposal."

"We could destroy *Ilario's Grimoire*," Marlow said. "The way it was *supposed* to have been destroyed centuries ago. A spellbook isn't just a set of instructions, right? It's the core of the magic that gives the spell its power. Destroy the spellbook, and the spells themselves cease to exist. Like burning a spellcard, but on a bigger scale."

Fisher shook his head. "That's true, in *theory*. But do you have any idea how difficult it is to destroy a spellbook as powerful as *Ilario's Grimoire*? It's not as simple as burning a spellcard. It has protections. Enchantments. Only an extremely powerful spell could destroy something like that for good."

"Okay," Marlow said, exchanging a look with Swift. "Well, you're a spellwright, aren't you? Let's make an extremely powerful spell."

Fisher cast his gaze up toward the gray sky. "It's not that easy."

"I didn't say it would be *easy*," Marlow replied. "What's the alternative, then, we just let Vale do as he pleases and upend reality to suit himself?"

"It's not that different from what the Five Families already do," Fisher ground out.

"The difference is that we can *do* something about this," Marlow replied. She looked him in the eye. "You want to. I *know* you do. Because you've been caught in the claws of this city your whole life and you've been forced to use the gifts you have to serve everyone but yourself. But you have a chance now to do the right thing. To do something *good*."

"You might get a kick out of stomping around the Marshes breaking curses, but I don't have the luxury of being a hero," Fisher said with a bitter edge. "I have people depending on me. I have my family to think about. And I can't—I *won't*—put them at risk. The Reapers—"

"Don't worry about the Reapers," Marlow said. "I'll take care of them."

Fisher shot her a dubious look. "You'll 'take care of them'? What are you, seventeen?"

"I'll be eighteen in a few months," Marlow replied cheerfully.

Fisher snorted, shaking his head.

"You're what, twenty-five?" Marlow mocked. "And you're one of the most brilliant spellwrights to ever work at Vale Library. Age has nothing to do with it. If I say I'll get you out of your deal with the Reapers, I'll get you out of it. I don't make promises that I can't keep."

Swift stepped toward him. "You can trust her," he said gently. "Whatever it is that's going on with you and Vale and the Reapers . . . she can help. It's what she does."

Fisher looked at them for a long, silent minute. Then he folded his hands together. "You'll have to get the ingredients for the spell."

Marlow blinked.

"I might be brilliant, but I don't know if I'll be able to pull this off alone," Fisher went on. "I'll need help. An assistant, at least—someone who knows spellcraft."

Marlow nodded.

"And I'll need a place to work, outside of the library. Too dangerous to do this right under Vale's nose."

"Actually," Marlow said, smiling, "I know just the place."

The tip of the cigarette flared bright red as Viatriz took a drag and then lifted it away from her lips. She tapped it idly against her ring finger and Marlow watched the flecks of ash dance in the low, bruised light from the window of the Mudskipper's basement.

"You left the book in the archives?" she asked, surveying Swift, Marlow, and Fisher sitting in front of her on the couch.

When Marlow had shown up with yet *another* unfamiliar face—two, actually, if you counted Swift, who technically Viatriz had never met—she figured there was about a fifty percent chance they'd kick her out and refuse to ever speak to her again.

To her surprise, the three of them had been quickly whisked down to Viatriz's lair to explain themselves.

"Just like you asked," Marlow confirmed, avoiding Fisher's curious glance.

"Well, then, I suppose that makes us square," Viatriz said.

"Sure," Marlow agreed. "And now that we're square, I need another favor."

Viatriz barked out a laugh. "Of course you do. What is it now? More spells?"

"Just one, actually," Marlow replied. "A spell to destroy *Ilario's Grimoire*."

Viatriz gaped at her, forgotten cigarette smoldering between her fingers. "I'm sorry. I must be hearing things. Because *last time* you were here, you told me that your mother already destroyed it."

"And you told me that was impossible," Marlow reminded her. "Which Fisher here confirmed."

Viatriz's gaze slid to the spellwright. "You've seen the grimoire?"

Fisher glanced at Marlow and waited for her nod before answering. "Yes."

He didn't say anything more, but Marlow knew Viatriz was pretty smart. Smart enough to know that the fact that Fisher had seen the grimoire meant it was most likely in Vale Library.

Viatriz rubbed the center of her forehead with two long fingers. "Okay. So the grimoire wasn't destroyed. Did you, perhaps, recall that the Black Orchid actually *wants* the spellbook? As in, all in one piece? Why the hell would we help you destroy it?"

"Because I'm . . . hoping you'll change your minds?" Marlow suggested with a guileless smile.

Viatriz shot her a flat look.

"Trust me," Fisher said. "Everyone's better off if that thing is destroyed. The magic it contains is far too dangerous to be entrusted to anyone. Even someone with the best of intentions."

"You're going to have to give us more than that," Viatriz said dryly.

Fisher shot Marlow a look. It was one thing to ask the Black Orchid for favors. But did she really trust them enough to reveal the existence of—as Fisher put it—a spell with the potential to grant its caster complete control over reality?

But the way Marlow saw it, they didn't really have another choice. If they had any hope of destroying the grimoire, they needed the resources of the Black Orchid.

"In the grimoire is a recipe for a Compulsion spell," Marlow said. "But it doesn't compel people. It compels reality itself."

Viatriz narrowed her eyes like she didn't believe Marlow and shot a questioning look at Fisher.

He nodded. "She's telling the truth. I've seen the spell. It's real. Whatever the spellcaster speaks becomes true. Whatever command he gives would act upon the world as though he'd cast a spell. He could simply order someone to die and their heart would stop. He could command the sky to fall to the earth. Or the sea to swallow up entire nations. He could enslave the entire world to his will."

The words settled over the room like a shroud of dread. A shiver of horror crept up Marlow's spine. Fisher was right. It was far too much power for anyone to wield. Especially someone whose true nature Marlow didn't know.

"Gods," Viatriz said faintly.

"Look," Marlow said. "It's pretty simple. You help Fisher with the spell to destroy the grimoire. In exchange, he'll help you figure out how to break the Five Families' enchantments on their libraries. That's what you want, isn't it?"

Viatriz pursed her lips. "It is."

She didn't say anything else. Marlow noted that Viatriz hadn't questioned any of them about Fisher's abilities as a spellwright and whether he'd even be capable of helping them break such powerful enchantments.

It more or less confirmed her theory that Viatriz had known exactly who Fisher was the minute they'd entered the Mudskipper. It was why she'd agreed to talk with them so quickly. Why she was even entertaining this offer. She obviously knew enough about Fisher to know he was one of the greatest spellwrights of his generation.

The Black Orchid had more than likely had their eye on him for a while. It made her wonder why they hadn't tried to recruit him to their ranks before now—although given Fisher's association with the Reapers, maybe that made sense.

Finally, Viatriz spoke again. "We do have our own spell workshop space here. And I can see if I can spare Gray and a few others to help with spell construction."

Marlow had only met Gray twice, but given the protections and spells Marlow had seen him use, she was sure he'd be up to the task.

"Great," she said. "I trust that you can pick people who can be . . . discreet about this. Swift and I will help gather whatever ingredients you need."

"Fisher," Viatriz said, addressing him directly for the first time since the negotiation had begun. "Why don't you stick around and I can show you to your new workspace? Swift, Marlow—we'll be in touch when we have that ingredients list ready."

"In touch how?" Marlow asked. "I don't think I need to remind you I'm literally living in Vale Tower right now."

Viatriz gave her an admonishing look. "So was your mother, when she worked with us."

Marlow's teeth clicked shut. She hadn't thought about that—how *had* the Black Orchid communicated with Cassandra in Vale Tower?

"You'll know when you see it," Viatriz promised. "Until then, take care."

She waggled her fingers at them, which Marlow took as their cue to leave. She glanced over at Fisher as she and Swift rose, just to make sure he was all right with them leaving him behind.

"Are you sure about this?" Swift asked in an undertone as he and Marlow climbed the stairs back to the main dining room of the Mudskipper. "I mean—trusting the Black Orchid?"

Marlow wasn't sure about trusting just about *anyone*, but for a shadowy organization of rogue spellwrights, the Black Orchid had actually proven themselves to Marlow in a few ways. They'd never directly hurt Marlow or anyone she cared about. When Marlow had first questioned Viatriz about Cassandra, she'd told her the truth—even if she'd been wrong on some points. And even though Cassandra had plainly betrayed them in some capacity, Viatriz had nevertheless extended some semblance of trust to Marlow.

"I think we could do a lot worse" was what she told Swift. "And if we're going up against Vale, we need all the help we can scrape together."

FIFTEEN

Marlow had promised Fisher she'd make sure the Reapers didn't pose a problem for him, so when she and Swift left the Mudskipper, it wasn't Vale Tower she headed toward, but back to Reaper Island.

Swift had wanted to accompany her, but Marlow figured if she was showing up unannounced, it was better to go alone. And she needed Swift back at Vale Tower to cover for her in case Vale came looking for her.

It took a while to find a water-taxi willing to take Marlow out to Reaper Island, and by the time she arrived, dusk had fallen. Lanterns had been lit on all the docks surrounding the island, and Marlow was caught off guard by the number of other boats moored there.

From within the mansion, Marlow could hear the faint strains of music, and through the glass-paned windows she caught glimpses of people moving about, dressed in fine clothing.

A Reaper party. Great.

Marlow plodded up the dock toward the crumbling mansion. Last time she'd been here, it had been under the cover of early morning darkness, stealing in like a thief.

Now Marlow strode through the open doors like she belonged there. She *wanted* their attention.

She quickly spotted Lady Bianca, wearing a long, dramatic gown in a deep, rich shade of purple with a slit up the side, offering glimpses of her shapely legs. Her long, dark hair was gathered in glossy waves over one shoulder, her lips painted a shade of bright vermilion. She was surrounded by men in suits sipping sparkling wine from crystal glasses.

It was not unlike an Evergarden party, aside from the fact that any one of these people would probably kill Marlow without a second thought.

Actually, maybe it was *exactly* like an Evergarden party.

Marlow could tell when Bianca had spotted her, because her dark eyes narrowed in her direction. She excused herself from the circle and strode over to Marlow, all thunder and grace.

"I think I would remember inviting you to this soiree," Bianca said as she approached.

"I didn't realize you had guests," Marlow replied. A quick glance around told her that now that Bianca was talking to her, she was no longer going unnoticed by the other guests. "Can we talk privately?"

Bianca swiped a flute glass off a passing tray. "We're amongst friends here. You can speak plainly."

Marlow glanced around—no one here was a friend to her. But Bianca was staring at her expectantly, and Marlow would rather spend as little time surrounded by Reapers as she had to.

"There's a spellwright working for you. Dominic Fisher," Marlow said.

Bianca took a sip of her wine. "Of course. The brilliant young Mr. Fisher."

"I want you and the rest of your gang to forget you ever heard that name," Marlow said. "Forget him, forget his family, forget every curse he ever made for you."

Bianca smiled, her dark-painted lips curving as sharp as a scythe. "Why in the Ever-Drowning Mangrove would we do that?"

"Because if you do, I'll give you my mother's ledger."

Bianca leveled her with an unimpressed look. "Do you think I'm a fool, Miss Briggs? I'm certain you've already made numerous copies of the contents of that ledger, so how exactly is that any help to me?"

"Of course I made copies," Marlow agreed. "And as it happens, that ledger doesn't just contain the names of Reaper spellwrights. It's also got the names of Copperhead spellwrights. You want to take care of your little Copperhead problem? You want the rest of the gangs in the Marshes to bow down to the Reapers the way they once did? This ledger is everything you need."

For the first time since Marlow had walked into the foyer, Bianca looked interested.

"It sounds to me," Bianca said, "that you're saying that *you* have everything you need to take care of our Copperhead problem."

"Yes, that's what I just—"

"As in," Bianca continued, "*you* take care of the Copperheads and you have yourself a deal."

Marlow gaped at her while Bianca took another slow sip of wine. "You—want *me* to get rid of the Copperheads?"

"Well, you have just as much reason to want them gone as we do, don't you?"

"I'm not—how exactly am I supposed to single-handedly take down one of the biggest gangs in the Marshes?"

Bianca smiled again. "You've proven yourself to be very resourceful, Miss Briggs. I'm sure you'll think of something."

Without waiting for Marlow's reply, Bianca turned to the string quartet and signaled them to stop playing. The room fell silent, all eyes on Bianca. And Bianca's eyes were on Marlow.

"Everyone," she said, in a voice much warmer and brighter than the one she'd used with Marlow. "I want to introduce you all to the girl who's going to take care of the Copperheads. No longer will the Reapers have to tiptoe around the whims of a thug like Leonidas Howell—not once Marlow has dealt with him. Let's all raise a glass to our bright new future—and to Marlow Briggs."

"To Marlow Briggs!" the guests chorused back, lifting their sparkling glasses into the air.

Marlow's gaze never left Bianca. She understood exactly what this was, and what Bianca's game was.

She was offering Marlow this deal because she thought there was no way in hell Marlow would be able to pull it off. And if she failed, the Reapers would get to keep their prized spellwright *and* they wouldn't have to worry about Marlow holding the ledger over their heads, because Marlow would be dead.

Bianca met Marlow's gaze with a poisonous smile and lifted her glass. "To Marlow Briggs."

SIXTEEN

Too often, the business of cursebreaking required patience, and that was the one skill Marlow had never been able to master. As it turned out, the business of spellcraft was much the same.

Until Fisher and the Black Orchid produced a list of spell ingredients, there was nothing for Swift and Marlow to do except wait. Marlow was anxious and impatient from the moment she woke each morning to the moment she curled up for a fitful night of sleep, and after just a few days Swift had to talk her down from storming back to the Black Orchid workshop to demand they pick up the pace. He claimed it would only antagonize them. Grudgingly, she had to admit he was probably right.

But there was one way she had found to exorcise her restlessness—Adrius. He had always been a distraction for her—now it was a welcome one. When she was with him, Vale and the grimoire and the gangs all sank beneath the rush of anticipation and excitement. She felt both in and out of control at the same time.

Over the next week and a half, they met up wherever and whenever they could—late-night trysts in the Vale boathouse, midafternoon rendezvous on Adrius's zeppelin, and one memorable evening backstage at the opera, where Adrius had gone to see *The Butterfly Queen* and ended up missing the entire second act. They were careful never to be seen together. Marlow stayed clear of Falcrest Hall, and Adrius never set foot inside Vale Tower. But the rest of Evergarden became a map of stolen moments.

After one particularly late night with Adrius, she returned to the apartment in the early hours of the morning and collapsed on the couch, her head full of thoughts of Adrius, the scent of orange blossoms and amber, the rumble of laughter in his chest where it had been pressed against hers.

When the front door of the apartment cracked open, she leapt to her feet so quickly she made herself dizzy.

Swift stood in the doorway, blinking at her, a paper bag clutched in his hand.

She noted that he was wearing the same clothes she'd seen him in the night before. "And just where have *you* been?"

He laughed. "What's with the judgmental tone, Miss Midnight Tryst? You've been off rendezvousing with Adrius the past four nights in a row. I'm not allowed to have fun in Evergarden, too?"

Marlow narrowed her eyes.

Swift rolled his. "Relax. I woke up early for some reason. Decided to go for a walk. I brought biscuits and gossip."

He waggled the paper bag in her direction, and only then did Marlow notice the magazine tucked under his arm.

She opened the bag and pulled out some sort of fancy chocolate-and-fruit tart dusted with glittery confectioner's sugar. It wasn't her usual chocolate biscuit from the little boat near the Bowery, but it would do. She bit into it gratefully.

"Take a look at this." Swift made a show of flicking out the magazine. Marlow recognized the font on the cover as the *Starling Spectator*. He opened it to a page and held it up to her.

Marlow almost spat out her tart when she realized she was looking at a picture of *herself*—she recognized the dress she'd worn to the Vale-Falcrest wedding. It must have been taken when she and Gemma had entered, although Gemma had been cropped out of it.

Suspected Falcrest murderer Marlow Briggs innocent? the headline read. Beneath that: *Sources close to the suspect claim she is being used as a convenient scapegoat for the real killer.*

She batted the magazine away. "I already knew about this. Amara planted some rumors that Vale used me to get to Aurelius."

Swift raised his eyebrow. "Well, the rumors have changed their tune."

"What?"

"They're saying *Adrius* killed his father," Swift said, flipping open the magazine. "And that you are just so in love with him that you agreed to take the fall."

Marlow stared at the article, and then at Swift. "It says Adrius did it?"

Swift nodded. "And there may or may not be a heavy insinuation that Amara orchestrated it to get control of the Falcrest family." He scratched the side of his neck. "I mean, it's not *that* far from the truth, right? Except it wasn't Amara, it was Vale."

"Let me see that again." She snatched the magazine, scanning the article. *Sources close to the suspect.*

That could only mean one person.

Vale didn't so much as flinch when Marlow slapped the magazine down on his desk.

"What the hell is this?" she demanded, arms crossed.

Vale looked surprised by her harsh tone. It was the first time she'd ever used such a tone with him, but Marlow was seething too hot to consider the consequences.

"It looks like a gossip magazine," he replied blandly. "I didn't think you were interested in such things."

"A gossip magazine where *you* planted a story implying that Adrius killed his father," Marlow said.

Vale leaned back in his chair, pressing his lips together. Marlow could almost see the thoughts churning through his head as he decided whether to try to deny it. Finally, he said, "After the lies that have been running lately, I thought it best to set the record straight."

With more lies. Marlow wanted to spit the words like venom, but as far as Vale was aware, Marlow didn't know the real truth.

"I can see you're upset," Vale said. "But I won't make apologies for protecting you."

Except it wasn't just Marlow that this story was protecting. It was Vale, too. By shifting suspicion onto not just Adrius but also Amara, Vale had perfectly positioned himself to seize control of the Falcrest family.

Once he completed the spell he was working on, nothing and no one would stand in the way.

Again, Marlow had to wonder—to what end? Was Vale just another power-hungry player in Evergarden, driven by simple greed? Or was there something else he was after?

"You think you know what really happened," Marlow said. "But you weren't there. Why are you so convinced I didn't do it?"

It wasn't the first time she'd directly challenged him on it. She knew by doing so, she risked Vale finding out that Marlow knew, or suspected, his involvement.

But his expression did not waver. "Because I think if you had done it, you wouldn't be nearly so determined to take the blame." He let out a deep sigh. "I know what it is like to want to protect something so badly you'd risk almost anything. I look at you and I recognize that same desire that lives in me. Just as you are driven to protect the people you care about, so am I. That includes you."

Marlow watched him closely. She didn't think this was an act—but then, nothing Vale had said to her seemed like an act. Every time she spoke to him, it twisted her mind in knots. It was the same way she'd felt, sometimes, about her mother.

With Vale, it was even more difficult to parse where the con ended and the truth of him began.

"In any case, Marlow, I'm glad you came to see me this afternoon," he said, rising from the desk. "There's something I've been meaning to show you."

Marlow didn't know what she expected exactly, but when the canal boat took a turn right toward the Industrial Quarter, her stomach dropped.

Surely, *surely* Vale didn't know about the Black Orchid workshop. She stole a glance at him, but he was wearing the same blithe expression he'd had on since they departed, as if nothing was amiss.

That didn't stop Marlow from imagining what could happen next. Vale would walk her directly into the Black Orchid's secret lair, reveal he knew exactly what all of them were up to, and then have every single person there killed in front of her to show Marlow not to cross him.

It was a chilling thought. Marlow fought to keep her trepidation from showing on her face as Vale smiled over at her.

But then the canal boat sailed past the turn into the Industrial Quarter and Marlow shut her eyes in relief. They wound along the waterways that filtered out into the Marshes.

"Here we are," Vale said as their canal boat pulled up alongside a pier. Beyond the pier Marlow could see a building, one that looked peculiar and out of place at the edge of the Marshes. With its shiny plate-glass windows and expertly designed facade, it looked like a building you'd find in Evergarden.

Vale stepped onto the dock first and held out a hand to Marlow. She let him help her onto the pier, her gaze still locked on the building.

"What is this place?" Marlow asked.

"It is—well, it *will* be—a school," Vale replied. "We just completed construction a few weeks ago. I've planned a dinner to celebrate the grand opening in a few nights, but I wanted to show it to you first, as you were actually my inspiration."

"I was?" Marlow asked.

"Of course," Vale replied. "I saw what a difference getting a good education made in your life—how much difference it *could* have made, if you'd remained in Evergarden. And I thought to myself—doesn't every child deserve that? So I began making plans for this school, which will be open to every child in the Marshes."

She stared at the school, and knew Vale was waiting for her to react. That he wanted her to be impressed. And she *was* impressed. "That's . . . wow."

Vale gave her a gentle smile. "Would you like to go inside?"

Marlow nodded. She'd known, when she and her mother first moved to Evergarden, that she'd been given an opportunity she otherwise would never have been able to access. But now Vale was giving that same opportunity to others like her—like Swift, like Fisher. She didn't know how to feel.

She'd always known that Vale prided himself on being a philanthropist.

And it had always seemed to her to come from a place of real caring. But now, knowing what she knew about Vale's true desire for power, she couldn't help but question if that was all just an act. Or was it real—and had Vale convinced himself of his own righteousness *because* he cared?

They walked up the broad, clean steps of the school and entered the shining front doors.

"Ah, there you are!" A chipper voice greeted them as a tall woman in bright-pink heels clacked toward them from down the hall.

"Marlow, you remember Laurel," Vale said.

Marlow had met this woman on a few different occasions. She was one of his many secretaries, and had a hand in organizing Vale's charitable efforts.

"Of course. It's good to see you again," Marlow said.

"Likewise," Laurel replied. "So glad you could make it to see the place. We've been working around the clock to get it ready for the students." She looked over at Vale. "Sir, there are a few things that we still need to get your approval on, if you'll just stop by the headmaster's office."

Vale nodded. "Of course."

"Marlow, I can show you the classrooms while he takes care of that, if you like?" Laurel offered.

"Sure, that would be great," Marlow replied.

Vale disappeared down a different corridor to the headmaster's office, and Laurel led Marlow back down the hall.

"So you've been working with Vale for a few years now, haven't you?" Marlow asked lightly.

Laurel nodded. "That's right, I was hired just a few months after your—" She cleared her throat. "After your mother. Actually, I only got this job because I used to work at the cannery over in the Industrial Quarter. The workers who lived around the factory were getting sick, and I was trying to get the factory owners to clean up the runoff, but they wouldn't budge. Until Vale stepped in. He had his spellwrights invent new spells to clean up the water and protect it from further waste. He'd seen what a fight I'd put up with the factories, and he offered me a job to help spearhead some of his other efforts around the city."

Marlow could tell, from Laurel's bright eyes, that her admiration for Vale was genuine. That her belief in the integrity of their work was real.

Laurel ushered Marlow inside one of the classrooms, which was set up with pristine wooden desks and a large blackboard across the front wall. Another wall had been decorated with a mural of various swamp animals. The third held a bookcase filled with a wide selection of volumes, from history to science to introductory spellcraft to poems and fiction. A portrait of Vale hung at the back of the classroom, as if watching over the students who would soon be seated there.

"Are you all right to stay here for a moment?" Laurel asked. "I have to go sign for a delivery out back—lots to do before the opening."

"Go ahead," Marlow said with a wave. Laurel ducked back into the hall. Marlow walked through the rows of desks, trying to imagine what her life might be like if she'd spent her childhood days in a place like this instead of helping her mother run cons and dodge landlords, loan sharks, and debtors. Maybe she'd be a spellwright by now. At the very least, she thought, she wouldn't be facing an impending trial for murder.

"You know, I never really considered much outside the borders of Evergarden before I met your mother," Vale said from the doorway. He crossed the threshold and came toward her. "I saw the life she had lived here in the Marshes and how hard it was for her just to scrape out a living. How few opportunities she had, despite how brilliant and resourceful she was. It made me realize how much I could help people like her, and use all the power and money of the Vale name for good."

Marlow remembered what her mother had written in the letter to Vale—the letter she'd delivered right before she'd died. She'd said Vale had fallen in love with a woman who didn't exist. Marlow had felt an ache in her when she read those words. Because more than once in her life she'd wondered if the woman she thought was her mother was really who she seemed to be, or if *mother* was just another role Cassandra had played like so many others.

And this—was this Vale's version of that? Playing the role of the wealthy philanthropist to hide his dark schemes and hunger for power?

Maybe the two of them did deserve each other.

"What really happened between you two?" Marlow asked before she could stop herself. "I mean . . . she never told me how you met."

Vale smiled. "She was trying to con me."

Marlow wanted to be surprised, but she wasn't.

"Well, actually, at first she was trying to con an acquaintance of mine—the son of a Vale vassal family—but the moment I met her, I couldn't get her out of my head," he said. "It sounds silly, but I fell in love with her immediately. She was like no one else I'd ever met. Not honest, of course, but *real* in a way that I felt the noblesse nouveau were not. She made me earn her respect, rather than giving it to me just because I was the Vale heir." He chuckled. "You're very much like her in that way, you know."

In the past, hearing she was like her mother would have filled Marlow with pride. Now, knowing what she knew about Cassandra, she wasn't sure what she felt. "What happened?"

"I found out the truth—who she was, what she was trying to do. And I knew—I *knew* I should walk away, but I didn't. The truth is, it didn't matter to me. It didn't matter that she'd lied. It didn't matter that she was after someone else. When I told her that, she opened up to me. Told me she was only doing it because she didn't have another choice. That she was, more or less, being forced into this con by a debtor who had seen how beautiful she was, how cunning she was, and wanted to use her for his own gain."

Marlow had never heard about that part of her mother's life. Cassandra had been a con woman for Marlow's whole life, but Marlow had never questioned how it started. That maybe it hadn't been a choice, but something forced on her.

But then . . . just because that was what she'd told Vale didn't mean it was true. Marlow recalled what Cassandra had written in the letter she'd found in Vale's desk drawer. *You wanted to save me. I wanted you to think that you could. That was the con.* Cassandra had seen how much Vale wanted to play protector, that she'd invented the role for him.

"I paid all her debts to him," Vale went on. "Every last pearl, and then some, for him to stay out of her life for good. My family thought I'd lost my mind—this was before my parents passed, when my father was still the head of the Vale family. But I didn't care. We fell in love . . . or so I thought. Even though I was already married, I knew I couldn't live without her. So I offered her a place in my household, a way to be kept safe from people like the man who had used her. I offered her a future."

"And instead, she left you," Marlow concluded softly.

Vale nodded.

"Because of me," Marlow said. She didn't know much, but she knew Cassandra well enough to know she hated to be tied down. A child, one who was the illegitimate daughter of a scion, would have put her in an impossible situation.

But still, she'd chosen to keep Marlow. Either out of real love for the man who'd fathered her, or for some other reason that Marlow would never know for sure.

Vale looked up sadly. "I don't know why she left. I'm only glad she returned. Glad that I was given the chance to know you—my daughter. I hope you know just how grateful I am for that."

Marlow was struck by the emotion in his voice. Ever since she'd discovered he was the one behind Adrius's curse, she'd spent every moment in his presence questioning his motives. But when it came to her, she couldn't deny the truth—he *did* care about her. He'd made it clear every moment since the one when he'd rescued her from imprisonment. The very building they stood in now was a testament to it.

"And I hope you will also understand that I will do anything it takes to protect you," he went on. "Even when you may not agree with my tactics."

Marlow understood. In Vale's mind, planting rumors in gossip magazines was the same as paying Cassandra's debt and offering her a place in his household.

"The school is . . . beautiful," Marlow said at last. "But it won't fix everything that's wrong in the Marshes. It won't protect anyone from the gangs, from the greed of the Five Families."

"You're right," Vale said simply. "It's but a small push in the right direction. It's a first step only. But I want to go further. I want to see a Caraza that is free of the gangs. Free of the Five Families' greed. A Caraza where anyone, regardless of where they were born, can flourish. I think that's what you want, too, isn't it?"

If such a thing were even possible. Marlow had grown up in the sinking mud of the Marshes. And when she'd grasped a rope to pull herself out, all it had done was show her that this city had no solid ground. The people who stood without sinking did so only by climbing over others. You could either exploit or be exploited, and even the folks with good hearts knew they'd have to pick a side eventually.

And the system that had made it this way started at the top—in Evergarden. With the Five Families.

"As long as the Five Families are in charge, I don't see that happening," Marlow said.

Vale smiled faintly. "Yes, I think you're right." He cleared his throat.

"This school may be a small first step, but it's also a symbol of everything I hope to accomplish in my lifetime."

Marlow stared at him and found only sincerity in his gray eyes. *This was what Vale planned to do with the power he would gain from Ilario's spell? Free Caraza from the forces of greed and corruption that had choked it for so long?*

It seemed too good to be true. Marlow had always been skeptical of idealists, people like the Black Orchid who wanted big change but refused to acknowledge the reality of what it would take.

But when you had the power to shape reality itself, you didn't have to worry about what was possible. You could simply make it so.

Fisher's voice came to her then. *The magic it contains is far too dangerous to be entrusted to anyone. Even someone with the best of intentions.*

Vale's intentions might be noble, but did that give him the right to reshape reality to his liking?

No, Marlow thought firmly. But she could not quite silence the voice inside her that wondered if Vale's spell was Caraza's only chance of ever changing.

SEVENTEEN

When Marlow returned to Vale Tower, she found an unwelcome presence lurking in her hallway.

With a fortifying breath, Marlow marched straight up to Silvan. "What the hell are you doing here?"

Silvan froze, his shoulders going up to his ears.

"Are you trying to spy on me or something?"

He turned to face her, his face a mask of cool indifference.

"Did your dad ask you to keep an eye on me?" Marlow asked. "Or maybe Amara?"

"I don't do Amara's bidding, *or* my father's, for that matter," Silvan replied acidly.

"Then you're just skulking around my apartment for your own gratification?"

"I don't have to explain myself to you."

"You absolutely do if you're trying to stick your nose in my business," Marlow replied.

"Not everything is about you, Briggs," Silvan replied scathingly. "Now if you'll excuse me, I have places to be."

He sauntered away, leaving Marlow befuddled and annoyed in his wake.

Silvan poking around wasn't exactly good news, but it was more of a nuisance than a true threat. Marlow shook her head, moving to the apartment door. Faintly, she could hear the soft strains of music coming from within.

Smiling, Marlow eased the door open and took in the sight of Swift washing dishes in the sink. The phonograph in the corner of the living room—a new addition since Swift's arrival—played a soft, soothing melody.

"Hey," Marlow greeted him, shutting the door behind her.

Swift looked up from the sink, startled. "You're back."

Marlow joined him in the kitchen. "I just spotted Silvan skulking around outside. He didn't come in here and try to talk to you, did he?"

She wouldn't put it past him to try to get information about Marlow out of Swift.

Swift dried a teacup and placed it carefully on the counter. "No, we didn't talk."

"It's not the first time I've seen him lurking around our hallway," Marlow said.

"Maybe he wants to bond with you," Swift suggested.

Marlow didn't dignify that with a response.

Swift cleared his throat and nodded over to the living room. "Something came for you." A handsome bouquet of flowers sat in a crystal vase on the coffee table. "Adrius is *really* besotted, huh?"

"These aren't from Adrius," Marlow replied, reaching into the bouquet and plucking out a single delicate flower from the center. A black orchid.

Swift looked down at it. "Oh."

In order for a delivery to have been made directly to Marlow's apartment, the vendor had to already be on an approved list. Marlow recognized the design of the bouquet—there'd been numerous bouquets just like it delivered when she and her mother had lived here.

This was how the Black Orchid had communicated with Cassandra, then. And now they were using the same method to send Marlow a message.

Marlow held the black orchid out to Swift. He touched one of the petals. They both jumped when the petals folded up into a tight furl and then burst open again, revealing a small, rolled piece of paper sticking out from the center of the flower.

Tentatively, Swift took it and unrolled it. He read it for a moment and then lifted his gaze to meet Marlow's.

"They have the list of ingredients for the spell."

When Marlow and Swift appeared in the Black Orchid's spell workshop, Fisher looked surprised to see them. Sheets of crumpled paper littered the table in front of him, scribbled with lists and diagrams that were crossed out and written over. Marlow didn't know enough about spellcraft to understand how one went about figuring out the ingredients needed for a particular spell, but it was clear from the bags under Fisher's eyes that it had been an exhausting process. He looked like he hadn't changed clothes in a few days.

"That was fast," he said, wiping his ink-stained hands with a handkerchief. "We only finished it last night."

"Well, what can I say, we're eager. Is that the list?" She gestured at the sheet of paper in front of Fisher, written in crisp ink.

He nodded, handing it to her.

Marlow scanned the list. With every new item, her heart sank a little lower.

"I can get a few of these from the library, but the rest will be up to you," he said.

These weren't the kind of ingredients Marlow could just easily pick up at the Bowery, or even Orsella's. Marlow tilted the list toward Swift and watched as he read through it. When he was done, he raised his eyes to meet hers and she knew he was thinking the exact same thing.

How in the Ever-Drowning Mangrove were they going to get their hands on all this?

Fisher's eyebrows rose. "Is that going to be a problem?"

Marlow folded the list and tucked it into her jacket. "We'll get it done."

He nodded. "As soon as you have any of the ingredients, bring them here. For a spell like this, each ingredient needs its own specific preparation, and some of them could take weeks."

Marlow didn't know if they *had* weeks—they had no way of knowing how far along Vale was on his own spell. Fisher had already refused to help create it, but that didn't mean Vale hadn't found another spellwright willing to do his dirty work. Part of Marlow wondered if they'd be better off if Fisher *had* said yes—but then, he was already risking enough.

She and Swift left the workshop, exiting through the Mudskipper and down to the dock to wait for a water-taxi.

"We need to go see Orsella," Marlow said.

Swift nodded. "That's what I was thinking, too. She'll know how to get her hands on . . . at least *some* of these ingredients."

Marlow held up a hand to wave over an approaching boat. "She has one of them in her shop right now."

Swift furrowed his brow. "Which?"

"A hidden desire of the heart."

"And how exactly do you know that?"

Marlow smiled wryly. "Because I sold her mine."

Hex Row was close enough to Copperhead territory that Marlow and Swift used two more Disguise spells. Fisher—or rather, the Black Orchid—had also gifted her with about a dozen wards and hexes to help them get in and out of the Marshes safely.

But the moment Marlow and Swift walked through the door to Orsella's shop, the Disguise spells dropped.

"New wards?" Marlow asked.

Orsella scowled at her from the other side of the counter. "So. You haven't managed to get yourself killed yet." There was no indication that she was at all happy about this.

Before Marlow could reply, there was a soft *meow* and Toad leapt up from behind the counter.

"Toad!" Marlow exclaimed, rushing to the cat, who sat licking her paws.

She immediately rubbed her head against Marlow's outstretched hand.

"Sweet girl, I missed you," Marlow cooed.

"She's been nothing but trouble, which I guess shouldn't be a surprise given who her owner is," Orsella groused. "I assume you're here to take her back?"

"Yes," Marlow replied as Toad stretched up to press her cold nose against Marlow's. "But also, this." Marlow drew the ingredients list out of her jacket and handed it to Orsella. "I need to know how to get my hands on everything on that list."

Orsella read through the list, eyes getting wider the farther she read. "Is this a joke?"

She directed the question at Swift, who was busy scratching Toad between the ears.

"No," Marlow replied.

"What the hell is this even for?" Orsella demanded. "Tears shed by a killer? A nightmare? A blade that has tasted the blood of a tyrant? Are you making a *curse*?"

"Not exactly," Marlow replied. "I can't really tell you what it's for."

"No doubt you've gotten in over your head. *Again.*"

"Orsella," Swift said pleadingly. "We could really use your help."

Orsella huffed in frustration. "Fine. I'll ask around and see what I can do. No promises, though."

"What about the hidden desire of the heart?" Marlow asked.

"What about it?" Orsella snapped.

"I sold you mine," Marlow said. "Or—traded it."

"And?"

"Well, I need it back now."

Orsella cackled. "Oh, you do, do you? And is that how you think trades work, Briggs? You get to call in a favor—a *big* favor, might I add; that Ward Key spell wasn't easy to get my hands on, on such short notice—and then just rescind your payment?"

Marlow rolled her eyes. "Obviously I'll *buy* it back from you," she said. "Name your price."

"Oh *ho*, look who's gotten all fancy living in Evergarden."

"Orsella, come *on*, I can offer you a better price than anyone in the Marshes," Marlow said. Whatever the going price for a hidden desire of the heart was, she was pretty sure it was pocket change for the noblesse nouveau. Not that *she* had access to that kind of money, but she could figure it out. She'd ask Adrius, if it came to that.

"As tempting an offer as that is, I'm afraid I can't accept it," Orsella replied. "I already sold your heart's desire."

"You did?" Marlow asked, stomach lurching. "To who?"

Orsella's lips thinned into something that almost looked like a scowl— but not the usual scowl she wore when she found Marlow particularly irritating. "Another curse dealer."

Marlow's finely tuned intuition told her that Orsella was avoiding giving her a straight answer. "Orsella," she bit out. "*Who?*"

Her mind flashed to the worst possible scenarios—that Orsella had sold it to the Reapers, or to Bane and Leonidas.

But when Orsella finally muttered a reply, Marlow almost wished it *was* Leonidas.

"Lucian Warner."

A cold shudder went through Marlow. She caught sight of Swift's horrified expression, which told her at least she was not alone in her dismay.

"Orsella!" he scolded.

Marlow groaned. "Please, *please* tell me you're joking."

EIGHTEEN

Marlow had first crossed paths with Lucian Warner a few months into breaking curses. It was a case that had come close to stumping her, a woman who suspected she was cursed because over the past few years, several people close to her had drowned. At the time, Marlow hadn't had a lot of experience with death curses, but after some sleuthing she'd deduced that the woman was cursed so that any man who fell in love with her would die.

It didn't take long after that for Marlow to find the culprit—a classic case of a jealous ex-lover—and break the curse. All in all, not a particularly remarkable case. Until a man had shown up at the Bowery asking for Marlow. She'd been on guard the instant the man entered the shop. Based on his fine clothing, he was much richer than the Bowery's typical clientele.

He'd introduced himself as Lucian Warner and had informed Marlow that the curse she'd just broken was one he'd created specifically for the woman's jealous ex-lover. He made some veiled threats and sneered at Marlow. Said she was a little girl who didn't know her place. The whole thing had left a bad taste in her mouth—the fact that he'd taken the time to track her down, the condescending way he'd berated her, the fact that he seemed to hold her responsible for his bruised ego. It all smacked of the kind of man who couldn't fathom a world where he wasn't the smartest person in every room he entered.

She'd since crossed paths with Warner a number of other times, and her opinion of him hadn't improved. He charged a steep premium for his bespoke services, and as such, he could afford luxuries that most people in the Marshes couldn't—he wore the latest fashions, ate expensive imported delicacies, and regularly brushed shoulders with the noblesse nouveau at the opera and the ballet. For some reason, he thought this made him better than everyone else around him. He was just about the most pompous, obnoxious, self-important person Marlow had ever had the displeasure of meeting—and that included everyone in Evergarden.

"I really," Marlow grumbled as she and Swift made their way back to Evergarden, "*really* would have rather dealt with Bane, or the Reapers, or literally *anyone* else besides Warner."

Swift made a noise of agreement. "Yeah, because he's a creep who's weirdly fixated on you just because you broke some of his curses." He blew out a breath. "I can't believe Orsella does business with him."

"I'm sure he pays well," Marlow said. "And the upside is, I know where he stores his spell ingredients."

Warner co-owned a speakeasy called the Spirit Lounge near the Honey Docks, which also served as his workshop for making curses.

Marlow tapped a nail against the side of the canal boat. "I just need to figure out a way to sneak in without getting caught. There has to be some way to distract him so I can get in, get the heart's desire, and get out."

"He knows both of us, though," Swift pointed out. "As much as it pains me to admit, he *is* actually smart. If one of us tries to distract him, he's going to get suspicious."

"Can't be either of us," Marlow agreed. "And he's such a pompous prick, he's not going to take a meeting with some random person without vetting them first."

"So . . . we need someone who he doesn't know, but who he'll defi-nitely take a meeting with?" Swift asked. "Who would that be?"

Marlow grimaced. "I think I might know just the person."

"*This is a* bad idea," Marlow said, not for the first time that evening.

Swift shot her a bemused look over the rim of his cocktail. "It was *your* idea."

"Are you saying I never have bad ideas?"

Swift snorted. "You have bad ideas all the time. It's just that usually you don't admit it."

Marlow rubbed her temple. "Well, this time I am. Why didn't you try to talk me out of this?"

"Relax," Swift said. He nodded over her shoulder. "Your boy is going to do great."

Marlow turned, following Swift's gaze through plumes of cigarette smoke, to where Adrius sat in the corner of the speakeasy dressed in a shot silk suit the color of oxblood. He looked effortlessly in his element, despite the fact that this speakeasy wasn't exactly an Evergarden social club, but rather the headquarters of a seedy curse dealer.

The plan was simple: Adrius was to distract Lucian Warner by pretend-ing to solicit his services. Marlow would swipe an empty glass from their table with Warner's thumbprint on it, which she and Swift would use to get through the wards on Warner's back office to search for Marlow's heart's desire. Adrius would keep Warner occupied until Marlow signaled that they'd found it.

A cocktail waitress wearing what could charitably be called a dress sauntered over to Adrius's table. Though Marlow was too far away for their voices to carry, the Eavesdrop spell on Adrius's watch allowed Marlow to listen in.

"What can I get for you?" the waitress asked, her gaze lingering over Adrius.

"A Blue Monsoon," Adrius replied.

Surprise flashed over the waitress's face before she smoothed her expression. "Of course," she purred. "Wait just a moment."

The drink was code, a way for Warner's clients to discreetly request his services as a curse dealer. And while Warner rarely took initial meetings with clients himself, Marlow knew he'd make an exception for Adrius Falcrest.

Sure enough, not five minutes later, Marlow caught sight of Lucian Warner coming down a staircase she knew led to his office and, more crucially, his store of curses and spell ingredients.

He wore a slightly ostentatious dark-green suit with gold embroidery. His carefully styled hair was tucked under his signature charcoal fedora, accessorized with a simple but expensive-looking black silk band.

"Well, I must say," Warner said, claiming the seat across from Adrius. "I never expected to see a Falcrest scion in my humble establishment."

Adrius looked up, giving Warner a quick once-over. "Lucian Warner, I assume?"

"The one and only," Warner replied silkily. "Before we get started, I have to ask—how did you even find out about my operation?"

Adrius smirked. "Let's just say your reputation precedes you."

Warner looked pleased.

Marlow smiled into her drink. Adrius was playing this perfectly—flattering Warner's ego and feeding his desire to be seen as *important*. If someone like Adrius Falcrest knew who he was, Warner had truly made it.

"So, what can I do for you?" Warner asked. "I would assume a Falcrest scion would have access to any curse he wants."

"Unfortunately," Adrius said, "that access comes at the price of discretion. But I hear you know how to be discreet."

Warner leaned over the table. "Well, I wouldn't be in business very long if I didn't, now would I?" He waved a cocktail waitress over with two fingers. "Bring Mr. Falcrest and me each a glass of our reserve whiskey." As the cocktail waitress retreated, he redirected his attention to Adrius. "What kind of curse are you in the market for?"

"Something unique," Adrius answered.

"Then you've come to the right place, my friend," Warner replied. "My curses aren't like anything else on the market. Each one is individually crafted to suit your particular needs."

Marlow resisted rolling her eyes at the self-important lilt in his voice.

"Impressive," Adrius said. "I'll be honest with you, though. I didn't just come here looking for a curse."

"Oh?" Warner's piercing blue eyes examined Adrius with interest.

"The curse is more of an . . . audition of sorts," Adrius went on. "An operation like yours seems lucrative. I'm sure it could be even more lucrative with access to the resources of a spell library."

Warner leaned back in his seat. "Well. I wasn't expecting this—although I have heard rumors that the Falcrest family was beginning to dabble in the curse business."

Marlow stiffened and shot a panicked glance at Adrius. To her relief, he didn't allow any surprise to show on his face. Did that mean Adrius already knew that Falcrest Library was producing curses? Curses that Marlow had found in the hands of the Reapers? Did that mean it was *true*, and that Amara had begun covertly selling curses on the black market?

"Well, in this case I suppose the rumors are true," Adrius replied smoothly.

"Speaking of rumors," Warner said, "I've heard that you and Marlow Briggs were the talk of Evergarden this past summer."

This time, Adrius failed to hide his reaction. His shoulders tensed, and even from Marlow's position by the bar, she could see the wariness on his face. "I suppose."

Marlow scowled into her drink. Of *course* Warner found a way to bring her up. Swift was right—he *was* fixated on her.

"I hear it ended badly," Warner went on with feigned sympathy. "I can't say I'm surprised. That girl is a tempest, bringing trouble with her wherever she goes."

The waitress returned with their whiskey tumblers. Flecks of gold danced in the amber liquid.

Warner lifted both glasses from the tray, handing one to Adrius.

"To our future riches," Warner said, lifting his tumbler.

Adrius just smiled thinly and toasted him without a word, gulping down a sip.

"I suppose I understand the appeal, though," Warner said. "Marlow certainly is *spirited*."

Marlow's skin crawled at the suggestive edge in his voice.

"I didn't realize you knew her," Adrius said, setting down his glass. A lie—Marlow had mentioned it, although she'd avoided going into detail about her past dealings with Warner.

"Oh, yes," Warner replied airily, oblivious to how tightly Adrius was now gripping his glass. "We've had a few run-ins, here and there. A rather tumultuous relationship, you might say. I'm sure you know how it is with girls like her. They might put up a fight, but truthfully all they really want is to be put in their place."

He grinned lewdly at Adrius. Marlow's stomach heaved with revulsion, but it was quickly overtaken by a different kind of alarm when she saw Adrius's face—and the dangerous fury simmering in his golden eyes.

If he lost his cool and went off on Warner, their entire plan might unravel.

Keep it together, Marlow thought desperately.

Adrius dropped his elbow to the table, jostling his glass and tipping it over. Whiskey splashed out onto the table, soaking Adrius's sleeve.

"Whoops," he exclaimed, jumping up.

Marlow's heart pounded. This wasn't exactly the plan—Adrius was just supposed to finish his drink and pass it off to the waitress, and Marlow would swipe it from there.

Clearly Adrius had other ideas.

"Excuse me for a moment," Adrius said in a brittle voice, grabbing the whiskey glass off the table. "Let me just get cleaned up and then we can talk business."

He strode away from the table, his gait stiff with pent-up hostility.

"What is he doing?" Swift hissed. "This isn't the plan."

Marlow shook her head and grabbed Swift's arm, pulling him across the bar to follow Adrius. They found him leaning against the wall by the bathrooms, his fist clenched around the whiskey tumbler.

"Here." He thrust the tumbler at Swift. "Should be a good print on the edge here. I didn't touch it."

Swift looked at Marlow questioningly, clearly confused by the change in plan. "What happened?"

"He talked to Lucian Warner for ten minutes. You'd need a break, too," Marlow cut in before Adrius could reply.

Adrius fumed. "You didn't mention he was so—"

"Horrible?" Swift suggested. "Odious? Repugnant?"

"He was talking about *Marlow*," Adrius said in a low, dangerous voice.

"Ah," Swift said with a nod, as if that explained everything.

Marlow nodded over to the stairs leading up to Warner's workshop. "Go on, Swift. I'm going to stay out here and keep an eye on them."

Swift gave a quick salute and climbed the stairs.

Marlow turned back to Adrius and, before he could say a word, cupped his face between her hands.

"Don't let him get to you, all right?" she told him. "Just stay calm and keep him talking for another fifteen minutes. Twenty, tops. It won't be difficult—he loves the sound of his own voice."

Adrius's jaw clenched.

"Hey," Marlow said, softer. Before she could reconsider, she leaned in and kissed him.

He kissed her back fervently, as if all his bridled fury had found its release. She shivered against him. Out on the bar stage, a honey-voiced chanteuse sang about lost love and stolen moments. The warm press of Adrius's body against hers was almost enough to make her forget that Lucian Warner was waiting at the table for Adrius to return.

She broke away with a gasping breath. Adrius wasn't deterred, his mouth charting a hot trail down her throat.

"Minnow," he said roughly. His hands were hot against her bare skin, tracing her spine down to the low back of her dress.

"Adrius," she said, intending it as a reprimand. Instead, it sounded like encouragement. Bracing her hands against his chest, she pushed him back an inch. "You need to focus."

"If you wanted me to focus, you should have worn a different dress."

She was wearing the same deep purple silk dress she'd worn once before, at another speakeasy. She flushed, remembering how Adrius had cornered her that night, how in her drunken daze she'd thought he was going to kiss her.

That had been the night she'd finally admitted to herself that she wanted him to.

She smoothed the front of his suit jacket. "Swift is counting on you."

He sighed and started to move away.

"Wait," Marlow said. "Did you know about what he said about Falcrest Library selling curses?"

Adrius shook his head. "Did you?"

"I saw a box of curses at Reaper Island," Marlow replied. "But I didn't know what to make of it."

"If Amara is really selling curses to street gangs in the Marshes, I'll find out," Adrius promised.

"One thing at a time," Marlow replied. "You need to go back to the table before he comes looking for you."

Adrius nodded and Marlow reluctantly let him go. She remained hidden in the alcove while Adrius returned to the table, hoping to get her breath and thoughts under control. It was too easy to get distracted when she could still feel the ghost of Adrius's touch on her skin.

Through the Eavesdrop spell, she heard Adrius return to the table and resume his conversation with Warner. He swiftly and skillfully moved the conversation beyond the topic of Marlow, instead prompting Warner to regale him with stories about creative curses he'd come up with—some of which, Marlow noted with amusement, were ones she'd broken.

"Why don't I show you?" Warner said, about ten minutes later.

"Show me what?" Adrius asked, exactly as if he had accidentally been tuning Warner out for the past few minutes.

"My workshop," Warner replied. "It's actually just upstairs. We can go right now. I can show you the curses I'm working on, and some of the spell ingredients I've managed to get my hands on recently. You can see a bit more about how my business works. Get a real feel for it yourself."

Marlow's panic returned full force as she realized Warner had risen from the table and was leading Adrius over to his office.

The same office that Swift was still searching for the heart's desire.

Fuck. Marlow couldn't go warn Swift—she couldn't get past the wards without Warner's thumbprint. Either Adrius had to come up with some compelling reason to stay in the bar, or—

Or Marlow was going to have to distract Warner to buy Swift more time.

Without pausing to think it through, Marlow flung herself through the crowd to intercept them. She quickly caught sight of Adrius's dark-red suit, and ahead of him, Warner making his way to the stairs that led up to his workshop.

Marlow charged toward the stairs, getting there just seconds before them, and only slightly out of breath.

"Well, well, *well*," Warner said, his gaze sliding over Marlow like slick oil. "Marlow. What an exquisite surprise. We were just talking about you."

"Warner," Marlow greeted him. "I was just looking for you." She blinked at Adrius as though she'd only just seen him. "Adrius?"

Adrius fixed her with an icy glare that Marlow sensed was only partially feigned. "Marlow."

"Evergarden suits you, Marlow," Warner said, his eyes following the dip of Marlow's neckline. Under Warner's leering gaze, she felt exposed. "It's been a while, hasn't it? You're all grown-up now."

Marlow felt like retching and had to fight to keep her expression from twisting in disgust. It never ceased to amaze her, the things that grown men would say to teenage girls.

"I have a new case," she said, injecting just enough impatience into her tone to sound believable.

"And you're coming to me for help?" Warner asked with a self-satisfied smirk. "Times really do change."

"It's a curse I haven't seen before," Marlow said, quickly inventing a lie. "I thought you might know something about it. Do you have a minute?"

"How can I turn down such an intriguing offer?" Warner asked.

"Nonetheless—I have business with Mr. Falcrest. But why don't you stay, have a drink, and you and I can talk alone when we're done. Catch up. Reminisce about old times."

His tone was just suggestive enough to get Marlow's hackles up—and Adrius's, she realized with a glance at him.

Still, she had to get Warner away from his office. "Why don't you buy me a drink now? I'm sure Adrius is very busy and has numerous other engagements to get to."

She made *her* tone pointed enough for Adrius to catch on.

"No, actually, my evening is entirely free," Adrius replied with a blood-less smile.

Marlow fought to keep her expression neutral. She was going to *kill* Adrius. He knew what she was trying to do, and like the stubborn idiot he was, he was going to ruin the entire plan rather than leave her alone with Warner.

"Go get yourself a drink, Marlow," Warner said. "On the house, of course. I won't be long, and then you can have me for the rest of the night for . . . whatever it is you like."

Gods, she really hated this man.

"You know," Marlow said, thinking quickly. "If you're showing Adrius your workshop, I'd love to see it, too. It could help with my case."

At the very least, if she couldn't keep Warner out of the workshop while Swift was still in there, she could find *some* way to distract him while Swift escaped.

Warner glanced at Marlow and then at Adrius, clearly sensing the tension between them—which hopefully he chalked up to them being recently broken up under contentious circumstances.

"In that case," Warner said, holding out a hand. "After you."

Marlow ignored his hand and marched up the stairs, intentionally making as much sound as possible to warn Swift that they were coming.

"I consider this place my own little kingdom," Warner said to Adrius as they ascended the stairs behind her. "Perhaps more of a principality compared to the majesty of Falcrest Library."

At the top of the stairs was a metal door. Marlow waited on the landing as Warner slid past her, unnecessarily letting his hand trail over her hip as he reached to open the door with his thumbprint. She resisted the urge to recoil.

A glance at Adrius told her he hadn't missed the movement. He glared thunderously at Warner's turned back, jaw tight.

Marlow held her breath as the door swung open to a high-ceilinged room with rows of shelves lit by green bioluminescent lamps. To Marlow's relief, there was no sign of Swift.

"Feel free to have a look around," Warner said over his shoulder as Marlow and Adrius shuffled uneasily inside. "I don't allow this kind of access to just anyone."

Marlow caught Adrius's gaze. *Find Swift*, she mouthed. He nodded, and they split up to each comb down a different row of shelves.

"Wow, this is . . . quite impressive, Mr. Warner," Adrius said loudly. "It must have taken you a while to build up this inventory."

Marlow rounded the corner of another shelf and nearly jumped out of her skin when she saw Swift crouched next to a barrel.

"Gods," Marlow hissed, dropping down next to him. "You need to get out of here *right now*. I'll find the heart's desire—"

He held up a small, heart-shaped bottle filled with rosy gold light.

Marlow gave him a look that she hoped conveyed just how thankful she was that he had decided, at seven years old, to be her best friend.

"Adrius and I will distract him," Marlow whispered. "Just get out of here."

Swift nodded, crawling out from his hiding place and creeping down the row of shelves the way Marlow had come. Marlow went the opposite direction and had only taken two steps around the shelf when suddenly Warner was right in front of her.

"Lucian," she said, breath catching in her throat.

Without saying a word, he grabbed her arm and shoved her roughly up against the shelf. His other hand clamped around her neck, pinning her there.

Marlow was too shocked to react, her heart slamming against her ribs.

"Why don't you tell me, Marlow," he growled, his hot breath wafting over her, smelling of smoke and whiskey, "what exactly you were planning to steal from me?"

NINETEEN

Adrius's blood pounded furiously as he raced down the aisle, Marlow's choked gasp still echoing in his head. He skidded around the corner, barely registering Swift charging in the same direction.

His vision had narrowed to a single point: Marlow, pinned against the wall, one hand scrabbling at the fingers clenched around her throat.

Blistering rage roared to life in Adrius's chest.

Swift yelled something, a spellcard brandished in his hand. Adrius blew past him, reckless, blinding fury driving him.

The next thing Adrius knew, he had seized Warner's collar with one hand, the other cracking across his face.

Warner yowled in pain. Adrius lost track of everything except the exhilaration lighting up every inch of his body, the thrill in his chest, the dizzying cocktail of anger and adrenaline rushing through his veins.

It had been a storm building in him for hours—or days, or weeks, or *years*—and now it thundered through him, flooding his senses.

It was the purest thing he'd ever felt and all he wanted was to drown in it.

His fists found Warner again, and again, and again, each strike surging through Adrius. Warner fought back, and oh—that was even better, each blow a bolt of lightning.

Vaguely, beneath the pounding of his own pulse, Adrius could hear shouting, could taste blood, although he didn't know whose it was.

And then, Marlow's voice in his ear, somehow clear beneath the roaring storm in his head. "Adrius, we have to go, get up, we have to get out of here."

Arms dragged him back, away from Warner. Adrius staggered. Marlow grabbed his hand, pulling him across the workshop, down the stairs, through the speakeasy, and out into the warm, thick night air.

The storm inside Adrius began to clear. His knuckles were wet with blood, pulsing with a low, dull ache.

"Get that to the Black Orchid," Marlow was saying. She wasn't talking to Adrius. "I need to get him back to Evergarden."

Swift said something in reply. Whatever Marlow's answer was, it was enough to convince him to leave. Something warm trickled down the side of Adrius's face. He wiped it away. Blood.

Marlow's face swam in front of him. They were on a canal boat cutting through the dark maze of waterways.

He jerked up toward Marlow, cupping her pale face in one hand. "Are you all right?"

She just looked at him, all that blazing focus fixed on him. "I'm fine," she said at last. "Adrius, what *was* that?"

Adrius swallowed. The storm may have cleared, but he could still feel lightning crackling under his skin. "He was hurting you. I didn't think. I just—he *hurt* you."

What he didn't tell her was how *good* it had felt, how alive and whole the anger and pain made him feel. He didn't want to know what she'd think of him, if she knew. If she found out that if she and Swift hadn't dragged him away, Adrius probably would have killed Lucian Warner, and he wouldn't have felt bad about it.

Why would he? He'd stabbed his own father and he didn't feel bad about that, either.

Violence, his father had always said, was the tool of the weak. But in that moment, he hadn't felt weak.

Even now, sitting in the boat beside Marlow, he craved the feeling of his fists hitting Warner's face. Hungered for it.

But there was something he hungered for even more, and she was sitting right in front of him.

He took Marlow's face between his hands and kissed her, pulling her on top of him. Her thighs slid to either side of his hips, the silk of her skirt like water running over his hands as he hiked it up. He clutched her to him, her scent and the weight of her body flooding his senses.

This, too, felt like drowning, and he wanted nothing more than to sink beneath the water and breathe only her.

"Adrius," Marlow whispered, pulling back. Her breath was labored as she gripped his shoulders and held him back against the seat, her gray eyes searching his.

She had a way of looking at him that made him feel exquisitely unraveled. Like he was a mystery she was determined to solve.

This time, whatever solution she found there cast a dark cloud over her face.

Her touch was gentle as she leaned in and kissed him again, softly. Adrius ached with the tenderness of it. It made his chest go tight, his stomach knot. Marlow didn't let anyone see beneath her armored shell. He didn't deserve this softness from her. He'd only poison it.

He broke away, turning his face toward the dark water of the canal. Away from her searching gaze.

"I'm fine," he said. And then, once more, almost quieter than the sounds of the swamp around them, "I'm fine."

———

His body aching and his blood still buzzing, Adrius pushed into his apartment in Falcrest Hall.

"Adrius." Amara's voice stopped him short.

He looked up and found her sitting primly on the settee in a violet dressing gown, her dark hair loose around her shoulders instead of up in the severe coifs she'd taken to wearing it in the last few weeks.

When she and Darian had married, Amara had moved out of their shared apartments in Falcrest Hall. This was now technically *Adrius's* sitting room.

So if Amara was here, it was because she'd come to see him. Adrius knew his sister well enough to know that meant nothing good.

"What are you doing here?" Adrius asked.

"The better question is what were *you* doing *not* being here?" Amara replied. "Where were you tonight?"

"None of your business," Adrius replied gruffly.

She peered at him more closely. "Did you get in a *fight*?"

Adrius had done his best to clean up on the boat ride back to Evergarden, but he knew he probably still looked rough. "None of your business," he repeated, with more heat.

"It's time to stop messing around, Adrius. Our situation is more precarious than you know. With Father—" She stopped, her hands clenching in her lap. "You and I are the only ones standing between this family and ruin."

He wanted to say, *With Father gone, you and I are the only ones left.* But to Amara, it meant they had to protect the Falcrest legacy. To Adrius, it meant they could be *free* of it.

But Amara had always, always wanted to please their father. To live up to the impossible expectations he had for them. He remembered a particular moment, when they were both just fifteen, and his father had been trying to tempt a Morandi vassal house over to the Falcrests. As part of Aurelius's negotiation, their families had dined together. Amara, eager to prove her usefulness to her father, had spent the entire dessert course outlining the advantages that the Falcrests had over the Morandis.

The head of the vassal house had not been impressed. At the end of the night, he'd told Aurelius in no uncertain terms that they would not be moving their support to the Falcrests.

After the other family had gone, Aurelius had torn into Amara. He'd blamed her for the failure, saying her tactics had made them look desperate.

"You are nothing but a child, a simpleton!" he'd raged. "You made us look like sniveling little swamp rats begging for scraps. Is that what you are, Amara? A pathetic little rat?"

Amara had just sat there, head down, taking the abuse.

But Adrius had been furious. "Don't talk to her like that! She was just trying to help."

Aurelius had wheeled on him, eyes black with rage, and for a moment Adrius had thought he might strike him. But instead, he'd just ordered them both out of the room.

Out in the hallway, Adrius had put his hand on his sister's shoulder. "Don't listen to anything he says, okay? He's just pissed that he failed."

Amara had turned, looking up at him, her dark eyes bright and almost feral. And then she'd slapped him across the face.

Adrius had been too startled to react.

"Don't you ever, *ever* try to defend me again," Amara had seethed.

Adrius realized, in that moment, what he'd done. By trying to stand up for his sister, to protect her, he'd instead made her look weak in front of their father. And that was something she couldn't forgive.

It wasn't a mistake he'd ever made again.

"We need to keep the Falcrest vassal families in line," Amara said.

"Which means you need to stop dragging your feet and pick a fiancée now. Or I'll pick one for you."

"You said I had until the end of the year to marry," Adrius reminded her.

"Which is in less than three months!" Amara spat. "And you haven't even begun courting anyone properly yet! You're not taking this seriously, just like you've never taken anything in our lives seriously."

Adrius bit down on what he wanted to say. That he was, in fact, taking this very seriously, because Marlow's life was on the line. Nothing else had ever been as important to him.

He didn't say any of that, though. Instead, he asked, "Are you selling curses to the Reapers?"

"What?" Amara spat. "What does that have to do with—"

"Answer the question," Adrius growled.

Amara's eyes flashed. "So what if I am? Someone in this family needs to take initiative. We need to show the vassals and the other Five Families that we are just as strong as we always have been."

Adrius shook his head. "Gods, Amara, you have no idea what you've done, do you? The gangs are this close to all-out war in the Marshes. People will be *killed*."

"What do I care about the Marshes?" Amara asked.

Adrius laughed humorlessly. "You are so desperate to prove yourself to a man who's practically *dead* that you'll destroy the whole city for it, and both of us with it."

"At least," Amara hissed, "I am trying to *do* something. What have you done, Adrius?"

I stabbed the man who made us like this, Adrius didn't say.

"You *will* pick a fiancée," Amara said darkly. "Or I'll make sure that your girlfriend is put to death for what she did."

When he didn't reply, Amara rose from her seat and stalked toward the door, her dressing gown billowing around her ankles.

"Don't test me, brother," she warned as she passed him.

And then she was gone, the apartment door slamming behind her as a final rebuke.

TWENTY

Over the next two weeks, Marlow and Swift succeeded in gathering three more spell ingredients—poison from a rare dart frog, which Fisher had smuggled out of Vale Library; a nightmare, which Swift had provided himself when he'd woken up one night from a dream that the Reapers still had him; and a piece of petrified wood, which Marlow had had a surprisingly difficult time tracking down through her various connections in the Marshes.

And, of course, Marlow's heart's desire.

That still left them with three more ingredients to find: tears shed by a killer, a blade that had tasted the blood of a tyrant, and the remains of the spellbook creator. Marlow and Fisher had slowly been working their way through a stack of books about Ilario, searching for clues as to where his remains might have been buried, but so far they'd had no real leads. In her most despairing moments, Marlow worried that Ilario's remains had been lost for good, and that everything they'd done to get this spell ready would be for nothing.

Today, though, she and Swift were going to see Orsella—away from Hex Row, because Marlow didn't want to risk a run-in with the Copperheads.

"Please tell me you've got something for us, Orsella," Marlow said when she and Swift pulled up to the dock where Orsella had agreed to meet them.

"Well, hello to you, too," Orsella replied, hands on her hips. Then she sighed, rubbing her forehead. "I've got a lead on your blade."

Marlow perked up at that.

"Next week, there's a black-market auction. It'll be held on Temple Island the night of the full moon," Orsella said. "Rumor is the Bride's Obsidian Blade is up for auction."

"The . . . what?" Swift asked.

"It was the knife that the bride of the . . . fourth? Fifth? Emperor of Corteo used to assassinate her husband on their wedding day," Marlow answered.

"Don't get too excited yet," Orsella cautioned. "Everyone's buzzing about it. The chatter around this means just about everyone's going to want to get their hands on it. And these auctions are exclusive events— they're not going to let just any riffraff in."

Swift and Marlow exchanged a glance.

"Can't *you* get us in?" Marlow asked.

Orsella sniffed. "And what's in it for me, hmm?"

"Orsella."

Orsella cleared her throat. "Even if I *wanted* to help you out—which I don't—I can't. I was . . . asked not to return by the auction house."

"You were *banned*?" Swift asked incredulously.

Marlow stifled a laugh. "What'd you do?"

"*None* of your business!" Orsella replied.

"Must've been something pretty bad if a black-market auction banned you for life," Marlow snorted.

Orsella narrowed her eyes. "There *is* another way to get in. This auction house sells more than just spell ingredients. They also sell secrets."

"You mean like . . . blackmail secrets?" Swift asked.

Orsella nodded. "The price of admission is a secret. Of course, it can't just be any secret. It has to be something *worth* something."

"Luckily," Marlow said, with more confidence than she felt, "secrets are my specialty."

"Look, just—be careful, all right?" Orsella said gruffly.

"Aww, Orsella, you really *do* care," Marlow cooed.

Orsella glared.

"We'll be careful," Swift promised.

They bid Orsella farewell and continued on their way to the Mudskipper so Marlow could deliver the petrified wood and give Fisher an update about the other ingredients.

"If we can get into this auction and *if* we can actually win the Obsidian Blade, that only leaves two more spell ingredients," Swift said.

"Still no luck on locating Ilario's remains, though," Marlow reminded him.

"Well, they've got to be somewhere," Swift replied optimistically. "And that just leaves . . . tears shed by a killer."

"I figure we can just head to the Blind Tiger and make some Copperheads cry," Marlow said.

Swift shot her an irritated look.

"I'm *kidding*," Marlow exclaimed. "Kind of."

Swift cleared his throat. "We could ask Adrius."

Marlow stiffened. "He's not a killer," she said sharply.

"I mean, technically, no," Swift agreed. "But it's only a matter of time before they stop keeping his father alive with enchantments, and then—"

"He didn't *choose* to stab him."

"I know that," Swift replied. "But I don't think it makes a difference for the spell. Hell, maybe we should've just let him kill Warner and then—"

"Swift," Marlow said abruptly. "Please."

The truth was, ever since Adrius had attacked Warner, a deep pit of worry had burrowed into Marlow's stomach. She had never seen him like that before—full of rage and wrath—and she had to admit that it scared her. Not because she feared what he would do with that rage, but because she didn't know where it had come from.

She'd had the sense, afterward, on the boat, that he didn't know where it had come from, either.

"You Marlow Briggs?"

Marlow startled at the voice. It took her a few seconds to register the man standing at the end of the plankway, partially concealed below a makeshift wood-and-rope bridge.

"Who's asking?" Swift demanded, marching right up to the man.

"Swift," Marlow cautioned, holding him back with a hand on his arm. Her gaze was focused on the scythe tattooed on the man's wrist.

A Reaper.

"I've got a message for you, from Lady Bianca," the man said. "She says you better get a move on fulfilling your end of the deal."

Swift narrowed his eyes, looking from the Reaper to Marlow.

"I'm working on it," Marlow said to the Reaper.

"Well, you better work faster," the Reaper replied. "Or our mutual friend is going to have some problems."

He meant Fisher. Marlow wasn't the only one who would pay if she couldn't find a way to take down the Copperheads. Fisher would, too. And his family.

"Tell Bianca I'm handling it," Marlow said brusquely.

The Reaper raised his eyebrows. "Lady Bianca isn't known for her patience. You've got two weeks."

Panic fluttered under Marlow's ribs. Two weeks to take down one of the most dangerous gangs in Caraza?

"Well, it might take a little longer than that," she said.

"Two weeks," the Reaper repeated, and then pushed past Marlow and Swift to retreat down the plankway.

"Marlow," Swift said. "What the hell are you going to do?"

"I haven't figured that out yet," Marlow said. She'd made a promise to Fisher, though, and she intended to keep it. "Look, just . . . don't mention this to Fisher, all right? It's only going to scare him."

Swift looked at her uneasily.

"I'm going to figure this out, Swift," she vowed. In the meantime, they couldn't afford to lose focus.

When they finally arrived at the Mudskipper and slipped off to the Black Orchid workshop below, Fisher was already waiting for them.

"Everything all right?" he asked. He'd probably picked up on the tense silence between Marlow and Swift.

"Fine," Marlow replied before Swift could say anything. She pulled out the petrified wood from her bag and unwrapped it.

"This is great," Fisher said enthusiastically. "We're more than halfway there."

"Yeah," Marlow said. "Except those last three ingredients won't be as easy to get."

She told him about the black-market auction.

"I can get us in," Marlow said. "But I think it'd be best if you came with us—just to make sure the blade is what we need for the spell. We'll be in disguise, so don't worry about that."

Fisher's brow creased. "What about the money?"

"I've got that covered, too," Marlow said confidently. Or she would, as soon as she talked to Adrius.

"All right," Fisher said. "I'll keep looking into Ilario's remains in the meantime. Is there anything else? I've got a class to teach in an hour."

Marlow hesitated. A question had itched at the back of her mind ever since they'd recovered her heart's hidden desire from Warner, but she wasn't sure if she really wanted the answer.

"I wanted to know . . . ," she began haltingly. "For an ingredient like the heart's hidden desire. How does that work, exactly?"

"What do you mean?" Fisher asked.

"I mean, for whoever it was taken from," Marlow went on. She hadn't told anyone, save Swift, that it was *her* heart's desire they'd stolen from Warner. "What happens to them, exactly?"

Swift shot her a look, but Marlow kept her gaze trained on Fisher. She didn't want to see whatever was on Swift's face—pity or horror or something in between.

"Well, it's pretty much like any spell ingredient," Fisher explained. "Once the ingredient gets used in a spell, it's gone. There's no reversing the process of making a spell."

"But . . . how do you lose your heart's desire," Marlow asked, "if that was never something you had to begin with?"

Fisher shook his head. "You're thinking about this wrong. The ingredient isn't the thing itself. It's the *desire* for it. So say if you put your heart's desire into a spell, and later on you actually got the thing you were desiring? You wouldn't want it. You'd get no contentment, no satisfaction from having it. You'd just feel . . . empty."

Marlow's jaw clenched as she tried not to think about what that meant.

Maybe it was for the best, though. When she'd traded her heart's most hidden desire to Orsella, she'd done so thinking it was something she'd never be able to have.

So maybe it was a gift, if she stopped wanting it at all.

———

"*Adrius,*" Marlow gasped.

Adrius's hand skated up Marlow's side, sending heat shivering through her. His lips trailed down her throat and over her collarbone, where her neckline dipped to expose it.

"Dinner will start soon," she reminded him.

His arms tightened around her. "Let's skip it."

Marlow's laugh came out a little breathy. "We can't."

"Sure we can," he replied. "No one will find us."

"And when neither of us shows up you don't think that'll look a *little* suspicious?"

Next door in the Vale Tower ballroom, the guests were already taking their seats. Marlow could hear the echo of voices and the clatter of glasses and silverware through the wall of the parlor she and Adrius had snuck off to.

Tonight was the Charity Gala to celebrate the opening of the Vale School in the Marshes. Members of all Five Families were attending, along with numerous other vassal families and city officials.

It was also the first public event that Adrius had been allowed to attend at Vale Tower. Amara hadn't been happy about it, especially since she knew Marlow would be there, but given the Falcrests' connection to the Vales, it would be insulting for them to miss it. Of course, that hadn't stopped Amara from declining *her* invitation, claiming a bout of illness.

"Before we go in there, I wanted to talk to you about something," Marlow said, smoothing her hands down the front of Adrius's waistcoat.

"Is it how dazzlingly handsome I look in this suit?" he asked.

"Yes, *exactly*," Marlow agreed, running a finger along the gilded embroidery. "But also, we have a lead on another spell ingredient. And we need your help to get it."

"Is that right?" Adrius asked. "Need me to charm some hapless Falcrest

Library custodian? I'm told I can be very charming." He said the last part into the curve of Marlow's neck.

"Actually," Marlow said. "We need money."

Adrius sighed dramatically. "I *knew* you only liked me for my riches."

"Obviously. What else would I like you for?"

Adrius's hand snuck up the slit in her dress, skimming over her thigh. "I can think of a few things," he murmured.

Marlow grabbed his hand and pulled it off her. "The money?"

"You can have all the pearls in the ocean if that's what you want," Adrius swore.

Marlow's face heated at the ardor in his voice. "I don't think we need quite *that* much."

"How much, then?" Adrius asked. "I'm assuming this is some kind of black-market deal?"

"An auction, to be precise."

"When?"

"A week from today," Marlow replied.

Adrius nodded. "All right, that shouldn't be a problem. Are we done with the business talk?"

"Yes, but—"

Adrius kissed her.

"We really should get back in there," Marlow said when they came up for air again. "Someone's going to notice we're missing."

Adrius sighed, but then he nodded. "Here. Your hair is—and your dress . . ."

Marlow could guess how she looked—like she'd been unraveled in Adrius's hands.

Adrius put her back together. He smoothed her hair away from her face and fastened it with her gilded comb. He lifted the strap of her dress back onto her bare shoulder. Gently, he swiped a thumb beneath her bottom lip, wiping off a smudge of lip paint.

Marlow said nothing, just watched as Adrius carefully erased the evidence of their rendezvous, putting Marlow's armor back on, piece by piece, until no one would ever be able to tell what he'd done to her.

"You go first," she told him, when he was done. "I'll wait so it doesn't seem suspicious."

Adrius nodded, but lingered a second longer.

Marlow reached out, her hand finding his shoulder. "Adrius."

Her hand trailed down his arm and to his hand, but before she could take it, he pulled away. "I'll see you out there."

A moment later, he was gone.

Marlow waited a few long minutes in the parlor before slipping out and into the ballroom, where luckily many people were still milling about with pre-dinner cocktails.

Her gaze almost immediately found Adrius over by the bar, surrounded once again by a cadre of elegantly dressed Evergarden girls. He caught her eye for a fleeting moment, and then turned to say something to a brunette girl in a sapphire dress beside him. The girl wrinkled her nose slightly and then laughed.

Marlow recognized her. Adrius had danced with her at the masquerade. She'd sat beside him at the courte paume match.

Marlow watched them. She knew Adrius was only playing along for appearances, but it still *hurt*, more than she anticipated. It hadn't bothered her, knowing that there were other girls vying for Adrius's favor. She knew she was the one he wanted, the one he snuck away to see at every opportunity.

But that was just the problem, wasn't it? She could have Adrius in the shadows, but she couldn't stand beside him in the light. Not like this girl, whoever she was, or whatever girl he eventually chose as his wife.

And who was to say that Adrius couldn't love this girl, if it wasn't for Marlow? There was a reason the Moon Thief was the villain of the story, after all. Maybe that was Marlow—pulling Adrius further into the darkness with her when she should be letting him go to seek the light.

She turned away, unable to stomach the easy smile on Adrius's face, or the sight of the girl's hand on his sleeve. Blindly, she wove through the sparkling ballroom, uncaring of the chatter around her.

She'd just reached a tower of appetizers when a voice suddenly pierced through her churning thoughts.

"Miss Briggs."

Marlow turned and found herself almost face-to-face with Emery Grantaire, Caraza's City Solicitor. He was smiling at her in that cheerful way of his.

"Or should I say Miss Vale?"

"Briggs," Marlow said quickly. "I'm still getting used to the whole Vale thing, I guess."

"And how have you been since we last met?"

The last time they'd met, Marlow had been covered in Aurelius Falcrest's blood.

"Better," Marlow replied. "Actually, I'm glad I ran into you. There's something I wanted to talk about."

Grantaire's smile faltered. "I'm afraid I really can't discuss the details of your case with you. I can tell you we're close to setting a date for the pre-trial hearing."

"Oh—no, that actually isn't—it's not about that," Marlow replied. "It's . . . kind of a delicate matter."

"Matters involving the City Solicitor always are," Grantaire replied. He reached into his suit pocket and handed her a crisp white business card. "Contact my secretary and you can set up an appointment."

Marlow took the card. It shimmered slightly, and Marlow could just make out a few glyphs, so it was clearly enchanted in some way. She slipped it into her clutch. "I will."

Grantaire tipped his glass to her and sauntered off toward one of the tables at the back of the ballroom.

Marlow found her own table and took her seat beside Swift.

"Hey," he said, leaning toward her. "Are you okay?"

Marlow nodded, patting his arm. "Fine. Glad you're here."

Swift had been invited to the dinner at Vale's behest, much to the chagrin of the rest of the Vale family. Most of the noblesse nouveau attending chalked it up to Vale's particular form of eccentricity, having someone like Swift dine amongst them. Some were very clearly offended by the entire thing, and others seemed somewhat curious about Swift. A few people commended Vale on his generosity. After all, the dinner was to support a school serving the Marshes—it did make sense to invite someone actually *from* the Marshes.

For his part, Swift seemed mostly unbothered by their attention, focused primarily on the free food and alcohol.

Across from him, Silvan was noticeably irritated—even for him. He glared at anyone who so much as approached their table, and practically burned a hole in Lila Morandi's dress for the crime of laughing at one of Swift's jokes.

Marlow couldn't help but be offended on Swift's behalf, although he didn't seem particularly bothered by Silvan's snobbery.

"Where's Darian?" Marlow asked, glancing around the table as if Darian would materialize.

"Not coming," Silvan replied. "Apparently his wife objected to *some-one* being invited."

Swift sighed deeply. "It was me, wasn't it?"

Marlow bit back a laugh, although she felt a pang of genuine remorse. Thanks to her very existence, Darian was being pulled between his father and his new wife. She had a sinking feeling that Amara was going to exploit that divide as much as she could.

Marlow glanced over at Vale, who was seated at the head of the table. Seated to his left, his wife, Elena, was staring right back at Marlow.

The first course appeared on their plates and Elena broke her gaze.

Dinner was served without incident. As their main course dishes were cleared away, Vale rose from the table and ascended the steps at the front of the room to a podium.

"Welcome, honored guests," he said into the enchanted microphone. "The Vale family would like to thank you all for being here tonight and supporting such an important cause. The Vale School will open next week, and it will be a beacon of learning and possibility to the under-served children of this city. We truly could not have done it without your support."

He clapped his hands together, and the rest of the room joined in on the applause.

"This cause is very near and dear to my heart," Vale said once the applause died down. "And that is because of one person—my daughter, Marlow Briggs."

He paused, as if waiting for more applause. But none came.

Marlow froze, fighting the urge to duck under the table. Vale hadn't warned her that he'd be singling her out during his speech. Everyone in the room had turned to stare at her, but she kept her gaze fixed on Vale, and her hand wrapped tightly around Swift's arm. She did, however, from the corner of her eye, catch sight of Elena's livid expression.

"I only recently learned Marlow is my daughter," Vale went on. "I know there have been more than a few rumors swirling around, but the important thing is that she is a cherished member of the Vale family. Her arrival in our lives inspired me to create the Vale School, and I have no doubt—"

The ballroom doors burst open, drowning out Vale's next words.

Every guest turned to peer at this new interruption.

Amara stood on the threshold, wearing a dark-red dress that looked like blood in the ballroom lights. Over the dress, she wore a structured black bolero jacket with sharp shoulders and spikes radiating out from the flared sleeves. Her hair was slicked into an impossibly sleek, elaborate chignon.

"Sorry I'm late."

"Amara," Vale said. "I'm glad you could join us."

"Are you?" Amara asked, sauntering slowly across the ballroom toward him.

"Of course," Vale said. "You're family now."

"Family," Amara echoed. "Interesting you should say that. Because *my* family—my father—is dying because of that girl." She thrust her arm out, pointing at Marlow. "The girl you call your daughter. And I guess I just can't understand how you expect me and all these fine people to sit here and act like you haven't asked us all to dine with an attempted *murderer*."

Vale's expression grew stormy. "I can understand your anger, Amara. Clearly, you are grieving. But this is a discussion for us to have privately."

"You made it a public discussion when you trotted her out in front of hundreds of *our* people," Amara barked. "You can't insult us all by parading your illegitimate love child out in front of all of Evergarden and expect us just to accept it!"

"You are young," Vale said. "And I feel for your pain, I truly do. All of us are praying your father pulls through. But that does not give you the right to spread malicious rumors. The truth will come out in the hearings. Marlow is innocent."

"*Innocent?*" Amara echoed. "She confessed!"

Vale's voice grew steely. "Perhaps you might consider why an innocent girl would confess to a crime she didn't commit. Perhaps we should all consider just who she might have been trying to protect."

He shifted his gaze to find Adrius at the table.

"That," Amara said viciously, "is a baseless accusation. My brother and Marlow were never even a real couple."

Marlow's face heated. How did Amara know that? Her gaze found Adrius. Had he told her?

But Adrius looked just as stunned as Marlow.

"Your father," Vale said, "threatened Marlow. He had her mother killed, and Marlow feared she was next."

Silence echoed through the ballroom.

And then Amara's brittle, humorless laugh split the air. "You *must* be joking. Is that her excuse? That my father had something to do with her mother's disappearance? I suppose you'll believe just about anything."

"I know it can be hard to accept that our parents aren't the perfect—"

"Cassandra Briggs isn't dead."

Marlow's heart leapt into her throat.

Even Vale was stunned into silence.

"Cassandra is alive," Amara said. "My father had *nothing* to do with her disappearance." Her gaze swung to find Marlow. "And that girl sitting at that table with your *family* is nothing but a liar and a killer."

TWENTY-ONE

Marlow felt numb as she fled the ballroom and retreated to her room. Vaguely, she knew Swift had followed her, but she was aware of little else.

She sat on the couch in the living room, staring at nothing, while Swift busied himself making tea in the kitchen. A few minutes later, he handed her a steaming cup. Toad hopped up on the couch, tucking her soft body against Marlow's knees.

"She's lying," Marlow said, holding the tea without drinking it. "Amara. She has to be lying, right?"

She met Swift's gaze for the first time since they'd gotten back to the room. He was looking at her like he was afraid she might break. "I don't know."

"I *saw* it," Marlow said fiercely, looking down at her cup. "I looked into Caito's memories and I saw her fall. I—" She didn't know how to say what she was really thinking.

That Cassandra couldn't be alive because it meant that she was out there, somewhere in the world, and that meant she had left Marlow.

She sipped her tea.

Cassandra had always been the great unsolved mystery of Marlow's life. She was a puzzle that never seemed to fully fit together. A cipher without a key.

A knock came at the door. Marlow glanced at Swift. She could only think of one person who'd be coming to see her right now—Vale. He probably wanted to check on her, but Marlow wasn't really in the mood to talk to him, and especially not about her mother.

"I'll get it," Swift offered, but Marlow shook him off. She put her cup down and went to the door, opening it without bothering to check.

But the person standing on the other side of the door wasn't Vale.

Or rather, it was *a* Vale, but it wasn't her father.

Elena Vale stood across the threshold, her light blond hair loose from its chignon.

"Hello?" Marlow said, as if maybe Elena had simply gone to the wrong door.

"I was hoping to speak with you," Elena said. Her gaze flickered over Marlow's shoulder to Swift.

Swift looked at Marlow. She gave him a small nod. "I'll just go out . . . side, then," he said, and slipped past Elena into the hallway.

When he was gone, Elena stepped over the threshold and Marlow closed the door behind her.

"What did you come here to say?" Marlow asked. She had no energy and no patience for decorum at the moment.

"I know you must think that I hate you, Marlow, but I don't," Elena began.

"I didn't think you hated me," Marlow replied. "I know you must have been blindsided by finding out your husband is my father. But just so you know, so was I. My mother never told me."

"That doesn't surprise me," Elena said. "And to be very honest with you, Marlow, I wasn't blindsided at all."

It took a moment for Marlow to understand. "You knew about their affair."

"My husband thinks he's capable of hiding many things from me,"

Elena said simply. "But I didn't just know about their affair. I knew about *you.*"

Marlow shrank back. "What do you mean?"

"When your mother got pregnant," Elena replied, "I was already far along with Silvan. I caught her during a bad bout of morning sickness and I guessed the truth. I knew, even then, that your presence here would only cause problems. For myself *and* for your mother. And I knew if she told my husband she was pregnant with his child, he would never allow her to go. So I told her to leave Evergarden."

"You threatened her?" Marlow asked sharply.

"No," Elena replied. "I simply told her the truth. That having a bastard child of a Vale would only create complications for her. That she was better off on her own than tangled up in the vines of Evergarden. I gave her money—enough to support herself for a few years—and then she left."

Cassandra hadn't been much older than Marlow was now when she'd had her. She couldn't imagine how alone she must have felt, how scared. Marlow could see why she'd taken Elena's money and left.

"Why are you telling me this?"

"Because I'm here to give you the same advice I gave her," Elena replied. "Leave. Leave Evergarden the way your mother did. If not for the good of my family, then for your own sake. Things will only get worse for you if you stay here—you know that."

If only she *could* just walk away. Return to the Marshes, or go somewhere else entirely and leave all this behind.

Elena was right. Everything would be simpler if she did.

"Thank you," Marlow said stiffly. "For telling me about my mother. But if you don't mind, I need to be alone now."

Elena nodded. "I'll let you get some rest." Then she paused and reached out, touching one of Marlow's curls that had escaped its styling.

"You look just like her," she said softly.

Before Marlow could reply, Elena went through the door and was gone.

The next morning, Marlow walked into the living room and found Vale already sitting there on the couch, nursing a cup of tea, scratching a complacent Toad between the ears.

On his left, Swift sat stiffly in an armchair, wearing a polite smile edged with panic.

"Good morning!" Vale greeted Marlow as she stepped into the room.

Vale hadn't come to Marlow's apartment since the night of their first abysmal attempt at a family dinner. The fact that he was here now made her uneasy.

"Good morning," Marlow replied warily. "I see you've met Toad."

Vale rubbed a knuckle against Toad's head. Her eyes flashed a pearlescent blue.

Shit. Toad could detect curses. And thanks to the protective enchantments on *Ilario's Grimoire*, Vale was technically cursed.

Marlow glanced back at Vale, but he hadn't seemed to notice Toad's suddenly glowing eyes.

"I—um, wasn't expecting you," Marlow said.

"Yes, I'm sorry to drop in on you unannounced, but I wanted to check on you after everything that happened last night," Vale replied.

Marlow came to the couch and sat down on the other side. "I'm all right."

"I thought we could go somewhere, just the two of us, if you're feeling up for it," Vale said.

Marlow hesitated. She was still feeling fragile after everything that had happened the night before. She didn't know if she was up for spending a morning pretending around Vale.

But she was also curious. "All right," she said at last. "Let me just get dressed."

———

Vale took her to a grove of old-growth live oak trees on the edge of the Outer Garden District. They meandered down the path, past the ancient, moss-blanketed trees with their twisted roots and plunging branches.

"I took your mother here once," Vale told her. "Back when we first began seeing each other."

"She must have liked it here," Marlow replied. Her mother had a special love for the natural world around Caraza—the swamp, the marshy land, the mangrove forests. All of it was beautiful to Cassandra. Their apartment was still decorated with various landscapes that had captured her interest. She'd always talked about the wonders of the world beyond Caraza, and how she wished to see them—snowcapped mountains, pink-sand beaches, rain forests thick with growth and life.

Marlow had to swallow against the painful realization that maybe her mother *had* gotten to see those places, after all. Without Marlow.

"Do you think she really could have left?" Marlow asked, the words coming out before she could think to stop them.

Vale looked down at her with a gentle expression tinged with sadness. "I don't know," he said. "Your mother . . . she was always a free spirit. More afraid of being tied down than almost anything else. When things between us got too complicated, she did leave, then."

"Yeah," Marlow echoed, because she knew that, too. She and her mother had moved around the Marshes more than once because Cassandra had gotten in over her head some way or other. But the difference was, none of those times had she ever left Marlow behind.

"When she finally returned after all those years, she told me she thought that leaving would be for my own good," Vale went on. "That I would be better off without her—without *you*—complicating my life in Evergarden."

It sounded like what Elena had said. Was that all she'd ever been to her mother? Was that all she was? A complication? Was that all she would ever be to Vale, to Adrius? Marlow had spent her whole life mucking things up for people. She was good at it.

"Well," she said quietly, "I guess she was right."

Vale came to an abrupt stop beside her, grabbing Marlow's shoulder gently but firmly and turning her to face him. "Is that what you think?"

There was a blazing look in his gray eyes. His usually smiling face was drawn and grave. She swallowed down the answer she wanted to give. *Yes.* She stirred up trouble because she didn't know how to let things go. She didn't know how to be any other way, and now she knew why—she'd been trouble since the day she was born.

Vale shook his head. "She was *wrong*, Marlow. Because no matter how complicated things become, I know down to my bones that my life would *always* be better with you in it."

Tears stung Marlow's eyes. She blinked them away before they could fall. But her father was looking at her with nothing but care and sincerity in his eyes, and Marlow couldn't help the ache that opened up in her chest.

Because Cassandra—if she really was still alive—had decided she was better off without the complication of her daughter.

And meanwhile Vale—who had more than enough reasons to resent

Marlow, to turn his back on all the trouble she'd brought to his door—had instead welcomed her in, shown her kindness, given her protection, given her *love*.

The kind of love Marlow wasn't sure she'd ever had before, save, perhaps, for Swift.

For all the awful things Vale had done, he truly did love her.

TWENTY-TWO

Marlow watched the sun set as she sat at a teahouse overlooking the Crescent Canal. Out on the canals, couples were enjoying the warm evening, or crossing over to Starling Street, where Marlow could just make out the golden lights illuminating the sky above the Monarch Theater.

Marlow, too, had plans tonight, but they weren't in Evergarden. Tonight, she, Swift, and Fisher planned to infiltrate the black-market auction and get their hands on the Obsidian Blade.

But first, of course, they needed pearls. And Adrius was taking his sweet time.

"Now, who would keep a girl like you waiting?" a familiar voice asked. "Whoever he is, he's not worth it."

Adrius slid into the seat opposite Marlow.

Marlow glanced around quickly. She was in her semi-disguise, hair colored dark, an elaborate headdress covering most of her face, but still, she couldn't be too careful.

"Did you bring the pearls?" she asked quietly.

Adrius grinned and plunked down a small money purse—obviously enchanted to hide the enormity of its contents.

It was more money than Marlow had ever seen in her entire life.

Marlow reached for the purse, but Adrius tucked it away quickly.

"What are you—?"

"So how are we getting to this place?" Adrius asked. "I'm assuming it's not in Evergarden?"

"We?" Marlow echoed. "You're not coming."

Adrius shot her an offended look. "I'm pretty sure I'm the one putting up millions of pearls for this little venture, so I think I'm coming."

"Adrius." She couldn't keep the frustration out of her voice.

"Minnow," he countered.

Marlow bit her lip. They still hadn't talked about exactly what had happened with Warner. Adrius seemed content to pretend everything was fine, but Marlow was too good at seeing through Adrius's many masks. She knew something was wrong, no matter how hard he tried to throw her off the scent. She just didn't know what to do about it.

But it seemed like a bad idea to bring him along to an exclusive, potentially dangerous black-market auction when his behavior was so unpredictable.

On the other hand, she didn't have time to argue with him about it. She needed the pearls. The sun was about to set, and she still had to go back to Vale Tower to change and fetch Swift. Fisher would be waiting for them on Temple Island.

"Come on," Adrius said. "It's all anonymous, right? So it's not like anyone's going to know I'm there. And besides—have *you* ever bid on anything at an auction?"

"*Fine*," Marlow acquiesced, pushing away from the table. "Let's just go before anyone sees us."

Adrius refused to wait behind while Marlow returned to Vale Tower, which meant she had to sneak him in through the hidden service elevator, cursing him silently the entire time.

"You know," Adrius said, keeping pace with her as she marched down the corridor to her apartment. "You didn't even thank me for getting together the money for this little venture."

"Thank you," she said, deadpan.

"You're so welcome, Minnow," he simpered.

She kind of wanted to punch him. Which, unfortunately, did not diminish her desire to kiss him. Even at his most obnoxious, she still, regretfully, found him entirely charming. Not that she was *ever* going to admit that to him.

She shoved open her front door. "Change of plans, Swift, it looks like Adrius is—"

She stopped talking abruptly as several things became very clear.

The first was that Swift was not wearing a shirt.

The second was that he was not alone.

And the third—

"Oh," Adrius said, stopping beside Marlow. "Hi, Silvan."

Marlow was struck speechless by the sight before them.

Swift lay sprawled on the couch, his chest completely bare and his dark hair plastered to his forehead and cheeks. Kneeling beside him, Silvan looked similarly disheveled, his pale skin flushed pink, his usually pristine ice-blond hair more rumpled and mussed than Marlow had ever seen before.

"Don't you knock?" he asked in an imperious tone.

"This is my living room!" Marlow spluttered. "You—what are you *doing* here!"

Silvan looked down at himself and then at Swift. "I should think that was obvious, considering it's the same thing *you* get up to any moment you have alone with Adrius."

"You know about—" Marlow cut herself off. "Never mind. That's. Just. I can't deal with *this*"—she made a broad gesture at the entire living room—"*situation* right now."

Silvan sniffed. "Well, seeing as it's actually none of your business—"

"Silvan, I swear to the Ever-Drowning Mangrove if you don't get out of my living room *right now*—"

Silvan picked himself off the couch and straightened his shirt, which, Marlow was dismayed to realize, was half-unbuttoned.

With another haughty look at Marlow, he leaned down and kissed Swift on the lips like they were a pair of doomed lovers in an opera. Then he straightened up and sauntered past Marlow and Adrius out the door.

"So—" Swift began from the couch.

"You could have picked," Marlow began in a low, tremulous voice, "*literally* any other person in Evergarden to make time with—*why* did you have to pick *him?*"

Swift rolled his eyes. "Don't be dramatic, Marlow. He's not actually that bad. At least when we're—"

"Any other person!" Marlow exclaimed. She stalked over to her bedroom. "I am going to get changed, and when I'm done, neither of you is going to speak to me until we get to the auction house."

Swift and Adrius nodded mutely.

Marlow fumed all the way to the cable car station. They took the cable car to the Pavilion stop in the Marshes, and then hired a private canal boat to take them the rest of the way to Temple Island.

Once they were seated in the canal boat—Marlow next to Swift,

Adrius facing them on the other bench seat—Marlow turned away from both of them.

Adrius cleared his throat. "Well, if Marlow's not going to say anything, I will."

Marlow shot him a suspicious look, but he wasn't talking to her at all. He was looking right at Swift.

"I'm sure you know what this is about," Adrius went on. Marlow had never heard him use this tone of voice before—he sounded authoritative and uncharacteristically stern, his arms crossed over his chest.

"Uh . . . no?" Swift answered unsurely, looking to Marlow as if she might have some guidance. Marlow was as clueless as he was.

"You and Silvan," Adrius prompted. "How long has it been going on?"

Swift leaned back, stretching his arm over the back of the bench. "I don't really see how it's any of your business, but if you must know, technically I guess two months."

Marlow's jaw dropped. "*Two months?* How is that even possible? You only moved in a few weeks ago!"

Swift threw up his hand. "*You* were the one who made me babysit him for an entire night after the Blind Tiger! We had to occupy ourselves *somehow* while you flitted off to the Honey Docks to hunt down Bane."

"While you *what?*" Adrius demanded.

Marlow ignored him. "You couldn't think of a way to occupy yourselves that didn't involve sticking your tongue down his throat?"

"It was either that or kill him," Swift replied defensively. "Kissing just seemed a bit less messy."

"Ugh," Marlow groaned. "I can't *believe* you didn't tell me."

"Well, I was pretty pissed at you at the time," Swift reminded her.

"I mean *after* that!"

"Oh, because *you're* so forthcoming."

Marlow turned away, hurt. If she was being honest with herself, she was mostly upset that she'd missed this. It seemed so obvious in retrospect—the way Swift was always calling Silvan *Your Highness*, which now sounded more like a pet name than an insult. The jealous way Silvan had glared at anyone who dared to talk to Swift at the Vale School charity dinner. Even—

"Gods below," Marlow said abruptly. "Is *that* why I caught him sneaking around our hallway? He was there to—to—" She couldn't even say it.

"Yep," Swift replied with some satisfaction.

Adrius stared between the two of them with the expression of someone fighting off an impending headache. "Okay, well—putting aside how and why this all started, it's obviously still going on—"

Marlow made a disapproving noise.

"So I want you to listen to me very carefully," Adrius went on.

Swift peered at him, eyes narrowed.

"I don't care if you're Marlow's best friend," Adrius said fiercely. "If you break his heart, I'll kill you."

A peal of laughter bubbled out of Marlow.

Adrius aimed a piercing look at her.

"Wait," Marlow said, choking back another laugh. "You're actually *serious*?"

"Of course I'm serious."

"But it's *Silvan*," Marlow said. "Does he even *have* a heart?"

Adrius's glare intensified.

"Look, I appreciate the concern," Swift said placatingly. "But we're really not—it's not like that."

"He likes you," Adrius said plainly.

"Uh, no," Swift said. "He likes making time with me."

Marlow wished for a boat accident.

Adrius shook his head. "Silvan doesn't *do* that. Not with just anyone. He likes you. So just—be careful with him."

Swift looked stunned. Marlow was still skeptical.

Adrius cleared his throat. "All right. Well, now, I suppose, it's your turn?"

"What?" Swift asked.

"Well, you know," Adrius said with a wave. "If you're worried that I'm going to—hurt Marlow. I can assure you—"

Swift burst into laughter. He clapped Adrius on the shoulder. "Adrius. Buddy. If you hurt Marlow, I'm not the one you need to be worried about."

Marlow smiled despite herself. Swift glanced over to catch her eye and she quickly schooled her expression, crossing her arms over her chest.

Thankfully, the dock light appeared through the mist not long after that.

The canal boat maneuvered over to it and moored beside another decked-out boat. Ahead, Marlow could see the dark outline of the Temple of the Ever-Drowning Mangrove, where the auction was set to take place.

Fisher was waiting for them on the dock.

"Sorry we're late," Marlow said, stepping off the boat to greet him. "Swift was *otherwise occupied.*"

Swift rolled his eyes.

"It's fine," Fisher said, looking apprehensive.

"This is Adrius," Marlow said. "Adrius, this is Dominic Fisher."

Adrius surveyed Fisher with a supercilious smile, the kind that would have made any noblesse nouveau crumble into dust on the spot. Marlow had told Adrius about the role Fisher had played in creating the Compulsion curse—she supposed he had a right to feel a little hostile toward the spellwright.

Fisher gave him a solemn nod. "We should get going."

As they filed up the dock, Marlow nudged Adrius and said under her breath, "Be nice."

"I'm always nice, Minnow."

As they approached the grandly carved doors of the old temple, Marlow touched the slip of paper tucked into her jacket pocket and glanced over at Adrius. Dread curdled in her stomach.

He didn't know what secret Marlow was going to hand over to the auctioneer to gain entry. None of them did.

She hoped it would be enough.

Before they reached the door to the temple, they passed through a temple gate glowing with enchanted glyphs. When they walked out the other side, they were each surrounded by an array of silver glyphs.

"What just happened?" Adrius demanded.

"It's an illusion enchantment," Marlow explained. "The auction is supposed to be completely anonymous, so they have it set up so that everyone who steps foot inside is disguised. Since we passed through the gate together, we can all see past each other's illusion, but no one else can."

"What does the illusion look like, then?" Swift asked, inspecting his arm as if he expected to see scales there or something.

"I'm guessing something like that," Fisher replied, nodding over to the temple doors, where a pair of people were approaching the bouncer stationed there.

Except the pair didn't exactly look like *people*. In front of their faces— or perhaps instead of their faces—Marlow saw the visage of two stone statues.

Marlow watched as one of them reached into their coat and handed the bouncer a slip of paper with a silver seal. The bouncer fed the paper into the pale green mist that flickered in a suspended orb above a plinth that sat before the doors of the temple. The mist engulfed the paper and then immediately began glowing red.

The bouncer sneered. "You expect to get in peddling some ridiculous rumor?"

"Wha—no, it's *true!*" the stone-faced man insisted. "I swear it's true!"

"Nice try," the bouncer replied. He nodded over at two other bouncers guarding the doors, their faces disguised in black marble. "Get rid of him."

The two bouncers advanced, seizing hold of the stone-faced man.

"No, please—I swear it's true!" he protested.

"You are hereby banned from the auction," the doorman said. "Don't try to con your way back here again."

The marble-faced bouncers dragged the man back to the docks.

"What is that stuff?" Swift asked Fisher, eyes fixed on the green mist.

"It's called Veritas Mist," Fisher replied. "It's an enchantment to detect falsehoods."

"Handy," Swift replied. He glanced at Marlow. "You're *sure* this secret of yours is true?"

Marlow looked away from Adrius. "Positive."

She led them over to the bouncer.

"Invitation?" he asked in a bored tone.

"I have an offering," Marlow replied, holding out her own sealed secret. "For entry for all four of us."

The bouncer took it and dropped it into the mist. Marlow could feel Fisher and Swift holding their breath. The mist remained green.

The bouncer took it out of the mist. "All right."

Adrius started to move toward the door.

"Not so fast," the bouncer said. "Your secret might be *true*, but that doesn't mean it's worth anything."

"And who decides that?" Adrius asked imperiously.

"The Auctioneer," the bouncer replied. "Wait here."

He opened the door slightly and slipped the secret to someone behind it.

Adrius leaned over to Marlow. "What do we do if this Auctioneer decides your secret's worthless?"

"Trust me," Marlow replied, her gut clenching. "They won't."

It was, after all, a secret Marlow herself had almost been killed over.

The bouncer made them wait inside the courtyard while he let in another group of people. These ones had silver and gold illusions over their faces. Another had a mask of opaque glass. Another group entered, with illusions of black obsidian. And another.

Then, just as Marlow was beginning to lose patience, the bouncer crooked his finger at them.

"You're in," he said gruffly, pushing the door open to let them inside.

Marlow sidled past him with a saccharine smile—which she belatedly realized he probably couldn't see beneath the illusion.

They were led into a grand atrium filled with other auction-goers milling about, sipping wine and other refreshments. With the protective illusions in place, it was impossible to identify anyone, but Marlow found herself scanning the crowd anyway.

And then she saw something that made her go cold.

"*Shit*," she hissed, grabbing Swift's arm.

"What?" he demanded, looking up from gorging himself on hors d'oeuvres.

Marlow glanced at him and then back at the auction guest she'd spotted. He looked like everyone else in the atrium, a mask of pure bronze hiding his true face. Except one thing was different.

"Did someone bring a pet *crocodile* to this auction?" Adrius asked incredulously.

On his other side, Fisher looked as spooked as Marlow felt. "Is that—?"

Adrius looked at the others, taking in their haunted expressions. "I think I'm missing something."

"That," Swift said faintly, "is *Leonidas Howell's* pet crocodile."

"Who?"

"The leader of the Copperheads," Fisher put in.

"And the man who's more than willing to start a gang war in the Marshes if it means he can kill us," Marlow added. "Me and Swift, that is."

Fisher snapped a glare at her. "You didn't tell me Leonidas is after you."

Marlow patted his shoulder. "Fisher, if I took the time to list every person in this city who wants me dead, we'd never get anything else done."

"So," Adrius said, "none of you stopped to think that maybe the leader of a curse-making gang might show up to a black-market auction selling *curse ingredients*?"

Swift and Marlow exchanged a rueful look. Adrius had a point.

"I thought everyone was supposed to be anonymous," Fisher said. "Why would he bring that thing? Even with the illusion, everyone's going to know who he is."

"I think that's the point," Swift replied, a slight brittleness in his tone. "Unlike most of the people trying to covertly buy spell ingredients, Leonidas *wants* people to know he's here. He wants them intimidated. Scared."

"Well, congratulations to him, it worked," Fisher said. "What are we going to do?"

"Just steer clear of him," Marlow replied. "He has no reason to think we're here. He'll be so busy trying to throw his weight around, he won't even notice us."

"Except that we're bidding on one of the most prized items in this auction," Fisher reminded them. "I'm pretty sure he'll notice us then."

He also had a point.

"Why is it one of the most prized items?" Adrius asked.

"Because of its history," Fisher replied. "The most potent spell ingredients are the ones that have strong emotions associated with them. That's why memories are so frequently used in spellcraft. An object like the Obsidian Blade has a lot of emotion associated with it—specifically *destructive* emotion. That emotion comes from the original user of the blade—the bride of the Cortesian Emperor who murdered her own husband—but also because that story is so well-known. The legacy of the blade makes it even *more* powerful of an ingredient. Especially for the types of spells I'm guessing most of these people are interested in making."

"The illegal type," Swift filled in.

"Is the spell we're making illegal?" Adrius asked.

"All invented spells have to go through a rigorous process of testing and regulation," Fisher replied.

"So, yes, definitely," Marlow replied helpfully.

"I couldn't help but overhear," a voice said from behind Marlow. "Were you just discussing the Obsidian Blade?"

Marlow spun around and came face-to-face with someone with a face of dark, lacquered wood.

Her heart kicked in her chest. Just how much had this stranger overheard?

"I was just explaining the more technical aspects of its use in spell-craft," Fisher said quickly.

"I see," the stranger replied. "And that certainly wouldn't be because *you* need it for spellcraft, now would it?"

Fisher glanced at Marlow.

Marlow let out a careless laugh. "I'm sure half the people here are looking to get their hands on it. We'd hardly be unique in that regard. And those who aren't looking to use it for a spell are probably hoping to keep it away from their competition."

The stranger held up his hands placatingly. "I can tell you're a circum-spect group. I meant nothing by it. I'll be the first to make my intentions clear—I *am* bidding on the blade. Nothing wrong with a little friendly competition, though!"

The illusion spell employed by the auction house worked on voices, too. But even though this stranger's voice was distorted, there was something oddly familiar about the way he spoke.

"You're a spellwright, I take it?" the stranger asked Fisher.

"Are *you*?" Marlow shot back.

"More of an . . . iconoclast," the stranger replied. "Or at least I'd like to think so."

A tray of canapés passed by, and the stranger plucked off a sugar-dusted cookie with a center of bright red jam.

"I just love these, don't you?" he asked, popping it into his mouth. The illusion of the mask made it seem like the food had simply disappeared into thin air.

Marlow's grip tightened on Adrius's sleeve.

Underneath the lacquered wood mask was *Vale*. That's why he sounded familiar.

And that meant Vale was here looking for the exact same thing as them.

"Honored guests," an authoritative voice boomed out into the atrium. The lights flickered red. "Please take your seats in the main hall. The auction is about to begin."

"I guess I'll see you all inside," the stranger—Vale—said, and then disappeared into the stream of people entering the auction hall.

Marlow tugged on Adrius's sleeve before he could follow.

"That was Vale," she said in an undertone.

"What? Are you sure?"

She nodded. "He must be after the blade for his spell."

"Well," Adrius said with a grin, "We're just going to have to outbid him, aren't we?"

He offered her his arm and led her into the auction hall after Swift and Fisher.

The doorman handed Marlow a bid paddle, and then the four of them took their seats.

The Auctioneer took the stage. "Honored guests. Welcome to the Midnight Auction. We have a wide array of exciting items up for sale this evening . . ."

Marlow tuned out the rest of the speech in favor of looking around the room. She spotted Leonidas, surrounded by who she assumed must be Copperhead cronies, near the front. Vale sat along the side of the hall, and he appeared to be alone.

As a big-ticket item, the Obsidian Blade wouldn't be up until later in the evening. The bidding began with a few other spell ingredients that were of little interest to Marlow.

An hour into the auction, she was starting to feel impatient, and she sensed Adrius was, too.

He leaned over to her and whispered, breath hot against her ear, "What are the chances we can find some place to sneak off to?"

Marlow's face warmed.

Before she could reply, the Auctioneer's boisterous voice rang through the hall.

"Our next item is a *very* tantalizing addition to our collection, added just tonight," he said.

Marlow's stomach clenched.

"A truly scandalizing, dare I say *ruinous*, secret about none other than the most powerful family in Caraza."

Marlow felt Adrius's sharp intake of breath.

"I can personally guarantee you that knowledge of this secret is worth a *very* pretty pearl . . . in fact, it might just be the most explosive secret we've *ever* auctioned off here."

"*Fuck*," Swift hissed on Marlow's other side. "Did someone else find out about the curse?"

Marlow shook her head. Her stomach seized with dread. She knew it wasn't about Adrius's curse. She knew exactly what this secret was.

Because it was the same one she'd offered up in order to get in.

"To entice you a little further," the Auctioneer went on, "I can confirm that this secret concerns an old scandal—almost two decades old, in fact. This is one deep dark secret that it seems Aurelius Falcrest *won't* be taking to the grave with him."

Marlow looked over at Adrius, who sat completely frozen in his seat next to her, his jaw a rigid line.

"We'll start the bidding at two hundred thousand pearls," the Auctioneer said.

"Adrius—"

"Two hundred thousand!" Adrius called, raising the paddle.

"Two hundred and fifty thousand!" someone near the back of the hall called.

"Two hundred and seventy-five thousand!" someone else countered.

Marlow grabbed at Adrius's arm. "What are you *doing*?" she hissed. "We need that money for—"

"Three hundred thousand!" Adrius called, ignoring her completely.

"Four hundred thousand!"

"Five hundred thousand!"

"One million pearls."

The last bid was said calmly, with a kind of finality that made the rest of the room fall silent.

Marlow swiveled around to stare at the bidder. Their face was obscured by a jade mask, but there was something almost familiar about the stillness with which they held themself.

Someone else countered at one million two hundred thousand. Another shouted out one and a half million.

"Two million," the same jade-faced bidder said calmly.

Adrius raised his paddle and opened his mouth.

Marlow grabbed hold of the handle, right above Adrius's hand.

"Don't," she warned. "You can't."

He met her gaze, mutinous, as more bidding ensued. He must have seen something in Marlow's eyes—seen some hint of her guilt, because betrayal flashed over his face.

"You—*you* did this?"

Marlow didn't try to deny it, her grip tightening on the bidding paddle. Adrius shook his head, jaw clenching, and then pushed out of his chair and stalked from the hall.

"Shit," Marlow muttered.

"Do I hear four million pearls? Four million pearls?" the Auctioneer called out.

"Four million," the jade-faced bidder said.

"Do I hear five million?"

Silence echoed through the auction hall.

"Four million pearls going once, going twice and . . . sold!" The Auctioneer cracked his gavel against the podium. "Honored guests, we will be taking a five-minute break before commencing bids on our top ticket item for the evening—the Obsidian Blade of the Emperor's Bride!"

Marlow shot to her feet as the crowd started to murmur and move around them.

"I'm going to find Adrius," she told Swift and Fisher. "If the bidding starts, *stall.*"

She hurried past the pulpit toward the exit, but before she could slip through the doors she heard something that made her pause.

"Tell me who gave you that secret or I will make you regret it."

Marlow whipped around, crouching against the wall where she was blocked by the edge of the stage. Above, by the pulpit, stood the Auctioneer and the jade-faced bidder.

"We don't reveal our sources," the Auctioneer replied.

"You will this time," the jade-faced bidder said threateningly.

"You won the bid," the Auctioneer said flippantly. "That secret is yours to do whatever you like with. Its source should be of no concern."

"It *is* of concern," the jade-faced bidder snarled. "Because what I'm going to do is bury this secret and anyone who knows about its existence. And if you stonewall me, that will include you and everyone who works at this establishment."

Marlow's heart thumped.

"I can't reveal our sources," the Auctioneer repeated. "Anonymity is the number one priority of our auction house."

Marlow sent a prayer to the Ever-Drowning Mangrove that the Auctioneer wouldn't capitulate.

"Now, if you'll excuse me, we're about to resume bidding."

Shit. Marlow had to find Adrius, and do it fast. Or this whole plan was going to fall apart.

TWENTY-THREE

Adrius marched through the foyer of the auction hall, unsure where he was going but knowing he had to get out of that room. He burst through the doors and stepped out into the courtyard, the muggy night air swallowing him. Lightning bugs glowed and then dimmed against the night sky.

He was furious, *livid*, but more than that he was hurt.

Perhaps he shouldn't have felt so blindsided, but he did. And part of him—part of him even wondered if the hurt had been intentionally dealt. The same worry nagged at him. That Marlow had never truly forgiven him for turning his back on their friendship. That she never would.

He wasn't sure how long he'd been standing outside when he heard careful footsteps on the stone ground.

"The bid that won won't tell anyone the secret," Marlow said.

Adrius turned to her and didn't answer.

"I . . . overheard them threatening the Auctioneer," Marlow explained, though Adrius hadn't asked for an explanation. "Sounded like they were pretty adamant that the secret stay secret."

"What was it?" Adrius asked. He locked eyes with her. "What was the secret, Marlow?"

To Marlow's credit, she didn't look away from him, even as guilt clouded her expression. "It was about your mother. That your father cursed her."

Adrius nodded. He remembered hearing Marlow accuse Aurelius of cursing his wife, and in the same breath accusing him of cursing Adrius.

She'd turned out to be wrong about the second part, of course.

"So it's true?" he asked. "I mean, the Veritas Mist seemed to think it was."

Marlow nodded. "It's true. I . . . I saw her myself."

"You *what*?" Adrius demanded. "You saw my mother?"

"It was right before Amara's wedding," Marlow said. "I tricked Caito . . . followed her. She led me to your mother."

"And you never *told me*?" Adrius demanded.

"When was I supposed to tell you?" Marlow shot back. "After you promised your sister you'd *never* speak to me again?"

"And yet I've spoken to you dozens of times since then, so yes, Marlow, I think you could've put aside a few minutes to tell me you know where my mother is and that she's—what? Been imprisoned by my father for fifteen years?"

"I thought I could—"

But Adrius wasn't finished. "Yet despite the fact that you couldn't find time to tell me where she was, you certainly had time to *sell* that secret to some stranger at a black-market auction. Without even telling me what you were doing."

"You weren't supposed to be here!" Marlow burst out. "I told you not to come, I didn't want—"

"You didn't want me to find out what you were doing," Adrius finished tonelessly. "Of course you didn't. Just like you didn't want me to find out you were searching my father's study for clues about your mother, or that you've made some kind of deal with the rogue spellwrights she used to work for—what else aren't you telling me, Marlow?"

Marlow's eyes flashed defiantly, which told Adrius all he needed to know. There *was* more she was keeping from him. He couldn't even find it in himself to be surprised.

"I'm sorry," she said in a low voice, "that I didn't say anything about your mother. I'm sorry I had to use that secret to get us in here. It was the only thing I could think of that would be worth something to these people."

"Because you knew it was worth something to me!" Adrius cried. "Did you even think what might happen if that secret gets out?"

"So *what*?" Marlow asked. "So what if everyone finds out who your father really is, what he's capable of? So what if they all know the truth?"

"They would have used it to blackmail us—me, Amara," Adrius said. "And Amara would do anything to protect our family."

"You think I don't know that?"

Her eyes caught on his, and in the silence that stretched between them Adrius heard the unspoken part. That Marlow knew exactly what lengths Amara would go to, to protect the Falcrest name.

Like strike a terrible bargain to force her own brother into marrying someone for political gain.

A bargain Marlow was still trying to undo, even though Adrius knew it was futile.

"She's been cursed too long for the curse to break," Marlow said in a low voice. "It's permanent now. Even if your father dies . . . any order he gave her will still be in effect."

Adrius's stomach dropped. "So there's no way to free her?"

"Destroying the grimoire is our only hope," Marlow said. "And the *only* way we can do that is with this spell. I did what I had to do, and I know it hurt you, but in the end it will have been worth it. *If* we can get the Obsidian Blade. So please, Adrius. Come back inside with me and help us do that."

Adrius looked off into the mist rising from the Marshes. "Where is she?" he asked quietly.

Marlow's reply was gentle. "Caito is keeping her in a house in the Outer Garden District."

Adrius swallowed down a sob that wanted to climb up his throat. His whole life he'd thought his mother was somewhere far away from him. Was it possible that she'd been so close this whole time?

"Then take me to her. I want to see her."

"It's dangerous," Marlow said. "Caito knows that I know, but if she finds out that *you* do—"

"I don't care," Adrius replied stubbornly. "I need to see her. Promise me that you'll take me there, and I'll come back inside."

Marlow fell silent, and Adrius wondered if she was thinking of her own mother, and the lengths Marlow had gone to try to find her.

Finally, she nodded. "All right. Tomorrow. I'll take you to her."

"Then let's go." He strode briskly past her back inside the auction hall. She followed as he stormed back through the doors.

The Auctioneer was jabbering to the crowd. "That's a bid of six and a half *million* pearls, going once, going twice—"

"Eight million pearls," Adrius called from the back of the room.

The counter came instantly. "Nine million."

Adrius glanced at the bidder who had countered. It was the same person Marlow had pointed out earlier, the one she'd suspected was Vale.

There was no way Adrius was losing to the man who had cursed him.

"Twelve million pearls," Adrius said.

A murmur rippled through the room.

"Twelve million five hundred thousand," Vale called.

The Falcrest pockets were deeper than Vale's, Adrius knew that much. But there was only so much he could spend at once without Amara taking notice. And twelve million pearls was definitely over that threshold.

He raised his paddle again. "Fifteen million—"

A sharp gasp from the audience cut him off. Adrius turned instinctively toward the sound and realized, a beat too late, that instead of the illusions enchanted onto the faces of the attendees, he was now looking out at a sea of faces.

They were looking back at him.

And then the auction erupted into chaos.

TWENTY-FOUR

Marlow held fast to Adrius's arm as the auction attendees streamed toward the exits. She couldn't see Swift and Fisher through the sea of fleeing people.

"Honored guests, please remain calm," the Auctioneer's voice boomed through the hall. "Someone has tampered with our illusion enchantments. Please make your way to the exits in an orderly fashion."

"Shit," Marlow said, realization washing over her. "Vale."

She didn't know if he'd seen her face before the chaos began. Or Adrius's.

And he wasn't the only one Marlow needed to stay away from. There was also Leonidas. And—*Caito*?

Marlow caught sight of her distinctive face paint. She seized Adrius's arm and backed up against the wall, pulling Adrius in front of her. Several more people pushed past them to get to the doors.

"Caito's here," Marlow said to Adrius. Over his shoulder, she could just make out her form, clearly distinguishable by the bright streak of green in her dark hair. Then it clicked. "She must have been the one who bought the secret."

It made sense. The Falcrest chevalier had a vested interest in a black-market auction to keep tabs on potential rogue spellwrights. And she'd have a good reason for wanting Aurelius Falcrest's secrets to stay secret.

But if she found out that Marlow was the one who'd put that secret up for auction . . . well, Marlow remembered what had happened the last time Caito wanted to silence her.

"We need to get out of here," Adrius said firmly.

"What about the blade?"

"What are we supposed to do?" Adrius asked. "The auction's obviously not continuing. We can't just *steal* it."

"Gods below," Marlow swore, realization dawning. "That's *exactly* what this is about. Someone must have tampered with the illusion enchantment to create a distraction so they could steal the Obsidian Blade."

"Who?" Adrius asked. "Vale?"

Marlow shook her head. Vale wouldn't need to steal the Obsidian Blade, and he had much, *much* more to lose by being seen at the auction than just about anyone else in attendance. If anyone knew Cormorant Vale was at a secret black-market auction, his reputation as an honest philanthropist would be ruined.

But there was one person who didn't care at all if they were seen. One person who was volatile and brazen enough to make such a bold move without considering the consequences.

Leonidas Howell.

"Find Swift and Fisher and find a way to get us off this island," Marlow instructed.

"Why? Where are *you* going?"

She didn't answer, just shoved Adrius back so she could slip out from the wall. Dodging around more panicked guests, Marlow carved a path to the front of the auction hall. She scanned quickly for any sign of the Auctioneer, but he'd disappeared. Her gaze caught instead on a display box made of dark wood, about eight inches long, sitting on the pedestal where the Auctioneer had been standing.

She scrambled onto the stage and lunged for the box.

It was empty.

"Looking for something?"

Marlow whirled and found herself face-to-face with Leonidas. His lean, rangy form was all coiled, potential energy, his coal-dark eyes like fathomless pits of cruelty. On his gold-chained leash, Sycorax stared hungrily at her, his tail swishing menacingly. In Leonidas's other hand, he held the shining black Obsidian Blade.

Fuck. She'd gotten here too late.

A moment after she spotted Leonidas, Thaddeus Bane, his right-hand man, appeared at his side. The last time Marlow had seen him, he'd been vomiting slugs outside a burlesque club in the Honey Docks.

"Marlow Briggs," Bane said, rolling her name in his mouth like a marble. "Now this is a very welcome surprise. We've been looking for you, Marlow."

Marlow's chest tightened with fear, but she tried not to show any of it on her face. "You'd think you'd find something better to do with your time."

"How badly do you want this?" Leonidas asked. The Obsidian Blade flashed with silvery light. "Tell you what. I'll give it to you in exchange for Swift."

Marlow bit back a growl, thankful that Swift was nowhere near them right now. Hopefully, he was headed off the island entirely.

"No?" Leonidas taunted. "Then how about this? Get on your knees and beg for it, and it's yours."

He grinned, teeth flashing in the low light. Bane guffawed.

One day, Marlow vowed to herself, the two of them were going to pay for every vile thing they'd ever done.

But it wouldn't be today. Marlow didn't even have any hexes on her— they hadn't been allowed at the auction.

"Come on, Marlow," Leonidas jeered.

He had her pinned, and he knew it. Marlow's heart thudded against her chest, panic threatening to drown her.

"Oh well," Leonidas said with faux disappointment. "It was worth a shot."

He laughed, loud and piercing, the sound like a thousand spiders crawling over Marlow's skin. Bane brayed along with him.

Still laughing hysterically, Leonidas pulled something from his coat. A crack split the air and the next thing Marlow knew was *pain*—ripping through her side, setting her ablaze from the inside out.

A scream tore from her throat. Her knees gave out from under her, and she collapsed to the ground. The pain only intensified.

Worth a shot, she thought faintly to herself. Leonidas had shot her—and judging by the burning pain, it was with a cursed bullet.

"Minnow . . . Minnow?"

Her mother's low, melodious voice floated over her.

"Mom?" Marlow said, woozy. She forced her eyes open. She hadn't even realized she'd closed them.

Cassandra appeared in front of her—her golden hair falling in messy waves around her face, her lips tilted into a familiar smile full of mischief.

Tears welled up in Marlow's eyes, and she was reaching for her without thinking. "Mom!"

Cassandra leaned toward her. "Shh . . . Minnow, don't move." Her fingers stroked gently over Marlow's brow.

"Mom . . ." Marlow choked. "Why . . . why did you leave? Why didn't you tell me you were going?"

"Oh, Minnow," Cassandra said. "I had to leave. I couldn't stay here, tied to a daughter who would only ever be a liability. You see that, don't you?"

"Wh-what?" Tears shook Marlow's voice.

"I couldn't do it anymore, Marlow," Cassandra said regretfully. "I tried, for sixteen years. But I just—I couldn't love you."

Marlow felt like her heart might shatter in her chest.

"The truth is, Marlow, I'm better off without you," Cassandra said. Her voice was tinged with pity. She pulled away from Marlow, out of her reach.

"Mom, *no*," Marlow sobbed. "*Please.*"

And then it wasn't her mother Marlow was looking at, but Adrius. "She's right, you know," he said. "I'm better off without you, too. All you do is hurt the people around you. I don't think anyone could really love you—you won't let them."

"I'm sorry," Marlow whispered, her voice choked with tears.

Adrius shook his head, his honey-gold eyes wistful. "You didn't think I *really* loved you, did you?"

Marlow shut her eyes, shaking her head.

A low rumble sounded from her other side. Marlow opened her eyes again and came face-to-face with Sycorax. He stalked toward her, his yellowed teeth gnashing into a mockery of a grin.

Marlow had the distant, far-off thought that this was the last thing she was ever going to see.

The sound of shouting voices filled the air around her. Sycorax paused and suddenly lashed out in a different direction. Marlow was too weak, too racked with agonizing pain to see what had drawn his attention.

"Minnow, Minnow, can you hear me?"

Adrius was back. Marlow let out a pitiful little groan and tried to reach for him.

"I've got you," he said. She felt warm hands on her side. "Come on, we've got to move."

Marlow shook her head—or tried to. "N-no," she whimpered. "No, I can't, please—"

"Come on, you can do it," Adrius urged. "I've got you."

He heaved her toward the edge of the stage and dropped down to the floor below. Then he hooked her arm over his shoulder and slid her off the stage and into his arms.

Pain screamed up her side.

"I know, I know, I'm sorry," Adrius soothed, carrying her through the auction hall as quickly as he could. "Swift and Fisher are waiting. We've got to go."

Marlow wavered in the margins of consciousness, the next few minutes coming to her in brief flashes.

And then they were outside the auction hall, the heavy night air like warm breath on her shivering skin. She could hear three people speaking in tense voices.

"Do you know what kind of curse it is?" *Swift*, she thought.

"If I had to guess, I'd say a Living Nightmare curse." Fisher.

Their voices faded out again as Marlow drifted.

"He's here," Adrius said at some point, minutes or maybe hours later. She felt him move, and he set her down on something hard and flat. The world swayed and rocked beneath her.

"What in the Ever-Drowning Mangrove happened to her?" a new voice asked.

It sounded almost precisely like Silvan, but that was impossible. Why would Silvan be here? She heard Swift reply but couldn't quite grasp the meaning of his words.

"Where are we even going?"

"Back to Evergarden?"

"No," Fisher's voice cut in. "She needs a counter-spell. If we don't cast it in the next two hours, she'll die."

They were the last words Marlow heard before darkness swallowed her.

TWENTY-FIVE

Marlow's head ached dully as she slowly came aware of herself. She blinked her eyes open. The room around her was dimly lit by violet bioluminescence, but she could make out the familiar shapes of the Black Orchid's workshop.

She was safe, then. For now, at least. Across from her, Swift sat in a wooden chair, head tipped back, eyes closed, mouth open. The tightness of Marlow's chest abated slightly upon seeing him safe.

Then Silvan appeared on his other side. Marlow watched with mounting disbelief as he approached Swift's sleeping form and placed a steaming teacup on the stool beside him. For a moment he just stood there, looking down at Swift with a slight frown.

It wasn't his usual scowl or sneer or contemptuous look. Instead, his expression was . . . the only word that came to mind was *worried*. His hand twitched slightly at his side and then he turned away from Swift.

Marlow shut her eyes before he could see that she was awake.

"Did you get *any* sleep?" he asked.

Marlow startled—but he wasn't talking to her.

It was Adrius's voice that answered, hoarse and weary. "I'm fine."

Silvan made a skeptical sound. Marlow waited until she heard his footsteps retreating before she turned and peered over the back of the couch at Adrius.

"Minnow!" he exclaimed, leaping from his chair to perch instead on the armrest nearest to her. His hands hovered over her as though he was afraid to touch her. "How are you feeling?"

Marlow sat up, wincing at the pain in her side. "What in the Ever-Drowning Mangrove is Silvan doing here?"

Adrius blinked, drawing back slightly at the question. When Marlow focused on his face, she could see the toll the last few . . . what, hours? Days? Had taken on him. His eyes were bloodshot, exhaustion plain in every line of his face.

"We had to get off the island," he explained slowly. "The boats were all gone. I had a Beacon spell on me—Silvan has its pair. We always have one on hand in case one of us needs to be rescued from boring social events."

"You couldn't think of any other way to get off the island than by calling *Silvan*?" Marlow demanded. "We can't trust him! He's Vale's son, he—"

"You were *dying*!" Adrius bellowed.

The raw pain in his voice made Marlow shrink back, her anger wavering. Her hand went to her wound. Fear climbed up Marlow's throat. She knew it had been a close call, but—something about the hollow terror in Adrius's eyes made it feel *real*.

"Marlow?" Swift's groggy voice broke the tense silence. "You're awake?"

Marlow turned toward him and watched a wave of relief wash over him.

"Are you all right?" he asked.

"I . . . I think so," Marlow answered. Adrius turned his face away from her, jaw tight. "What happened?"

"The Copperheads got you with a cursed bullet," Swift said quietly. "Fisher said it was a Living Nightmare curse."

Marlow remembered with a sharp pang seeing her mother in front of her. It hadn't been real, she understood that now. Just the curse showing her her darkest fears. She didn't look at Adrius.

"We managed to get you here and make a counter-spell before the curse took you," Swift went on. "Fisher said if we'd waited any longer, you'd be dead."

"How . . . how long was I out?" she asked finally.

"The whole night," Swift replied. "It's morning now—at least, I think it is."

A new sense of panic quickened Marlow's pulse. *Morning.* She squeezed her eyes shut. She was supposed to meet Vale for tea this morning. The events of the night before came back to her in flashes. "The auction. Vale." She looked at Adrius. "He saw you. He might have seen me, too."

"Maybe," Swift agreed. "But there's nothing we can—"

"I have to get back to Vale Tower," Marlow said frantically. "If he sees that I'm gone—"

"You're not going anywhere right now."

It wasn't Adrius or Swift who answered, but Orsella, shuffling into the room like she belonged there.

Marlow had had enough surprise visitors today. "Orsella? What are you doing here?"

"Turns out there aren't that many places you can get last-minute spell ingredients for a rush counter-spell," Orsella answered. "Luckily, your boy here pays well."

She nodded over at Adrius.

Marlow knew Orsella well enough to know she'd probably upcharged him by nine or ten times the regular cost for whatever they'd needed to get. Not that Adrius couldn't afford it—after all, he'd had about twelve million pearls on him for the auction.

Shit. The auction.

"What happened to the Obsidian Blade?" she asked. "Leonidas took it, and then—I don't know what happened after he shot me. I don't even know how I got away."

"The auction had its own security," Adrius said. "They came in, distracted the Copperheads long enough for me to get you out. But after that, I don't know. The auction might have gotten the blade back."

"Or Leonidas still has it," Marlow said darkly. "Gods below. What are we going to do?"

"Well, if Leonidas has it, at least Vale doesn't," Swift offered helpfully.

Which brought them back to Vale again. Vale, who might have seen Marlow last night at a black-auction market. If he *had* seen her, she was going to have to come up with a damn good excuse for her presence there, or he was going to know what she was up to. That she was working against him.

And what might he do to her then?

Her head pounded.

They could figure out what to do about the Obsidian Blade later. Right now, she had to find out what Vale knew. What he suspected.

"Get Silvan," she said to Swift. "We're going back to Vale Tower."

Swift nodded, hurrying out the door. As it swung open, Fisher entered the room.

"I need to talk to you," he said to Marlow.

"Can it wait?" she snapped.

"No, it can't."

"Fisher, we'll figure out what to do about the Obsidian Blade later," Marlow said hurriedly. "Right now, I need to get back to Vale Tower and—"

"It's not about the blade," Fisher said. Marlow had only heard him use this tone once before—when he'd accused her of picking up where her mother had left off.

Marlow went silent.

"Why didn't you tell me the Reapers threatened my family?" Fisher demanded.

"What?" Marlow asked.

"I went to see my father this morning," Fisher said. "And he told me that the Reapers have someone *watching* him. Following his every move. They're not even trying to be subtle about it—they *want* him to know."

"They're . . . they're just trying to scare him," Marlow said, with less confidence than she felt. "I'm—I still have a week left to get the Reapers what they want. They won't touch your family. I'm handling it."

"Are you?" Fisher asked. "Because you nearly just got yourself killed going up against the leader of the Copperheads. I have no idea why I thought it was a good idea to trust a seventeen-year-old girl when she said she knew what she was doing. You're in over your head, and worse—you've dragged me in with you."

Behind Marlow, Orsella snorted. "That's what I'm always trying to tell her."

Marlow let out a shaky breath, not sure what she was feeling—anger or fear or guilt or some brackish mix of all three. Her head pounded. She felt like she might throw up.

"And it's not just me," Fisher went on. "It's Swift, and it's the Black Orchid, and even Adrius—you've dragged us all into this mess. *Your* mess."

He was right. This was who Marlow was at her core—she was a hurricane, blowing into people's lives and bringing trouble to their door.

She swallowed, meeting his gaze. "I'll fix it, Fisher. I swear to you."

He just shook his head, his face grave and weary. "I know you'll try. But you'll die trying. And we'll be the ones left to deal with the fallout."

Vale was waiting for her. He sat in the parlor, hands folded, the teapot steaming gently in the center of the table in front of him.

Marlow's heart jumped into her throat. Was it her imagination, or was he scrutinizing her?

"I thought you'd forgotten about tea," he said lightly.

Marlow sat stiffly across from him, trying not to wince at the twinge of pain in her side where the cursed bullet had struck her. "I just overslept."

A plate of cookies dusted in sugar and cocoa powder sat next to the teapot. Marlow took one, just to keep from fidgeting beneath Vale's assessing gaze.

"Late night?" His tone was just this side of sharp.

Did he know? Had he seen her?

She took a bite of the cookie and chewed carefully, biding time. She didn't want to lie and say she'd been in Vale Tower when she hadn't—he might know that much, at least, even if he hadn't seen her at the auction.

He waved at the teapot and it lifted off the table, tipping warm, rich brown tea into each of their cups.

Marlow watched the steam swirl up. "I took Swift to the ballet," she said at last. "He's never been before."

"What did you see?" he asked.

Shit. What were they showing now? Marlow couldn't think, her head still throbbing from the aftereffects of the Living Nightmare curse.

"*The Ballad of the Moon Thief,*" Marlow blurted. It was the only ballet she'd ever seen. They had to still be performing it, right? It had only been up a few months.

Vale sighed, plunking his teacup down in its dish. "Marlow. I thought you and I agreed we would endeavor to be honest with each other."

Marlow's heart stuttered. Her fingers gripped the edge of the table. "I . . ."

"I know you were at a black-auction market last night."

Panic was a living thing inside Marlow. What reason could she give for being there? What might Vale believe? Her mind was suddenly, terribly blank.

"It's all right," he said gently. "You don't have to explain. I know you must have had your reasons for being there. Just as I did."

Marlow stared at him, stunned. Not only was he admitting to being at the auction—he was letting her off the hook?

"I know that, because you're like me, Marlow," Vale went on. "Everything you do, you do because you believe it is *right*. Because you want to make this city better than it is. Because you want to protect the ones you love."

He rose from his seat and turned to gaze out the window behind the desk. Down at Evergarden, at the canals and streets of Caraza below. "I've been working on something. Something that could change the world. Once it's completed, the gangs, the Five Families . . . they won't be in control anymore."

He turned back to her, his expression frantic, almost manic. "I can protect you, Marlow. I can make sure you'll stay safe."

Marlow pulled in a shaking breath. "What . . . what do you mean you're working on something?"

"A powerful spell," Vale replied, his gaze fixed on her. Marlow could hardly believe he was telling her this. Telling her the *truth*.

And if he was being honest with her—really, actually honest—then she wasn't going to waste this opportunity.

"You mean like the spell you cursed Adrius with?"

She watched Vale's face go utterly still. Then his mouth curved into a rueful smile. "I should've known you'd figured that out. You're smart, Marlow. Like your mother. Like me."

"I'm not like you," Marlow spat. "I would never compel someone to murder their own father."

Vale sighed wearily. "It was never something I wanted to do, Marlow, you must understand that. It was for the greater good."

Marlow could understand how Aurelius's death might be for the greater good—she might even agree on that front. But it was no excuse for cursing Adrius. "Why drag Adrius into it? Why put him through that?"

"It was the only way," Vale said softly. He looked away, his face creased with remorse. "I wish I hadn't needed to do that to him. For all his flaws, for all that the Falcrests have done, Adrius didn't deserve it. But there was no other way."

Marlow folded her arms in front of her. "You could have stabbed Aurelius yourself if you wanted him dead that badly."

But Vale shook his head. "It wasn't Aurelius's death that I needed. It was his blood."

"What?"

"The blood of the father, spilled by the son," Vale said, almost as though he were reciting it. He met Marlow's gaze again. "It's one of the ingredients in the spell I'm creating. And this spell . . . if you knew what it could do. It could save you, Marlow. It could save all of us."

"What do you mean *save* us?" Marlow asked.

"The corruption and rot of this city run deep," Vale replied. "And there are few who can see beyond it, as you and I do. Few who can even begin to envision a world where compassion, and not greed, guides our everyday actions. Where the most vulnerable are protected, rather than exploited. Where the ones who try to exploit them are punished, rather than rewarded. This spell would not just allow us to envision that world, but to make it *real*."

Marlow had gone her whole life believing that such a world was impossible. Fear and greed would always win out—not because she believed people were inherently greedy, but because greed was rewarded, and compassion punished. People like Swift and like Fisher—people who were good to their core—were trapped inside a brutal system that forced them into servitude and violence. And people like Marlow's mother—people who, perhaps, *could* have been good if they'd been given that choice—were drawn into the same cycles of corruption that had taken that choice away from them. And people like Aurelius Falcrest were the ones who made the rules, unleashing all their cruelty and rapacious greed on everyone else.

But in the world Vale wanted to create, Swift wouldn't have to live in fear of the Copperheads. Fisher wouldn't be indentured to the Reapers. His family would be safe. And Adrius . . . Adrius wouldn't be chained by his family's machinations. He would be free.

Free to be with Marlow, maybe. If that was still something he even wanted.

It was hard to sit there in front of Vale and try to tell him that creating such a world would be a mistake. Marlow wasn't sure it was.

"The curse I put on Adrius will haunt me for the rest of my days," Vale said. "But as you know well, everything in this world has a price. And if a black mark on my soul is the price of creating a better world, then . . . I am willing to bear it. There are no easy answers, Marlow. I believe you know this better than anyone."

"The kind of magic that would make that possible," Marlow said slowly. "It's dangerous."

Vale nodded. "This is not something I am undertaking lightly. This magic must be used only sparingly. Wisely. And only by the right people."

Could such a power really be used for good? If anything could pry Caraza from the grip of the gangs, the Five Families, the morass of corruption that had festered there for so long, it was Vale and this spell.

Fisher had said that Marlow was in over her head, and maybe he was right. Maybe she'd been a fool to think she could stop this from happening.

The spell would give Vale the ability to shape reality to his liking. And if this was the reality he wanted, then Marlow had to wonder—even if she *could* stop him, *should* she?

TWENTY-SIX

Adrius disembarked the boat and stared at the nondescript house in front of him.

"This . . . this is where she's been this whole time?" he asked.

To think that for over twelve years, he'd been told his mother had abandoned him, had traveled halfway across the world, only to find out she'd been a twenty-minute boat ride away the entire time.

"I think your father wanted her close," Marlow replied. "So he could keep an eye on her in case she found a loophole and escaped."

Vicious fury roared to life in Adrius's chest. He had the wild thought that if Aurelius were standing in front of him now, he wouldn't hesitate to sink a knife into his heart again.

Marlow touched his arm gently and Adrius turned to meet her worried gaze.

"Are you sure you want to do this right now?" she asked.

Adrius just nodded.

Marlow led him up the path to the house, through the wrought-iron gate, past the manicured lawn and the carefully pruned hedges.

At the front door, Adrius stopped.

"What if she—"

He swallowed. What if his mother didn't want to see him? What if she didn't recognize who he'd become? Someone so cold, so lacking in feeling that he couldn't even mourn his own father.

Isme would see right through him. She'd see how much Adrius was like her husband, the man who'd imprisoned her here. She would send him away once she realized who her son really was.

"Adrius." Marlow's voice broke through the angry swirl of his thoughts. "When I saw your mother, she'd been locked up in here for . . . a long time. And the *only* thing she asked for, the only thing she wanted—it wasn't her freedom. She just wanted to see you and your sister."

Adrius took a breath, letting the words sink in. But what if what Isme really wanted was the Adrius that she'd known? The little boy who cried when his sister hit him and sat in his mother's lap asking for treats and stories and hugs? The Adrius that existed only in her memory, not the person he was now.

"We don't have to go in," Marlow said softly. "We can come back another time."

But Adrius shook his head. If he lost his nerve now, he didn't know if he'd ever get it back.

"Okay," Marlow said, and then pushed open the door.

There was no greeting from within. Marlow stuck her head into the foyer.

"Hello? Isme?" she called into the house. Adrius remained in the doorway as Marlow crept farther inside.

And then Adrius saw her through the archway that led into a sitting room. His mother. She wore a deep purple dressing gown. Her dark hair was now streaked with gray, gathered in a braid over her slim shoulder.

She gripped a candlestick in one hand, as if it was a weapon.

"I'm not here to cause you harm," Marlow told her.

Isme's grip on the candlestick tightened.

"Hi, Mom," Adrius said softly.

The candlestick dropped to the ground. His mother dove toward him. Adrius moved to catch her.

She collapsed into his arms, weeping with huge, heaving sobs. The kind Adrius could feel down to his bones.

"Adrius," she sobbed, over and over. "My son. My son." She pulled back, her bony hands clutching his face. "It's really you. My gods."

All at once Adrius was hit with a wave of grief so profound, he might have collapsed to the ground if he weren't still holding his mother.

It felt as if this pain and sorrow had been locked in his chest for so long, buried so deep, he'd let himself believe he didn't feel it at all. But now, looking into his mother's eyes for the first time in over a decade, it broke over him in a relentless flood of grief.

"Yeah," Adrius said, his voice tremulous with unshed tears. "It's really me."

"You're all grown-up." She burst into fresh sobs, tears streaming down her cheeks.

Her tears made Adrius's fall freely.

"I'm sorry," Adrius wept. "I'm so sorry."

His mother pulled back, cupping his face in her hands. Adrius closed his eyes against the tenderness of her touch, the grief in her eyes. "Sorry? Whatever are you sorry for? None of this was ever your fault."

Hot tears slid down Adrius's cheeks. "I'm not who you think I am. I'm not—" His voice hitched. "I . . ."

"You are my *son*," she said fiercely. "That is all I need to know. That is all that matters. You are my son and I love you so much."

Adrius shook his head. "You don't know what I've done. What I've become."

She stroked his cheek. It made Adrius feel like shattering. "I may not know you anymore, Adrius. But I know your heart. I know you are good."

She pressed her lips to his forehead. Adrius held on to her and wept.

It felt like he had been starving for this his whole life. He'd told himself he didn't need it, didn't want it. Didn't deserve it. That he'd just take whatever he could get—Amara's ire, his father's scorn. A fake relationship with a girl he could never be with for real. Scraps and cast-off debris that he could cobble together in place of love.

But now as he wept in his mother's arms, he knew that it didn't matter what he tried to build in its place. Love would always find a way to shatter it. And he would be left in the wreckage.

TWENTY-SEVEN

Adrius and his mother were too wrapped up in their reunion to notice Marlow slip out of the house. She shut the door gently behind her and followed the path from the house blindly toward the dock, her own tears gathering in her eyes.

As glad as she was for Adrius to see his mother after all these years, it broke something open in her. Because she knew exactly how desperately Isme had wanted to see her children during her long imprisonment. It was, as Marlow had said, the *only* thing she'd asked for.

And Marlow couldn't help but think of her own mother, maybe somewhere halfway across the world. Did she even miss her daughter?

Even if she did, even if she thought of Marlow as often as Marlow thought of her, she had still chosen to leave.

Marlow's mother loved her—she knew she did. She just didn't love her enough. Didn't love her the way Isme loved her children.

Marlow wiped her eyes and stared down at the clear waters of the canal. Wherever Cassandra was, Marlow hoped she was happy. She hoped she was safe.

But she wasn't going to spend another second thinking about her.

She turned back toward the house—and then froze.

Standing at the other end of the dock was Caito.

"Marlow Briggs," she said, satisfaction lacing her voice. "I know it was you who sold the Falcrests' secret at the auction."

Marlow set her shoulders in a tense line. "Why do you even care anymore, Caito? Aurelius is as good as dead. You don't have to be his guard dog anymore."

Caito's lip curled in a snarl.

"Why are you even loyal to him?" Marlow asked. "You've seen what he's done."

"You mean, why remain loyal to the richest and most powerful man in the city?" Caito sneered.

"Why be loyal to a man who would imprison his own wife and scorn his own children?"

"Isme is weak," Caito said. "And I know that the only way to survive in this world is to find the person with the most power and the fewest qualms about keeping it and make yourself indispensable to them." She smirked. "Your mother knew that, too."

Marlow wanted to protest, but she heard the whisper of Cassandra's own words in her head. *In this city, there are victims and there are survivors. And we are not victims.*

Wasn't there some truth to that? You either found a way to climb out of the muck or you let yourself be pulled under by it. And sometimes climbing out meant pushing someone weaker down instead.

Everything in this world has a price.

Caito had looked at her options and had made the calculation that aligning herself with Aurelius was the price she was willing to pay to survive.

And maybe Marlow was doing the same. If she ever wanted to live in a world that wasn't divided into victims and the people who would step over them to survive, then maybe the price was letting Vale win. Letting him cast his spell. Letting him create that world.

"Marlow?"

Both Marlow and Caito turned toward the sound of Adrius's voice, calling from the gate.

His gaze landed on Caito and hardened. "Caito."

Marlow watched Caito's face as she assessed the situation. With Adrius here, the worst she'd try to do to Marlow was make threats.

"You helped him keep her locked up here, didn't you?" Adrius demanded, his hands curled into fists at his sides.

"Of course," Caito replied coolly. "There's no one else in this world that your father trusted as much as he trusted me."

Adrius's shoulders went taut, his jaw tightening.

"Adrius," Marlow called. "Let's just go."

Adrius kept his thunderous gaze on Caito for another tense breath. Then, without a word, he stalked past her, down the path, and onto the dock. He didn't look at Marlow, just shouldered past her to board the canal boat.

"You should take care, Marlow," Caito called as Marlow stepped onto the boat behind him. "You insist on digging up everyone's secrets, and you're going to be the one who ends up buried."

"*Are you all* right?"

Marlow waited until they were far away from Wisteria Grove before asking. They were taking a circuitous route back to Evergarden, avoiding the canals that would take them through Pearl Street and other more populated areas to avoid being seen together.

Adrius just shook his head. His eyes were red from crying, his fists clenched tight in his lap.

"Thank you," he said quietly, "for finding her. For—for figuring out what he did to her."

Marlow nodded. She could tell there was more he wanted to say, so she kept quiet.

"My whole life I—I just assumed she wanted nothing to do with us," Adrius said. "That she stayed away by choice because—because like my father, she didn't . . . love us. But now I know the truth." He looked up at Marlow. "I wasted so much time trying to earn my father's attention or—or convincing myself I didn't want it. And all along, she—" He broke off, wiping his face furiously.

Marlow curled a hesitant hand around his shoulder.

"It's just, if I'd known," Adrius said. "If I'd known this whole time that she loved me, I think things would have been different. *I* would have been different."

Marlow had never allowed herself to wonder the same. What if Cassandra had never left Vale the first time? What if Marlow had been raised knowing who her father was?

But none of that really mattered. It didn't change who she was now.

"You don't have to be different, Adrius," Marlow said. "Your mother loves the person you are *now*."

He swallowed, jaw clenching. "And what about you?"

"I—what do you mean?" Marlow stuttered. But she knew what he was asking. She could see it, when he turned to her, his whiskey-colored eyes fixed on her.

"I mean that we've been sneaking around, stealing every moment we can together, and I still don't know what it is you want from me."

She couldn't look away from his dark gaze. Neither could she summon a reply.

He tugged a hand through his windswept curls. "Look, just—forget about the deal with Amara. Forget about our families, for just a minute. If there was nothing standing in our way, if we could really be together—would you even want that?"

"Would I . . . ? Where is this coming from?"

"Just answer the question," he said, pained. "Please."

It felt like a trap, somehow. "What does it matter, Adrius? We can't—"

"I know that," he snapped.

"What do you want me to say?" she asked.

"The truth," he said, sounding weary. "You demanded the same from me once, remember?"

How could she forget?

"I told you how I feel about you," he said. "I held nothing back. And now I think it's only fair that you do the same."

What kind of game was this? "You know how I feel about you," she said, her voice trembling slightly.

"I don't, actually," Adrius replied. "Do you think you're so easy to read?"

For Adrius, yes. She always felt like he knew just how to get under her skin.

"I claimed responsibility for your father's death so that no one would find out about the curse," she said. "I put myself on the line for you. I risked my *life* for you."

"Yes," Adrius replied. "Which you do for any number of people in any number of circumstances. You've done it for clients, you've done it for Swift—hell, you even did it for Silvan once, and you don't even like him."

"I—how do you know about that?"

"Swift told me," Adrius replied with a wave. "Don't change the subject."

This had to be a ploy, some way of getting the upper hand on Marlow. Anything else didn't make sense. He *had* to know how she felt about him.

But then she considered things from Adrius's perspective. He had poured his heart out to her. Disowned his family for her. Pledged himself to marry some girl of his sister's choosing for her. Broken a powerful curse because of his love for her, which shouldn't have even been possible.

And Marlow had done . . . what exactly? She'd made no declarations, hadn't made her desires known to him beyond these illicit, stolen moments.

She'd risked her life, yes, but Adrius was right—for Marlow that was less a declaration of love than a hazard of her job. In the grand scope of their relationship, Adrius had put everything on the line and held nothing back. And in return, Marlow had done what she always had—she'd guarded her heart.

Even now that she had him, Marlow played it like a hand of Ruse, never letting Adrius see what cards she really held.

It struck her then. He wasn't toying with her at all.

She was the one toying with him.

"No games. No lies. Just the truth," Adrius said. "What do you want from me?"

"I—" The words caught in her throat. It wasn't fair. How could he ask that of her, when they both knew it was something they might never have? How could he force her to say the words when all it meant was that they'd both know just how much her heart would break when he promised himself to someone else?

Adrius nodded, his jaw tight. "Right." He turned away.

"Adrius . . . ," Marlow began, but she had nowhere to go from there. He wanted something from her that she'd never be able to give.

She could have a fake relationship with him. She could have moments stolen in the dark.

But she could never have him for real. She'd always understood that. But she saw now, for the first time, how selfish she'd truly been with him. She *was* the Moon Thief, after all—holding the Sun King captive in her court of shadows.

And she knew how that story would end.

TWENTY-EIGHT

Marlow slept fitfully that night, plagued by thoughts of Isme and Adrius and Vale and the Copperheads and the Reapers. It was all a tangle in her mind.

The Reapers were still after Fisher. Adrius was still bound by his deal with Amara. They couldn't complete their spell—and now Marlow wasn't even sure they *should*.

She'd been in dangerous, messy situations before, but she'd always known how to get out of them. Solve the mystery. Break the curse.

Now she had no idea what to do.

"Can I ask you something?" Marlow asked Swift over a breakfast of tea and plain biscuits. She couldn't stomach much else.

"Yeah, of course," Swift replied.

Before she could talk herself out of it, Marlow said, "Do you think we're doing the right thing?"

"What do you mean?"

"I mean, with this spell," Marlow said. "Trying to stop Vale. What if . . . what if he's actually right? What if the city would be better off if he was calling the shots?"

Swift's eyes went wide and he set his teacup down so hard, it sloshed out onto the table. "You're serious?"

Marlow nodded. "He could get rid of the gangs. Take away the Five

Families' control of magic. I mean . . . would that really be worse than the way things are now?"

Swift was silent for a long moment, staring down at the table with an unreadable expression. "Marlow," he said at last. "You've never been forced to do something against your will. You've never had your choice taken away like that. And let me tell you, there is no goal noble enough to justify that."

Marlow met his gaze. She knew there was truth to what he said, but she still couldn't help but wonder. If people like the Copperheads and the Reapers and Aurelius Falcrest were the only people willing to do the unjustifiable to get what they wanted, then wouldn't they always win? If there were no lines that they wouldn't cross, then wouldn't everyone else have to live with the rules they made?

A knock at the door broke the tense silence. Marlow went to it with trepidation. The only person she could think of who would be at the door was Vale.

But when she opened the door, she was relieved to see Gemma.

"Oh," Marlow said in surprise. "Did we have plans?"

"No," Gemma replied. "I just wanted to come by and see how you are."

"Um, come in," Marlow said. "Would you like some tea?"

Gemma swept into the apartment and stopped when she saw Swift at the table. "Oh, Silvan was looking for you," she said.

Swift then did something Marlow had never seen him do before. He *blushed*.

"Right," he said, standing from the table. "I'll just—I should go find him."

He hastened out the door while Gemma looked on with mild amusement, and Marlow with mild horror.

Once he was out of earshot, Gemma said, "I don't think I've ever seen Silvan this hung up on someone. I just hope he doesn't get his heart broken."

Marlow recalled Adrius's warning to Swift. She still could not quite fathom the concept of Silvan having actual feelings for Swift, and considered if perhaps it was all an elaborate prank on her.

She closed the door and gestured Gemma over to the table, where she poured them each a fresh cup of tea.

Gemma stirred her little golden spoon in her teacup, peering at Marlow from across the table.

"I couldn't help but notice," she said, setting the teacup down, "that you haven't asked for my help in over a week."

She meant her help in arranging a place and a time for Marlow and Adrius to meet up in secret.

But before Marlow could come up with an answer that wouldn't invite any more questions, Gemma continued, "Did you two break up again?"

"Again?" Marlow echoed. Then she blinked, realizing, abruptly, that Gemma didn't know the whole story between her and Adrius. "Gemma, Adrius and I . . . we weren't really together."

Gemma's forehead creased in confusion. "Then why have you been sneaking around with him?"

"No, I mean—before that," Marlow amended. "Before Amara's wedding. When everyone thought we were—it was like with you and him. It wasn't real."

Gemma snorted. "I'm pretty sure it was nothing like with me and him, actually. But . . . why were you pretending?"

Marlow took a sip of her tea. "It's complicated."

Gemma gave her an unimpressed look.

"He needed my help with something," Marlow said. "And I needed a convenient way to come back to Evergarden. I thought it made sense at the time."

"Maybe a little *too much* sense," Gemma said.

Marlow laughed. "I convinced myself I was over him, but . . ."

"Hard to get over a Falcrest," Gemma said knowingly. She was looking down at her teacup, a brooding expression on her face.

"Yeah, I guess it is."

"I'm fourth in line to the Starling family," Gemma said. "My older sister is married already, with a baby on the way, so it's unlikely I'll ever be heir. Which means I can basically do whatever I want. And I do. I kiss girls at parties and go on expensive shopping trips and gossip about the rest of the noblesse nouveau. I think I'm over Amara." She swallowed. "And then I see her across the room, or I—hear something that makes me want to tell her about it. And it's like my heart breaks all over again."

"Gemma," Marlow said gently, covering her hand.

Gemma met her gaze, tears swimming in her eyes. "I regret it, you know? Every day, I regret it."

"Falling for her?"

Gemma shook her head. "I regret not putting it all on the line. Not telling her what I felt and what I wanted."

Marlow looked down. "Do you think it would've made a difference? Do you think she would've chosen not to marry Darian?"

"No," Gemma replied, no hesitation in her answer. "I know it wouldn't have changed anything."

"Then why regret it?" Marlow asked, her voice breaking. "Isn't it better that you still have your pride?"

"You don't think there's any pride in being honest?" Gemma asked. "Isn't that what you're all about, Marlow? The truth?"

Marlow looked down at her tea.

"I'm just saying," Gemma went on. "Even if there's nothing I could have done to change things, I wish I'd told her. Just to put it all out into the open. Just so she knew, *really* knew, what she was walking away from. It's not like I had anything left to lose."

———

The sky blazed with hot-pink clouds as Marlow stepped out onto the roof of the Malachite Building. Adrius was already waiting for her, his back to her as he gazed out across the glittering Evergarden sunset.

The last time they'd been here together was over a year ago, the night of Adrius's seventeenth birthday. They'd sat and watched the sun rise over the city and Marlow had felt like something was beginning.

She'd been wrong.

"Thanks for coming," she said.

"Gemma said you wanted to tell me something," Adrius replied, turning to her.

She watched him pause to look at her, as if drinking her in. His eyes felt as warm as the evening air on her skin.

Gemma's words echoed in Marlow's head. *Isn't that what you're all about, Marlow? The truth?*

Marlow was brave, but not like this. Not with her heart.

She looked toward the distant bay glittering in the waning evening sunlight. "This isn't easy for me. Swift told me once that the more I feel vulnerable to someone, the less I trust them, and I think he was right about that."

"You feel vulnerable to me," Adrius surmised. "You don't trust me."

"I don't want to be like that," Marlow said. "I don't want to be like my mother, never letting myself love someone all the way. One foot always out the door. So, I need to tell you the truth."

She cupped his face in her hand. He leaned into the touch. She wanted to memorize the way he looked now, golden light splashing across his curls, soft hope glowing in his eyes.

"The truth, Adrius," she said haltingly, "is that we can never be together."

For a moment he just stared at her, stunned. She watched as his hope extinguished. "Because of Amara?"

Marlow shook her head, a sob building in the back of her throat.

"Because . . ." Adrius's voice shook. "Because you don't want me?"

Marlow just shook her head again, tears spilling freely down her cheeks. "Because I do," she whispered.

Confusion clouded his gaze.

"The spell ingredient we stole from Warner," Marlow said, fighting through her tears. "It was mine. The most hidden desire of my heart. I traded it to Orsella for . . . well, it doesn't really matter."

"Marlow," Adrius said, his voice scraped bare. "What was it?"

"The one thing I want that I could never say aloud." Her voice shook. "But I'm saying it now, even though there's no hope that I'll ever have it." She didn't let herself look away from him. "It's you, Adrius. A future with you."

Before she could say anything more, Adrius kissed her. It felt different from every other time they'd kissed, like she could feel his desperation, his longing.

And just as abruptly as he'd kissed her, he stopped, drawing back, but not far. Close enough that Marlow could feel his labored breath against her cheek.

"Adrius," she said desperately, still holding his face in her hands. "We need to end this."

His cheeks were wet, from her tears or his own she didn't know. She could hear his breath shake as he drew it in.

"The funny thing is," she said, though it really wasn't funny at all. "When I traded my heart's desire, I didn't think it would matter. I knew there was never a future for us. You knew that, too, didn't you? You've always known. That's why you pulled away from me that day. The morning after we came here the first time."

The morning after he'd come to her on his seventeenth birthday. The morning they'd watched the sun rise over Caraza together. The morning he'd turned his back on her and acted like she was nothing to him.

Adrius shut his eyes, as if it pained him, too, to look at her. "What . . . what would have happened if I hadn't been a coward? If I'd told you the truth that night?"

"Adrius, don't," she said, pulling away. But he didn't let her go far, holding her tight against him.

"If I'd kissed you?" he asked desperately, his voice breaking, his golden eyes blazing. "Would you have stayed in Evergarden? Would we have had a future then?"

Marlow shook her head, her tears coming hot and fast. "No. Come on, Adrius. You know we wouldn't. That's why you didn't kiss me that night. Because there was never a chance it would have worked out. All of this was just . . . we were still playing pretend."

"Don't say that," Adrius bit out fiercely. "It was real—it was *always* real to me."

Marlow just looked at him. He was never more beautiful than when he let himself fight for something. And she wanted him to fight for her, for *them*, even if it wouldn't change anything.

But she couldn't let him do that to himself.

"It was always real to me, too."

He made a noise like she'd struck him. And slowly, from one breath to the next, they parted, until only their fingers were still entwined. This might be the last time she ever touched him, she realized. He held her hand tight for a moment and then she slipped from his grasp, allowing herself one final look at him against the brilliant sky.

TWENTY-NINE

Night had fallen by the time Marlow returned to Vale Tower to find Swift and, regrettably, Silvan in her living room.

"Oh, good, you're back," Swift said as Marlow walked through the door.

"Oh, good," Silvan echoed without any of Swift's sincerity.

"This was delivered today," Swift said, holding out a crisp white envelope to Marlow. When he laid eyes on Marlow's tearstained face, his expression creased with concern. "Are you all right? What happened?"

Marlow snatched the envelope from him and turned toward the kitchen. "I'm fine. I don't want to talk about it."

"Weren't you meeting up with Adrius?" Swift asked.

Marlow ignored him, ripping open the envelope.

"Oh *no*," Silvan said dramatically. "Please don't tell me Adrius is going to be all mopey now. I hate when he gets like that."

"Because *you're* such a bright, cheerful kind of presence," Marlow muttered, scanning the contents of the letter. It was an official summons from Grantaire's office for Marlow's hearing, to begin in a week's time.

"As much as it truly—and I mean *truly*—pains me to say this," Silvan said. "Adrius is . . . happier, when he's with you. More himself."

Marlow recalled Gemma saying something similar to her once. *Different* was the word she'd used.

"Well, it doesn't matter," Marlow replied, folding the letter back up and setting it aside. "He's marrying someone else."

She didn't look up to see Silvan's or Swift's reaction to that.

"Fisher was right about me," she said to the kitchen counter, her fists clenched at her sides. "I really do just drag everyone into my mess."

"What?" Swift asked. "He said that?"

Marlow leaned her elbows on the counter and put her face in her hands. She nodded miserably. "The whole reason I became a cursebreaker was because I thought I was good at it. That I could solve mysteries and right wrongs and *help* people. But maybe what I'm really good at is mucking things up."

Swift came around the counter and took Marlow by the shoulder. There was a fierce, steely look in his eyes. "Are you kidding me? Marlow, if you hadn't come back into my life, I'd still be under Leonidas's thumb. If you hadn't agreed to help Adrius, he'd still be cursed."

She shook her head. "And now Adrius is marrying some vassal's daughter because of me. *You* can't even go back home, thanks to what I did. Fisher's family is in even more danger because I thought I could protect him from the Reapers. And my mother—" She stopped, swallowing back tears. "Well, basically all I did was complicate her life from the minute I was born. It's no wonder she wanted to stay away from me. That's what I do—I come into people's lives and I just—make a mess of them."

"She kind of has a point," Silvan put in.

Swift shot him a glare. "Listen to me," he said, gripping Marlow's shoulder. "You're right. You *are* good at causing problems for other people."

Marlow met his gaze, surprised and a little hurt.

"You still want to fix this thing with the Reapers and Fisher, right?"

She nodded.

"So let's do that," Swift said. "Let's cause as many problems as we can for the Copperheads."

Marlow blinked up at him, struck by a fierce appreciation for how much faith he still had in her. Her gaze fell on the official hearing summons. And then drifted to her mother's writing desk, and the ledger that was still hidden behind the mirror above it. A plan began to take shape.

Swift grinned, clearly recognizing the expression Marlow wore when she was plotting. "Let's go make a mess of things."

"*This is* . . . very interesting," Grantaire said, turning another page of Marlow's mother's ledger. "*Very* interesting. Where did you get ahold of this?"

"It was my mother's," Marlow replied. "She'd hidden it in our apartment in Vale Tower. I just recently found it after I moved back in. I've verified all the names in there myself."

"We'll have to make our own verifications—you understand," Grantaire said.

Marlow nodded. "Of course. But I'm not handing this information over for free."

Grantaire's eyebrows rose. "Miss Briggs, I can't grant you leniency in your hearing just because you gave this to me."

"Well, that's fine, because I'm not asking for leniency. I want something else."

Grantaire closed the ledger and sat back in his chair, expectant.

Marlow didn't exactly trust Grantaire, but she did trust that her read on him was correct. That she knew what he wanted, and that she could convince him she could give it to him. The same way Cassandra would do to her marks.

"With the information in that ledger, you could take down the Copperheads *and* the Reapers. The two biggest gangs in the Marshes. You'd be a hero to the city."

Grantaire maintained the mild smile on his face, but Marlow could see a glimmer of hunger in his eyes. He was young for his position as City Solicitor, and he'd had something of a meteoric rise, making grand promises to clean up the city and root out corruption. That was what he'd staked his reputation on, and Marlow had just handed him a way to turn those pretty promises into a reality.

She knew City Solicitor was simply a step in a larger plan Grantaire had for himself. If all went well, the mayorship could be next.

He folded his hands neatly in front of him. "If the information you've provided checks out, then I don't think anyone will have to worry about the Reapers and the Copperheads anymore. You have my word that my office will do everything in our power to cut the gangs off at the knees."

"That's all I needed to hear," Marlow said. She stood from her seat.

"Can I call you a boat to take you back to Vale Tower?" Grantaire asked, rising as well.

"I'm fine, thanks."

"All right," Grantaire replied. "If you would wait just a moment before you go?"

He slipped out the back door of his office before Marlow could reply.

She glanced out the wide paned windows that framed his desk, overlooking Old Caraza Square. The corruption of Caraza had been a part of its fabric since its very founding. It was almost impossible to think that could ever truly change.

But if Vale was right . . . if he could fix it and take control away from the gangs and the Five Families, maybe Caraza could be the kind of place where justice really did exist. Where the powerful could be punished for wrongdoing and the defenseless had somewhere to turn. Maybe all of Grantaire's lofty promises about rooting out corruption didn't have to be a fantasy.

Grantaire returned just a few moments later.

"Here." He handed her a sealed envelope. "The official notice for your hearing."

Marlow looked down at the envelope. "Your office already delivered one to me last night."

"Oh, did we? My mistake." He smiled brightly, putting a hand on her shoulder. "You have nothing to worry about, Marlow. Just tell the truth, and everything will sort itself out."

Marlow wanted to laugh at the bold naivete of such a statement, but she just smiled. "I can see myself out."

She walked out of the office and into the comfortable waiting room, where Swift sat nursing a cup of tea that one of the secretaries bustling about the office must've brought him.

"How'd it go?" Swift asked as Marlow approached.

"Good," she said with a small grin. "The Copperheads and the Reapers have no idea what's about to hit them."

Swift got to his feet and followed her out of the office, down the elevator, and out the main concourse of City Hall. But as they cut through Old Caraza Square toward the canal, Marlow felt a familiar prickle of unease.

Before she could even identify what had triggered it, two men stepped out from the shadows.

Marlow went cold. She knew these men. The Ferryman and Nero, two of the Copperheads' favorite bruisers.

"Well, if it isn't Marlow and Swift," the Ferryman said gleefully. "Sure wonder what business someone like you has at City Hall."

"Marlow," Swift said in a low, warning voice, his hand on her arm.

Marlow darted a glance around and saw that the Ferryman and Nero weren't the only Copperheads here. That she and Swift were surrounded by them, creeping out from the shadows and closing in.

She didn't have time to wonder how they'd found them. She didn't have time to question what they were doing in the middle of downtown Caraza, instead of in the Marshes where they belonged.

All she had time to do was reach for the hex card in her pocket and scream, "*Divertere!*"

Her hex struck the ground in front of the Ferryman, setting it ablaze with a line of flames. In the next second, Marlow grabbed Swift's arm and hauled him back the way they'd come, sprinting toward the square.

And then she felt another hex strike her between the shoulders, sending shocks up her spine that froze her.

"Swift, *go!*" she cried, using her last bit of strength to shove him away from her.

"*Avendra!*"

A flash of red glyphs streaked toward her and then everything went dark.

THIRTY

Marlow woke up lying on a cold metal surface, an ache pounding through her head. With a groan, she opened her eyes and knew almost immediately where she was.

Inside the dreadnought where the Blind Tiger was housed. But she wasn't in the speakeasy—she was in another part of the ship.

The brig.

A metal grate kept her penned into her own cell. The other two cells were empty—but there was a man sitting by the door, counting out strings of pearls.

Though his face was in shadow, Marlow recognized the exuberant purple-and-gold-printed suit he wore. Thaddeus Bane.

Marlow let out a soft groan and tried to get to her feet.

Bane looked up. He grinned. "Ah, she wakes."

She glared. "Where is Swift and what did you do to him?"

He let out a barking laugh. "Oh, I knew this would be fun."

Marlow leaned her forehead against the metal bars of her cage and closed her eyes. The cold metal helped with her headache a little. "How'd you know where to find us?"

"We got a heads-up," Bane replied. "From your pal Grantaire."

Marlow looked up, startled. *Grantaire?*

"Think maybe he wants you dead?" Bane asked.

Why would he? He'd rescued Marlow from being imprisoned, on Vale's account.

Her head was swimming too much to make sense of it.

"Don't worry, sweetheart," Bane said with a nasty grin. "Leonidas will see you soon."

The words struck cold terror into Marlow's heart. Bane was terrifying enough, but Leonidas—he was cruelty incarnate.

She didn't want to know what he had planned for her.

The metal door to the brig creaked open before Marlow could reply. Another Copperhead, one Marlow vaguely recognized, stepped into the brig and gave Bane a nod.

"Ah," Bane said, his eyes sparkling. "Looks like the time has come."

He walked over to the cell door and unlocked it.

Marlow didn't move.

"Come on now," Bane said, waving her toward the door. "Let's not keep him waiting."

Numb with terror, Marlow stepped toward the door. Bane pushed her forward with a sharp shove to her back.

Later, Marlow wouldn't remember a single second of the walk from the brig to the captain's quarters, where Leonidas waited.

He sat in what looked like a grand throne, like the Cortesian Emperor might sit in, surrounded by dozens of Copperheads. He wore his signature dark charcoal suit without much adornment. In one hand, he spun a blade between his fingers.

Marlow's heart dropped. It was the Obsidian Blade.

Sycorax, his giant crocodile, lay on his belly at Leonidas's feet, his yellowed teeth stained red as he gorged himself on what looked like human blood and viscera. Marlow's stomach turned.

"Marlow Briggs," Leonidas said. "I've been waiting for this moment for a long time."

Marlow couldn't speak. She could barely stay standing, she was trembling so hard.

"What?" Leonidas asked, leaning forward. "No snarky comeback?" He tsked. "I expected more from you, Marlow."

"Where's Swift?" Marlow asked, her voice trembling.

Leonidas grinned. "Swift? That coward turned tail and ran away. He *left you*, princess. Just like he left us. So much for loyalty, right?"

Marlow sucked in a shaking breath—the first proper breath she'd taken since she woke up. Swift wasn't here. He hadn't been caught. He wasn't at Leonidas's mercy. He was *safe*.

"You really thought you could take us down, didn't you?" Leonidas asked. "Stupid, naive Little Miss Cursebreaker. You've always managed to wiggle your way out of trouble before, but not this time." His gaze went cold and dark. Marlow felt like she was looking into a fathomless void. "Not this time."

He reached into his suit pocket and pulled out a spellcard. "*Moriare!*"

Long, claw-like scratches split the flesh of Marlow's arms. She screamed, clutching at her arms as if she could keep the blood from flowing.

Leonidas leapt off his throne and stalked toward her. Marlow scrambled back, slipping on a pool of her own blood and crashing to the ground. Leonidas grabbed her by the throat and pinned her down.

Marlow scrabbled at his hand, tears stinging her eyes, lungs heaving. Terror like she'd never known before gripped her chest as she stared into Leonidas's dark, empty eyes.

"Don't worry," he said softly. "I'm not going to kill you just yet."

Marlow sobbed, kicking her legs out futilely as Leonidas increased the pressure on her throat and with his other hand pulled out another spellcard.

"Ah, here we are," Leonidas said. He put the spellcard in front of Marlow's face so she could see it. "You know, after my favorite spellwright went"—he whistled—"*off* in the head, it took me a while to find one who could make this spell for me again."

Marlow didn't need to look at the spellcard to know what Leonidas was talking about.

"So, what do you say, Marlow?" Leonidas asked. "You want to be a Copperhead?"

The curse he'd used on Swift. The one that had rotted his flesh for every order he refused.

"*Please,*" Marlow gasped, knowing it was useless. "*Please* just kill me!"

Leonidas grinned down at her. "Now where would be the fun in that?"

A scream built in Marlow's chest as Leonidas raised the spellcard.

"*Maledire.*"

Deep red glyphs oozed from the curse card, surrounding Marlow's wrists and crawling up her arms. Terror gripped her tight in its claws.

Leonidas wrenched her back to her feet. "Why don't you do a little spin for us, Marlow?" he said mockingly.

Marlow didn't move. This couldn't be happening.

Her right hand started to tingle, almost like it had fallen asleep. When she looked down at it, the very tips of her nails were starting to turn a festering green. She knew what this was. She'd seen Swift's arm after the Copperheads had used this same curse on him.

Every second that passed when she didn't follow Leonidas's order, the rot would creep up her hand.

She swallowed a whimper and spun in a circle.

Leonidas and Bane clapped and broke into guffaws. The other Copperheads laughed along with them.

"Very nice," Leonidas said approvingly. His dark eyes went flat and cruel. "Now hit yourself in the face."

Marlow squeezed her eyes shut, her entire body quivering in fear. Leonidas was just getting started. He would spend hours torturing her, humiliating her. And then he'd feed her to Sycorax.

She'd be lucky if he killed her first.

She raised her open palm and slapped herself across the face.

"Harder," Leonidas ordered.

Marlow slapped herself again.

"Harder!"

And again. Her cheek stung. She tasted blood.

"Look at me," Leonidas ordered.

Marlow opened her eyes. His cruel black eyes bored into hers. A sob built in her chest, bubbling into her throat.

Leonidas held up the Obsidian Blade. Violet light glinted off its edge.

A loud boom shook the dreadnought. For a moment Marlow thought Leonidas had done it somehow, but he blinked, startled.

"What was that?" Bane asked.

Leonidas waved him off and then beckoned to another Copperhead. "Go find out."

The Copperhead scrambled over to the hatch and disappeared into the corridor.

Leonidas refocused his attention on Marlow.

"Come here," Leonidas beckoned.

Marlow gasped in a sharp breath and shut her eyes. As if she could block this nightmare out.

"*Marlow*," Leonidas chided in a singsong voice. "Let's not make this difficult. Come here."

Marlow's fingers began to tingle. Squeezing her eyes tighter and balling her fists, she inched toward him. Closer. Closer.

"Good girl," Leonidas crooned. She could feel his hot breath against her face. And then the cold edge of the blade against her cheek. "Don't worry. This won't hurt much."

Another boom rocked the ship, this one hard enough that it jerked Marlow off balance and sent her stumbling to the ground.

Leonidas narrowed his eyes. "What have you done?"

Marlow shook her head, panic stealing her breath.

The Copperhead Leonidas had sent to check reappeared in the doorway. He just stood there a moment, swaying.

"Well?" Leonidas snapped.

The man's head toppled from his shoulders and thumped onto the ground.

Marlow screamed.

The man's headless body collapsed in the doorway. A shadowed figure stepped over his body and into the light.

For a moment, Marlow almost thought it was an illusion.

But then the illusion spoke.

"I'm looking for Leonidas," Vale said. His gaze fell on Leonidas. "Ah. That must be you."

"Well, well, well," Leonidas said, getting up from the ground and stepping over Marlow's body. "Is Daddy here to save his little girl?"

Without even waiting for his signal, the other two dozen Copperheads swarmed Vale.

Vale took a calm step backward and drew a hex card out of his pocket. He murmured an incantation, too quiet for Marlow to hear.

Sickly green glyphs glowed out from the spellcard and enveloped the Copperheads in a bright explosion of light. Marlow heard several screams, and when the light faded again, she saw that the Copperheads were all—there was no other word for it—*melting*.

Angry red boils erupted on their skin and began to bleed. Their flesh dripped onto the floor in thick globs as they shrieked in horror and pain.

"*Sventrare!*" Leonidas roared, casting his own spellcard.

"*Sciogliere*," Vale said calmly.

More sickly green glyphs engulfed Leonidas. Marlow watched in horror as the same curse struck him, sloughing off his skin in bloody chunks. She squeezed her eyes shut, stomach heaving.

Terror froze her, and for a moment all she could do was sit there on her hands and knees, listening to the screams of the other Copperheads as Vale cast his curse over and over again.

Move, she told herself. *Do something!*

She knew she had to get the curse card Leonidas had cast on her. It took every ounce of her strength to crawl toward him—or what was left of him. His body lay in a mangled heap in front of the throne. Sobs pushed their way out of Marlow's throat.

A scaled tail whipped past her before she could reach Leonidas.

Tethered by his golden leash, Sycorax made a swipe for her, his powerful jaws snapping down, tearing into her jacket, but thankfully not her flesh.

Marlow screamed again and lunged to hold his jaws shut, remembering what the Brash Buccaneer had once told her—crocodile jaws were immensely strong when it came to closing, but weak when it came to opening them again.

She could feel Sycorax struggling against her hold, but his jaws remained shut. Marlow closed her eyes and concentrated on holding his jaws closed, trying to block out the sounds of carnage in the room around her. She was shaking hard, but she gripped his jaws tight, gasping in panicked breaths and trying not to vomit.

Suddenly, his struggling ceased. Marlow opened her eyes. She looked down at the crocodile head she still held in her hands. The rest of Sycorax's body had been torn to shreds.

She shrieked and let go. She was shaking so hard she didn't know if she could move, but she had to get the curse card. Sucking in as much air as her trembling lungs would take, she reached into the heap of blood and melted flesh that had once been Leonidas. She was crying hysterically as she searched for the curse card, a powerful wave of nausea rolling through her entire body. And just when she thought she couldn't take the horror anymore, her fingers grazed the edge of a card.

She pulled it from the grisly mess and reached inside her pocket for her lighter. Her hands slippery with blood, she tried once, twice, three times to get the lighter to catch. The horrific sounds of the other Copperheads falling prey to Vale's curse filled the air.

With a cry of frustration, she sucked in a deep breath and clicked the lighter a fourth time. The flame caught, and Marlow held the curse card to it.

The card glowed a sickly green. The same glowing aura surrounded Marlow and then drew toward the curse card, peeling away from her. The card absorbed the curse, and then the glow extinguished. The card faded to a dull ash color.

Relief poured over Marlow. She sucked in a few steadying breaths, and realized the room had gone quiet.

Then Vale's voice spoke. "Marlow?"

Marlow choked out a whimper.

"Marlow, it's all right," Vale's voice said gently. She could hear that he was moving closer.

She blinked open her eyes.

Vale stood about ten paces away from her. His neat, cobalt suit was drenched in dark blood. The Copperheads' bodies lay in puddles of deliquescent flesh on the floor.

In one hand, he held the Obsidian Blade. His eyes met hers and he tucked the knife away.

"It's all right," he said, kneeling on the ground beside her. "You're all right now. You're safe. They won't *ever* touch you again. You're safe now."

Marlow could only stare at him, at the fresh streaks of blood and flesh on his suit, the horror of what he'd done—what he'd done to protect *her*—hollowing her out.

He reached out with a gentle hand and pulled her into him, cradling her head against his shoulder and rocking her gently, like she was a colicky infant in need of comfort.

"I'll always protect you, Marlow," he murmured. "Always."

THIRTY-ONE

A loud crash ripped Adrius from sleep.

At first he thought the sound had been entirely in his dream—a blurry, indistinct swirl of images and feelings he couldn't parse on this side of waking.

But then another crash shook the room, this one followed by the sound of shattering glass or porcelain. Adrius shot out of bed, still only half awake, and stumbled through the sitting room to the front entrance of his quarters, the enchanted lights illuminating as soon as he stepped inside.

Another crash sounded and Adrius burst into the hall. It sounded like the noise was coming from the other end of the hall—from Amara's quarters.

"Adrius."

Adrius turned, and there in the dark was Darian, standing a few feet from the entryway of his and Amara's quarters. Like Adrius, he was clearly wearing the clothes he'd gone to sleep in. His golden hair, usually so perfectly coiffed, was a mess.

Adrius had almost never seen Darian look anything less than perfectly put together and polite. Now he looked scared.

"What's going on?" Adrius demanded. "Is Amara all right?"

Darian hesitated. "I don't know if I should be the one to tell you."

Adrius advanced on him. "Tell me *what*?"

"It's your father," Darian replied. "About an hour ago he . . . succumbed to his injuries."

Adrius felt the bottom of his stomach drop. His father was *dead*. After weeks of waiting for this news, it didn't feel real.

"Let me in there," Adrius said, motioning toward the entryway.

Darian pressed his lips together, his brows creasing. "She wanted to be alone."

The crashing noises stopped, but somehow that only made the dread in Adrius's gut deepen. "Darian."

Darian dropped his gaze and nodded, brushing past Adrius to unlock the door to his and Amara's quarters.

When Adrius stepped inside, he could see immediately what had caused all that noise.

Amara had overturned the chairs, the table. She'd smashed the cabinet full of glasses and plates. A wooden chair lay in splinters across the rug. Shards of glass glittered in the moonlight bleeding through the paned window.

At the foot of the couch, hunched over on the ground, sat Amara.

Her hair was a wild mess around her face. Her cheeks were tearstained, but she wasn't crying, not anymore. Instead, she was staring out at the room with a blank face, her arms folded around her knees.

"Amara?" Adrius said cautiously.

When she didn't make any indication she'd heard him, he crept closer.

And then, when he was about an arm's length away, she made a noise like an aborted sob and looked up at him.

"What am I supposed to do?" she croaked. And then she lowered her face into her arms and wept.

In that moment, Adrius understood his sister better than he had in years. Perhaps better than he ever had. Because Aurelius had not been a father to him or to Amara. He had been a *god*—one that Amara had worshipped and Adrius had defied.

And now he was gone.

In the wreckage of his sister's rage and grief, Adrius crumpled.

Grief hit him like a wall, something solid and insurmountable. He thought he could evade it, could shut himself off from it, but it had always been there. He didn't know for what he grieved—his father, his sister, his mother, himself, the child he'd once been. The love that grew, stunted and twisted but there all the same, for the people who had only ever failed him. He didn't know if the feeling in his chest was relief or devastation, to be finally free of the man Adrius had defined himself by and against his entire life.

But the one thing he did know, without a single doubt, was that right now, in the wake of this devastation, there was only one place he wanted to be.

THIRTY-TWO

The bathwater in Marlow's apartment was enchanted so it never got cold, but even though Marlow had been sitting in the bath for almost two hours, she still didn't feel warm.

Or clean.

The scent of the lavender soap was giving her a mild headache, but she didn't want to move.

Every time she closed her eyes, all she saw were the twisted, melted corpses of the Copperheads.

A soft knock on the washroom door drew her back to the present.

"Marlow?" Swift's voice came, gentle and muffled through the door. "Are you still in there? You didn't drown, did you?"

It took all of Marlow's strength to reply. "I'm still in here."

"Are you planning on coming out at all tonight?"

Marlow didn't reply.

When she'd first arrived back at Vale Tower, Swift had been pacing their living room, wild-eyed and panicked. He'd explained that when the Copperheads kidnapped her, he'd managed to get away before they took him, too. He'd gone directly back to Vale Tower, where he'd told Silvan what had happened.

Silvan was the one who'd told Vale.

Marlow hadn't told Swift much about what had happened once Vale showed up at the Copperheads' dreadnought, but he'd been able to tell just from looking at her that it had been bad.

He'd asked her what Leonidas had done to her.

"Nothing as bad as what Vale did to them," Marlow had replied.

Swift hadn't pressed for details.

"Look, I . . ." Swift started through the door. "I was going to go see Silvan. He's . . . actually pretty worried about you. But if you want me to stay here, I'll—"

"No," Marlow rasped. "It's all right. I'm all right. You should go."

She could hear him hesitate outside the door.

"I'll see you in the morning, then," he said quietly, and then Marlow heard the sound of his footsteps quietly retreating.

She didn't know how long she remained in the bath after Swift left, but eventually she did get out, wrapping herself in a cloud-soft robe and taming her wet hair into a loose braid.

Just as she stepped out from the steamy washroom, there was a quiet knock on the front door.

Marlow froze. The clock on the living room wall said it was past midnight, and she couldn't think of anyone who would call on her at this hour.

There was only one person she *wanted* to see, and she knew he wasn't at the door.

Still, a fragile hope propelled her across the living room and made her unlatch the door. She pulled it open and there, impossibly, standing in the darkened entryway, was Adrius.

He looked almost as unraveled as Marlow felt. Instead of his usual pressed suit, he was wearing sleeping clothes—a button-down shirt tied with a sash, and a silk sleeping robe. His eyes were red-rimmed and tired, his curls wild around his drawn face.

"Hi," he croaked, swaying in the doorway. "I know I shouldn't be here . . ."

Marlow didn't answer. Instead, she wrapped her arms around his shoulders and pulled him through the threshold and into her arms.

He stumbled into her, holding her just as tightly as she held him. His warmth bled into her. Marlow trembled.

He pulled back a little, just enough to look her in the eye, cupping a hand around her cheek.

"What happened?" he asked. "Something happened."

Marlow shook her head. "It doesn't matter. You're here."

"I had to see you," Adrius said. "I . . . my father. He's dead."

Marlow sucked in a sharp breath. She couldn't say she was surprised. And maybe it was horrible, but the first thing she felt was relief. "Do you want to talk about it?"

Adrius traced her cheek with his thumb. "I just want to be here."

She leaned up and kissed him, gently. "Is this—"

He didn't let her get the question out, kissing her more urgently. Heat blazed between them. He wrapped an arm around her waist, pulling her into him.

Marlow stumbled back, dragging him with her. He pressed her up against the wall, kissing her until she felt like she was on fire.

She slid her hand to his chest and nudged him back, breaking the kiss. For a moment they just looked at each other, breathing hard in the dark. As if daring each other to stop what they both knew would end in heartbreak.

But instead, Marlow took his hand and led him to the couch.

She pushed him down onto it and climbed onto his lap. It didn't matter how this would end. All the reasons they couldn't have this faded into the gray of the night.

They were here. They were alive.

That was enough.

Marlow kissed him again, slow and indulgent. She reached for the sash of her robe.

Adrius reached for her wrist, gripping it. "Are you sure?" he whispered against her mouth.

Marlow nodded. "Yes. Are you?"

He released her wrist, cupping her face between his hands. "Of you? Always."

THIRTY-THREE

Marlow hadn't expected Adrius to stay the night. It was too risky. But there was a part of her—a small part—that'd thought maybe he would anyway. That after the way he had touched her and held her and called her *his* the night before, that he might not be able to bear leaving her.

It was a pathetic, lovelorn thought, and she hated herself a little bit for the disappointment that curdled in her stomach when she woke up alone.

She knew what last night was. It was a moment of weakness for both of them. A goodbye. It changed nothing about the impossibility of them. It only made it harder to bear.

But Adrius hadn't left her empty-handed, she realized when she glanced across the rumpled covers and spotted something sitting on the side table that hadn't been there before.

It was a small, clear vial, the length of Marlow's thumb. She picked it up and turned it over in her palm. It was filled with a clear liquid.

Tears, she thought suddenly. Tears shed by a killer. Aurelius was dead, and that made Adrius his killer.

She gripped it tightly in her fist. Ever since Vale had told her his plans and how he'd wanted to transform the city, she'd been asking herself if trying to stop him was even the right thing to do.

But after last night, and the brutal, horrific way he'd dealt with the

Copperheads, after she'd seen the burden he'd put on Adrius by forcing him to kill his own father, she knew her answer.

She dressed quickly, slipping the vial of Adrius's tears into her jacket pocket. She went to the kitchen, shoving a stale biscuit into her mouth, and then out the door, marching down the hall.

She took the elevator up to the Vales' private residence, only mildly surprised when she was allowed access. She knew there were two wings of the residence: one that Vale and his wife occupied, and the other belonging to Silvan and formerly to Darian.

She marched down the corridor to Silvan's rooms and then stopped in front of the door, knocking vigorously.

When no one came to open it, she grew impatient and pulled out a Lockpick spellcard.

The lock gave easily to the spell and Marlow barged inside, strode through the sitting room, and slammed open Silvan's bedroom door.

"What the hell!" Silvan yelped, pulling the sheet over himself and gaping at Marlow in the doorway.

Beside him, Swift wore an expression of blind panic, his hair sleep-rumpled and his chest bare. "Marlow?"

Silvan groaned and flopped back against the pillows. "Ugh, it's *you*." He pulled the sheet higher, over his face.

"Is everything all right?" Swift asked, concern lacing his tone. "Are *you* all right?"

"Yeah," Marlow answered. "I mean, no, probably not, but I will be."

"Uh, so is there a reason you barged in here?" Swift asked.

"Yes," Marlow replied. "We need to go to the Mudskipper. Even if Fisher can't help us anymore, we *need* to finish that spell." She glanced at the lump of sheets where Silvan was, all too aware that he didn't know the exact nature of their deal with Fisher and the Black Orchid, or that it had anything to do with Vale.

283

"Uh, okay," Swift answered. "Of course. I'll just . . . let me just get up and we can go, yeah?"

Marlow waited. Swift didn't move.

Silvan's head burrowed deeper into the covers. "Is she gone yet?"

"Nope," Marlow answered.

His answer was a groan of frustration.

"Give me ten minutes, okay?" Swift said.

From beneath the covers, Silvan's voice came out muffled. "Only ten?"

"Why would you need more than—" Marlow began, and then thought better of it. "Never mind, do *not* tell me. *Never* tell me. Just get dressed and meet me back at the apartment."

Half an hour later found them aboard a canal boat on their way to the Mudskipper.

"Hey, Swift?" Marlow said after ten minutes had passed in uncharacteristic silence.

He turned toward her. "Yeah?"

"Do you actually *like* him or something?"

Swift looked surprised by the question. "Who, Silvan?"

Marlow raised her eyebrows. "You been spending time in anyone else's bed lately?"

Swift flushed. "No."

"Gods below," Marlow said, a little amazed. "You *do* like him."

"Shut up," Swift said. "He's . . . you know, he's not so bad when you get to know him. Kind of like a cat—you just have to earn his trust. And once you do, he's actually kind of . . . sweet."

"*Sweet?*" Marlow echoed incredulously. She could not think of a word that described Silvan less. But then again . . . she recalled how adamant Silvan had been about accompanying Marlow to track down Swift. He'd played it off as suspicion of her, but maybe the truth was that he'd been *worried*. And the other night, after the auction, when Marlow was cursed, he'd come to their rescue.

Maybe there was more to him than his sharp exterior. Maybe he made Swift happy. If anyone deserved something good and uncomplicated like that, it was Swift.

"What?" Swift asked, and Marlow realized she was still staring at him. She shook her head. "Nothing. Just—*smitten* is a new look on you."

Swift blushed harder and reached over to thwack her on the shoulder.

They reached the Mudskipper not long after that, and each gulped down a cup of enchanted tea to pass through the hidden entrance to the Black Orchid's workshop. Marlow stopped short when she spotted Fisher bent over a worktable, a few books scattered around him.

"Fisher?" Marlow said.

He looked up from the table. "What are you doing here?"

"I was about to ask *you* that," Marlow replied. "I thought you said you were done with this."

He shook his head. "The Reapers released me from the contract this morning. I thought you had something to do with it."

Marlow started to deny it and then paused. The Copperheads were dead. Which meant as far as the Reapers were concerned, Marlow had held up her end of the bargain.

"It was Vale," she said at last. "He . . . he killed the Copperheads." *Slaughtered* would have been a better word for it. *Massacred.* "We can't let him finish that spell. I've seen what he's capable of now, and it's . . ." She shivered. "He can't be allowed to have that kind of power."

She had seen the price of Vale's Caraza, and it wasn't one she was willing to pay. There was no such thing, she realized now, as a just world built on a river of blood.

"I have this," Marlow said, pulling the vial of Adrius's tears from her pocket and placing it on the table in front of Fisher. "But Vale has the Obsidian Blade now. I saw him take it."

"I've been thinking about what to do about the blade," Fisher said. "I may have a solution."

"We're not just going to find another blade used to assassinate a tyrant lying around," Swift said.

"Not exactly," Fisher said. "Although . . . actually, yes. Sort of."

Marlow and Swift exchanged skeptical glances. "Explain, please."

"Back in the old days, before the spell libraries existed and spellcraft became codified, no two spells were exactly alike. Each individual spell-caster brought their own thoughts, beliefs, and impressions to the spells they created. Two different spellcasters could use the same components to create two different effects."

"Makes sense," Swift said.

"So," Fisher went on. "What happened when spellcards were invented was that the spellwright and the spell*caster* were no longer the same person. This creates an inherent dissonance between the process of creating a spell and the process of casting it. And the whole point is that spells now had to be built such that they could be cast anytime by anyone. The ability of the spellwright to imbue their own beliefs into the spell became muted, because they were no longer the ones necessarily casting the spell. Still with me?"

Marlow nodded. She recalled Fisher lecturing about a similar topic in the class she'd sat in on.

"Therefore, the types of ingredients used in a spell started to change, because they had to hold the same meaning regardless of who was casting the spell. It became common to take blood, or memories, or emotions themselves in order to sort of . . . artificially imbue spells with meaning."

"What does that have to do with the Obsidian Blade?" Marlow asked.

"Well, think about it," Fisher said. There was a note of excitement in his voice that Marlow only ever heard when he was talking about spellcraft. "We're the ones creating this spell *and* we're the ones casting it. Even the ingredients we're using—many of them came from us. Swift's nightmare, Adrius's tears, your heart's desire . . ."

"So you're saying we don't have to use the Obsidian Blade because . . . if we're the ones casting the spell, we can use an ingredient that holds the same meaning but to *us*, specifically?" Swift asked.

Fisher nodded. "The ingredient is 'a blade that has tasted the blood of a tyrant.' The Obsidian Blade would have worked perfectly for that because almost everyone agrees that the emperor killed by that blade was a tyrant. It holds the same meaning no matter who is casting the spell. But if we're the ones casting the spell, then the ingredient only has to hold that meaning to us."

"So we need to find another blade that has 'tasted the blood of a tyrant,' except the *tyrant* part just has to be something we all believe?" Marlow asked. She paused, and then it clicked. "Gods below. You want to use *my* knife, don't you?"

The knife that Adrius had used to stab his father through the heart.

Fisher was right, though. Aurelius Falcrest *was* a tyrant—at least, Marlow believed that, and she was sure Adrius, Fisher, and Swift would agree.

Fisher nodded.

"And that will work?" Swift asked.

Fisher nodded again. "I don't see any reason why it wouldn't."

"Okay," Marlow said slowly. "Small problem, though—the knife was taken as evidence. I don't know where it is."

The three of them fell silent for a long moment.

Then Swift said, "Isn't your hearing next week? If the Five Families vote to dismiss the case, can't you get the knife back then? It *is* still yours."

"Sure, but . . . that's a week and possibly more to wait," Marlow said. "And we don't know how close Vale is to finishing his spell, especially now that he has the Obsidian Blade."

"Well, we still need to find Ilario's remains, too," Fisher reminded her. "If we can't do that, it won't matter anyway. But I think this is the best plan we have."

They only needed two more spell ingredients. And after seeing Vale's capacity for ruthless violence, Marlow had never felt more determined to stop him.

"All right," she said. "After the hearing, I'll get my knife back. In the meantime, we keep searching for Ilario's remains."

———

Marlow sat alone inside the courtroom. The whole room was perfectly circular with a domed glass ceiling. The back of the room was a wall of paned glass that looked out on Old Caraza, and Evergarden beyond it. It had the effect of making Marlow feel like a bird trapped inside a glass enclosure.

Behind her, about two hundred noblesse nouveau, court reporters, and other interested parties sat watching the proceedings. In front of her, on a high platform, sat representatives of each of the Five Families.

It had been one week since the incident with the Copperheads. One week since Adrius had snuck up to Marlow's room in the dead of night.

A lot had changed in one week.

Aurelius Falcrest had been entombed in the Falcrest mausoleum. Darian, Silvan, and their father had attended the funeral. Marlow hadn't.

Part of her had thought that Adrius might find his way back to her apartment after the funeral, but he hadn't showed. And then two days later, he'd announced his engagement to Iris Renault in the papers.

Marlow wasn't exactly proud of it, but she'd set the newspaper on fire.

She knew why he'd done it, of course. It had everything to do with today—her hearing. When the heads of the Five Families would vote on whether or not Marlow would stand trial for Aurelius's murder.

She hadn't even been sure if Adrius would be at the hearing, but she'd caught a glimpse of him in the crowd, sitting with Silvan, Gemma, and Iris.

He wore all black—mourning garb—and he looked as if he hadn't slept at all in the week since she'd seen him last.

Not that Marlow herself had managed much sleep.

At the front of the room, the judge called the court to order.

"As it concerns one of their own, the court recognizes the authority of the Five Families in determining whether or not this case goes to trial," the judge intoned. "The court recognizes Zeno Morandi, representing the Morandi family. Dahlia Starling, representing the Starling family. Cormorant Vale, representing the Vale family. And Amara Falcrest, representing the Falcrest and the Delvigne families. A unanimous agreement must be reached to take the case to trial. Now the court will hear brief statements from the prosecution and the defense."

Grantaire stood, smoothing his jacket.

Fury filled Marlow at the sight of him. He'd tried to get her killed, and here he was, pretending like he personally balanced the scales of justice.

"Only a full exploration of the facts of this case can allow true justice to prevail," Grantaire said.

Yeah, right, Marlow thought to herself. Grantaire didn't want justice, he wanted to discredit Marlow for good in front of the entire city. He wanted her locked up, or better yet *dead*, so she could never reveal that he'd sold her out to the Copperheads.

"If it pleases the Five Families, I will make sure no stone goes unturned in determining exactly what happened and who is ultimately responsible for the death of Aurelius Falcrest."

Grantaire returned to his seat and then Marlow's representative, someone Vale had hired, who Marlow had met only once before, rose.

"The facts of this case, Mr. Grantaire, are clear to anyone," she said. "Miss Briggs acted only in self-defense. The death of Aurelius Falcrest *is* a tragedy, for which he has only himself to blame. Let's not waste any more of these people's or the court's precious time by putting on a theater show to arrive at the conclusion that has already been made apparent."

The representative took her seat.

Amara stood. "I'd like to address the court."

"Lady Falcrest," the judge said. "This is most unusual."

"I understand," Amara replied. "But I believe there will be a grave miscarriage of justice if I do not point out that Cormorant Vale is unduly biased in this case. He should not be allowed to vote on this matter, as the defendant is his own daughter."

Murmurs rippled through the room.

Vale leapt to his feet. "Now, Amara—"

"We cannot simply strip one of the Five Families of their vote," the judge replied evenly.

"That's not what I'm proposing at all," Amara said. "Cormorant Vale should recuse himself in favor of his heir."

Marlow's stomach sank. Darian was sure to do whatever Amara told him to do. She resisted the urge to turn and look at Adrius. The whole reason he'd announced his engagement was so that Amara would stop this trial from happening.

Why, now, did it seem that she was maneuvering to make sure the trial went forward?

She was going back on her word, Marlow realized bitterly. She couldn't

290

find it in herself to be surprised, but when she finally found Adrius's face in the crowd, he looked livid.

"Vale is not only biased in favor of his daughter, he very well might be the mastermind behind the entire plot to kill my father," Amara went on.

"That is *quite* the accusation," the judge said.

"He has preached about cleaning up the city, but the truth is, he doesn't want to clean up the city at all—he wants to destroy it," Amara said. "He wants to get rid of the other Five Families and dismantle everything we've built. He has already tried to forcibly take over the Falcrest family as an *adviser*, and I will not sit idly by and let it happen."

The judge looked thoughtful. "There is some precedent for this. If a majority of the Five Families wills it, the court will recuse Cormorant Vale in favor of his heir, Darian Vale."

"The Morandi family seconds the motion," Zeno Morandi said.

Vale looked stunned, but Marlow wasn't surprised. The Morandis were insulted by Marlow's very presence in Evergarden.

"That's three votes, Your Honor," Amara said.

"The motion passes," the judge said. "Lord Vale, please step down."

"Your Honor," Vale said. "The precedent for this—"

"The decision has been made," the judge said. "Surely you trust your eldest son and heir to execute his duties faithfully?"

Vale pressed his lips together and nodded. He smoothed the front of his suit jacket and stepped down from the platform.

Darian rose from the audience and walked up to the front of the room. As he passed his father, Vale paused, putting a hand on his shoulder and saying something too quiet for Marlow to catch. Amara's eyes narrowed.

Darian's jaw tightened and he nodded. He looked nervous climbing the stairs onto the platform. Conflicted. Marlow studied his face, trying to figure out where his loyalties now lay—with his father, or his new wife?

"If there's nothing else," the judge said. "We'll proceed to the vote. A vote 'no' is a vote to dismiss this case. A vote 'yes' is a vote to take the case to trial. Zeno Morandi, how do you vote?"

"The Morandi family votes yes," Morandi said.

"Dahlia Starling?"

Dahlia cleared her throat. "The Starling family votes yes."

Marlow wasn't surprised by this, either. The Starlings owned half the tabloids in the city—what better way to sell magazines and newspapers than a sensational trial?

"Darian Vale."

Darian leaned forward nervously. He didn't look at his father. "The Vale family votes yes," he said in a quiet voice.

"Amara Falcrest?"

Amara's gaze found Marlow. Something vindictive and satisfied burned in her dark eyes. "The Falcrest and Delvigne families vote yes."

THIRTY-FOUR

"Amara!" Adrius roared, bursting into the foyer of Falcrest Hall.

Amara sauntered out onto the mezzanine above, looking as calm as ever. As calm as she had up on the dais in the courtroom, condemning Marlow.

"We had a deal!" Adrius spat. "What the hell do you think you're doing?"

Amara went to the banister, looking down at Adrius, and clapped slowly, the sound echoing through the foyer. "Oh, bravo, brother."

Adrius mounted the stairs. "What is that supposed to mean?"

"It means I'm enjoying this little performance of outrage," Amara replied. "But did you really think I didn't know? You've been secretly meeting up with Marlow for *weeks*."

Adrius froze at the top of the stairs.

"Oh, I see," Amara said coolly. "You really thought you were getting away with it, didn't you?"

How had Amara found out? He shook himself. That part didn't matter right now—Marlow was what mattered.

"That's over," he said. "I'm engaged to Iris now. Like you wanted. I did what I said I would, and *you* went back on your word."

Amara scoffed. "I'm not the one who went back on my word. Our deal was that you stayed away from Marlow. Which you *didn't*."

Adrius stiffened. "I'm not going to see her anymore. It's over. I swear it."

"That's right, Adrius, you *won't* be seeing her anymore. Because she'll be locked up where she belongs," Amara spat. "I don't understand how you can even *look* at her when she killed our father."

"She *didn't*," Adrius said, before he could consider the words. He sucked in a breath, jaw tightening. In a clear, crisp voice he said, "Marlow didn't kill our father. I did."

Amara went still. "Don't," she said in a low, dangerous voice. She took a step back. "Don't lie about something like that, Adrius. Don't—"

"It's not a lie," Adrius said quietly. "It's the truth. And I should have told you weeks ago."

He should have told her the moment they'd arrived back at Falcrest Hall after her wedding. But every time he'd come close to saying the words aloud, it was like he just shut down, and he'd find himself hours later, polishing off a bottle of wine alone in his room. Was it guilt that had kept the words buried? Grief? Or just plain cowardice—the kind that his father had always seen so clearly in him?

"No," Amara bit out. "*No.* You didn't kill him, Adrius, you didn't—"

"I wasn't—I didn't want to," Adrius said. "I was cursed. There was a Compulsion curse put on me—"

"Then *she* is the one who cast it!" Amara raged.

Adrius shook his head. "She's the one who broke the curse." He stepped toward her. "Amara, our father—he wasn't who you thought he was. The curse that was used on me . . . he used it on our mother. She's here, she's in the city, he's had her locked up for *years*. I—"

"Stop it," Amara demanded. "Stop this, I don't want to hear this, just—*stop it*!"

The desperation in her voice made Adrius obey. "Amara."

"I don't want to hear it!" she shrieked.

Adrius drew in a breath. He could see the tight line of tension in her body, the pain marring her face. The truth of who their father was coming up against her love for him. She didn't want to believe it could be true, because what would it mean to know that the man she'd idolized all her life was a monster?

"Fine," Adrius said. "But if you won't call off this trial, then I'm done. I was right to renounce the Falcrest name when I did. I don't want any part of this rotten family."

Before Amara could reply, he descended the stairs and walked out of Falcrest Hall.

THIRTY-FIVE

Marlow dragged herself through the front door of her apartment and stumbled over to the couch, where Toad was curled up. She mewled when Marlow approached and turned over, stretching out and displaying her striped belly.

Marlow scratched her idly and Toad purred, eyes slitted in contentment.

"At least someone in this place is happy," Marlow muttered.

The trial had dragged on for five days. Five days of listening to Grantaire spew blatantly false accusations against Marlow, twisting the truth to suit his narrative. In between appearances in court, Marlow used every waking moment to furiously track down leads about where Ilario's remains might be.

So far, she'd come up empty.

Tomorrow, Grantaire would call Marlow to speak. She knew whatever he asked her, he'd try to spin her answer.

A knock at the front door of the apartment shook her from her dark thoughts.

She was too exhausted to deal with a visitor. Especially if it was Vale. She stormed over to the door and threw it open. "*What?*"

Adrius stood on the other side. It took Marlow back to the night he'd shown up at her door. The night they'd cast aside everything keeping them apart and stolen a moment of moonlight-soaked hours together.

Until the sun had risen, and with it, the cold light of reality.

"Amara went back on our deal," Adrius said, staring at her from the doorway.

Marlow took him by the hand and pulled him inside the apartment. "Yeah, I sort of noticed that."

"I told Amara the truth," Adrius said. "About my father, I mean. About the curse. I should have done it ages ago."

"Adrius—"

"There's something else," Adrius rushed to say. "I . . . I don't know how to say this, but . . ."

He turned toward the door and called out, "You can come in now."

Marlow watched, frozen with shock, as her mother stepped into the room.

"I . . . I found your mother," Adrius said haltingly. "I thought . . . I don't know. That you'd found mine for me, so . . ."

Marlow shook her head mutely, certain that this was some trick, or that perhaps the drama of the day was causing her to see things that weren't really there.

But it really was Cassandra, standing on the threshold. Her hair was cut much shorter than Marlow remembered, but aside from that, she looked the same as she ever had.

A lump rose in Marlow's throat.

"I'll just . . . I'll give you two a moment," Adrius said, and crossed the living room to retreat into Marlow's bedroom.

"Minnow," Cassandra said. She crossed the threshold at last, sweeping Marlow into her arms. "I missed you so much."

Marlow didn't hug her back, but she didn't push her away, either. "I thought you were *dead*."

Cassandra pulled back just enough to look Marlow in the face, stroking her hair gently. "I know. I'm sorry for that. I made so many mistakes . . . too many. I didn't want to pull you into my mess. I thought, if everyone thought I was dead, you'd be safe."

"You could have told *me*."

"You would've wanted to come with me," Cassandra replied. It was true, and it *hurt*, because all it meant was that Cassandra hadn't wanted Marlow with her.

"Then why come back at all?"

"Adrius told me about the trial," Cassandra replied, holding on to her. "About his father and the Copperheads and—Minnow, what have you gotten yourself into?"

Marlow pulled out of her mother's embrace. "I don't have to explain myself to you, of all people. You never bothered to explain *anything* to me. Not even who my father really is."

Cassandra's expression flickered with hurt. But then she crossed her arms over her chest. "What is it you want to know, then?"

"How about how you managed to convince everyone—including *me*—that you were dead?" Marlow said.

"I never intended to make you think I was dead," Cassandra said.

"I saw Caito's memory of that night," Marlow replied. "I saw you go over the bridge, into the canal. How did you survive?"

"I swam," Cassandra answered. "I had an Endless Breath spell on me. I thought I might encounter trouble, so I took precautions."

"And how did Vale end up with *Ilario's Grimoire*?" Marlow asked. "You must have given it to him."

"Not how you think," Cassandra said. "Yes, you're right—I did hand it over to him. I realized too late what I'd gotten myself into by stealing it, and I knew if I handed it over to the Black Orchid, Falcrest would kill me. So I did the only thing I could think of—I went to Cormorant. I told him . . . as much of the truth as he needed to know. And he promised to return the spellbook to Falcrest and smooth the whole thing over."

"Well, he didn't," Marlow said. "He kept it."

"Yes, I figured that out when Caito found me and demanded I give the spellbook back," Cassandra replied. "At that point, I figured my only option was to get out of the city."

"You could have taken me with you," Marlow said before she could stop herself. "You didn't have to just . . . *leave*."

"And turn my only daughter into a fugitive?" Cassandra asked. She shook her head. "I couldn't make you live a life like that."

Marlow bit back what she wanted to say, which was that she might as well be a fugitive now.

"And what about Grantaire?" Marlow asked.

"Grantaire?" Cassandra asked sharply.

"Yes," Marlow replied. "He wants me dead, or locked up at the very least, but I don't know why. I know why the Copperheads wanted me dead. I know why the Falcrests do, too. What I *don't* know is why the second I turned over evidence of you extorting rogue spellwrights, Grantaire tried to get Leonidas to kill me."

Cassandra's face went very still. Then she tilted her head and opened her mouth, and before she'd even spoken a word Marlow knew whatever she was about to say was complete bullshit.

She knew her mother and she knew what it looked like when she conned someone.

"The truth," Marlow bit out. "You owe me that."

Cassandra drew in a breath and nodded, looking away. "Grantaire was a . . . business partner, of sorts. Before he was the City Solicitor he was a cop—a pretty dirty one, though he managed to keep his dealings well-hidden. I didn't know much about him, but I remember even the first time we crossed paths realizing he was a lot smarter than any other cop I'd dealt with before. He managed to figure out what I'd been doing with the spellwrights and, like any dirty cop worth his salt, he *offered* to help cover it up. As long as I cut him in, of course. The more he rose in the ranks, the more protection he was able to offer me—but also, he'd begun carving out a reputation for himself as a reformer. And we both knew if anyone figured out what he'd been up to, what he'd done for me, his reputation would be ruined."

"So I'm guessing the ledger I turned over to him proved he was involved," Marlow said. She closed her eyes briefly, remembering what she'd seen. There had been two columns of payments in the ledger. "The second payments."

Cassandra nodded. "It might not have proved it entirely, but I kept track of his cut out of every payment. I'd guess that a cursory dig through Grantaire's finances would reveal he was getting payments in exactly those amounts, even if he'd disguised them as something innocuous."

"And now he's the solicitor trying to prove my guilt in a murder trial," Marlow said. "Great."

"I won't let him bring you down just to cover up my mistakes," Cassandra said. "I won't let anything happen to you."

Marlow had seen the way her mother solved problems in her life, and she wanted nothing to do with it.

"I don't need you, or Vale, to try to protect me," Marlow said. "I can protect myself."

Cassandra stared at Marlow, guilt plain on her face. "I guess you've had to do a lot of that since I left."

Marlow turned away. She didn't want to get into everything she'd done and everything she'd felt since Cassandra had disappeared. What difference would it make?

The door of Marlow's room clicked open, and Adrius stepped out.

"I'm sorry," he said. "I didn't mean to eavesdrop, but Minnow—I can't let you take the fall for killing my father. I'll tell everyone the truth."

"It won't matter," Marlow replied. "They'll just say you're trying to protect me. Or that I've got you under some spell. There are political reasons why Amara and the Morandis and Grantaire want me gone, and those won't just go away."

Adrius drew in a breath. His eyes locked on hers. "If they want you gone, then let's *go*. We can leave the city. We can go anywhere."

"Adrius," Marlow said. "We can't just—"

"Why not?" he demanded. "Why can't we? Fuck the Five Families. Fuck the city." He surged toward her, cupping her face between his hands. "Nothing matters here except you."

Marlow couldn't stand to look at him, his eyes shining with hope. A part of her felt angry at him for even saying this—for dangling the possibility in front of her. For believing in it himself.

"And what about Vale?" she asked quietly. "If we leave, he'll cast his spell and—"

"Fisher and the Black Orchid can deal with him," Adrius insisted. "They've almost completed the spell, haven't they? Do they even really need us now?"

"Adrius . . ."

"Run away with me, Marlow," Adrius said. "We can start over."

That same anger kindled in her gut. She reached up to Adrius's hands and gently moved them away from her face. "Do you even know what you're offering? You want to *start over*? Give up everything—your money, Evergarden, your name?"

"I already gave up my name," Adrius said darkly. "I don't care about any of it."

Marlow crossed her arms over her chest, like it might help her hold everything she was feeling inside. "You say that now."

"I mean it," Adrius insisted. "What has money and power ever done for me? It's only destroyed everyone in my family. My mother. My father. Amara. It would be a *relief* to leave it behind."

"What happens a few months from now? When we're far away some-where, with barely enough money to feed ourselves? Where are we even going to *go*? What would we do?"

"We'll figure it out," Adrius said. "You're the smartest person I know. This city isn't the only place that needs the services of a cursebreaker."

For a moment, Marlow let herself think of it. A new life, somewhere far from Caraza. Breaking curses, with Adrius at her side.

Cassandra stepped toward them. "I can get the three of us out of the city. And I have . . . money. Enough of it to start over."

Marlow shook her head. "Adrius, even if we *could* get out of Caraza, you know we don't have a future together. I gave that up."

"It's not too late to take it back," Adrius pleaded.

"You know I can't do that," Marlow replied, heated. "They need it for the spell."

Cassandra looked between the two of them. "What are you talking about?"

Adrius's gaze flicked over to Cassandra. When it became clear Marlow wasn't going to answer the question, he said, "Marlow gave up the most hidden desire of her heart as a spell ingredient. Our friends are using it to create a spell to destroy *Ilario's Grimoire*."

Cassandra's eyes met Marlow's. She took a step forward. "Use mine instead."

"What?"

Adrius looked even more stunned than Marlow felt. He turned back to her. "See? We can do it. We have everything we need."

Marlow looked between the two of them. She could *see it*. Her life, somewhere else. A new city, a new home. Maybe she'd keep breaking curses, or maybe she'd do something else entirely. But she would be with her mother. With Adrius.

And maybe Adrius was right. Maybe he *wouldn't* miss his life here.

Maybe he'd be suited to another life, a free life. One where he could take control of his own destiny. Where he wasn't mired in the failures and the rot of his family's legacy.

He deserved that. Maybe Marlow did, too.

And Cassandra—maybe she deserved the chance to make up for her past mistakes. She was looking at Marlow now with an expression so familiar to her, tender with affection for her daughter. She *wanted* Marlow with her. She *had* missed her. Maybe they could start to rebuild that relationship, the one that had been Marlow's constant, her touchstone, her whole life.

Marlow wanted to say yes. She *ached* for it.

But that yes belonged to a different person. Someone she wasn't, and never would be.

"I can't leave," she said simply. There was no anger in her words, no heat. It was just the truth, plain as it would ever be. "I don't run from trouble. And I don't leave my messes for someone else to clean up. That's not who I am."

Marlow wouldn't be a victim of this city. But she wasn't satisfied with just surviving it, either. She had always sought a third option—to fight back against the inherent cruelty of the world in any way she could. By breaking curses. By digging up the truth, no matter how ugly, no matter how painful.

To leave would be to bow out of the fight—and that was worse than losing.

"Marlow," Adrius croaked. "If you stay, you'll be convicted. You *know* you will. You said it yourself."

He was right. With Grantaire and Amara both bent on getting her locked up, she didn't stand a chance.

She had only one hope. One sliver of a chance to save herself, and Adrius.

She had to go see Vale.

THIRTY-SIX

It was just after dinner at the Vale residence when Marlow stepped into the foyer. Through the archway Marlow could see the dining room. Vale was seated at the table, Elena and Silvan beside him. Their plates had not yet been cleared away.

"Marlow," Vale said in surprise. "We weren't expecting you this evening. Have you eaten? I'm sure we could—"

"I need to speak with you," Marlow said urgently. "It's very important."

Vale sat very still for a moment, gazing at her. Then he turned to his wife. "Why don't you and Silvan retire for the evening?"

"They can stay," Marlow said abruptly. Then, with just a hint of sarcasm, "We're family, aren't we?"

Vale watched her carefully as she circled the table, facing all three of them.

"Grantaire is calling me to speak tomorrow at the trial," Marlow said. "As I'm sure you know. And I wanted to let you know that I plan to tell the truth. I'm going to tell everyone who's really responsible for Aurelius's death."

She kept her gaze trained on Vale, but she could see Elena and Silvan shift beside him.

"Cormorant, what is she talking about?" Elena asked.

Vale folded his hands on the table in front of him. "Marlow," he said gently. "There is no proof."

"I know," Marlow replied. "No one will believe a word I say. Which is why I've come here to ask *you* to say it."

"Marlow," Vale said bracingly. "I swear to you, you will not take the fall for this. I would never allow that. If you would just trust me, and be patient—"

"Do you want to tell them, or should I?" Marlow asked.

Vale fell silent.

"Tell us what?" Silvan asked. His face was pinched with unease.

"You say you want to create a more just Caraza," Marlow said. "Well, here's your chance. Own up to what you've done."

Vale slammed a hand down on the table, springing to his feet. "I will fix it," he said fiercely. "You won't be locked up for this, Marlow, I swear it. I will protect you."

Marlow knew exactly how he meant to protect her. The spell. Once he completed it, it wouldn't matter if Marlow was convicted and sentenced to death. He could stop it with a simple command.

"Protect me by telling the truth," she said.

"What is she talking about?" Silvan asked. Then, in a softer voice that made him sound much younger than his eighteen years, "Dad?"

But Marlow had had enough. She whirled toward Silvan. "He's the one who cursed Adrius. He admitted it to me. And he ordered him to kill his own father."

Silvan shrank back. "That . . . that can't be true."

But Elena didn't look stunned like her son. Either she'd known all along what Vale was up to, or she knew her husband well enough to know he was capable of it.

Silvan turned to his father. "It isn't true . . . It's *not* . . . Is it?"

Vale moved toward him, grasping his shoulder in one hand. "I promise you, it was for the best. It was *necessary*."

Silvan jerked away from him, fury taking over his sharp features. "Don't come near me."

Hurt flashed across Vale's face before he closed his eyes and wiped his expression carefully blank.

"There are things you do not understand, Silvan," he said brusquely. "Sometimes we must do things that seem morally repugnant in order to—"

"Adrius is my best friend," Silvan spat. "I don't care what your reasons were—you could have gotten him *killed*."

"Silvan—"

Silvan shook his head, backing away. "No. I don't want to speak to you again."

Before Vale could say anything else, Silvan stalked out of the room.

Elena rose from her seat. "Cormorant. Your actions have put this family at risk—surely you see that."

"I have my reasons, Elena," Vale said forcefully.

She laughed scathingly. "I'm sure you do. And I'm sure they're very noble. I just hope they're good company when you look up and realize you're alone."

"Elena—"

"I am tired of cleaning up your messes, Cormorant," Elena said, with a vicious look at Marlow. And then she, too, was striding from the room.

Leaving Vale and Marlow alone.

"Are you trying to turn my family against me?" he demanded. "Is that what you want?"

Marlow hugged her arms close to her body. She wanted to say that Vale had done that all by himself, but she wasn't sure it was true. Maybe Elena would have overlooked this transgression more easily if she hadn't had to stomach weeks of Vale parading his illegitimate daughter around their house. Maybe Darian wouldn't have had to choose between Amara and Vale if it weren't for Marlow.

Maybe Marlow *was* the reason.

"I thought I was your family," Marlow replied. "Isn't that what you said?"

"You *are*," Vale insisted. "Of course."

"Then protect me," Marlow said. "Come to the courthouse tomorrow and turn yourself in. Tell everyone the truth."

"If you would just listen, you would understand that—"

"*Please*, Dad. You're the only one who can save me."

What was it Vale had said? That just as Marlow was driven to protect the people she cared about, so was he. He wanted to be a savior—a savior to Cassandra, to the people of Caraza, to Marlow. She knew this about him, and she wanted to use it against him, but—it wasn't just that. It wasn't *just* a manipulation.

"If you really love me, then do this for me."

She wanted it to be true. She wanted him to prove her wrong about him, to show her that when it came down to it, she was more important to him than his plans, his ideals, his *vision*. That she was his daughter and he would do anything to protect her, even sacrifice himself.

Vale closed his eyes, bowing his head. "All right," he said at last. "I will."

Marlow paced outside the courtroom, nerves churning.

"Where's your father?" Swift asked, glancing around the hallway where they waited to be ushered inside. The room was already full of onlookers, but for Marlow's safety she had to be escorted inside after everyone else.

"I don't know," she replied, glancing around the empty hallway. "I thought he'd be here."

Bitter disappointment flooded her. She should've known. Vale was never going to turn himself in for her. And now if Marlow tried to get up on that stand and tell everyone the truth, it would sound like she was making the whole thing up. At best, she'd be convicted anyway. At worst, she'd implicate Adrius along with her.

"Miss Briggs?" the bailiff asked, poking his head back into the hall. "It's time to go in."

Marlow swallowed. "Thank you."

She cast one last glance at the empty hallway and then turned away, following the bailiff into the courtroom. She kept her head down, aware of hundreds of pairs of eyes on her.

At the prosecutor's table, Grantaire sat smiling, as he always was. Marlow felt a chill go down her spine.

She took her seat at the stand.

"The court is now in session," the judge said. "The prosecution may begin."

"Miss Briggs," Grantaire said warmly, like they were old friends. "Can you begin by telling us how you came to be acquainted with Aurelius Falcrest?"

"We weren't, really," Marlow said. Her voice was magically amplified to reach the entire room. "My mother was an employee of Cormorant Vale for some years, and so I'd seen Aurelius and met him once or twice, but that was basically it."

"And his son, Adrius Falcrest?" Grantaire inquired.

"We were classmates," she answered. "Friends."

"And when did that relationship become more than just friendship?" Grantaire asked.

A complicated question if there ever was one. "Right around the time of the Summer Solstice Classic Regatta this year."

"And when did that relationship end?"

Another complicated question. "Shortly before the Vale-Falcrest wedding."

"Is that so?" Grantaire asked. "Because I have sworn testimony from several people, including Gemma Starling, that claims you and Adrius Falcrest were never actually together."

Gemma. Marlow didn't try to find her in the crowd. She knew Gemma had just been doing what she'd been told to do—tell the truth. It wouldn't have been fair to expect her to lie for them.

"*She* claims it was all a ruse," Grantaire went on. "Is that true?"

Marlow took a breath. "There may have been some aspects of our relationship that the gossip columns got wrong. But my feelings were always real."

She looked at Adrius again and he was looking right back at her, the pain evident on his face.

"Ah," Grantaire said. "And did you have romantic feelings for him before that? When you were living in Evergarden the first time?"

Marlow gritted her teeth, her face heating with the humiliation of having to recount this in front of all of Evergarden. "I did."

"And yet you weren't together then? You were just friends, as you said?"

"That's right."

"Why was that?"

Marlow looked down at her fist, clenched tight in her lap. She couldn't fathom how cruel Grantaire had to be, to make Marlow say it.

"I suppose because Adrius didn't want to be in a relationship with me," Marlow replied.

"Did he tell you that?" Grantaire asked.

"Not in so many words," Marlow answered. "But he made it clear enough."

"How exactly?"

Marlow wanted to rip that stupid smile off Grantaire's face. Instead she gritted her teeth. "Because he stopped talking to me and acted like he wanted nothing to do with me."

"I see," Grantaire said, his tone sympathetic. "That must have been very hurtful."

Marlow didn't say anything. She'd made her peace with what Adrius had done back then. She knew why he'd done it. She didn't even really blame him anymore. Because hadn't he been right, after all? Hadn't they both realized that no matter how much they might want to be with each other, there would always, always be greater forces keeping them apart?

And wasn't it easier, then, to stay away?

"Which brings us back to this counterfeit relationship," Grantaire went on. "Now tell me, Marlow, why would you pretend to date a boy who had humiliated you and betrayed your trust so thoroughly?" He let the question linger, but not for long. "Was it, perhaps, so you could get close to his father? You suspected Aurelius Falcrest had something to do with your mother's disappearance, didn't you?"

"I didn't—it wasn't until later that I suspected him," Marlow stammered.

"But you *did* suspect him," Grantaire said. "You even had proof, didn't you? Sworn testimony from Alleganza Caito states that you had an altercation with her in which you accused her of murdering your mother. Is that true?"

"If you call being followed and attacked an 'altercation,' then yes," Marlow replied dryly.

"Witnesses also say they saw you fleeing Aurelius Falcrest's study the evening before his death," Grantaire said. "What did you two discuss?"

"He handed me a cursed cup of wine and made some veiled threats," Marlow said.

"Threats?" Grantaire asked.

"He said I knew what a dangerous place the world is," Marlow said. "And that there comes a point when courage begins to look like foolishness."

"And you took that as a threat?" Grantaire asked, his brow creased with confusion.

"Well, coupled with the cursed wine, yeah, I guess I kind of read between the lines there," Marlow replied, unable to stop the sarcasm spilling from her mouth.

Grantaire didn't look amused. "Then you showed up at his daughter's wedding the next day—a wedding you most certainly were not invited to. Which the bride, in fact, informed you of and had you escorted out. Why did you go to the wedding, given that your presence was not wanted by the bride herself?"

"I went to see Adrius."

"But you two weren't in a relationship. And even if you were, by your own admission, you two had 'broken up' the night before," Grantaire said.

"I thought he was in danger and I came to warn him," Marlow said. "In danger from his father."

"*Was* he?"

"No," Marlow admitted. "I was wrong."

"But you still poisoned Adrius against his father, didn't you?"

"I'm pretty sure Aurelius did a fine job of poisoning his son against him himself."

Grantaire smiled. "It sounds an awful lot like your grudge against Aurelius was about more than just your mother."

Grantaire was taking his godsdamned time with his questioning, and Marlow just wanted to be *done*. This was all a farce anyway. Her fate was already decided.

"Look," she said. "Did I like Aurelius Falcrest? No. He was a bully and a bad father and overall a pretty terrible person. I'm hardly the only person sitting in this room who knows that. But I didn't murder him."

Grantaire smiled mildly. He strolled back over to the prosecution's table and picked something up.

"Miss Briggs," he said, placing a sheathed knife in front of her. "Can you please tell me what this is?"

Marlow stared at the knife. *Her* knife. The exact knife they needed for their spell. Her hands twitched in her lap.

"A knife."

"*Your* knife," Grantaire corrected her. "Isn't it?"

"Yes."

"And this was also the knife that dealt a mortal wound to Aurelius Falcrest," Grantaire went on. "Is that correct?"

Marlow gritted her teeth. "Yes."

"And why *did* you have this knife with you? I don't know how they do things in the Marshes, but as far as I'm aware, wedding guests in Evergarden generally don't come armed," Grantaire said. The crowd tittered at the jab.

"I told you, I was there to protect Adrius," Marlow said.

"A boy you weren't dating. A boy who broke your heart—twice—and humiliated you. Even if he was in danger, as you say, why would any of us believe that you would protect him?"

For the first time since Marlow had sat down, she let herself look at Adrius. He was staring right back at her, his golden eyes aflame.

"Because," Marlow said, without taking her eyes off his. "Because I love him. Because no matter what happened in the past between us, I forgive him. Because if the choice were mine, if there was nothing standing in our way, I'd want to be with him. Because I will always do everything in my power to protect him."

It was a relief, to finally say it. Gemma was right, after all—there was pride in putting the truth out there. Even if it changed nothing.

Adrius stood from his seat abruptly. For a moment Marlow thought he was about to walk out of the courtroom, but instead he said, loud enough for all the court to hear, "Marlow didn't kill my father."

"Adrius, don't—"

"I did."

Stunned silence rang through the courtroom.

"Marlow Briggs is innocent," Adrius went on. "She has been covering for me this entire time. I'm the real murderer. I killed my father. My only regret is that I didn't come forward sooner."

"Your Honor," Grantaire protested. "This is ridiculous. This is clearly just a last-ditch effort to waste our time with this nonsense. No matter what this boy says, we have more than proven our case against Miss Briggs."

The judge tapped his gavel. "Let's have some order and some propriety, please," he said irritably. "This is a courtroom, not a—"

The doors flew open. Vale stood at the threshold. Hope soared in Marlow's chest.

But then she took in the full picture of him. The cursemarks on his arms—cursemarks Marlow had seen only once, in the Mirror of Truth—were fully visible, like tendrils of shadow wrapping around his arms, his neck, even feathering the sides of his face. And his *eyes*—they were no longer the stormy gray that matched Marlow's, but glowing a luminescent green.

There was a book tucked under one of his arms. Marlow had never seen it before, but she knew instantly what it was. It was thick, bound with black leather and embossed with curling gold designs. The same black tendrils wove around it, tethering it to Vale.

Ilario's Grimoire.

"Excuse me!" the judge exclaimed with more heat. "We will *not* tolerate these unauthorized interrupt—"

"*Silence,*" Vale said with a wave of his hand.

And to the shock of the entire courtroom, the judge went silent.

Calmly, Vale made his way down the aisle to the center of the room. "This court is corrupt and illegitimate. I'll be taking over from here."

Marlow's mind went white with panic.

Swift locked eyes with Marlow. The expression on his face said it all.

Something had gone very, very wrong.

"Cormorant," Zeno Morandi said darkly. "You can't do this, and you know it."

"Is that right?" Vale asked. "Will you be stopping me, then? *Sit down,* Zeno."

Zeno sat, his craggy face alight with alarm and horror at his own obedience.

It wasn't a spell. Silencing the judge hadn't been a spell, either. Vale was simply . . . issuing orders.

And reality itself was obeying.

Vale had cast his spell. They were too late.

THIRTY-SEVEN

"*Things are going* to be different around here," Vale said to the room at large. "It's about time someone fixed the rot that has taken hold of this city."

"And you think you're the man to do it?" Grantaire asked.

Vale turned slowly toward him. "As opposed to whom? You, Emery?"

Grantaire smiled.

"I did find you useful, once," Vale admitted. "But then you made a grave error—you tried to get my daughter killed."

Grantaire paled. "I—I don't know what you mean."

"Rest assured, I will not tolerate anyone who goes after my family," Vale said. "*Turn around.*"

Grantaire obeyed, turning toward the wall of windows behind them.

"*Walk,*" Vale commanded. "*And don't stop walking.*"

Grantaire marched forward. "No," he pleaded. "Please, don't—"

Marlow saw what was going to happen. She squeezed her eyes shut as Grantaire collided with the plate-glass window. She heard it shatter, and then the gasps and cries of horror from the crowd that followed.

When she opened her eyes, all she saw was the jagged edge of the window, smeared with blood where Grantaire had walked directly through it and fallen to his death.

Panic choked the rest of the room as the crowd realized just what Vale was now capable of.

"There's no need to be afraid," Vale said. "I assure you, Emery Grantaire deserved what he got. He was a rat and a liar and the worst kind of corruption that plagues this city."

The crowd panicked anyway, droves of people fleeing toward the exits, screams filling the courtroom.

Thinking quickly, Marlow reached out and snatched her knife from where it sat on the witness table in front of her. She ducked low to the ground and, while Vale's back was turned, darted over to Swift.

"The Five Families must be relieved of the outsized power they wield, for the good of the city," Vale said. "Amara Falcrest. Zeno Morandi. Dahlia Starling. *Step forward.*"

From the chaos of the courtroom, the three other heads of the Five Families stepped toward Vale.

Marlow's stomach twisted. What was Vale going to do to them? The same thing he'd done to Grantaire? To the Copperheads? Something worse?

"*Kneel,*" Vale commanded. "Your spell libraries will now be under my control."

"We need to get out of here," Swift hissed.

"Not without Adrius," Marlow said firmly. She nodded toward the door. "You get out of here and get to the Mudskipper. Take this to Fisher." She held out the knife. "We'll be right behind you."

Swift hesitated, but Marlow shoved the knife at him and gave him a little push, and then he was joining the mayhem, scrambling out the door.

"It's time to prepare for a new era," Vale declared. "I will lead us all to a fairer and more just Caraza."

Marlow spotted Adrius crouched amidst the shattered glass and debris. She crawled her way over to him.

As soon as she was close enough, Adrius pulled her into him. "Are you all right?"

Marlow nodded. "I'm fine. But we need to get out of here."

Adrius's gaze strayed over to Amara, where she knelt at Vale's feet with the other heads of the Five Families.

"He's not going to hurt her," Marlow said, with more conviction than she felt. "We're the only ones with any chance of stopping him. We have to go *now*."

Adrius sucked in a breath and nodded. "Yes, you're—you're right. Okay."

Grabbing Adrius's hand, Marlow pulled them both to their feet and made a break for the door.

The hallway was a rushing stream of people fleeing the courtroom. She gripped Adrius's hand tight as they fought across the current of panicked people.

"Minnow!"

Marlow turned to find her mother emerging from the crowd to join them.

"What are you doing?" Marlow demanded.

"What I should've done before," Cassandra replied. "Protecting you. We can go—we can get out of the city. But we have to go now."

"*Go?*" Marlow said. "*That's* your solution? You want to run again?"

Cassandra's expression was steely. "We don't have a choice."

"You are the reason Vale has the grimoire in the first place," Marlow spat. "You *gave* it to him. This is on you."

"I never should have trusted him," Cassandra said. "I know that now. If I'd had any idea he was capable of this—"

"Marlow," Adrius cut in. "We need to go."

Marlow nodded. "You're right. Mom, you're coming with us."

"Where are we going?" Cassandra asked.

Marlow smiled grimly. "To see some old friends of yours."

"So, " Viatriz said as Marlow, Adrius, and Cassandra stumbled down the stairs to the Black Orchid's spell workshop, "I guess you're *not* dead, after all."

She was glaring at Cassandra, and she wasn't the only one. Fisher also looked none too pleased to see her.

"Viatriz," Cassandra greeted her coolly.

"Can we get to the reunions later?" Marlow asked. "We have slightly more pressing issues right now. Such as how the hell we're going to finish this spell and stop Vale. He's already getting access to the other spell libraries as we speak. He'll have the entire city bent to his will before nightfall if we don't do something."

"What do you propose we do?" Fisher said. "We're still missing a spell ingredient."

"Will our spell even still work?" Swift asked. "I mean, now that he's already cast *his* spell, is it too late?"

Fisher shook his head hesitantly. "No, I don't think so."

"You don't *think* so?" Adrius demanded.

"The spell isn't actually cast on Vale," Fisher explained. "It's cast on the grimoire itself. The *grimoire* is what gives him control. But Vale is able to use that power by putting some of his own blood within its pages, effectively tethering him to the grimoire's power. So theoretically, if we destroy the grimoire, it *should* end his control and destroy the spell for good."

"But that's only if we can do it without Vale knowing what's happening," Swift said grimly. "Because the second he realizes, he can just . . . command *our* spell not to work."

Fisher nodded.

"But none of this really matters," Adrius cut in. "Unless we can get the final ingredient, right?"

"Can't we just . . . figure out a loophole?" Marlow asked. "Like we did with the blade?"

"I'm afraid not. The only way to destroy the grimoire is with the remains of the person who wrote it. And we're no closer to figuring out where to find that than we were a month ago."

"The remains of the person who wrote the grimoire?" Cassandra asked. "*Ilario's* remains?"

Marlow whirled on her. "Do you know something about them?"

"Not . . . exactly," Cassandra said. "But when I was trying to track down the grimoire in Falcrest Library, the spellwright Montagne let slip that the Falcrests had other artifacts belonging to Ilario. Maybe that includes his remains."

"Of *course*," Marlow breathed. "Ilario was so obsessed with protecting his grimoire, he probably made sure he was buried with it. Which means however the Falcrests got their hands on it, they must've gotten their hands on his bones, too."

"But Falcrest Library is the size of a city," Fisher said. "Where would we even start looking for something like that?"

"I don't know," Cassandra admitted. "But Montagne might."

Marlow shook her head. "Montagne's not going to give us any answers in the state he's in. Caito took his memories."

And then the real answer bloomed in Marlow's mind.

And apparently in Cassandra's as well, because at once they both said, "*Caito.*"

"She was the closest thing Aurelius Falcrest had to a confidant," Cassandra said. "If anyone would know if the Falcrests kept Ilario's remains, it's her."

"You're right," Adrius said, a note of unease in his voice. "Caito said it herself—there was no one my father trusted more than her."

"Well, she's not exactly either of our biggest fan," Marlow said. "But it's the best chance we've got of finishing this spell. We have to try."

"I can talk to her," Adrius said. "I can convince her to help."

Marlow locked eyes with him and nodded. She didn't know if Caito would listen to him, but out of everyone, he had the best shot of swaying her. He was the son of the man she'd sworn her loyalty to—maybe that would count for something.

"Okay," Marlow said. "Adrius will go find Caito and convince her to help us. The rest of you will gather up all the spell ingredients we already have and meet them at Falcrest Library. We can finish the spell there."

"Wait," her mother said. "There's something I need to do."

Marlow clamped down on her frustration. "We don't have time—"

"Minnow," Cassandra said with so much emotion in her voice that Marlow fell silent. "Please, just—just listen."

She reached out and stroked her fingers through Marlow's hair, the way she'd done so many times before. It made something open up inside Marlow, a well of longing for the past version of herself who had never found out the truth about her mother, who still believed there was no problem Cassandra couldn't solve.

"I know . . . I know I haven't always been there for you," Cassandra said haltingly. "I know you think I abandoned you, but the truth is I thought you'd be better off without *me*. I've messed up my own life so many times. I don't want that to happen for you."

"Mom—" Marlow began, but Cassandra cut her off.

"You deserve to have everything you want for your life," Cassandra said. "And I meant what I offered before. I'll give up my heart's most hidden desire so you don't have to."

"Mom, *no*."

"You were right, Marlow," Cassandra said. "The only reason Vale has the grimoire is because of me. This is the least I could do." She looked over at Fisher. "You know what to do."

Fisher nodded hesitantly.

"Mom . . ." Marlow closed her eyes. "What . . . what is it? Your heart's most hidden desire? Is it . . . Vale?"

Cassandra shook her head. She stroked her thumb over Marlow's cheek. The gesture was so tender, Marlow felt like she was seven years old again, listening to her mother's stories of schemes and close calls, listening to her deep, full-throated laugh. "It doesn't matter what it is."

Marlow swallowed. She was right. It didn't matter. Marlow would *never* solve the mystery of her mother. She would never understand her completely.

But that didn't mean she didn't still love her.

Viatriz cleared her throat. "All right. So Cassandra will stay here with us. We'll gather the rest of the spell ingredients and meet you at Falcrest Library."

The rest of them nodded and started to disperse. Adrius reached for Marlow's wrist, halting her.

"Don't think I didn't catch that," Adrius said. "You said *the rest of you*. What are you going to do?"

Marlow set her jaw. "I'm going to get the grimoire from Vale."

"That's a bad idea," Swift said at once.

"He's right," Adrius said. "You can't go alone. It's too dangerous."

"That's why I *have* to go alone," Marlow said. "I'm the only person here that Vale won't hurt."

Adrius held on to her wrist. "Are you sure of that? I mean—he's your father, but he's—"

"He won't hurt me," Marlow said with conviction. "Please, just—trust me."

"Do you even know where he is?" Viatriz asked. "He could be anywhere in the city."

"Vale vowed to take down the Five Families and get rid of the street gangs," Marlow replied. "He already took out the Copperheads. That means the Reapers are next."

"So you're going to Reaper Island?" Swift asked. He exchanged a worried glance with Fisher. "Marlow, I *really* don't like this. At least let me go with you."

Marlow shook her head. "This is something I have to do alone."

THIRTY-EIGHT

Walking through the front gate of Falcrest Hall felt like walking into the jaws of a beast. Adrius had vowed not to return here twice before, but each time he'd found himself back within its walls. Maybe he was a fool to believe it would ever truly relinquish its grasp on him.

He tried not to think about Marlow, going to face Vale alone, as he ascended the staircase. Surprise and relief rushed over him as he caught sight of Amara on the landing. Despite everything, she was still his sister.

She looked just as surprised to see him. "Adrius?"

He had the sudden urge to pull her into a hug. He didn't think they'd embraced since they were children.

"You're all right?" he asked. "Vale didn't hurt you?"

She shook her head. "He just ordered me to return here, and not to leave. Adrius, it's just like I said, he—he's going to take *everything*."

Adrius pressed his lips together. "I'm not going to let that happen."

She narrowed her eyes. "And what exactly are *you* going to do?"

Adrius wanted to laugh. Even now, Amara couldn't imagine that Adrius was capable. He had no interest in trying to prove himself to her—to anyone, anymore.

Instead he asked, "Where's Caito?"

"What? What does Caito have to do with—"

But Adrius didn't bother to hear the rest because Caito had emerged into the hall behind Amara.

"Caito!" Adrius called, bolting toward her.

"What can I do for you, Adrius?" she asked in a flat tone.

For as long as Caito had been working for Aurelius, Adrius had had very few interactions with the woman. She kept to herself, attended to Aurelius's orders, and generally made it clear she had no interest in interacting with either of his children. For Adrius's part, she had always somewhat creeped him out, with her piercing stare and affectless demeanor.

And now that he knew the role she'd helped play in keeping his mother imprisoned, Adrius couldn't say his opinion of her had improved.

"I need you to tell me if Falcrest Library has the remains of the sorcerer Ilario," Adrius said.

Amara shot him a look of bewilderment, but Adrius kept his gaze trained on Caito.

"If anyone would know, aside from my father, it's you," Adrius went on. It stung to admit it, but he realized now that Caito was the only person in the world his father ever truly trusted. He'd never trusted either of his children. But Caito—maybe she was what he'd always wanted Adrius and Amara to be. Ruthless, cunning, and without weakness.

Caito's eyes narrowed. "Why would you want to know that?"

"Because we need it to stop Vale," Adrius replied.

Caito scoffed. "*We?*"

"You were loyal to my father for a reason, right?" Adrius asked. "Vale is the reason he's dead."

Caito's eyes flashed dangerously. And that was when Adrius knew. Caito had claimed her loyalty to Aurelius was a simple calculation—he had power and he knew how to keep it. So she had made herself indispensable to him. More essential than his own children.

But in some twisted way, that ruthless, self-serving loyalty had transformed into something else. Caito had dedicated her entire life to helping

Aurelius achieve his dark goals. Even if she didn't bear the Falcrest name, she had a better claim to Aurelius's legacy than any of them.

"He trusted you, Caito," Adrius said, almost pleading now. "Until his very last breath, he trusted you wouldn't let him down."

Caito's lips thinned into a terse line. "All right. I'll take you to Ilario's remains."

Adrius nodded, once, and started to leave.

Amara grabbed his arm, pulling him back to look her straight in the eye. "You had better stop him, brother. I'll die before Vale takes control of our family's library."

Stopping Vale was about so much more than that, but Amara had made it clear time and again where her priorities lay. She released him, and then Adrius turned and walked out of Falcrest Hall.

Fisher, Swift, and Viatriz were waiting for them at the gate to Falcrest Library. They each wore a satchel slung over their shoulders.

"You didn't mention this was a group outing, Adrius," Caito sneered.

"We need them," Adrius replied firmly. To Swift, he asked, "You have everything?"

Swift patted his satchel.

"Let's go, then," Adrius said, and led the way through the great black archway that would take them inside Falcrest Library.

The five of them stepped through the portal and instantly found themselves on a landing in the middle of the library's vast atrium.

Fisher, Viatriz, and Swift were all staring up at the zigzagging walkways and tessellated staircases with something like awe.

"What?" Adrius asked, impatient.

Fisher was the first to shake himself out of it. "I've never been in here before. I knew it was huge, but . . . this place is surreal."

Adrius knew what he meant. Falcrest Library was so large that its true size couldn't fit inside Caraza without some very clever enchantments to make the library's actual footprint much smaller than the space contained within it. The result was this—a central concourse composed of impossible walkways and staircases, where you might at any moment find yourself in a completely new geometric relationship with the space around you.

He remembered when he'd taken Marlow here, what felt like ages ago. She'd hated the way the atrium made her question which way was up or down.

"Stay close," Caito advised. "Ilario's remains are hidden deep inside the library. Wouldn't want anyone to get lost."

The last part was said with just a hint of sarcasm.

They set off, traversing the strange puzzle of the atrium. An elevator rocketed them up through what felt like endless levels of crisscrossing paths and stairs. The enchantments on the library had been designed such that you should have been able to get almost anywhere in the library with virtual ease—since everything in the library was crammed on top of itself in complicated configurations.

But wherever Caito was taking them was clearly not so easy to access. They wandered through hallways and across courtyards. At one point Adrius became convinced they were somehow underwater.

Finally, they reached the entrance of a cavernous antechamber of black marble, with archways surrounding them on every side.

"All right," Caito said, coming to a halt. "This is it."

"This place feels like a mausoleum," Swift said with a shudder.

"It *is* a mausoleum," Fisher said, pointing up at a carving above the central archway that read *Mausoleum of the Falcrests.*

"This isn't the Falcrest Mausoleum," Adrius said. He'd just *been* to his family's mausoleum, not a week ago, when his father was entombed there. Yet as he walked around the antechamber, he could see each archway was labeled with the name of a Falcrest ancestor. Unease prickled over him.

"It used to be," Caito replied. "They moved it outside the library a few generations ago. But this was the original mausoleum."

Swift raised his hand. "Does anyone else think it's weird that Ilario's remains would be inside the original Falcrest mausoleum?"

"Maybe not," Fisher said faintly, standing in front of the very last archway.

Another shiver crawled up Adrius's spine as he hurried over to where Fisher stood. Carved into the black marble above the archway were the words *The Tomb of Ilario Falcrest, Founder of Falcrest Library.*

Adrius stared up at them, unable to grasp any sense of meaning from the words.

Vaguely, he felt Swift join him there.

"Ilario *Falcrest?*" Swift said in disbelief.

"Adrius, did you know about this?" Fisher asked in a hushed tone.

Adrius just shook his head, unable to speak. Ilario, the person who had invented the Compulsion curse, one of the most evil and reviled sorcerers in history, was his *ancestor.*

The corruption in the Falcrest family went back further than Adrius ever knew. Theirs was a tree that was rotted at the root.

"Should we . . . go in?" Viatriz asked.

Adrius squared his shoulders and stepped through the archway and into the tomb. It was a round, vaulted room made entirely of the same black marble the archway was cut from. In the middle of the room sat a white marble sarcophagus, covered in a thick layer of dust.

Adrius went to one edge of the sarcophagus, which he realized was just a simple stone box with a heavy slab top.

"Help me move this," he said.

Fisher, Viatriz, and Swift each took a side, and together, with great effort, they slid the top open. A cloud of dust plumed up from the sarcophagus. Adrius stumbled back, shutting his eyes and coughing violently.

"Grave robbers."

Adrius nearly leapt out of his skin at the sound of the gravelly, creaking voice. He whirled. The particles of dust had resolved into a shape—an almost human shape, although it looked half-beast. Two sharp, curved horns protruded from its head. Its eyes glowed red.

"Grave robbers," the phantom rasped again.

Swift clutched at Adrius's arm. "Please tell me that's not a ghost."

It had taken Adrius a moment, but he recognized the figure now. Marlow had made him read a dozen books about Ilario the Terrible. He knew Ilario was said to have worn a horned crown, and some accounts of him included glowing red eyes.

It *was* a ghost. Ilario's ghost.

"It's not a ghost," Fisher said. "It's an enchantment. Look." He pointed at a stone tablet carved into the end of the sarcophagus. There were carvings in the stone tablet that glowed like spellcard glyphs.

"Ilario must've created this enchantment before he died, to ward people off from doing . . . exactly what we're trying to do," Fisher said.

"Steal from my grave and you will be cursed forevermore."

Adrius shivered. Enchantment or ghost, the specter spoke with Ilario's voice.

"We really should have guessed that a sorcerer famous for inventing curses would have cursed his own tomb," Viatriz said. "What do we do now?"

Adrius looked at the others, dismay written across their faces. They'd come so far, and gotten so close. Vale *couldn't* win.

And if that meant someone had to be cursed for an eternity, then it was better that it was Adrius. Ilario was his ancestor. This was his legacy.

He stepped toward the sarcophagus.

"Are you kidding me?" Swift demanded, yanking him back. "Marlow will *kill* me if you get cursed again."

Adrius shook his head. "I have to do this. If Vale wins, then the entire city is cursed. Better that it's just me."

"*My mortal body may be rotting inside this coffin,*" the phantom croaked. "*But my power and my magic live on. My spirit will haunt whoever trespasses into my tomb.*"

"You *really* want to have *that* hanging over you for the rest of your life?" Swift demanded.

Adrius shook him off. "If I have to."

He stepped toward the tomb again. Peered into the dark compartment. Bones and dust lay at the bottom.

"*I will be your constant companion,*" the spirit hissed. "*Wherever you go, I will go. I will never leave your side until the day you die.*"

Adrius paused. Slowly, he turned to Fisher. "How does an enchantment like this work?"

"Well," Fisher said uncertainly. "Before he died, Ilario would've had to imbue an object—in this case, a stone tablet—with some of his own essence."

"So this"—Adrius gestured at the phantom—"is really him?"

"In a sense," Fisher replied.

Adrius smiled grimly. "Any of you have a chisel?"

"What for?" Viatriz asked.

"We don't need Ilario's bones," Adrius replied. "We need whatever *remains* of him. And it sounds like this—enchanted ghost, or whatever it is, fits the bill."

Viatriz glanced at Fisher.

"He's right," Fisher said, sounding surprised. "It will work for the spell."

"Here," Swift said, reaching into his bag and handing Adrius a knife and a small mallet from the spell ingredients satchel.

Carefully, Adrius placed the edge of the knife against the bottom of the tablet and began chiseling it from the sarcophagus lid, while Ilario's spirit castigated him for desecrating his tomb.

When he was done, Adrius wrapped the enchanted tablet in a spare cloth and shoved it back in Swift's bag.

"Does that mean he's also coming with us?" Swift asked with a wary glance at Ilario's spirit, who was still shrieking at Adrius in anguish for profaning his grave.

"Looks that way," Adrius said. "Let's go make a spell."

THIRTY-NINE

Reaper Island was silent as Marlow pulled up to the dock. Usually there were patrols by foot and boat to ward off unwanted visitors, but no one stopped Marlow from simply mooring her boat and walking along the plankway to the mansion.

If she'd been unsure about her assumption that Vale would be here, that uncertainty was long gone now. The only question that remained was whether she was too late.

Mist wreathed the crumbling mansion. Despite the heavy heat of the air, Marlow shivered. She didn't want to know what kind of scene waited for her within. Images of the Copperheads' twisted, mangled bodies flashed through her mind. Marlow choked down her nausea.

She entered the sunken mansion through the same second-story balcony she'd come through on her first visit. She was only just through the door when she saw the first body. A man, lying on his side, face pressed into the tile floor.

There was nothing gruesome or horrific about the body, only that he was clearly dead. Marlow didn't even see any blood on him. Another body lay a few paces away, also untouched.

But the bodies were all the more chilling for their lack of visible wounds. With the power of Ilario's spell, Vale could have easily commanded their hearts to simply stop beating. They would have been dead before they'd even hit the ground.

She had to step over a third body that was slumped in the doorway. More bodies lay scattered along the mezzanine, a trail of them, leading to Vale.

His back was to Marlow. The black, shadowy tendrils tethering him to the grimoire shifted and slid around his arms.

In front of him stood Lady Bianca. She was weeping, her son Elio clutched in her arms.

"*Give him to me,*" Vale commanded.

Bianca choked out a sob, trembling as she held the child out to him.

"Don't!" Marlow couldn't stop the desperate cry from leaving her lips.

Vale lifted Elio into his arms, cradling him gently to his chest. He turned to face Marlow.

"Don't hurt him," Marlow pleaded, stepping toward them.

"Hurt him?" Vale echoed. "You think I would harm a child? Do you believe I'm some kind of monster?"

Marlow met his glowing gaze. "Yes."

Vale's face crumpled with hurt. "I have only ever wanted to keep you safe," he said softly. "Don't you see that? Don't you see that this is the only way to protect you from the dangers of this world?"

"You've killed dozens of people in cold blood," Marlow said.

Vale's expression hardened. "Only those who deserved it."

"And you're the one who gets to decide that?" Marlow asked. "What about my mother? She's conned people and extorted spellwrights for *years.* Are you going to kill her, too?"

"Marlow," Vale said, an edge of frustration in his voice.

He set down Elio, who crawled immediately over to his mother. Bianca scooped him into her arms and stumbled back against the wall.

Vale paid them no mind. "Don't pretend you don't understand the difference between her and these people."

"Then what about the innocent people you've hurt?" Marlow demanded. "What about Adrius? Who else are you willing to sacrifice?"

"That is the point, Marlow," Vale said. "Now that I have this power, there will be no need to sacrifice the innocent on the altar of greed."

"There's another way," Marlow said. "You want to do good in this city and you *can*. Just not like this. The spellbook you're using is full of dark magic. The spell you cast was created by a man motivated by nothing more than a hunger for power. That's not you—I *know* it isn't."

She knew Vale wasn't driven solely by a selfish hunger for power. Nor was he driven solely by good. He was like the brackish water of the Marshes—not purely one thing or the other, but a mix of them both.

Some part of her still wanted to believe there was enough good in him to win out.

"Magic is just a tool," Vale replied. "And in my hands—the *right* hands—it can be used for good. I'm so close to making this city what it should be."

"And then what?" Marlow asked. "Will you let this spell go? Will you destroy the grimoire like it should have been destroyed? When do you stop?"

Vale shook his head. "You still don't understand, do you? It is only the existence of this power, the threat of it, that can keep this city in line. Without it, people's darker natures will always prevail. Deep down, you know that. Some people are simply irredeemable—and it is people like *us* who must keep them in line."

"And who keeps you in line?" Marlow asked. "Who is it that makes sure you don't go too far? That you won't become like Aurelius, or even Ilario himself?"

"Is that what you're afraid of?" Vale asked, his voice softening. "I could have easily killed the other heads of the Five Families. But I spared them. I am not a monster, Marlow. Perhaps this power scares you, but you will see, in time, that everything I have done will be worth it."

Marlow swallowed. "If you want me to believe that, then swear to me that you won't kill anyone else. No matter how irredeemable they may be."

Vale bowed his head. "I suppose that's fair. Very well. I swear to it."

Marlow was stunned by his simple agreement. Maybe he wasn't as far gone as she thought. Stopping Vale completely meant handing the city back to the Five Families and the gangs. But maybe there was a way to use the grimoire's power—use *Vale*. After what she'd seen him do to the Copperheads, she'd been so terrified by his brutality that she'd failed to see that the key to it was *her*.

She had the power to temper his worst impulses.

"Let's—let's go back to Vale Tower," Marlow said. "You can explain it all to me. Properly. Everything you want to do with this power."

His eyes suddenly narrowed, suspicious.

Unease roiled in Marlow's stomach.

"Oh . . ." Vale said softly. "I see now. You didn't come here to reason with me at all. You came here to *stall* me. *Tell me the truth. Why did you come here?*"

If Marlow had ever wondered, late at night, how Adrius had felt in that moment she had ordered him to divulge his secrets to her, she didn't have to wonder anymore. Words spilled from her mouth with no hope of holding them back.

"I came to get the grimoire," Marlow said. "We're creating a spell to destroy it."

"We?" Vale echoed. "Who is we? *Tell me who you are working with.*"

"The Black Orchid," Marlow replied, unable to stop the answer from coming. "Dominic Fisher. Swift. Adrius."

"*Tell me where they are now,*" Vale commanded.

Marlow tried to choke back the words, but Vale's power gripped her, forcing them from her throat. "Falcrest Library."

Vale made a noise of frustration, waving an arm through the air. "*Open to Falcrest Library.*"

There was a strange ripping noise, and then the air in front of Vale tore in two. In a space that had once been empty, Marlow saw, as if through a doorway, the twisting labyrinth of the Falcrest Library atrium.

Before Marlow could even comprehend what had just happened, Vale stepped *into* the atrium.

The ragged edges of the portal—or whatever it was—began to close. Without pausing to think, Marlow threw herself after him.

FORTY

The Falcrest spellcraft laboratory was a vast, capacious hall with a soaring ceiling, the floor gridded with hundreds of spellcrafting circles. A lit brazier blazed in the center of each circle. It was at one of these that Fisher had been standing with their spell ingredients along with a dozen different tools, for the past hour.

The rest of them—Adrius, Swift, Viatriz, and Caito—stood on the perimeter of the spellcrafting circle, watching him work, along with Ilario's phantom enchantment, which had been dragged along with them for the ride by the tablet Adrius had carved from the tomb. Adrius was impressed by Fisher's knife-sharp concentration, even as the phantom hurled abuses at him.

"*You, pitiful child, will never succeed in destroying my grimoire,*" the phantom crowed. "*I am the greatest sorcerer who ever lived. My legacy has survived five hundred years, and it will survive five hundred more!*"

Impatience itched at Adrius—he did not want to be here, watching what looked like incredibly tedious work, listening to the mad ranting of a ghost. He wanted to be with Marlow. But this was what she had tasked him to do, and he would just have to trust that she was right about Vale—that he wouldn't hurt her.

Fisher had just finished feeding the third ingredient—poison from a dart frog—into the brazier, when the entire room began to shake.

"Is that supposed to be happening?" Swift whispered.

"No," Viatriz said at once, her gaze going to the ceiling.

"It's an intruder," Caito said, in the same passionless tone she said everything. "Someone is messing with the enchantments on the library, trying to tunnel through the concourse instead of following the correct path."

"Vale?" Swift asked.

"He must have figured out what we're doing," Adrius said. "He's trying to find us."

Swift cleared his throat. "Uh, Fisher? Any way we could speed this up?"

The room shook harder.

"It takes as long as it takes," Fisher replied, half-apologetic and half-irritated. He fed Swift's nightmare into the flames. The flames flickered black, and a flash of images appeared in them—two cruel, grinning faces. A sudden, wrenching pain shot through Adrius. He cried out, but then it was over just as soon as it had begun. He glanced around, realizing he hadn't been the only one affected. Swift was paler than Ilario's ghost.

"Just two more," Fisher told them through gritted teeth.

He fed Marlow's mother's heart's desire to the flames next. A sudden, potent despair swirled through Adrius, and then dissipated.

Finally, Fisher held up the tablet Adrius had carved from Ilario's tomb. As he held it to the flame, the phantom let out a terrible, inhuman shriek that rattled Adrius's bones. Blue flames engulfed the specter, and then disappeared into a cloud of smoke.

The flames in the brazier leapt and then calmed again.

Fisher dipped a stylus into the ashes below the blue flames and then crouched on the ground, writing out a spiral of glyphs around the brazier.

"He's getting closer," Caito warned.

"Almost done," Fisher replied through gritted teeth. The stylus trembled in his hand as he wrote out the last arm of the spiral. The entire thing lit up with bright-blue light. The flames in the brazier roared higher, so bright, Adrius and the others had to shield themselves from the heat and the radiance.

Fisher pulled out the final ingredient—Marlow's knife. He held it into the flames. The blue glyphs on the ground began to swirl in dizzying spirals, ribboning around the blade. And with a mighty gust, the flames extinguished.

"It's done," Fisher said, holding the knife, which now glowed a faint blue. He glanced around at the others. "We might only get one shot at this."

"It should be Adrius," Swift said. He locked eyes with him for a moment, in which a sense of understanding passed over Adrius. "He's the one Vale cursed in the first place. And his mother is still under the same curse. He should be the one to destroy the grimoire."

Fisher held the knife out. Adrius closed his fingers around the handle. He could still remember how it had felt in his hand when he'd plunged it into his father's chest. He might always be haunted by that memory, but now he *knew*—it hadn't been his fault. It hadn't been his choice. But this—this was. Severing Vale's power. Making it so that he would never be able to control someone the way he'd controlled Adrius.

He nodded at Swift. "I'll do it."

The room shook again.

"Let's get out there before he turns this whole place inside out," Viatriz said. They hurried from the laboratory into the vast hallway outside. The walls and doors along it flickered in and out as they walked, the hallway growing longer and then shorter, as if it could not decide what it was.

"This way," Adrius said, leading them up a set of stairs that seemed to stretch up endlessly, until at last they spilled out into the atrium.

Adrius spotted Marlow before he spotted Vale. She was racing along one of the walkways, but it kept changing directions in front of her.

"There's Vale," Viatriz said, but Adrius had already taken off running.

It was futile trying to navigate the ever-shifting pathways across the atrium, but Adrius did it anyway, cutting a haphazard route toward Marlow. It was as he approached the end of a walkway that dropped off in a sheer ninety-degree angle that he finally spotted Vale. He stood on the landing of a long, diagonal staircase. He wasn't moving—instead, the atrium's crisscrossing paths moved around *him*.

"Adrius!" Marlow cried. She was about two levels above him, on a pathway that ran almost vertical to his own. Adrius looked up and saw a steep staircase above him. He shut his eyes and leapt, not knowing if the ground would be there to meet him.

The world turned over on itself. He landed hard on the stairs, stumbling up a few steps before he opened his eyes. Marlow stood on the landing above him, her hand flung out to him. Adrius grabbed it, and she pulled him toward her.

"Did you do it?" she asked, eyes burning.

Adrius nodded, touching the hilt of the knife.

All at once, the atrium stopped shifting around them. The landing Adrius and Marlow stood on lifted toward Vale. From the corner of his eye, Adrius saw the walkway the others were on reorient toward him, too.

"I know that you all have come here to try to stop me," Vale said. "But you should know, not only is that endeavor futile, it is contrary to all your interests."

His gaze passed over all of them—Fisher, Swift, Caito, Marlow, Adrius—before pausing on Viatriz.

"And who are you?" he asked.

Viatriz stopped, eyeing Marlow. "Viatriz Darza."

Vale's eyes flicked over her, lingering on her hand. Adrius followed his gaze and saw a black tattoo on her wrist.

"I've heard of you," Vale said slowly. "Your group. What do you call yourselves? The Black Orchid?"

Viatriz nodded.

"I think you'll like my plans for the city."

"I doubt that."

"The Five Families must be relieved of the outsized power they wield," Vale said. "I can do that."

"And then who gets to be in charge?" Viatriz asked. "You?"

Vale smiled. "For the good of the city, I'm willing to take on that role. But don't worry—you and your spellwrights will get a voice in the new order. I only want what's best for this city. For all of us."

Adrius eyed the grimoire tucked under Vale's arm and the ribbons of shadows binding it to him.

"What if he's right?" Marlow asked suddenly. She turned to the others. "This city is never going to change unless someone *makes* it change."

Adrius stared at her in disbelief.

"Because of him, the Copperheads and the Reapers are gone. The Five Families have surrendered their control of the libraries. He says he wants to make the world better, and I . . . I do believe that." She turned back to Vale. "Dad. I believe you."

She took a step toward Vale.

"What are you saying?" Fisher demanded harshly.

"You were right," Marlow said to Vale. "I *am* afraid of what this power can do. But we can't just hand this city back to the Five Families. If we destroy the grimoire now, then everything goes back to the way it was. I don't want that."

Vale placed a hand on her shoulder. "I knew you would understand." He looked back at the others. "Where is the spell to destroy the grimoire? *Show me.*"

To Adrius's horror, he found himself stepping forward.

"I see," Vale said. "*Hand it over.*"

Adrius's hands shook. It was just like being under the Compulsion spell again, his own body betraying him. His own mind, his own *will* rendered a helpless onlooker as he held out the knife to Vale.

Over Vale's shoulder, Marlow met his gaze for a brief, blazing moment.

"*Disarmare!*" she cried.

A bewildered pause ensued as Marlow, Adrius, and Vale all watched the grimoire go sailing out of Vale's hands.

Marlow dove after it.

Vale's eyes darted wildly from the grimoire to the knife. After a split second's hesitation, he snatched the blade from Adrius's hands and lunged after Marlow.

Marlow twisted, throwing her hands out in front of her. The knife clipped her across the arm. Vale froze, face twisted in horror.

The spray of Marlow's crimson blood filled Adrius with white-hot rage. He rammed his shoulder against Vale's chest. Vale reared back, doubling over. Adrius charged again. Vale slashed forward.

The knife caught Adrius just below the ribs. Pain ripped through him. Vale's eyes widened.

Then his expression went flat and hollow as he twisted the knife deeper.

FORTY-ONE

A scream built in Marlow's lungs as she watched the knife go through Adrius. She stumbled to her knees.

Vale let go of the knife, backing away in horror as he watched blood pour from Adrius's chest.

Adrius collapsed. Acting on pure instinct, Marlow stumbled forward to catch him before he hit the ground.

His eyes were open but vacant, staring at nothing. His chest rose and fell with rapid, thin breaths. He had minutes left, if that.

"What did you do?" she asked, tears stinging her vision as she looked wildly up at her father. "*What did you do?*"

"I-it was an accident, Marlow, please—it was an accident," Vale choked. His face was twisted with despair and shock, and Marlow could not tell if it was real.

But it didn't matter. Adrius couldn't die. Marlow wouldn't allow it. She cupped his face in her hand, her thumb brushing over the ridge of his cheekbone, his jaw. *Hold on, Adrius*, she thought fervently. *Please just hold on.*

A weak breath rattled his chest.

This could not be his end. Desperation gripped her.

"I—I can heal him," Vale said suddenly.

Marlow jerked her head up to look at him again. His eyes, gray again instead of that glowing green, were cold and sure.

"I can heal him," he said with more certainty. "I can save him." He took a step toward her. "But you must hand over the grimoire."

Marlow looked down. The grimoire lay open beside her. A smear of blood marred the page. She could see the magic radiating from it—dark glyphs spiraling into tendrils that tethered its power to Vale.

Her gaze drifted over to the knife, glowing bright blue and covered in Adrius's blood.

She could destroy the grimoire now and strip Vale of its power. That was what they'd come here to do. What she'd sworn to do.

But Adrius would die. The light was fading quickly from his eyes. She feared each awful, gurgling breath might be his last.

She had the sudden, unbidden thought that if he died, she would never recover from it. It would be like the sun itself had been extinguished.

There was no choice, no possibility, but to save him. Even if it meant Vale won.

Marlow picked up the grimoire.

"That's it," Vale said gently. "Give me the grimoire and I will save him."

Marlow looked down at the gash in her own arm, blood streaming steadily from the wound. She pressed her palm against the flow of blood.

"Marlow," he said sharply.

Marlow slammed her bloody palm onto the open page of the grimoire. Dark-red glyphs glowed on the page. The grimoire grew warm in her hands as the glyphs surrounded her, suffusing her with the same power it had given Vale. Black tendrils wound up her arms.

"*Don't move,*" she said to him. The spell curled around her words and compelled him to obey.

She went to Adrius's side, no longer frantic, but filled with calm purpose. There was nothing to be troubled about. The spell would allow her to save him.

The spell would allow her to do almost anything.

His brown eyes gazed up at her, unseeing. His chest rose and fell shallowly.

Marlow placed her still-glowing hands over his heart.

"*Heal,*" Marlow commanded the wound in his chest.

The flesh of his chest knitted itself back together. Adrius gasped and sat up, staring down at himself like he couldn't quite believe it. Then he raised his gaze to meet Marlow's, something like awe or maybe fear in his eyes.

"Do it now, Marlow!" she heard Fisher call. "Destroy the grimoire!"

She could. Adrius was all right now. She didn't need its power anymore. She looked down at the spellbook in her hands.

But even if they stopped Vale, even if they took this power from him . . . he was hardly the only thing that plagued this city.

Vale wasn't wrong to say the city needed to be changed. To be *fixed.*

There was still the Five Families. Grantaire himself might be dead, but there were dozens of others just like him, ready to exploit whoever they could to make a few pearls. Corruption grew in every corner of Caraza, Marlow knew that well.

"What are you doing, Marlow?" Swift demanded. "Destroy the grimoire!"

She could feel the grimoire's power pouring into her. Limitless. *Real* power—the kind no one could take away from her.

A way to bend this miserable world to her will.

Vale wasn't the person to fix things. But maybe Marlow was.

How could she give that up? She thought of all the curses she had broken in her life. All the people she had helped. That she had *saved.* She could save countless more with this power. No one would have to live in fear of the gangs, the loan sharks, the predators that stalked every muck-filled canal of the Marshes.

Maybe Vale had been right. Maybe the threat of this power was the only way to ensure that people's darker natures didn't prevail.

The future opened up in front of her, limitless. A future where Swift never had to fear the wrath of the gangs again. Where a bright, brilliant kid like Fisher would never end up caught in the claws of the curse trade. Where someone like Cassandra would never turn to extortion and cons in the name of survival.

Marlow could create that future.

She looked back at Adrius.

He didn't say a word, just stared back at her, his eyes filled with unwavering trust.

And she couldn't help but remember the night she had looked him in the eye and ordered him to tell her the truth for no other reason than because she wanted it and she *could*. Because she'd been hurt and humiliated and terrified that she'd been a fool again. Because she'd wanted some way to wrench control back, to make herself believe she wasn't helpless.

And she remembered the sick feeling that had followed when she'd realized what she'd done. The shame of realizing she'd let her doubts and mistrust goad her into doing something unforgivable.

Her mother had always taught her that the world was divided into victims and survivors. Vale wanted her to believe that it was separated into the righteous, like him, and the irredeemable.

But Marlow knew them both to be wrong. People were mostly some mixture of selfish and selfless, of good and bad. Not purely one thing or the other, but a brackish blend of complicated motives and values.

This power was too great to trust to someone like Vale, who believed himself a savior and could justify any act of violence for the greater good.

It was too great to trust to the Black Orchid, or Fisher, or even Swift.

It was too great for Marlow to trust to herself.

She seized the enchanted knife from the ground and drove it through the grimoire.

Bright-blue flames—flames that felt cold instead of hot on Marlow's skin—engulfed the grimoire. They burned bright and fast, and when they were out, nothing was left of the grimoire except ash.

FORTY-TWO

Adrius stood at the gate of the house in Wisteria Grove and let out a breath. The hours since Marlow had destroyed *Ilario's Grimoire* had been a flurry of activity.

Vale had been quickly detained by Caito and taken back to Falcrest Hall, where he would be a prisoner until the other Five Families decided what to do with him. It wasn't really justice, but it was perhaps as close to it as they could manage for now. Adrius knew Amara would see to it that Vale was punished for his crimes, and the other Five Families would temper her hand.

Destroying the spellbook hadn't just destroyed Vale's spell—it had also significantly weakened the protective enchantments on all the spell libraries. Viatriz and the Black Orchid had moved quickly to secure the library spellbook collections before the Five Families could try to seize them again.

But Adrius's only thought had been of his mother. The moment the grimoire was destroyed, the Compulsion curse that had been placed on her decades ago had finally been lifted. Adrius had come to take her home.

Marlow had offered to go with him, but Adrius had wanted to do this alone.

With measured steps, he made his way across the lawn and up the front steps of the house. Nerves buzzed beneath his skin as he raised his fist and knocked on the door.

"Mother," he said. "It's me. Open the door, please."

There was a long pause, and then he heard the quiet click of the lock. The door creaked open slowly.

His mother stood on the other side, her expression shocked. For almost two decades, the curse had prevented her from opening the front door.

"What . . . how . . . ?"

"You're free, Mom," Adrius said gently. "We . . . we destroyed the spellbook responsible for your curse. There's . . . a lot more I need to tell you, but that's the most important thing. You're free now."

She stared at his face, as if she could not comprehend his words.

He took her hand, held it tight in his. "Come on," he said. "Let's get you out of here."

This house had been a prison to her for so long. Adrius vowed to himself that she would never have to set foot there again.

"Where will we go?" she asked.

He led her over the threshold. "Anywhere you want."

———————————

It was five days before Adrius saw Marlow again. Four days since she'd returned to her tiny, creaking flat above the Bowery Spellshop and left Evergarden behind. Three days since Marlow had been formally acquitted of all charges.

On the fifth day, Adrius sent a note, asking to meet her on the roof of the Malachite Building at midnight.

She was already waiting when he arrived, looking out at the city.

"You know," Marlow said as Adrius approached. "I never really think about it, but from up here, the city is kind of beautiful."

She was right. Even the Marshes was breathtaking, with its dark pocks of floodwaters reflecting the deep purple and turquoise glow of the bioluminescent lamps.

But Adrius's gaze wasn't drawn there, or even to the glittering towers of Evergarden. Instead, it rested firmly on Marlow's face in the pale moonlight.

"My mother's curse is broken," he said. "Thanks to you."

She turned to him. "To *us*. I didn't do any of it alone."

Adrius dipped his head in acknowledgment. "How is your mom?"

Marlow shrugged and looked out toward Tourmaline Bay. "Gone. Left before the dust even settled. It was that or go to jail. I don't blame her for making that choice. She's got too many scores to settle in this city. And I think . . . I think maybe she deserves a fresh start."

Adrius swallowed. "I get that. I think . . . I think my mother does, too. She's been a prisoner so long."

He paused, not quite sure how to voice the next thought. Marlow just looked at him, waiting him out. That searching look on her face.

"I feel like I've been one, too," he said at last. "Evergarden is a prison. This city is. A fresh start would be . . . good."

Marlow nodded. A breeze blew a few strands of her tied-up hair into her face. She tucked them behind her ear.

Adrius's heart kicked in his chest. He didn't get *nervous*, but that was the only word he had for what he felt now.

"There's an airship headed out in three days," he pressed on. "We're going to be on it. My mother and I. Her family has a country home on the Cortesian coast. I think we're going to go there for a while."

"Okay," Marlow said, her voice barely a whisper. Her gray eyes looked resigned.

"You could come with us."

Marlow didn't say anything for a moment, and Adrius barreled on. "I know—I know what you said before. About how you don't run. But it doesn't have to be running. It's like you said. A fresh start. And we—we would be together, without the gossip columns and Evergarden, and we could see the world and leave this place behind. This city—it's never brought you anything but pain."

The look on her face made him stop. She was smiling, but there was something heartbreaking about the expression.

"You're right," she said. "But this city, for all its flaws, made me who I am. And I can't abandon it. I think I belong here—in the muck, in the broken places. Caraza is a part of me, and I'm a part of it. And I want to stay. I want to stay and make things better for whoever I can, however I can."

Adrius knew that this was her answer—he'd known it before he asked.

"If anyone can do it, it's you," he said.

"Adrius, I—" she started. She shook her head. And instead of saying anything else, she reached up and lifted a chain from her neck. At the end of it was a small, heart-shaped bottle filled with softly glowing pink light.

Adrius looked at the bottle and then at her. "Your heart's desire?"

She nodded and held it out to him. "Take it. It's yours, anyway."

He took it, ducking his head into the chain and tucking it beneath his waistcoat. "I guess it's only fair. You stole mine first."

She smiled, but the expression crumpled almost immediately. Her hair was again blowing into her face and Adrius reached out and brushed it away for her.

"I'll keep it safe for you, Minnow," he murmured. And then he couldn't help it—he stepped forward and kissed her.

"Stay to watch the sunrise?" she asked when they parted.

Adrius nodded, and took her hand.

EPILOGUE

Marlow gave her hair one last squeeze to get out as much of the swamp water as possible before shouldering open the front door of the Bowery.

Silvan looked up from a stack of spellcards as she entered. "What the hell happened to you?"

"What does it look like?" Marlow asked irritably. "Where's Swift?"

Silvan put the spellcards back inside their display case. "Somewhere. Doing something." He shrugged. "I'm not his keeper."

"No, but you're his . . . something," Marlow retorted. Swift and Silvan had never really outright defined their relationship, at least not to her, but after eight months, Marlow was running out of hope that Swift would get tired of Silvan the way he had with every other person he'd ever been involved with.

"What are you even doing here, then?" Marlow asked.

"I'm helping," Silvan replied primly.

"No, you're not," Swift replied affectionately, appearing in the doorway to the back room and circling around the counter to drop a kiss into Silvan's hair. He paused when he caught sight of Marlow. "Did you take a swim in the Swamp Market again?"

"Suspect dropped his curse card in the water when he realized I was onto him," Marlow replied.

"Well, did you get it at least?" Swift asked.

She smiled. "Come on, Swift, you're talking to the best cursebreaker in Caraza. Of course I got it."

Just because the Five Families didn't control the libraries anymore didn't mean there weren't still curses out there.

And as long as there were curses, Marlow would go on breaking them.

"Well, you stink," Swift said, plucking a spellcard out of Silvan's hand. "*Ripulire!*"

The light-blue glyphs surrounded Marlow, wiping her clean from all the mud and swamp water and leaving her smelling fresh like flowers.

"Thanks," Marlow said. "How's inventory going?"

Swift sighed. "We're *still* working through the backlog of Hyrum's old system, but I think this is the last time we'll have to deal with the old man's sorry excuse for organization."

Six months ago, Hyrum had abruptly announced he was retiring from running the Bowery and had ceded it all to Swift.

"By the way, did Fisher stop by?" Marlow asked. "He said he'd drop off a few new spellcards for me."

When he wasn't teaching budding new spellwrights with the Black Orchid, Fisher made special wards and hexes to help Marlow on her cases. His way of atoning for all the curses he'd made under the Reapers' thumb. Now instead of making curses, he helped break them.

"Haven't seen him yet," Swift replied. "But I was just upstairs—looks like you have a new client."

"Seriously?" Marlow asked. "It's been nonstop lately."

Swift shrugged. "What did you expect when you stopped charging for your services?"

"I didn't stop charging," Marlow replied. "I still charge. When they're rich."

"You want me to turn them away?" Swift asked.

"No, it's fine," Marlow said, waving him away. "I'll see what they want. And if Fisher stops by—"

"Don't worry, I'll get you your precious spells," Swift replied. He reached out and ruffled Silvan's hair. "I'll send my messenger boy up with them."

Marlow laughed. Silvan batted Swift's hand away. All three of them knew Silvan would not be delivering those spellcards under any circumstances. While he enjoyed hanging around the Bowery to flirt with Swift and irritate Marlow, he was loath to actually make himself *useful*.

"I'll see you two later," Marlow said. She trudged up the rickety stairs to her flat. She may have been clean now thanks to Swift's spell, but that didn't stop her from wanting to sink into a nice, hot bath to wash the day away. Her most recent case had been exhausting, and she rather felt she deserved a long nap—which she'd be taking just as soon as she took down this newest client's information. After all, Swift was always telling her she needed better boundaries around work.

But when she pushed open the door to her flat, what she saw shoved all plans of naps and baths aside.

Someone was sitting at her desk, feet propped up, scratching a very happy Toad between the ears.

Someone she hadn't seen in eight months.

Adrius's skin was sun-warmed, richer and darker than she remembered, his hair taking on a golden sheen. He wore a casual outfit of linen trousers and a white collared shirt—so different from the embroidered suits he'd worn in Evergarden. He looked relaxed. He looked pleased. He looked—*real*.

He swung his feet off the desk, setting them on the ground. "Hi, Minnow."

His warm, familiar voice unfroze Marlow. She crossed the room in three brisk strides.

Adrius rose from his seat to meet her.

Marlow seized the front of his shirt, shoving him back against the desk.

Adrius stared at her, wide-eyed and bewildered, his hands coming up to catch her by the elbows.

"Minnow—"

She cut him off with a fierce kiss, pouring every lonely minute she'd missed him into it. It was easy to lose herself in the heady scent of orange blossoms and amber, in the soft give of lips against hers.

But then she remembered herself and swiftly broke away, mortified that she hadn't even stopped to wonder what he was doing here, or if this was even what he wanted anymore.

Adrius just laughed into her mouth, cupping her face. His hands were rougher than she remembered, but everything else about him felt wonderfully familiar.

"Welcome home to me," Adrius said, a little breathless, when they parted.

"You didn't tell me you were coming," Marlow said, but she couldn't manage to make her voice sound chiding, not when she was so ferociously thrilled to see him.

He'd written her nearly every day of the past eight months. Marlow always wrote back, whenever she had a spare moment, telling him about her cases, the curses she'd broken, the latest thing Silvan had done to annoy her. He'd made no promises to her in his letters, although his letters had spoken often of missing her—sometimes in such detail that Marlow had to make sure she was alone when she read them.

"You're back," Marlow said dumbly. "Are you back?"

"I'm back," he breathed.

"For good?"

He hesitated. "That kind of depends."

"Wait," Marlow said, a terrible thought striking her. "Swift was kidding about you being a client, right? You didn't get cursed again, did you?"

"Sort of," Adrius said.

Marlow let go of his shirt and pushed him a step back. "You have *got* to be kidding me. What is it this time?"

"Well, you see," Adrius said, his expression one Marlow recognized well from all the times he would flirt with her back when their relationship was just a ruse. "I've been cursed to eternally yearn for a girl I left back home." He pulled her close again and murmured against her lips, "But I hear you're a pretty good cursebreaker."

ACKNOWLEDGMENTS

It's hard to believe that this is my fifth book. If I ever thought that writing books would get easier as I went, that notion has been thoroughly disabused by *Masquerade*. I owe so many thanks to the people who kept me going and who worked so hard to make this series what it is.

Thank you to Hillary Jacobson and Alexandra Machinist for being the most amazing partners and advocates. Thank you to Sarah Mitchell, Josie Freedman, Berni Vann, and the rest of the team at CAA.

Thank you to my editor, Brian Geffen. This series would not be what it is without your hard work, enthusiasm, and unwavering faith in me. A huge thank-you to Samira Iravani and Michael Rogers for another gorgeous cover. Thank you also to the rest of the team at Holt Books for Young Readers and MCPG: Carina Licon, Tatiana Merced-Zarou, Gaby Salpeter, Naheid Shahsamand, Starr Baer, Alexei Esikoff, Jie Yang, Amber Cortes, Maria Snelling, Ann Marie Wong, Jean Feiwel, and the many others involved in bringing this book to the world.

As always, thank you to the rest of the writing crew: Tara Sim, Meg Kohlmann, Alexis Castellanos, Erin Bay, Amanda Foody, Janella Angeles, Kat Cho, Amanda Haas, Mara Fitzgerald, Swati Teerdhala, Charlie Herman, Melody Simpson, and Madeline Colis. Special thanks to Ashley Burdin for reading an early(ish) draft and reassuring me that the entire thing was not complete dreck. Akshaya Raman and Axie Oh, I hope I never have to face a deadline without you two.

Thank you to Erica for the many, many walks in the redwoods spent untangling the morass of Caraza. Thank you to the rest of my family for the unwavering support you've always had for me: Mom, Dad, Sean, Riley, Julia, Wilder, Charlotte, and Rosemary. And to Curry, for providing constant snuggles throughout the writing of this book.

One final thank-you, from the bottom of my heart, to every reader, librarian, bookseller, and bookstagrammer who has picked up a copy of *Garden of the Cursed*. Your enthusiasm for Marlow, Adrius, and the rest of Caraza has kept me going even through the darkest moments.

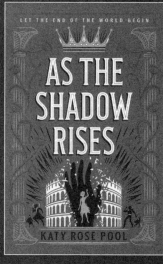
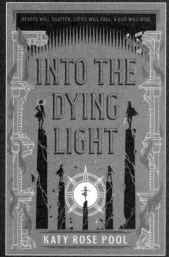